IRON & FIRE

#2, SILK & STEEL SERIES

ARIANA NASH

Iron & Fire, Silk & Steel, #2

Ariana Nash

Dark Fantasy Author

Subscribe to Ariana's mailing list & get the exclusive story 'Sealed with a Kiss' free.

Join the Ariana Nash Facebook group for all the news, as it happens.

www.pippadacosta.com

Please note: Crazy Ace Publishing monitors popular international pirate sites for infringing material. If infringement is found (illegal downloading or uploading of works) legal action will be taken.

CHAPTER 1

Silver, Bronze & Gold,
The dragons of old,
The first to come,
Our world undone.
Betrayal and devastation,
Birthed a new creation,
The worst was done,
The Jeweled reign begun.

- Elven folksong

ysander

"LET me out and we'll call this an unfortunate misunder-standing." Lysander added a teasing smirk, the kind that had won over countless dragons in the past. Unfortunately, Chloe was human, and currently standing on the outside of his cage with her eyebrows raised, clearly unimpressed.

"Or I'll destroy this little rebel village once I *break* out. Let me out now and you have my word it won't come to that." It was a bluff, of course, Lysander had thrown his weight at the cage bars, as man and dragon, and not a single one had shaken loose. Too narrow to slip through, too heat resistant to burn through. He'd tried it all. Bluffing was all he had left, and that didn't appear to be working either.

Chloe's lips thinned into the same judgmental line as her narrowing eyes.

Making a grab for her was useless. He'd tried that too. She was fast, for a human.

She finally managed a thin imitation of a true smile. "You'll have to promise more than that, dragon."

Chloe had a look about her that said she'd lived a long time on the fringes of war. Repair-patches dappled her trousers and shirt. Wrinkles and scuffs marked her boots the same way as they did her face, making her seem older than he suspected she really was. Even her hair was chopped off, having it out of the way her only concern. Her appearance spoke well of the hard woman behind it.

Lysander shifted his seated position against the back of the cage and spread his arms. "You want to take my boots too? Or the shirt off my back? I have nothing else to offer."

She huffed a dry laugh and muttered something in her native French language as she often did around him, knowing he had no hope of understanding. "You are the amethyst prince," she finally added, her accent sharp, making *the* sound like *zah* and *amethyst* sound sultry and exotic. "What I am seeing in you is not all you are capable of."

He dropped his head back and blinked through the bars above. If the cage wasn't enough, they'd built it inside a warehouse with only the smallest of narrow windows placed way at the top, near the roof. He couldn't see outside. Captivity hadn't been so bad to begin with. After all, it was just another cage, and he'd been raised in his mother's crushing emotional prison. But it had been days now, weeks even. They hadn't tortured him. He supposed that was a blessing, but boredom alone was its own kind of torture.

"You commanded the queen's monstrous flights," she continued. He ignored her, keeping his eyes up at the ceiling. "You've killed thousands, and I'm supposed to just believe you won't hurt us because of *your word?*"

She wasn't wrong. He had commanded the queen's flights. *Killed thousands* was a little overdramatic. These days, in the absence of humans, his flights had mostly kept order among dragons, protecting the tower from the occasional wild northern interloper while occasionally dispatching any elven assassins venturing into the barrenlands.

Lysander pulled a knee up and picked at his boot. But that was all before his brother Akiem witnessed Lysander killing their mother, the queen. Everything had gone to shit since then. He'd practically handed the humans their victory on the beach, told them about the bronze forges they could use to ruin the bronze's underground warren, and at the time, he'd had every intention of giving himself up peacefully. They'd shot him, dumped a bag over his head and marched him to this one: Chloe.

"If you want out of this cage, you must give us more," she said.

In the beginning, he'd stubbornly refused to acknowledge her questions. But the cage had grown wearisome, and he had little love for his kin, so why protect them by keeping their secrets? Some amethyst he could stomach, some he even admired, but none had any love for him. These days, they'd all kill him on sight. Then there was Dokul, the bronze chief and his ruthless daughter, Mirann. Lysander had planned to manipulate them from inside their brood, but instead, had only managed to narrowly survive them. It seemed wherever he turned, dragons of all kinds wanted a piece of him, and he had no idea why.

He lowered his gaze. She'd stepped closer, this fierce human with her dragon-teeth daggers clipped to her belt. Daggers Eroan had taught them how to harvest and wield.

Thinking of the elf brought a twisted smile to his lips. He'd had a lot of time behind these bars to think of Eroan. If he hadn't let Eroan live, hadn't tried to save him time and time again, that elf would have died in the queen's bed and the elves wouldn't have learned how effective dragon-teeth were against dragonscale. The bronze wall would still be intact. If Eroan had died—as he'd seemed so determined to do—little would have changed. Elisandra might have still been alive. Or, had Lysander still snapped and killed his mother, he'd have fled to the bronze line where Dokul's brutal affections awaited. So, all things considered, maybe this cage wasn't so bad a place. Maybe he'd always been destined to end up right here, staring at the little human woman.

"I don't know what you expect from me?" he asked. "Anything I tell you, you'll assume to be lies..." They would

4

never trust him. Then it struck him: He wasn't getting out of this cage. Ever. Only fools trusted dragons.

Rising to his feet, he approached the bars. Eye to eye with the human, she stared back, unafraid. "Don't expect anyone to come for me, if that's what you're hoping for."

She glared back at him. He'd known members of his own flights like her. Utterly cold. Ruthless. She'd do whatever it took to save her people. He could admire that, one soldier to another.

"You're their prince, their heir." She tucked her thumbs into her trouser pockets. "They'll come. And we'll kill them when they do."

Laughter tickled the back of his throat. He swallowed before it could burst free. "You grossly underestimate a dragon's ability not to give a shit." He leaned as close as the bars allowed and watched distrust shadow her eyes. She'd take one of those daggers at her belt and strike at him in a heartbeat, once she got her answers. "Nobody is coming for me. They'd all prefer I rot in this cage."

Finally, some flicker of emotion darted through her gaze, briefly softening it before her guard slammed back up. "The old tales tell of how your kind took human form and infiltrated our ranks as spies, long before the world fell, when people still reigned from huge cities. Your kind made those people believe things. Some of my friends say *your* green eyes have magic in them. That you can make us believe things... Is that true?"

If he possessed that trick, then it was clearly broken, like the rest of him. Hypnotic gazes? Next she'd think he could turn into a snake and slither through the bars. He clamped his fingers around the bars and lowered his voice, adding a smooth rumbling just for her. "I hate to break it to you, but you caught the wrong brother if you want to lure my kin here. So do with me what you will. Let me out or let me die." Pushing off, he backed away. She watched like she was waiting for him to reveal his true power. Like he was supposed to be some important dragon prince who had all the answers, the key to turning the tide in their useless war. By nights, they'd fucked up. Akiem was who they truly wanted. His brother always had been the center of attention, the one every dragonkin wanted to know, to serve. The *preferred* amethyst prince.

He whirled, sunk his hands into his ragged hair and kicked at the bars. For once, just once, before it all ended, he'd like to be the one in control of his life. He couldn't remember a single moment in all his years when he'd been free enough to make choices. And now this place and these humans... were these four walls the last he'd ever see?

"What happened to your wing?"

The question whipped him around.

She'd moved up close to the bars, her human eyes softer than before. Lysander sprang off his back foot and lunged. He shot a hand through the bars and grabbed at her, but she darted away, barking an alarm. Her warriors poured in, their movement spilling into his peripheral vision. He knew what came next.

He let a growl rumble free. "Let me out now or I swear, when I do escape, I'll kill you all!"

"And that's the truth behind your lies!" Her icy glare locked with his. "You are never leaving this cage."

He threw the weight of dragon behind his stare, darkening his presence with threat and subtly altering his appearance, adding a sharpness to his pretend human edges. He looked less like them now, less civilized, more *unknown*. She wanted the truth? The shift threatened to tear him open and fill the cage-space with a mass of enraged dragon. The humans saw it, saw the air ripple, felt the intangible magic surge, maybe even tasted its lemony bite on their tongues.

The sting of the dart jolted him from the madness. He tore the little feathered bolt from his arm and threw it back at them. Bastards. They'd started with the darts not long after he'd first shifted, after seeing a dragon up close had made them scurry into the shadows like the frightened mice they were.

His vision of Chloe swayed and tipped. The bars were the next to go. Darkness swirled. He was never leaving this box. He reached for those bars now, and missed, fingers sailing through the air until his shoulder hit hard iron instead. He couldn't shift now if he'd wanted to. All of him was drifting apart and sinking to where the dreams waited. His knees hit the ground, then a hand. He reached his other hand through the bars, so at least part of him was free when the darkness swallowed him whole.

roan

THE MASS of dragon had crashed through the tree canopy and slammed into the ground, heaving up a great blast-wave of roots and dirt. When they fell, they fell hard. Eroan regarded the dead amethyst in silence, his gaze sliding over its narrow snout and glassy, open eyes. Eyes easily the size of an elf's head. Blood and sizzling acids dripped from the gaping hole in the exposed firepit, low in its throat.

They'd been getting bolder, of late, and more reckless. Desperation, he guessed.

To his right, hidden in the brush, a huge ballista sat camouflaged among vines, hidden from above. Its enormous dragon-teeth-tipped arrow had been the end for this amethyst, striking it clean in the neck, tearing out its firepit and much of its throat, knocking it from the sky. The dragon had hit the ballista as it landed, by chance more than skill. The weapon would need fixing before its next use.

His pride of elves muttered their congratulations to the shooter, an Assassin of the Order, one of Cheen's best, as she had proven with this kill. She took the pats on the back and handshakes with humility and caught Eroan's eye for a few moments. He nodded once. The full celebration would come later, back in the safety of Cheen village. For now, the deed was done and the dragonkin had lost another of their number. Glittering excitement shone in the eyes of his Order brothers and sisters. But more than that, honest hope. The tide of war was turning one dead dragon at a time.

"Take its teeth," he ordered. "And be quick. Wolves will descend soon."

The carcass would be ripped to shreds overnight and fully devoured within days. Should another dragon come looking, it would likely turn away from the stench of its fallen kin.

"We'll fix the ballista tomorrow." He turned from the dead beast and adjusted the dragonblade at his back. "Next shift, take your places." Order assassins melted back into the shadows, unseen until it was too late if you happened to be dragonkin. His heart swelled at the thoughts of how things had changed in a matter of a few months.

Of course, it wasn't enough. One village picking off two or three dragons wouldn't make much of a dent in their numbers. All the villages should be doing the same. An organized force should be gathered, trained, educated with these new weapons, to make a push on the tower. Someone needed to be dispatched to Ashford to deliver the knowledge he'd gathered across the sea and rally the

Higher Order into action. Eroan suspected that someone should be him.

"That was one of the biggest I've seen yet." Seraph dropped from the tree canopy to the forest floor beside him and fell into step along the narrow, winding animal track. "Did you see its neck?" She made a clawing, sweeping gesture at her throat. "All gone. Nasty." Her dark hair had grown out the last few months. She wore it in a high horse-tail, unashamed to bear the scar of her missing ear-tip.

Eroan made an agreeable sound, but his thoughts were still lodged firmly in the future, in responsibilities, in waiting for someone to step up, someone who wasn't him. The last time he'd *done the right thing* he'd lost his home, lost people he cared about. His chest tightened. But change wasn't happening fast enough.

Signs of an early spring poked through the under-growth, green shoots through leaf litter, leaf buds swelling in the skeletal canopy above. More daylight hours meant more active dragons. The Order would need to prepare. The amethyst brood's behavior had become unpredictable now their queen was dead. So far, their appearances had been sparse, but with winter fading, and the days growing longer, that would soon change.

Seraph hopped over gnarled roots ahead. Her sword sat neatly on her back, its handle poking above her shoulder. The twin to Eroan's. She never left her hut without it. The sight of it reminded him of everything he'd lost and the mistakes he'd made. Both swords had belonged to the only dragon he wished he hadn't killed. These blades were the very reason the elves had begun to make a difference.

Seraph fell back into step and beamed next to him, her teeth bright in the dappled and fading daylight. She

11

thumped him playfully on the arm. "Smile, a dead dragon is a good thing. Your ballistae are working."

"It is," he agreed. "And they are."

"But...?" Her smile faded a little, but she clung to it, not willing to allow his sour mood to spoil hers.

"Nothing, I just... We can do more. We must do more."

"More?" she chuckled, "We've killed three in the last few weeks, that's more than we did in years back at..." The rest of her smile fell away, and her gaze fell to the forest floor, the word "home" unspoken.

Eroan didn't reply. Woodsmoke filtered through the trees. Cheen was close. Woodsmoke meant home, but after he'd returned from the bronze lines and seen what remained of his village, woodsmoke triggered different emotions. Ash and bone. Scorched, blackened earth where nothing would grow for years to come. The handful of survivors who had made it to Cheen described the dragon who had led the slaughter, a beast with scales of obsidian, as black as the night, eyes of gold. They hadn't seen the dragon until it was on top of them, and by then, it had been too late.

"Good hunting?" Janna's familiar voice rose above the others welcoming them back through Cheen's outer-barricades. He searched for her greenish-tipped blond hair among the barricade lines and spotted her toss a wave his way, her smile bright. He briefly nodded but slipped through the open gates quickly enough that she wouldn't be tempted to draw him into a conversation.

Seraph shot him an arched eyebrow. He ignored her too, although he'd learned ignoring Seraph led to more questions later. His student had become a friend after they'd survived the dragons together. That friendship loosened her tongue more these days than it had when he had been solely her Order leader and someone not to be argued with. It was Seraph's earring he still wore high up at the tip of his ear as a reminder of the time before. Removing it hadn't felt right, despite its obvious twinkling disadvantage among the undergrowth.

"You should speak with her," Seraph suggested as they passed one of the central pathways linking the scattered huts. Cheen's layout appeared chaotic. Huts huddled along paths and beneath trees. Some stood on stilts, others seemed perched in trees, but the design deliberately sprawled to prevent dragon-fire from destroying everything in a few blasts.

"And you should stay out of my business," he grumbled.

"It's just... you were always so close."

Eroan shrugged off the sword and pushed through his door into his hut. The hearth was cold, the hut moreso. Seraph followed, immediately gravitating to the array of various shaped dragon-teeth scattered about tables and leaning against the hut's walls. She picked up a tooth with a serrated edge as long as her forearm. "That's a mean blade. You made all these?"

"Trying to." Eroan set his dragonblade against the hearthside and paused, his gaze drifting to the small window. Of course he should talk with Janna. The fact she was alive had almost brought him to his knees when he and Seraph had staggered into Cheen months after they were both presumed dead—again.

"It's that Ross, isn't it?" Seraph chatted idly. "He's nice. He fishes. He has a pet hawk. He's funny too—"

"It's not Ross," he cut off her Ross appreciation assessment before catching her wry grin, sensing he'd been played.

Maybe it was Ross. Ross and Janna had forged a bond

since they'd fled the flames. She could do worse. Ross seemed nice. He wasn't a hunter or an assassin. But he did have a hawk. The male was harmless enough. Janna had found someone who could love her back the way she had always wanted, and that was the best he could have hoped for. Add to that her slightly rounded belly and it seemed better for them all that he stayed away.

"I overheard Xena talking about you once."

Eroan half-turned from the cold fireplace and regarded the young order assassin who had seen and endured more than most elves saw in their lifetimes. She'd been near death when the humans had found her below the bronze warren. Now, her face was flushed from a day in the winter sun, her eyes bright.

"Is there anything you don't overhear?"

She continued to examine his half-finished blades and shrugged. "Hut walls aren't thick. She said you were one of the best assassins she'd ever known, but you're terrible at being an elf."

He snorted. Xena had been full of little personal gems. She had liked to dangle cryptic bait and see who grabbed at it. "What is *that* supposed to mean?"

"I wasn't sure until I got to know you. Anything outside of the order you're *krak* at."

He blinked at her. "Because there is nothing outside the Order."

"There didn't *use* to be." She dropped the knife and reached to open the drawer beneath the table.

"Hands off," Eroan warned. Her curious nature would get her into trouble one of these days.

Eyebrow arched, she left the drawer alone, leaned back against the table, and folded her arms. "Now there's plenty outside the Order. Now we don't just live to die trying to kill the dragon queen. She's gone." She shrugged again. "Now we live to fight back. Now... we *get* to live. Thanks to you."

He breathed in, filling his lungs, taking the time to filter out too many unwanted emotions. "You know exactly why you shouldn't thank me, Seraph." He'd been honest with her about everything. She was the only soul alive who knew it all. His failures, his disgrace. He hadn't been the hero they all believed him to be. If anything, that had been Lysander, the dragon prince he'd had killed on the beach. *Kill him. Make him suffer.*

Guilt and regret knotted low in Eroan's gut, making him want to curl around the pain. He turned to the cold hearth instead, and taking up a stick, poked at the ashes. Had he been alone, he'd have given in to the guilt and let it eat at his insides.

"I often think about him," Seraph said. "The dragon who saved me."

He paused and rested back on his heels.

"Do you think Lysander's still there with those horrible bronze? I feel like I left him somewhere terrible—"

"He's with his own." He stabbed at the burned bits of log, wishing he could stab at the memory of having Lysander killed. "Leave me, Seraph. I... I have those blades to heat and shape, and my shift starts at midnight. You should be well rested for your shi—" His hut door slammed, and with a labored sigh he dropped onto the floor.

Kill him.

Make him suffer.

Closing his eyes, he rubbed at his forehead, massaging away an ache. Alone, in a hut that didn't feel like his own and probably never would, he silently wished that moment

15

on the beach had been different. If the humans hadn't used a bag to cover Lysander's head, if they'd let him speak, Eroan would have known who he'd condemned to death. He'd been so close... the prince who had saved Eroan, time and time again. The prince who had endured, who hadn't let his wretched existence beneath his tyrant of a mother beat him down. The prince who had saved Seraph from the worst they could do and saved Eroan in more ways than one.

A knot blocked his throat. He swallowed hard to clear it and opened his eyes, seeing only an empty hut full of shadows.

The past was done.

The future was where he needed to be.

Inside the Order house, eight young elves, each clutching small dragon-teeth daggers, performed their routines. Curan observed from the back of the longhouse, his scarred face grim. He spotted Eroan and held up two fingers as a silent signal to wait. Eroan hung back, keeping to the edges of the house so as not to distract the group, but observed them each in turn. They moved in perfect harmony, each step smooth and precise. Sped up, these age-old sequences would kill. Eroan knew them like he knew how to breathe. A few of the trainees needed some polishing, but most were brilliant, as Eroan would expect of Curan's students. Eroan had been his student too, once.

With the sessions over, he greeted those who spoke with him until eventually the last had filed out, leaving Curan behind.

"They're ready for the field," Eroan said.

"Some are," Curan grumbled, turning away from Eroan to collect the students' wooden training weapons, replacing them on the racks. Curan wore his age well, although why he didn't join the elders, Eroan couldn't fathom. He'd earned that right years ago. Perhaps he and Curan were more alike than he'd realized.

"And they thought me a harsh teacher?"

"What brings you here, Eroan?" Curan and him... there had been some harsh words spoken, after which Eroan had left for the bronze front-line with no intention of returning. Curan had remained icy, and regarded Eroan now with cool, professional detachment.

Eroan guarded his heart against the inevitable hollow sense of losing his sassa—a teacher and friend he respected. "We should employ a messenger to take the ballista designs to the Ashford Higher Order."

"It's too risky this time of year." Curan slotted one of the trainee's wooden batons home in the rack with a dull *thunk*.

"If we wait until spring, we'll have lost weeks of preparation time."

Another *thunk*. "No."

Eroan waited until all the weapons had been stowed and held the male's gaze. It had been Eroan's idea to collect the dragon-teeth in bulk, an idea Curan had argued against, saying it would alert the dragons to their presence. Curan had been right. The dragons had come and Eroan hadn't been there.

"Cheen has good messengers," Eroan persisted. The trek to Ashford was easily ten days through the dense forests. The journey would be a long and rough one, especially at this time of year when the weather could turn vicious. It was a risk.

Curan sighed wearily. "I said no, Eroan. Now, unless you have something else you need to speak with me about, please leave."

His guarded heart ached. "I've made mistakes, I know that..."

Curan's jaw ticked. "We've been engaged in open war with the dragonkin for countless generations. Waiting a few more weeks, until the days are longer, is the right decision. I do not have to explain this to you."

"Dragons are more active when the days are longer."

The older elf's look soured. Eroan wasn't telling him anything he didn't already know. "The night I found you... the skies opened and dumped a month's worth of rain in a few hours, do you remember?"

Eroan swallowed. He didn't recall much of that night, he'd been too young and knew only that he'd been walking for what felt like his whole life, afraid and full of rage. His boots had been so wet they weighed as much as rocks and his clothes had rubbed him red-raw.

"You had a look about you, even when small, like you'd cut through anyone and anything which stood in your way." Gentle fondness thawed some of the coldness in Curan's gaze. "I knew then you'd be trouble, but the kind of trouble that makes an excellent assassin. You have one of the most ironclad stubborn streaks I've ever seen, but it drove you on when all others would have given in. You're a formidable male, Eroan, but I fear I was wrong in tutoring you."

Eroan winced. "You weren't wrong." Without Curan's guidance, Eroan would be nothing. He owed him everything, which was why that regretful look in his eyes cut him to the bone now.

"Then prove it. Be grateful Cheen's elders allowed you

back into the Order. Had it been my decision, you'd be with the fisher-folk working the shores each morning."

The dry, shocked laugh escaped Eroan before he could stop it. "So tell them everything and see it done. I'll row a boat into the estuary each morning and catch fish for the rest of my days. Is that what you want of me? Is that all I'm good for?"

"Don't tempt me, Eroan. I know who you really are."

The words stung so badly they momentarily stole Eroan's voice.

He'd arrived in Cheen all those weeks ago and landed in his own myth. Of how Eroan Ilanea had risked it all to get the word regarding the dragons' weakness to their own teeth across the seas to the humans, of how the bronze wall had fallen because of his actions, of how he'd been there, on the ships, alongside the humans, shooting dragons from the skies. He had told Seraph everything in earnest, and she had quickly passed all that on, building him up. But Curan had known why Eroan had left, how his own self-hatred had driven him away, how inside he had *liked* what the dragons did to him. It wasn't heroism that drove Eroan, it was cowardice.

"We're grateful for everything you've done," Curan's tone dismissed.

"But it's not enough."

The old elf's eyes clouded with regret, then pity. "It's more than enough."

He snuffed his useless anger out. "Any word from the humans of France?"

"The last the elders heard was how they've captured a dragon." Curan puffed a small incredulous laugh. "I can't imagine how they've contained it."

Eroan remembered the cage he'd seen during his time

with the band of human fighters from the outpost of *Le Touquet*. He'd learned much from them. How to super-heat the teeth and fast-cool them, making them briefly brittle enough to shape, their ingenious ballista weapons, their motorized wheeled machines. Part of him wondered whether it would be better to return to them, but they were not his people, and they didn't need him quite like his own did. He had responsibilities here.

Things only he could do.

If Curan wouldn't send a messenger, Eroan had no choice at all. "You're right, it's too dangerous for a messenger." He headed for the door.

"Eroan?" Curan's voice stopped him. He turned to find too much emotion in his old teacher's face. "I don't blame you for what happened," Curan said. "I agreed to harvest the teeth. I was the Order leader. It was my decision."

Inside, guilt twisted like a clenched fist. Curan's words made no difference. Eroan's home and his friends were dead because of Eroan's choices. He nodded, appeasing Curan's guilt, and left before he had to listen to any more.

STANDING on a flattened branch forty feet off the ground, Eroan stared through the oak's naked branches at the crisp star-scattered sky above. The breeze was soft tonight, a whisper from the cooler east. Occasionally, distant owls hooted, and below his perch, mice rooted through dried, leaf litter. The weight on his soul lifted in the quiet forest. His muddled thoughts stilled.

Ashford. A ten-day journey if he traveled day and night. Cheen wouldn't miss him. The ballistae were in place and working. It made perfect sense for him to go now. What else was there here? Any elf could perform guard duty while he could be spreading the word, making a difference to other villages, rallying others to fight back instead of doing what they'd always done: hide, hoping never to be seen.

Generations before him, in a time when elves hid among humans, protecting them from the end of the world they never saw coming, they'd always been the hidden people. It was in their nature.

But times had changed. Hiding accomplished nothing but having the dragons pick them off one by one. He regretted his actions, walking away from his home, leaving Curan with the task of collecting dragon-teeth. A task that had gotten elves killed. But without Eroan, the bronze wall would still stand, humans would still be assumed dead. Actions had consequences. And in war, those consequences were often costly.

Tomorrow.

He'd tell the elders of his journey tomorrow. They'd argue against it, but they wouldn't—couldn't—stop him. Most of them looked at him like he was some kind of mythical creature anyway. He'd done the impossible, survived the dragons—twice, brought them new weapons, killed a queen... He had more sway with the elders than most.

A different kind of rustle pricked his ears from behind. A muted noise. Almost too quiet to hear over the breeze. His lips lifted at one corner and he waited, eyes on the skies, until a heavy branch behind the tree's trunk groaned under a new weight.

"You moved from your usual post," a whispered male voice teased into his right ear. His smile grew and the smallest flicker of lust sparked low down, distracting his thoughts from tomorrow and leading them firmly into the current time.

Eroan leaned into the voice and without looking, whispered back, "I'm not making it easy for you."

Nye's laugh was dark and rich. "Oh, I've known that for a long time, *Eroan Ilanea*."

Warm fingers eased around Eroan's neck, settling at his nape. Nye's breath fluttered against Eroan's ear, tightening Eroan's lust with promises that touch would deliver on, kindling his need into a hotter and hungrier force.

Eroan dutifully kept his eyes on the sky as a warm mouth brushed his ear, then the wet tip of a tongue tickled, sucking the lobe between soft lips. Teeth nipped, eliciting a small, involuntary hiss from Eroan.

Nye shifted from a side-branch, filling Eroan's view. Dressed in all-black leathers with a few gray patches, Nye was a creature cut from the forest at night. Inky black hair fell to his jaw in messy angles, shorter than most preferred to wear it, accentuating a jawline Eroan stroked his fingers along now. Nye's eyes may as well have been dark too now he was all in shadow, but his crooked, knowing smile was bright and the points of his elven teeth sharp.

"My watch isn't over," Eroan said. *Regrettably*, he thought. He found himself fascinated by that smile and the lips forming it. Teasing, kissable lips.

Nye planted an arm against the tree trunk over Eroan's shoulder, and braced himself, trapping Eroan between his chest and the tree. "There are others on-watch..." He plastered himself closer, nudging his knee between Eroan's so all Eroan could feel was the warm, hard press of male.

He shouldn't give in, but he'd stopped saying no when he'd found Nye had survived their home being razed to the ground. Nye had made the long, winter nights considerably more enjoyable.

"Hm...?" Nye's query teased across Eroan's lips, then the male's hand dropped to Eroan's hip and spread there, owning, teasing. Eroan knew that hand would soon wander inward to find evidence of his own wanting.

Nye turned his head, the line of his jaw twitching, and suddenly pushed off. "Or, I could just leave—"

Eroan hooked an arm around the male's waist, tugging him back before he could escape. "You're not getting away that easily." The kiss was a claiming, Eroan's hands on Nye's face, his mouth taunting, opening, luring Nye in closer so there was nothing between them.

Nye shifted his hips, brushing against Eroan's trapped arousal. Delicious friction sent a shudder through Eroan and dumped the rest of his reasonable thoughts from his mind. He sank his hands down Nye's back and cupped his ass, grinding him in tighter. Nye threw his head back. The restrained groan that escaped him summoned a sly smile to Eroan's mouth. He nipped at the male's jaw and swirled his tongue down the column of his neck. Nye's pulse fluttered against Eroan's mouth, light and fast. Eroan mouthed that vulnerable spot, drawing a pleasured hiss from between Nye's teeth, his duty long-forgotten.

"You're a bad influence..." Nye remarked, chest rumbling with the depth of his voice.

Eroan chuckled and Nye's grip tightened on his hip. "You came to me," he reminded. But maybe he *was* a bad influence. These moments they had recently stolen together, moments during Order duties... He would never have discarded his duty like this before. And then continue to neglect the way of the Order to chase personal pleasures. But life was too short to squander it. A dragon prince had taught him that.

If they were caught, they'd both be out of the Order. The risk made Eroan want to turn Nye around and take him hard against the tree, raw and unprepared. The thought alone sent a throbbing pressure to his arousal and pealed a telltale growl from the back of his throat. Nye shifted back enough to spread his hand over Eroan's trapped cock. Eroan tensed, but only because he needed to control the pace or else this would get noisy real fast.

Nye's mouth captured his, sweeping away his tight, panting noises.

When he withdrew, leaving Eroan breathless, a lustful wickedness flashed in Nye's eyes. He liked this. Liked it a lot, if the bulge in his trousers was any indication.

Nye lifted a finger and pressed it to Eroan's lips. "Quiet…"

Eroan nipped at his finger, enough for Nye to yank his hand back. Nye's footing slipped. His eyes widened.

Eroan swooped an arm in, scooped him around the waist, and swung him against the tree, saving him from falling. And now it was Eroan's turn to brace an arm behind Nye's shoulder, smothering the male, trapping all of him.

Nye's rich, nervous chuckles must surely have been designed to torment because hearing them made Eroan's throbbing, aching need turn maddening. He loosened his grip on Nye's waist and traveled his hand to the hard ridge inside Nye's trousers. Nye's smile vanished and his eyes widened for a different reason. He liked to be caught.

"You seem to be in *need of assistance*," Eroan whispered against his cheek. He leaned against his side, leaving enough room to pop open Nye's belt's toggle buttons. Nye trembled beneath his touch. Drenched in a visceral want, Eroan took Nye's arousal firmly in hand and eagerly stroked. Nye's entire body hardened, pulled taut like a nocked arrow. Eroan made sure to brush the silken head with his palm as he sank his fingers lower, circling and caressing warm balls.

Nye dropped his head back, surrendering. Dark lashes fluttered closed. Eroan would have liked to have dropped to his knees and take him in his mouth, but a tree branch forty feet off the ground was not the best place to go down on Nye—they'd both most certainly fall. But by Alumn, he wanted to bring him to the edge and hold him there until Nye begged him for more.

Nye's smooth pre-seed moistened Eroan's strokes. Nye's lips parted, his breaths hastening. All signs that heightened Eroan's desire.

He bumped his chin against Nye's and whispered into the corner of his mouth. "I want you in my bed where I can spread you without falling out a tree." With every word, he caressed Nye's taut erection, sweeping wetness off the slit with his thumb. Shudders spilled through Nye. His sharp little teeth bit into his bottom lip and Eroan's own arousal throbbed hotter, aching for attention.

"I'd never make it." He opened his eyes, dark pupils swelling.

"No?" Eroan tightened his grip and Nye's hand shot out to clutch at Eroan's shoulder, fingers digging in. Their gazes locked, Nye's full of half-lidded desire. All the silent glances, the lingering looks—unanswered questions had always simmered between them. Eroan had pushed them aside once, but not anymore. He needed to be loved, to be with someone, to chase the past away. When alone, his failures stalked him. He couldn't be alone.

Eroan shifted his grip, curling his fingers around Nye's erection again, trapping his prey against the tree. Nye's body heaved against his, his breaths panted close to Eroan's ear. He writhed and twitched; wound so tightly he would soon come for Eroan.

An unfamiliar noise barely registered through Eroan's scorching lust. His instincts ticked, distracted, until Nye's free hand clutched at Eroan's forearm, trying to slow him, to control him. None of that was about to happen. Eroan had him completely at his mercy.

The same unusual noise whispered in on the breeze again and this time Eroan's instincts chimed louder. He'd heard it before, many times, like sheets drying in the wind... but strange to hear it in the forest. *Wrong*, his instincts told him. *Out of place. Danger.*

There. Again.

Eroan abandoned Nye's arousal and clamped his hand over Nye's mouth. The male's eyes shot open, pleasure quickly veering toward alarm.

Eroan shook his head.

The breeze stirred a few dried leaves below. A fox screamed somewhere far off. And there, that sound: sheets flapping.

Nye's eyes widened.

Eroan slowly, quietly, turned his head. Naked winter branches clawed at the night sky. Stars silently flickered. But as Eroan scanned the dark, some stars vanished and reappeared.

It wasn't sheets he heard, but wings.

Enormous wings designed for near-silent flight, belonging to a dragon as black as night and almost invisible in the dark.

Akiem.

Eroan's heart stuttered. Memories fought to undo his control. It couldn't be the prince. Not here, not now.

Panic plucked at him. The dragon's golden eyes, his deep, smooth voice ordering Eroan's torture, the blast of dragon-fire in the queen's tower that had almost consumed him. But more than all of that, Akiem had destroyed his home, killed people he'd loved, taken Seraph and Xena to the bronze. Akiem was everything Eroan despised, everything he was forged to kill.

Nye shifted, trying to close his fly. Eroan gave him the barest of head-shakes, mouthing, "*No.*" Any movement would be seen from above. With any luck, if they stayed still and silent, the dragon would grow bored searching for its prey and move on.

Unless he had already seen them.

Wing beats thumped. The downdraft began to whip up dried leaves and grit from the forest floor, whisking the debris into a storm. The dragon was descending.

If it was Akiem, they wouldn't stand a chance at surviving what came next. Eroan looked up, into Nye's eyes. "Run."

Eroan dropped from the tree, landing in a crouch and springing into a run with Nye a blur to his right. The dragon let out a howling roar so loud it thundered through Eroan's skull. A warning cry. Other dragons would hear it and come.

Eroan's thoughts raced. *No, no, not again...* Cheen needed to be protected. He would not be the cause of more elven deaths.

Eroan ran, carving through the spindly brush, legs and lungs burning. Nye was a blur just off to his right, and then he was gone, having veered off toward Cheen.

"No!" Eroan barked. The dragon above screamed its rage at having its prey split up.

The wind tossed branches and dirt into a swirling wall, raining grit into Eroan's eyes, but still he ran. "Not Cheen!" he yelled. That's what the beast was waiting for, why it hadn't blasted them with fire. For them to run back to Cheen, to lead it straight to the village. Akiem was smart. Eroan hadn't forgotten that. Hadn't forgotten any of it.

A branch thrashed him in the cheek. He raised an arm, fighting through, and spotted Nye, heading back in. Nye's quick glance flashed understanding as he dashed over roots just ahead of Eroan and down hollows. Eroan whistled through his teeth and took an old animal track heading far away from Cheen. Nye followed. A ballista station was up ahead. The Order assassin manning it would have heard the dragon's cry and be searching the skies for the beast. If Eroan could lure Akiem in range...

Night fell from the skies, dropping a wall of smooth black scales into Eroan's path. He skidded to a stop and flung out an arm, blocking Nye from plowing ahead. Vast jaws opened, exposing glistening racks of curved, brilliant white teeth. Golden eyes glowed, as large as two suns, and the dragon's wings spread like enormous ship sails.

The glowing, churning firepit low in Akiem's long neck drew Eroan's eye. Behind obsidian scales, the fire glowed a rich purple—amethyst. Akiem's shallow, soulless eyes trained on Eroan and flickered with recognition. His lips drew back in a smile or a sneer—this close, Eroan couldn't tell. Akiem remembered too. He huffed, blasting Eroan with hot, wet air.

"Go," Eroan urged Nye under his breath, holding the dragon's glare.

Akiem's broad, crowned head cocked one way, then the

28

other—a hunter sizing up whether its tiny morsel was worth the effort.

"No," Nye hissed back.

"*Go.*" Unable to look, to force the order home, Eroan silently willed Nye not to be a fool. But Nye's presence lingered in the corner of Eroan's eye. He was going to make this difficult. "He wants me," Eroan said, keeping his voice low, hoping Akiem wouldn't hear under the sound of his own bellows-breaths. "Go, he won't follow. If other amethyst arrive, they'll hunt us to exhaustion. Go now, while you can."

"I'm not leaving you." Nye's growl held its own dangerous edge.

"You're an Assassin of the Order." Eroan's snarl tightened. "Do the right thing and *leave* while you can!"

Akiem breathed in, expanding his vast chest and rumbled something that sounded like a deeper, foreboding warning.

He has our scent. A body of water could shake him off their trail, but there were no rivers nearby, unless they made it the few miles to the estuary. Akiem would kill them before then. They'd be lucky to make it half a mile.

Eroan broke eye contact and swung his glare at Nye. *"Damn you, Nye, go!"*

The male snarled back, dragon-daggers in-hand. "Never!"

The passion and defiance burning in Nye's gaze tripped Eroan's fierce instincts to protect. If Nye wanted to die here, so be it. Dying was, after all, what Order assassins were good at.

Eroan plucked the dragonblade off his back, stepped forward, and lifted the sword, showing it to the beast.

Akiem's head lifted. His eyes sparkled at the sight of a sword he surely recognized.

"You want to finish what you started, dragon?" Eroan flicked the fingers of his left hand behind his back, signaling to Nye to take the animal track behind them. "You'll have to catch us first," he grinned and bolted onto the track, Nye a shadow beside him.

The ground rolled, dipped and climbed, through roots and brush and gullies. Anything outside the track fell away and all Eroan could see was the next turn, the next tree he had to careen around. Faster and faster. His chest burned. Ahead, large evergreen pines hid their retreat.

He could no longer hear the dragon, but it didn't matter, Akiem had their scent: hiding from sight wasn't enough.

"Where... are... we going?" Nye panted.

No time to answer. Returning to Cheen was out of the question, the coast was too far and with no water nearby, there was only one way out of this, and even then, it may not work.

Another dragoncall shattered the quiet and moments later, another boomed, answering from a distance. Akiem screeched, just meters above. The fine hairs on the back of Eroan's neck prickled. *Too close.*

He glanced back. Nye had fallen behind.

Fire flooded the sky and sizzled down the evergreens, backlighting Nye against purplish flame. Pine needles popped, hissed, and spat. Tall, thin shadows danced around the forest floor. Akiem didn't yet know where they were. The flame was meant to flush them out.

Nye put on a burst of speed. Ahead, the purplish fire-light illuminated the dragon carcass from earlier in the day, still lying where it had fallen. In the hours since their absence, something had torn the beast's middle open and spilled its pink insides across the ground. Eroan looked to the skies. Either Akiem would see them or he wouldn't, there was no other option. Vaulting over one of the dead dragon's forelegs, he skidded on the slippery entrails and scrambled toward the gaping, torn belly, now bloated with decay. Parts of the rib cage shone white among the gore, but the cavity was intact. Eroan took his blade to the belly-scales, thrust the sword in and tore through the flesh, ripping open the hole large enough for two. He lifted the two-inch thick skin, opening the hole wider. Nye, without a second's thought, plunged inside.

Eroan climbed into the dark, slippery, stinking hole. His stomach flipped, trying to heave up a stench so thick it painted his throat and lungs. He smothered his mouth and nose in the crook of his arm and leaned back into the curved inner ribs.

His eyes streamed, wetting his face. Squeezing them closed, he buried himself in the mind-space he'd used in the tower dungeons, the space that carried him away to a home that no longer existed.

Nye's hand nudged at Eroan's knee, then his thigh, until he finally landed on his hand. Nye's fingers squeezed closed. Eroan squeezed back, hoping to alleviate some of Nye's shuddering. And they waited in the dragon's belly for Alumn to decide their fate.

CHAPTER 3

*L*ysander

"You said none of them would come for you."

Chloe was looking smug today. Lysander returned her grin with a droll look of his own and went back to stewing in silence. Outside of a few insults and some colorful threats, he'd done nothing to these people and still they treated him like an animal. Perhaps he shouldn't have threatened to roast them all. They seemed a little sensitive to the thought of him eating them.

Humans tasted like chicken, or so he'd been told. Unlike his ancestors, he'd never eaten one to know for certain. The thought brought a smile to his lips. Maybe he would have, had he been hatched in another time, when the humans were everywhere, like ants. Elisandra had told him humans were a delicacy and hard to come by. There wasn't much meat on Chloe. She'd probably be all gristle and bone. And bitter. Definitely bitter.

She crouched outside the bars, bringing her eye level with his seated position at the back of the cage. "Where was the big bronze when we attacked the line?"

He dropped his head back against the cold iron and closed his eyes. More questions. Always with the questions. He'd tried asking about her. Did she have any family, any little kits, but she'd blanked him with her hard eyes.

"We thought it strange their chief wasn't there. A stroke of good luck for us. So where was he?"

These questions were new, but why bring up Dokul's absence now? What was her angle? Since the bronze line had fallen, they hadn't seemed that interested in the chief's brood or their defenses. They'd wanted to know about the tower, about the number of amethyst flights.

"How should I know where he was?" he grumbled, keeping his eyes closed. If he stared into the dark long enough, he could pretend there was no cage, pretend he was free to stretch his wings, even broken as one was. Gods, he wanted to shift and stretch every muscle from nose to tail and maybe roll around in the dirt to get the smell of human off him.

"Maybe you can tell me that?"

He sighed, his fantasy no good if she was going to keep twittering. He opened one eye, squinting at her. "Like I told you, I'm a nobody. In fact, you talking to me is the most attention I've been given in... since I can remember." Both eyes open now, and her smirk still there. "You haven't tried to fuck me or kill me in all this time, this cage is a fucking paradise." Her little human nose screwed up at his crass language. As her smile died, his grew. "Maybe you should come in here and rough me up a bit, huh?" He let his smile slip sideways and lowered his lashes, turning up the heat. "Make me feel at home?"

Her top lip curled. Disgust. That was rich, seeing as she was the one keeping him here.

"If you're a nobody, why is the bronze chief searching for you?" she asked, her strange lyrical accent thickening.

Lysander's smile cracked. "What?" His heart thumped a little harder. Dokul was actively looking for him? His heart stuttered.

She nodded. "He's hunting for the dragon we took from his beach."

His lapse in guarding his expression only lasted a moment. He plastered his smile back on his face and waited for his heart to slow its racing. "He's called Dokul and he's not a dragon you want to fuck with."

"The last of the first metal dragons. Yes, we know of Dokul. We've spent the last few decades studying him in fact. He wants you back enough to use his human appearance to try to infiltrate us and get answers. Unfortunately for him, he's as distinctive as human as he is as dragon."

A huge, hairless brute of a male with a fondness for battered metal armor did tend to stand out among these little cloth-wearing humans. Lysander recalled the smell of him. Wet metal, like blood. He could taste him too, warm and salty. It was only the young elf, Seraph's, intervention that had saved him from Dokul's rabid affections.

"He destroyed one of our northern-most camps when he didn't get his answers," she continued.

Dokul wasn't the problem here. The humans knew his appearance. He wouldn't be getting any information from them. No, it was Mirann they should be more concerned with. If Dokul was looking for Lysander, then so was his daughter and she could slip among their number like a snake in the grass. He looked at the warehouse door. She could be right outside now.

If Mirann found him first, she'd release him, but kill everyone here. If Dokul found him... He'd probably fuck Lysander in the cage and make the humans watch, then kill them all, including Lysander. Either way, Chloe and her little group of rebel fighters were living on borrowed time.

"Say this Dokul learns of my location and he comes here," Lysander swallowed. "How do you intend to kill him?" He kept his tone light, hiding the creeping sense of panic.

"We have our ways." She smirked, her accent potent.

Shooting a few unprepared bronze dragons out of the skies was one thing, stopping a dragon like Dokul and an organized flight was entirely another.

These humans were all dead and Lysander was stuck in a cage like the pet Dokul and his daughter had made him out to be. This Chloe thought she was smart, but she had no idea the lengths Dokul would go to.

He suddenly knew how this would all end and it wasn't the way she hoped. "You're making a mistake. You should let me go and save yourselves the pleasure of Dokul's company. He'll follow me away from your camp."

"We should, huh?" She stood and brushed down her trousers. "Of course you would say that."

He fake-grinned back. "Just trying to help you live, seeing as there aren't many of you left."

"We might surprise you, Lysander *Bronze*."

Ah, so Dokul had let that little name-change gem drop somewhere the humans could find it. Wonderful. Now how was he going to argue he no more wanted Dokul here than they wanted to die anytime soon. "Lysander Bronze," he repeated, chuckling to himself. That horrific spectacle of a coupling with Mirann still hurt him, even now.

"You said you were worthless, but it seems it's your lies that are worthless."

He didn't watch her leave, just stared through the bars at the warehouse wall. If he didn't get out of the cage, the bronze would come, and while he could manage Mirann for a while, Dokul was another matter. Lysander hadn't intended to leave the ancient dragon with a new smile in his throat and his own cock in his hands, but then, he hadn't intended to get caught handing over an elf to the humans either.

And even if he did get out of this cage, then what? It wasn't as though he could conveniently fly back home. And it was a long fucking walk.

What was there for him to go back to anyway? Everywhere he looked, the cage bars closed in.

roan

"WHAT IN-THE-NAME-OF-ALUMN HAPPENED TO YOU?" Curan barked as Eroan trudged through Cheen's gates. In the crisp light of dawn, Nye beside him looked as though he'd been chewed up and spat out. Eroan could only assume he looked as wrecked and smelled as revolting as Nye did.

"We had an encounter." Eroan flicked something wet and sticky off his fingers. His face itched, and when he scratched at it, brown mucus flaked off, embedding under his nail.

Nye fidgeted, lips turned down in a miserable grimace. Blood and dragon-innards had dried in his hair and coated his neck. Crusted bits of things Eroan couldn't identify stuck to his leathers. Nye crunched as he walked.

"Can we get cleaned up before you start with the questions?" Eroan asked Curan.

"Where's the dragon now?" Curan asked Nye, deliberately avoiding Eroan's glare.

"Gone." Nye licked his lips. Grimacing, he spat to the side. "We waited it out. Cheen's safe."

Curan considered them both long enough for the warmth of the sun to soak through Eroan's clammy leathers and lift more sickening odors into the air. If Eroan didn't know better, he'd think Curan was punishing them, but the male had never been petty. Still, things changed.

Finally, Curan gestured for them to leave. "Go, get cleaned up, but I want a full report as soon as you're ready."

They attracted a few stares as they headed across the village. The young ones pointed and giggled. Nye tossed them a wave, sending them into fits of more squealing. It wasn't every day a pair of assassins returned covered in dragon entrails.

"Come by my home." Eroan nodded ahead. "I have hot water."

"*Hot* water, huh?" Nye grinned. "I'd kill for that."

Slipping ahead to follow the winding paths through the trees, Eroan led him to his hut. Inside, he stoked the embers in the fire-grate back to life and tossed on a few more logs. "Give it a while to heat the water."

"What's this?" Nye eyed the pipe jutting from a raised steel tank, running around the top of the walls and down into what looked like a closet.

"A rain closet. The water heats up, runs through that pipe and comes out the head in there."

"You learn this from the humans?" Nye asked.

"Some of it." Eroan stood by the fire and carefully plucked off his ruined jacket, trying to minimize disturbing the gunk. "I added a little modification."

Nye opened the closet door and eyed the small rain-room inside. "Is there enough water for two?"

"Just one... You go first." Eroan dumped his jacket by the front door in a pile he'd later toss out, and tore his undershirt off, over his head, dropping that onto the pile too. It would all need to be burned. Sinking his fingers into his hair, he tried to run them through and snagged on solid chunks that had his gut tripping over itself again.

"That was quick thinking... last night," Nye said behind Eroan. His jacket landed on the pile, then his shirt, and as Eroan turned, Nye flicked open his trouser fastenings and pushed the trousers down over his hips. He kicked them off, leaving him virtually naked. Just a pair of loosely slung underpants covered him. Blood streaked his lightly muscled chest, but not as much as had dried on his forearms and face, anywhere exposed to dragon insides.

Nye blinked, and Eroan realized Nye was waiting for him to say something. Had there been a question? Because all his thoughts had ground to a halt when he turned to find Nye naked and bloody. "The er..." He cleared his throat and tried again, "It was the only way to mask our scent." He worked at his own trouser fastenings, trying to think around the temptation standing just a few feet from him. Nye's gaze tracked him, making his skin heat. The truth was, he hadn't known if hiding in the carcass would work. They both could just as easily be dead. Akiem was no foolish lower. And he wouldn't give up tracking them either. Now that he knew Eroan was alive, he'd likely be back. And he'd keep on looking until Cheen was discovered. Eroan needed to think of a way to stop that from happening.

Nye's fingers settled on Eroan's at his belt, prompting him to look up. His thoughts had been so lost in Akiem, he hadn't seen Nye close the distance between them. He wasn't even sure if Nye had said anything, though from the pitying look on his face it seemed likely.

He'd thought he'd gotten over his ordeal at the tower, thought he'd hardened himself to the past, but now he could feel the horror of it all creeping back in like a phantom in the dark.

Eroan caught Nye by the back of the neck and pulled him chest to chest, planting a messy kiss on the male's wet mouth. He tasted of all things Nye, but also the saltiness of dragon, of blood, and that lemony bite of dragon magic. The myriad of scents wrecked his restraint. Sudden, scorching lust ripped out all thought. He wholly needed Nye beneath him.

Nye gasped and gently pushed at Eroan's chest. "Eroan Ilanea, I love you, but you smell like a dragon vomited you up." He laughed, dragged Eroan by the wrist toward the little shower room, and shoved him inside. "Get in the hot rain already." Grabbing the dangling rope, he pulled, dumping hot water from the makeshift rainhead above over Eroan's head and shoulders.

Eroan hissed at the sudden sensory blast, grabbed for the still-laughing Nye, and pulled him inside the tiny space before his wretched memories could sink their claws in. Nye let out a very un-male-like yip and laughed harder, wet and writhing in Eroan's hands. The sight of Nye—hot water streaming through Nye's hair and down his face, plastering dark cow-licks to his cheeks— entranced Eroan. Nye lifted his face, letting water wash off the dirt, inviting luscious thoughts Eroan quickly lost himself in. He kissed Nye's neck, unable to resist—tasting water, blood, dragon, and elf—and mouthed down to his collarbone. Nye sucked in a breath and clutched at

Eroan's upper arms, either holding him back or holding him still. Eroan's already racing heart thumped harder, driving hot blood through his veins. He wasn't going to be able to play games, not now, not after last night. He needed the old memories gone, smothered beneath the hard and soft feel and sweetness of Nye on his tongue. Nye's hands stroked over his chest and down his back, pulling him close.

Nye's back arched, hips pushing, and Eroan answered that need, cupping Nye's erection through his sodden undergarments. The fabric became too much a barrier. Eroan tugged the cloth free, Nye's scandalous mouth attacking his. Cotton ripped. Eroan had Nye's hot, hard need in his palm. The male groaned into Eroan's mouth and Eroan took it in, took everything Nye gave, knowing his grip was too hard, his fingers too deep, but unable to loosen any of it.

"Eroan..." Nye reached between them, angling for Eroan's trapped arousal. "Let me..." Nye's words clipped off. He lifted sultry eyes and whispered, "Won't you try it?"

Eroan batted his hand away, shoved him back against the shower's flimsy wall, ravaged his mouth, and danced a trail of biting kisses down Nye's chest. Nye wanted Eroan beneath him, something Eroan had never allowed and wasn't about to start now. Eroan dropped to his knees, taking Nye between his lips and in deep, as he'd wanted to at the tree before Akiem had ruined the opportunity.

Nye's hands speared into Eroan's hair, fingers twisting. The male muttered words scattered between groans, but it wasn't enough. Eroan needed to hear him cry out, wanted to bring him to the edge and hold him there until it *hurt*. He angled Nye's arousal against the roof of his mouth and slid the head back, deeper, before withdrawing, curling his tongue, listening to Nye's ragged breathing and nonsense words.

Nye's thigh, trapped beneath Eroan's steadying hand, tensed as hard as rock. His hips rolled, thrusting his erection deeper, faster. Eroan took it, teased it, rolled and worked his tongue until Nye's shudders betrayed him, revealing how close he was to the edge. Eroan straightened, licking his way up, over Nye's solid abs. He twisted Nye by the hips and spread his ass. Nye braced an arm against the wall, back arched. Water beat against Nye's tableau of golden muscles. Eroan might have explored that back if the demand to take hadn't been driving him out of his mind. Inserting a finger, testing the resistance, Nye groaned, and lust sparked through Eroan's arousal. He tore at his own trouser fastenings, took his swollen erection in hand and guided its head against Nye's hole, barely managing to hold himself back from thrusting too deep, too fast. The wetness helped ease the tightness. Eroan slowly pushed in. Pleasure crackled, the tightness a direct link to that part of his mind that shattered into raw, unthinking pleasure. Reaching around Nye's hip, he stroked Nye's erection, finding it still deliciously hard and Nye just as open and wanting as before. Then Eroan eased deeper, hips driving himself into the tight, muscled sheath. Erotic sensation shivered through him and he thrust, losing control. He wasn't going to last and didn't care. He chased the pleasure, slowing only when he feared he'd lose himself too soon. When Nye spat a curse and his ass, cupped against Eroan's thighs, clamped, Eroan fell forward against Nye's back and hastened his pumping on Nye's cock until the male lost control. Nye cried out, losing his seed into Eroan's hand.

Eroan's restraint broke. He owned Nye by the hips and

fell into the rhythm that drove all the madness away and dumped him somewhere filled with numbing pleasure and nothing else. The cresting release loomed, too soon, too close. Tight, aching need spooled closer, building, rising. It snapped. Eroan threw his head back, teeth clenched, and groaned out as the unspooling release broke him, momentarily shattering coherent thought, setting him free from the guilt, the memories, the hurt, the wrongness of his own mistakes.

All too soon reality began to seep back in, leaving Nye a shuddering, panting wreck in his hands.

"I hurt you?" Eroan pulled back. He should have slowed, should have been gentler. Nye was smaller, in many ways softer. By Alumn, since his return from the tower, his mind had been harder, his wants sharper. "I'm sorry—"

"No." Nye caught his hand and threw a look over his shoulder, lashes low, smile slanted to one side.

Eroan withdrew with a small, shivering gasp as the dregs of pleasure finished him off and Nye turned in Eroan's lose grip. His half-smiling mouth brushed over Eroan's, mingling their racing breaths. "Didn't you say something about a bed?"

NYE LAY PRESSED against Eroan's side, his head pillowed on his chest, an arm slung over his waist, a leg hooked over Eroan's. Moments ago, someone had knocked on the door, but with no answer, that someone had taken off again. Seraph or Curan, Eroan assumed. Curan probably, or one of the Order on Curan's order to find where they'd both gotten to.

"I used to daydream about moments like this," Nye said, his voice low and hoarse. Hearing the gravel in it, Eroan wondered about the thickness of the hut walls and if anyone had heard them. "You remember when we were young... You were always so focused. Even back then. Any task, no matter how small, you threw yourself into it. You beat me at *everything*."

Eroan remembered Nye's scowling face every time he'd finished second in a race or was second back to the Order house after a night's scouting. Always second place. Eroan smiled at the memories and circled his fingers on Nye's warm shoulder. They'd argued when younger. Clashed in many ways, leaving Curan to separate them.

"Chasing you made me a better assassin."

A niggling, uncomfortable thorn poked at Eroan's mind. "Nye—"

"Everyone else saw it..." Nye's fingers traced lazy circles near Eroan's pectoral muscle. "But you never saw me that way. And then there was always the Order rule... Us? ...It was never going to happen."

Eroan let his gaze crawl over the roof trusses. He'd known Nye had always looked at him with more than respect in his eyes, but they'd been different people then. They were still different people. And something Nye had said in the earlier madness, before they'd washed the blood off, had gotten its claws in Eroan. He hadn't allowed himself to hear it then, but he couldn't forget it now.

I love you, Eroan Ilanea.

"Alumn brought you back..." Nye's stroking fingers wandered lower, over Eroan's abdominal muscles, stirring desires back to life. "I'm grateful, every day I'm grateful. I doubt I would have ever gotten ov—"

"I'm leaving for Ashford today."

Nye's fingers froze.

Eroan closed his eyes and winced as a new stab of guilt hit him. He shouldn't have let this thing with Nye go on this long or go this far. But he'd wanted it, needed it. He couldn't have been alone, he'd have lost his mind to the demons on his back. And Nye, he was good, and... he'd been willing.

Eroan rolled away from Nye's warmth and planted his feet outside the bed, sinking his fingers into his mussed-up hair. The bed rocked and lifted, Nye's weight gone.

"Were you going to tell me if I hadn't come to you last night or were you just going to run out on us like you always do?" Anger clipped each of Nye's words, ending them in a blade's edge.

Eroan rubbed at his face. He was a rotten piece of work. He'd known this wasn't just a distraction for Nye and still he'd let it happen. "I must tell the Higher Order about the weapons and see if there's been any word from France."

Nye snorted. "You *must*? Of course you must. And it has to be you, Eroan Ilanea, the elf who'll single-handedly save the entire known world. It couldn't be a messenger or someone else from the Order? No, it always has to be you."

Eroan's anger bristled. He'd tried to convince Curan. He was trying to do the right thing here. "It's more than that. Akiem knows I'm alive and he'll come looking. I need to move on, to lead a trail away from Cheen." He looked behind him to find Nye hastily snatching some of Eroan's own clothes from a fresh stack—his own were ruined. The too-long trousers bunched around his bare feet. He threw one of Eroan's shirts on, avoiding Eroan's gaze.

Nye was better than this, he knew what had to be done and he knew why the Order insisted on no personal attachments. "We're still Assassins of the Order," Eroan said. "Duty must always come first."

Nye's laugh sounded bitter and broken. "The same excuses, Eroan. Why don't you just admit it? What am I to you, really?" Nye straightened from fastening the shirt and held Eroan's gaze, his jaw twitching. "Were you bored? Was that it?"

"Nye, no."

"And I'm easy?"

Krak, he hadn't wanted this. "Nye..." Eroan grabbed at a pair of discarded trousers and tugged them on, stumbling in his haste as Nye headed for the door. "Wait. It wasn't like that... I... Don't leave things like this between us."

Nye tugged open the door. Sunlight poured in, high-lighting his mop of dark hair, ill-fitting clothes, and lack of shoes. He squinted into the light, messing up any chance Eroan had of reading his face. "Leave them how, Eroan? Me in love with you, and you just passing the time before running out again?"

Eroan stalled, pants half on, hands hitched at the belt. He owed Nye the truth. Stringing him along wasn't going to help either of them. Eroan was leaving and Nye should accept that. It would hurt, but he'd heal. "You and me, we... It needs to end." He sighed. "I'm sorry."

"You're sorry?" Nye's brows tightened, eyes hardening to cover the pain. "Don't be. I'm a fool for giving my heart to someone like you." And then he was gone, the door swinging open so the breeze could filter in, bringing with it the village sounds of laughter and idle conversation.

Eroan stared into the sunlight until his gaze slid to the racks of half-designed weapons and regret solidified into a new resolve. He'd already wasted too many hours with Nye and abandoned his duty for too long. He needed to see Cheen's elders. Now.

"Ah, Eroan, we were just discussing you."

Cheen's elders had the same poise and old-soul look about them as most village elders, at least when compared to the few Eroan had met. He'd been told the group of Cheen's five used to be six, but one of their number had died over a year ago when she'd been hunted by wolves. The sixth seat at the round table was empty and Eroan tried to fight off the unsettling feeling as the remaining elders smiled their polite smiles in his direction.

Still at the door, he bowed his head and caught sight of Curan among the side seats. There were a handful of other important elves here too, figures he barely lingered on. Why did this feel as though he were featuring in his own trial?

Anye, the female who had spoken when he'd arrived, was perhaps the same age as Curan, maybe a little older, if the crinkle lines around her eyes were any indication of her age. She reminded Eroan of Xena, and that too set his nerves on edge. He continued to feel Xena's absence like a hole in his heart.

"Greetings, elders." Eroan approached the long, oval, oak table.

"The impact of your arrival among us has been a profound one," Anye said. "And we are honored to have you in our number." She wore light gray gowns and bore a small Celtic tattoo on her neck in the same way many of the Cheen villagers liked to ink themselves. Not long after he'd arrived, he'd asked her what it meant, and she'd given him a look telling him never to ask again. Eroan assumed the ink was a reminder of something lost.

Standing before her now, his instincts itched. If they were about to ask him to take a seat at that table, he was afraid he'd say something that would likely get him tossed out of the elder house and possibly out of Cheen altogether. Xena had managed his wild tongue but he was still new to Cheen, his roots still settling in. He knew to keep his words careful, but that wasn't usually his way.

"Ashford should be made aware of the success of our additional weapons," he blurted before any of them could reveal what it was that had them all smiling thin smiles. "I'd like to head out today and take the details to them."

"Yes, Curan made us aware of your insistence on this matter."

Eroan swallowed and kept his eyes on the elders, avoiding Curan's simmering presence. Maybe they were about to tell him he was out of the Order and was to report to the shores tomorrow for his first day on the boats, catching fish. Not that feeding the village wasn't important. He had the utmost respect for any and all of his kin, but he was no fisher. Patience was not his best trait.

"Our messenger has agreed to relay all your findings to Ashford just as soon as you can teach him the necessary—" Anye said.

"Your messenger?"

Chair legs scraped, drawing Eroan's eye to the dark-haired figure he'd skimmed over earlier. The male locked gazes with Eroan and dipped his chin, leading Eroan's gaze to the lines of tribal tattoo near his collar. Recognition briefly tripped Eroan's thoughts. He hadn't seen Trey in...

years. But hadn't forgotten him. Trey was the kind of male difficult to forget. He'd cut his hair shorter, so even though it was tied back, most of it fell forward, framing a handsome and distinctive face. He'd also gained a scar and something of a haunted look in his eyes that hadn't been there in his youth. It was a wonder he was still alive. Village messengers died as regularly as assassins.

Eroan's mind turned over. He looked down, trying to reorganize how this should go. He hadn't expected them to say yes and certainly hadn't expected to be sending Trey into danger. But he'd wanted this, hadn't he? "That's not necessary," he heard himself saying, and with it came the strength of knowing he was right. Murmurs tittered around the hall. Eroan raised his voice. "The time it would take me to tell Trey everything I've learned is time better spent traveling."

"It's my job," Trey drawled, the elf's emotive eyes full of confidence.

Eroan ignored him. Another elf wasn't going to die for his ideas. He'd do this himself. "I'm leaving today with or without your blessing."

The titters turned to vocal denials. Cheen's people clearly didn't like the idea of losing someone they considered an asset. "Since my arrival, I've given you much." He addressed the room, scanning over them all. Nye was here, standing at the back, almost completely hidden in shadow. Janna too, with her partner Ross seated beside her, his hand on her knee. "It's time I shared the knowledge with others, saving more lives, and spreading the tools we need to win this war, not just survive it."

"Quiet please..." another of the elders urged the crowd.

When the chattering died down Eroan waited for the verdict. He didn't need their blessing, but he'd prefer to leave with it. Perhaps Anye knew that, because as she stared back, he saw the moment her mind changed. Her rigid mouth and cool eyes warmed.

"All right," she said. "Go, but not alone. Another must travel with you."

"I don't need—"

Anye's glare sharpened whip-quick. "As long as you are an Assassin of the Order, you follow their teachings. Assassins must always travel in prides of two or more. Is that not correct, Eroan?"

"Yes," he replied, feeling like an elfling in Order training all over again.

"I'll go with him," Nye's voice rang out from the back of the hall.

Eroan clenched his teeth.

"Unless Eroan objects?" Nye approached the table, keeping a respectable distance between them. Just two Order assassins doing their duty.

Eroan wanted very much to object but Nye was a capable assassin and the Order rules to run in prides of more than two applied for a reason. His chances of getting the information to Ashford doubled if he wasn't alone. He could ask for another of the Order, but Curan *would* object when Nye had already volunteered for the dangerous trek.

"No objections," Eroan said.

"Good, then it's settled." Anye beamed. "You leave as soon as you're ready. May Alumn's light guide your path, assassins."

Nye filed out of the hall directly behind Eroan. Eroan made it halfway across the village before turning on his heel. "I don't need an escort, Nye. Your talents are better spent here, keeping Cheen's people alive. By Alumn..." Eroan backed away. "You know we're over, so why drag it out like this?" A few village-folks glanced over, having heard Eroan's words.

Nye waited. "Are you finished?"

Eroan bit into his cheek. He was far from finished, but nothing he said was going to change anything. Nye was nothing if not stubborn.

"This has nothing to do with *us*." Nye stepped closer. "And everything to do with getting your information to Ashford. If you trek there alone, you're at risk of failing and you're the only one who has the knowledge. If it wasn't me, you'd ditch anyone else who volunteered or sneak off without them so you can continue your crusade alone." Nye paused, waiting for Eroan to deny it. "You think you can do it all alone, but you can't. Stop being so stubborn and see this for what it is. I'm here to help you get the task done. Nothing else. You said it yourself, we're Assassins of the Order and that must come first. I am capable of doing my job without emotional attachment. I've been doing it all my life."

He was right. Eroan was wrong to doubt his motives and wrong to think he could do this alone. It still felt like a mistake, but Nye had made sure Eroan's choices were limited. "We leave at dusk."

CHAPTER 5

$\mathcal{L}$ysander

LYSANDER CRACKED AN EYE OPEN. He'd chosen to sleep as dragon, mostly because they hadn't given him a bed and the floor was damned hard unless you had scales to bear the weight.

Chloe paced outside the bars, worrying her bottom lip between her teeth.

He watched her through narrow lids. She chewed on her thumbnail then picked at the wick. He could smell her fear, a zingy scent that quickened his heart, making him want to pounce and chase. It was the first time he'd smelled anything like it on her. She hadn't been afraid on the beach. She hadn't run screaming from the warehouse when he'd shifted the first time. What had her spooked now?

He huffed through his nose, alerting her to how he was

awake. She jolted and for a brief second, the fear was all over her, in her face, her eyes, her rod-straight back. Instincts plucked at him to leap and maul. Like this, she exuded *prey*.

Lysander gave his head a shake, clearing the urges, and rumbled low in his throat. Not a growl. This noise was meant for lesser kits, an alert or a small warning to kick them into line, nothing aggressive.

She approached the cage.

If he churned the fire, he could probably stir up enough in a few seconds to blast her before she made it to the door. She'd be dead in seconds. She really was afraid if she wasn't thinking clearly. But not afraid of him. Something else stalked Chloe.

He considered shifting but thought better of it when her wide eyes roamed his face, distracting her thoughts. His own reflection shone green in her eyes. Green scales, green eyes. The fan of his broad, spiked crown.

"You understand me like this, don't you?" she asked.

He huffed again, a gentle puff from the nose that stirred her hair and brought a smile to her hard mouth.

"But you can't talk?"

He rolled his eyes and set her laughing. Of course, he couldn't talk. He had a mouth and tongue designed to break prey and crush bones, not form intricate human words. As she chuckled at her own idiocy, he stretched out a foot, claws gleaming, and planted it close to the bars. His foreclaws, the larger front claws, were half the size of her. One swipe, and he could cut her in half. She carefully eyed the rack of deadly weapons. Few humans had ever gotten so close to a dragon and lived to speak of it.

When she didn't approach, he planted his head next to his foreleg and peered down his snout at the little human woman. Even with his head this low, she was still smaller than his eye level.

"You have beautiful eyes." She folded her arms. "But if you think I'm coming any closer just because you're giving me those sad eyes, you can think again, *mon lézard*."

He couldn't be sure, but he was fairly certain she'd just called him a reptile. He grumbled and grinned, revealing sparkling rows of devastating teeth. It was the wrong thing to do. She swallowed and backed away, the scent of her fear spiking again.

Before he lost her altogether, he summoned the shift, calling his form into itself and crushing the great weight of him into his thumping heart and long-limbed meat-sack, revealing the illusion of a man. She'd looked away, as most human did from visceral magic. He grabbed the bars. "I can help you stop him."

"Who?"

He frowned at her stupid denial. "We both know Dokul is coming. You can't stop a dragon like him. He's an ancient, the first to wake from the ice. I can barely stop him, but he wants me. So, let me go, I'll draw him away and nobody needs to die."

All her warmth had frozen over again. "If I let you go, you'll kill us all for him, Lysander *Bronze*." She started pacing again.

"I'm not a bronze."

"He says otherwise."

"He's insane."

"And you're not?"

Insane? He almost laughed. He only felt like it some days. "Have I hurt any of you?"

"You've been in there." She flapped her hand at the cage.

This human female was impossible. How could he prove good intentions to her? "I delivered the elf to the beach. I didn't attack any of your people. I could have shifted on that beach and killed the lot of you."

"No you couldn't. You were shot. You didn't want to risk the bolt moving to your heart. I know how it works..."

He tightened his grip on the bars. "Chloe, if I'd wanted to hurt you, I could have. There were what? Six, eight of your men in that tunnel beneath the bronze warren? I could have shifted and slaughtered every single one. The elf too. Your little dragon-teeth knives might have slowed me down, but the outcome would have been the same. I gave you the elf—"

"An unconscious elf. For all I know, you did that to her and you were taking her to the beach to eat. Her leader told us to have you killed so he clearly thought the same."

Lysander rolled his lips together and bought himself a moment to school his emotions, keeping them far from his face. "Eroan is an assassin, he was hardly going to advise you to let me go."

She stopped her pacing and squinted. "How do you know his name?"

"Eroan Ilanea. I know his name because I saved him from the queen. Did you see his swords?" Her eyes narrowed. "Those were mine. He learned about dragon-teeth from *me*." That was a little stretch of the truth, but technically not a lie.

"And yet he gave the order to have you killed? That's hardly the behavior of someone who knew you and believes you to be good. Was that another misunderstanding?"

He bowed his head and bumped it against the bars. "Damn it, human, would you just believe me? Dokul is...

He wants me, but not for the reasons you think. I'm not some important heir. Dokul wants me for some sick fascination he has and because I've slipped through his fingers at his every try to have me. If he finds me, he'll kill me."

She mulled over his words, chewing on her thumb again. "*Il est illusoire de s'imaginer que.* I can't let you out."

"Then you'll die!"

"No, he'll come and we'll kill him."

"Tell me you know that, for certain. That you have some amazing new weapon that goes beyond dragon-teeth, because those teeth won't be enough. He's not just any dragon, he's a force of nature. The earth cradled the first three dragons for thousands of years. A few fancy arrows won't stop him."

She shook her head and headed toward the door. "I can't let you out, Lysander."

"You can," he called. "I'll help you stop him!"

The door slammed behind her. He punched the bars and growled at the resulting pain rippling up his arm. "You're all dead!" His shout echoed.

She was gone, and with her, his last chance and theirs at surviving what was to come.

CHAPTER 6

 roan

THE RAIN SET in immediately after leaving Cheen and hadn't let up in the two days Nye and Eroan had been on the move. The trek would take them first down to the coast, where an inlet divided rolling hills, and then upward, into open moorland, until eventually down again into the valley that sheltered Ashford.

Starting a fire had become near impossible, and when the flames did catch, they weren't worth cooking on. Rabbits were plentiful but eating them raw wasn't nearly as appetizing as roasted. That left foraging for winterberries and ripe acorns.

The relentless rain muffled any sound they made, but also hindered listening for dragons and other predators. The temperature dropped two days into the journey, turning the ground to ice and fresh rainfalls to fat, dallying snowflakes. Spring's early shoots soon disappeared beneath the snowfall.

Nye nursed a campfire, trying to coax the flames higher. He blew into his hands. "This is why I'm not a messenger. Can you imagine living like this?"

"I prefer killing dragons." Eroan huddled against a tree, breath misting as he listened outside of Nye's complaints. Naked trees reached skyward into the endless gray. The sky was as gray as the ground, blurring where one began and the other ended. Easterly snowfall like this wasn't rare, but its timing, at the end of winter, meant wolves would be hungry, bold, and on the lookout for travelers. The fire, should Nye get it built up enough, would keep most predators away.

Nye muttered another complaint, along the lines of having wet feet.

They'd spoken little, and that was fine by Eroan, though he'd caught Nye's long glances and caught himself doing the same often enough. During the long march across the land, Eroan's thoughts had wandered back to Nye, wondering if he'd been too hasty in cutting him out. It wasn't that he didn't care for Nye, he cared for him the same way he cared for all elves in the Order. Nye was honorable, strong, brave. There was no reason not to love him, and yet Eroan couldn't bring himself to commit to more. It wasn't Nye, it was him. Nye had been right. Eroan went looking for battles to fight. He always had, since Curan had found him as a youngling, wet and alone, born of a storm, his only memory that of a dragon's savage attack that took his parents. Maybe after that, he didn't know how to love? He'd ruined what he had with Janna and had now done the same with Nye. Or maybe Alumn believed he didn't deserve to find love?

A twig snapped, pricking Eroan's ear. Eyes narrowed, he straightened away from the tree, waved Nye's concerned glance away, and started maneuvering his way between snow-blanketed trees. Eroan's all-weather coat, a dapple of grays, blended in well with the surroundings, but so did a wolf's. No dragon could tread lightly. The sound had to be that of a larger animal. He ventured through the dense trees to where a stream steamed in the cold air, fogging his line of sight.

A trail of small boot prints led up the stream's bank and then farther down, stopping behind a tree.

"Come out, Seraph." His soft voice traveled until the muted quiet swallowed it up.

"How did you know?" She emerged from behind the tree, wrapped head to toe in a fur-lined hooded coat, sword on her back, as always, nose pink and lips pale.

He smiled. "I didn't, but I had an idea a day back when someone spooked a deer herd."

She plodded over, snow crunching underfoot. "Yeah, well, you forgot to wait for me, so of course I was going to follow you."

"Forgot to wait for you?" He arched an eyebrow. He'd had no intention of waiting for her, or even telling her he was leaving, knowing this exact situation would have happened. And here she was anyway.

She thumped him playfully on the arm. "Where you go, I go. We're a pride now."

"Is that so?"

She shrugged and stomped back through Eroan's tracks toward the slither of smoke rising from Nye's small fire. "No way am I staying in Cheen without you." She turned and linked the little finger on each hand together. "We're like this, right? We bonded at the bronze wall. Don't tell me we didn't or feed me some nonsense about going back to Cheen for my *own safety*." She mocked his voice, the one he'd used to scold young and foolish trainee assassins.

"Right." He patted her on the head and jogged ahead. "Come on then, if you can keep up."

"Ha, keep up? I'd have been there by now if you two hadn't slowed me down."

Nye looked up from the fire, flashing a broad grin. "It's about time you stopped messing around in the woods, Seraph."

She frowned at him, then at Eroan. "I wasn't messing around."

"You need to work on softening your footing," he added. "For someone so small, you make a lot of noise."

Her scowl hardened. She threw her hands down, gesturing at the snow melting on her boots. "Snow crunches. I don't have wings—"

"No," a new male voice said, "but I do." A tall figure emerged among the trees, his armor so black it looked like a hole in the snow. Ruffles of black wolf-fur lined his collar and wrists. Long, unbraided black hair fanned about his shoulders, reaching halfway down his arms.

Akiem.

Eroan's instincts roared to the surface. He freed his sword, surging forward, making a barrier between Akiem and Seraph. The last time Eroan had seen Akiem, he'd ordered Eroan's torture. Seeing him here, now, hands raised and walking into their camp like it was perfectly acceptable, summoned a terrible, wild recklessness: To kill, to protect. He bared his teeth. "Take a step closer and I'll gut you where you stand."

Akiem's left eyebrow twitched. "Please, your threats are worthless. Even with my brother's sword you couldn't overpower me, *elf*." He had snarled *elf* as an insult. Dark eyes skipped to the sight behind Eroan, taking in Nye and Seraph.

He couldn't be alone. Akiem was no fool. There would be others nearby. But where? Which direction?

Eroan scanned the sky. The low, gray clouds could easily hide a flight of dragons.

His heart thumped. Memories crowded close: Akiem ordering Red-Eye to start cutting and the sizzling agony that followed. Akiem's words had left their scars.

He moved in.

"Not another step, dragon," Eroan warned.

Akiem lowered his hands and stopped his approach. "I'm not here to hurt you."

"No?" Seraph snarled, voice quaking. "You destroyed my home! You took me to the bronze! I remember you!" She bolted around Eroan and unleashed a roar, all fire and fury.

Eroan hooked an arm around her waist, pulling her back, into his arms, trapping her flailing sword-arm at her side. She bucked and kicked. "Stop..." he growled out. "Stop, Seraph."

"Let me go!"

"You can't fight him now... Not here." He wanted to. The fire in his blood demanded vengeance. He could taste it, like acid on his tongue. But the risk was too great and his mission too important. The dragon could have killed them all by now, so clearly he didn't want them dead. They could still survive this.

Her struggles subsided. He kept her trapped, knowing her too well to fall for her submissive act. The second he let her go, she'd lunge at Akiem.

"And I remember you," Akiem said. "The fiery little

65

elfling the bronze chief took a liking to. You escaped him, I see. I'm intrigued as to how you managed that."

"I'm not telling you a damned thing, monster!"

"You both have my brother's swords." Akiem mused, his smile razor thin. "Where you are, elf," his gaze flicked to Eroan, "Lysander follows. So tell me, where is he?"

Eroan swallowed. Could it be Akiem didn't know Lysander was dead? "Why should we tell you anything?"

He breathed in, nostrils widening. "If you don't, it would be nothing for me to crush all three of you. There are no dragon carcasses nearby for you to hide in."

He'd known. And he'd let them go. He hadn't wanted to kill them outside Cheen, he'd wanted answers. But being dragon hadn't worked. And now he was here, looking a human, though he could never fully imitate them. He stood too still, his gaze unblinking.

"We can soon make one." Nye moved up to stand close behind Eroan.

Akiem chuckled, "You elves really are very entertaining." He examined a piece of grit under his nails, then stretched his fingers, rippling them, like Eroan had seen dragons do with their claws. "I can see why Lysander would keep Eroan as a pet." His gaze lingered now on Eroan. "You're easy on the eye, at least. My mother recognized that in you."

Old memories swirled, old wounds reopening. A cool sweat dampened Eroan's skin. A leather collar clamped around his neck. A knife carving through his chest. "Lysander is dead."

Akiem's smile vanished. "How do you know this?"

"I killed him myself."

Purple fire flashed in his eyes. "When?"

"When the bronze line fell. On the beach..."

Seraph tensed in Eroan's arms. He should have told her before now, but some part of him had hoped he'd never have to.

Akiem tilted his head, studying Eroan. "That was months ago. Lysander is not dead. He was captured on that beach. You were there, elf. You will tell me where he is. *No more lies.*" A rumbling growl bubbled from the dragon, a sound no man could make.

"He's dead. I…" Eroan hated the break in his voice, the stammer in his words. Seraph bucked again, and this time he let her go. She stumbled back, away from him and Akiem, toward Nye. Eroan couldn't look at her, knowing the horror he'd see on her face. "I had him killed," he admitted. Confusion muddied Akiem's expression. "I thought he was just another dragon. He's dead."

Akiem sighed hard. "You believe it, but you're wrong. Dokul would not be tearing great swathes in the land to find Lysander if his body had been discarded on that beach. He's alive, elf. But clearly, you're of no use to me." Akiem turned away, black cloak whipping around him. "Be gone from these hills by morning when I will be hungry for elf."

Seraph pushed forward and opened her mouth to fling what would probably be an insult at him. Eroan shook his head. "Don't." He had more reason than any of them to want Akiem dead, and one day he'd see it happen, but not here. They were not prepared and igniting Akiem's ire while he was leaving would only see them all killed. "Let him go. Our mission comes first."

"Let him go!? Who even are you because there's no way Eroan Ilanea would have let that beast just walk away!"

Eroan kicked at the fire, instantly dousing it under snow. "We move now, and we keep moving."

"He's the reason Xena was killed!"

"I know!" Eroan snapped back, jolting Seraph in surprise. Fear fluttered her lashes. Fear of him, he realized. Replacing the sword on his back he set off on the track away from the camp. "Nobody wants Akiem dead more than me."

"*You* killed Lysander?" Her words echoed through the silence, chasing him down. He pulled his coat tighter and trudged on.

"Hush," Nye said. "Let's not draw more beasts to us."

Seraph barged by Eroan and stomped into his path. "Tell me. I deserve to know. He saved me, Eroan. And he kept on saving me and you... he saved you, and you killed him?" Her big eyes glistened.

"Yes. And I've thought of little else. Now get. I'm done talking about it. We keep moving—"

"Did *you* do it?" She squared up to him. "Did you?" She shoved at his chest, rocking him on his feet. "Well, did you kill the one dragon who's only ever helped us?"

A shuddering sigh melted the rage away, leaving him cold and wretched. "You were unconscious and they brought a dragon out. He had a bag over his head." Alumn, he remembered what that felt like. The suffocating lack of air, the disorientation. "I didn't know who he was... until you said he'd saved you." That same heartfelt pain tried to crush him now. "I told them to have him killed. It's done." *Kill him. Make him suffer.*

"Then what that dragon said could be true?" she asked. "He could be alive, right? The humans might have him."

Eroan shoved her out the way and marched onward, boots crunching through the snow. "None of that matters... Our duty is here."

But it did matter. He could feel the little flicker of

back. Eroan freed one of the daggers of his own design from the sheath at his hip and held it out, handle first. The guard's scrutinizing gaze took the blade's curve and serrated edge in, then equally critically roamed over Nye and Seraph.

"I'm Sentinel Venali. We have heard of your accomplishments, Eroan. You and your companions are welcome at Ashford. Follow us." The guard whistled and his pride of elves wordlessly closed ranks behind them, escorting them down a hillside toward what appeared to be a mound of grass-covered earth. Eroan had been here before, long ago, when Xena decided to have him see the rest of elven society—likely grooming him for a seat on the elder council. The mound sheltered a covered door, one of several well-guarded entrances to Ashford's underground center. From the outside, Ashford was no more than a rolling landscape of grass and gorse with the occasional odd bump in the earth, but below the surface beat the cavernous heart of elven society.

"What is this place?" Seraph asked as they trekked down what appeared to be a metal staircase burrowed through the earth. Where the metal had rusted away, industrious elves had patched the holes with timber. Strange metallic ribs poked through the dirt walls. Parts of the old, human-made walls, Eroan assumed.

"It used to be a human meeting place." Eroan recalled Xena's teachings. "A temple or some kind of communal gathering area where they traded goods. Hundreds of years ago, it was above ground, like all their huge settlements were."

The tunnel opened into a vast open space made up of several galleried floors. In the center of the atrium, an enormous tree reached through the floors and up to where light poured from a domed glass ceiling. Dust motes dallied in the air like snowflakes might and a few wintering butterflies twitched and skittered between the tree's budding branches. Little had changed, Eroan noticed, as Nye and Seraph approached the safety rail. Vines and flora still dangled from the higher levels. Moss coated much of the surfaces, hiding whatever the structure behind. Once, he'd been told, the levels flowed with hundreds of people, each visiting the internal rooms to buy goods. There were hundreds of rooms here, some large, some tiny. So many that most were closed off, the elves only used a third of the space excavated over the years.

"Please, follow us." Venali urged them on toward an official entrance where they were asked their names and village and waved on through the heavy iron doors. Venali's pride dissipated.

"Have you been to Ashford before?" Venali asked.

"I have," Eroan replied, "many seasons ago."

"You'll find the residential wing in the same place. Head straight there and you'll be assigned temporary quarters for your stay. I'll inform the Order of your arrival. You'll be summoned to an audience with them shortly."

Eroan nodded and led Nye and Seraph down the staircase from one floor to another, passing many elves. Some were marked like Cheen's villagers, others had paler skin, some with darker skin and narrow eyes. But all wore layered clothing that seemed to indicate importance, like villager elders. Eroan wished he'd paid more attention to Xena all those years ago.

"I've never seen anything like this ..." Seraph muttered, wide-eyed. She caught the rail of the first floor and peered up through the central atrium and reaching branches to where they'd originally entered on the levels above. "It's huge." Columns of light plunged straight through the center, making the tree appear to glow. Murmurs from the residents going about their business kept the quiet at bay, peppered by the occasional laugh. Elves strode from place to place or loitered in the light at the atrium's center. "It's... *magical*."

Eroan leaned against the rail and took a few moments to admire what the Ashford elves had built here. There were more of them than he remembered. He counted thirty at a glance, with many coming and going. Hunters, elders, guards, but few children. This was no place for elflings.

"That tree must be hundreds of years old. How have the dragons not discovered this place?" Nye whispered.

"Only esteemed elders and messengers are permitted inside," Eroan said. "Ashford's exact location is kept hidden from anyone who doesn't need to know."

"Elders, messengers and *you*." Nye's mouth quirked around a smile.

"Xena brought me here," he said, trying to imply their entry had nothing to do with his reputation when they all knew no elf would have turned Eroan away.

Their quarters were ample-sized windowless rooms fitted with simple cot beds and plumbed water systems, very different to their village huts. Seraph squealed with delight and plunged her hands into a basin of warm water, then sat on her bed and bounced a few times before flinging herself backward onto the clean, puffy sheets with a sigh. "I've died and found Alumn's garden."

Eroan smiled at her glee. He wouldn't have traded an Ashford room for his own hut. He needed the light, the breeze, the earth beneath his feet. Most elves didn't stay in Ashford for long, the center was a place of business, of rule-making and council meetings. Elves were not designed to be hidden below ground, which was likely why no dragon had thought to look for them here.

After having his wet coat collected for cleaning and drying, and fresh clothes left for him to change into, he was collected and taken to the Higher Order's council chambers. Tapestries hung on the walls, making the Order chamber feel small despite being four times the size of Cheen's Order house.

The Order assassins greeted him as Cheen's had, with relief and respect. He let them tell of how his own myth had grown, smiling at their polite greetings and delight in his arrival.

Once they'd settled, he told the dais of elders the knowledge he'd gained from the humans, their ingenious weapons, and the designs of dragon-teeth weapons. Question after question came next. They wanted details of his stay with the humans in the land called France, the layout of the amethyst tower, the number of dragons he'd seen, and the names of those he'd met. The meeting went on for hours, until the light had faded and the torches and candles were lit to chase away the night. He should have expected it but dredging up his time in the tower left him drained, and the memories fresh in his mind. Finally, the Order dismissed him until the morning, and he left them deliberating everything among themselves.

"I wondered if they were keeping you forever." Nye stood propped against the bannister outside Eroan's room, uncaring about the drop through the atrium to the ground floor behind him.

"Felt like it." He entered his quarters, leaving the door open behind him. Perhaps he should have let it click closed, but exhaustion clouded his thoughts. Being alone with the memories so close felt like a death sentence. He filled the room's small basin with cool water and plunged his hands in, then splashed the water over his face. They'd wanted to know it all. So many questions... so much he'd tried to forget.

Would the horror of the tower ever leave him?

A hand settled on his back, between his shoulders and although Nye couldn't have known how his touch brushed the whip scars beneath, Eroan had to fight the urge to brush the touch away—to push Nye away. The memories were close, crowding in. The whip cracks, sounds he'd thought he'd forgotten sounded again, making muscles jolt.

"They wanted to know it all?" Nye softly asked.

He removed his hand, allowing Eroan to finally breathe and settle his nerves. Before the dragon queen, he'd been stronger than this, better than this. Nothing had rattled him. But now... He ran a wet hand around the back of his neck, cooling flushed skin. "All of it."

He hadn't told Nye half of what had been done to him, but much of it had been obvious in the scars he now carried, outside and in.

"Did you tell them?"

"Some." Some things were too painful to tell but he was sure they read between his words.

"It will get easier." Nye leaned against the wall and folded his arms. "Give it time."

Eroan felt his mouth curl into a wry smile. Xena had said the same. Now she was dead. "With the knowledge I've just given them, they can make a real difference." He straightened and ran a wet hand through his hair, pulling it back from his face. "They'll send messengers to other villages. The Order will have a purpose again, but this time it will be to end the dragons, for good. Elves have weapons now... just not the numbers, but it can be done... if we partner with humans." He hadn't broached that with the elders yet, and they'd likely be reluctant, but it was the only way. He had to make them see the potential in working with the humans again—like elves had once before.

"Xena would be proud, you know?" Nye said. "She always was, but to see all you've accomplished... She is with Alumn, and she sees you."

So why did he still feel like a failure? "It's not enough."

"Only to you." Nye reached out and lay a gentle hand on Eroan's shoulder. "Don't be so hard on yourself."

Nye's gaze was full of too much understanding. Eroan had seen the same look on Xena's face, like everything would be all right if he just gave it time, but time wasn't going to change his past, time wasn't going to fix the future. Time did nothing without action. Eroan needed to act.

Nye turned his face away, toward the door, contemplating leaving. Not so long ago, Eroan would have pulled Nye close and kissed him on the neck, right where Nye couldn't help but give in. They'd have fallen into one another, into the place Eroan could go to forget.

He took Nye's hand from his shoulder and lowered it between them, but held on, not wanting to let go. Nye looked down at their joined hands. His dark hair fell forward, hiding his expression, then his fingers slipped from Eroan's and with a regrettable smile, Nye left. The door closed behind him with a definitive click.

It was for the best, but that didn't make it easier. And now Eroan was alone with the memories.

He threw on his coat, headed out of his room and

knocked on Seraph's door. She answered moments later, bleary-eyed and yawning. "Did you just get back?"

"Walk with me?" He forced a smile and hoped if he wore it long enough, it would stick. "I'll show you Ashford. At night, the moonlight filters into the atrium. It's beautiful."

Her mouth stretched into a grin. "Yes!" She bounded back inside and reemerged moments later, her hair dampened down and her eyes a little brighter. With her alongside him, her chattering full of wonder, the bad memories finally fell away.

TALKS PERSISTED FOR DAYS. Eroan sketched out the plans for the ballista weapons and others he'd learned from the humans. Messengers were dispatched. A war council was to be summoned to Ashford, and Eroan would be on that council as a ruling member. Progress. It felt good, better than good, it felt right. And yet he still couldn't shake the feeling it wasn't enough.

Sunlight poured in through the atrium and Eroan took a few moments between meetings to sit and soak up the light among a few other elves doing the same. Lying back among the roots, hands laced behind his head, he watched the dust motes drift on the breeze. He should have been at peace, but something had his body and blood restless.

Seraph dropped into a cross-legged position beside him. "How's it all going?"

"Good." With the sun behind Seraph, he squinted at her, catching part of her smile in front of the glare. Whatever she'd gotten up to over the past few days, it agreed with her. She glowed in the warm light. "You?"

"Awesome." She flicked her scarred ear. "They all want to know how I got this, so naturally I told them how I killed the dragon who did it. Then I told them how I was at the bronze wall when it fell and now, I'm like... some kind of hero or something. *Seraph Brennan,*" she gushed, "*partner to Eroan Ilanea, Slayers of Dragons.*"

He smiled and closed his eyes, basking in the warmth. The council would be calling him back soon. He just needed a moment in the light to feed his bones and shake off the growing sense of unease. Tiredness, that was all. It would pass.

"You know..." Seraph began, in a way that told him she was about to ask for something. "I heard they've had a new message from France."

Eroan kept his eyes closed. His smile faltered.

"The bronze chief is closing in on Lysander's location. The humans have some plan to kill the chief. The guard I spoke to wouldn't tell me any more. I er... I might have listened in anyway. The elders think the plan will fail. They've tried to advise against it. Like always, the stupid humans aren't listening." She let that sink in and said, "He'll get Lysander."

Eroan's breathing stuttered, despite his best efforts to calm it, along with his treacherous heart trying to race ahead of his thoughts. "There's nothing I can do."

"You know where he is, don't you?"

How had she figured that out? He cracked an eye open to find her peering down at him. "I have a good idea, yes. The humans I stayed with, they built a substantial cage to keep a dragon."

"And those are the same humans who took the bronze wall with you?"

He nodded. "If he's alive, he's there."

"And you're just going to let that beast find him?"

He wet his lips and closed his eyes again to keep her from seeing him falter. "He'll be where he belongs, with his own kind." They were his words, and they sounded like something he should say, but they tasted bitter and wrong, like something poisonous.

She made a disgruntled huffing noise. "His own kind? It seems to me, from everything I've heard about your time with him, and from what I saw myself, Lysander is *nothing* like his own kind."

"He's a dragon prince, Seraph. For all we know, what we saw was an act." Still his words. Still lies.

"To what end?"

It wasn't an act. He wasn't even sure why he was saying these things. He clearly remembered the prince who had tried to get him to eat, telling him he'd need his strength. The same prince who appeared drunk when Eroan was trussed up against the queen's wall, his eyes full of sorrow and want. The prince who was to be sold to the bronze in some strange dragon ritual. One he had clearly not wanted. The prince so hollow, he'd so desperately wanted not to be alone anymore. Eroan knew exactly what that felt like. You could be surrounded by people and still be alone.

"He vowed to keep me safe, and he did, and you don't know how he did it, because I've not told you, but you should know—"

"Seraph—"

"He sold himself to the horrible dragon for me. The things Dokul will do to him... He wants Lysander, like it's some kind of madness. I can't sleep, Eroan. I can't stop thinking about what's going to happen to him. I have to do something. You know that feeling, you follow it all the time. That inside part of you that tells you it's right. That part is telling me I owe him to at least try to help him."

Eroan sat up, pulling a leg to his chest. "You can't go."

"The bronze wall has fallen. How hard can it be? I know the way back. I'll find a boat or something..."

"Seraph, it's too dangerous."

"You did it."

He winced. "That was different."

"Why?"

Because he hadn't cared if he'd lived or died, but he cared for Seraph. "What are you going to do if you get there? Just let him out of that cage? The humans won't allow it."

Her brows pinched. "They'll listen to you."

"My place is here. We're making progress. Soon we'll be able to assault the dragon tower—"

"Come with me."

"I can't, and you can't go either. What you're suggesting is madness." He couldn't listen to this nonsense any longer and climbed to his feet. She blinked up at him. "You musn't go, Seraph. Give me your word you won't."

"He'll die," she said. "I know you wanted him dead on that beach, but I saw the look on your face after Akiem said he was alive. He's good. Can you live with yourself knowing you could have done something to save him and didn't?"

He is the future. Alumn, why couldn't he forget that old dragon's words?

"I never wanted him dead," Eroan admitted quietly. "All this time I thought I'd killed him... and when Akiem said he was alive ... I was *relieved*, yes. But that's all." It wasn't all. Akiem's words had left him with more than relief, they'd left him with feelings he didn't dare examine, the same feeling of restlessness that itched even now. He closed his hands into fists. "You can't save him. I can't save him. We are Assassins of the Order. No elf shall aid a dragon." He gritted his teeth, hearing the words and somehow hating them.

"You have to do something. He has no one else." She got to her feet too and stared up at him, her mouth set in a firm, determined line. "You're Eroan Ilanea. You're the only one who can save him."

"I do not save dragons. I kill them. And so do you." His voice shattered the quiet, silencing the chatter among the others seated around them and drawing their curious glances. "Forget this nonsense or I'll inform Curan of your indiscretion and you'll be struck from the Order."

Unshed tears gleamed in her fierce eyes.

Regret was a stone on his gut. He steeled himself against that wretched, empty feeling. Her foolish ideas would get them both reprimanded or worse.

"You know I'm right!" she snapped. "You're afraid!"

He turned away from her and the truth in her words.

"You feel it, just like I do! You'll never forgive yourself, Eroan!"

Her words rang in his ears and deeper, into the raw wounds he'd carried with him since leaving the queen's tower and Lysander to die.

He was Eroan Ilanea, Assassin of the Order. He saved elves, not dragons.

Lysander, wherever he might be, was on his own.

CHAPTER 7

$\mathcal{L}$ysander

SCREAMS and the oily smell of smoke roused Lysander from a deep, dreamless sleep. He blinked his dragon-eyes open and squinted into a bank of fog rolling into the warehouse. Not fog, he realized, heart sinking. Smoke. The dragonkin were here.

As dragon, he threw himself at the bars, rattling the cage structure, but it held. Again and again, he struck until his ribs ached from the impact and the smoke was almost too thick to see through. Then a dragon's roar shattered the night, calling to the depths of his soul. A roar of victory, so thunderous it shook the warehouse floor and walls.

Dokul.

Gods no...

Lysander shifted to human, hoping that form might be

more useful if any human arrived first. Chloe. He needed Chloe to come. She'd come with the keys and let him out. She was smart. Stupid too, but also smart. She knew he was her only hope at surviving this.

"Hey!" He gripped the bars. "Hey!"

Nobody came. The screams faded until all he could hear was fire burning and devouring.

Chloe stumbled in, rifle in her grip.

"Let me out now, Chloe!" He thrust an arm through the bars. "Quickly."

She staggered, spluttering breaths, and was halfway to the cage when a huge figure emerged from the rolling clouds of smoke.

Dokul seemed larger backlit by roiling flames. Broad shoulders carried his muscular bulk. His face sneered his victory. Like every time Lysander had seen him, the male wore one bronze pauldron, the rest of his upper body and head were bare, hairless, and gleaming in the firelight. A pale scar smiled across his neck where Seraph had cut him.

"Stay back or I'll kill Lysander," Chloe stammered, making it another few steps. She aimed the rifle at Lysander.

Lysander gripped the bars. "Let me out." Calm and steady, if he pushed too much, she'd run.

She glanced his way, eyes wide with panic. *Let me out,* he tried to convey with his eyes alone. *You can still live but you have to let me out now.*

Dokul's liquid laugh filled the warehouse. He strode closer, boots clunking. The metal adornments clipped to his belt rattled and chimed. "That little weapon of yours will not kill Lysander the same as it couldn't stop me."

Dokul's gaze fell to Lysander. The male's eyes darkened. His pink tongue wet his lips. The weight of his desire was a reeking, visceral thing, clearly visible in the outline of the huge erection pushing at his trousers.

Lysander ground his teeth. Disgust inched its way up his throat. "Chloe, unlock this door. You can still live."

She swung the rifle toward Dokul and fired. The bullet punched him low in the chest and out his back. Dokul barely missed a step. Blood dribbled from the bullet hole and the big male just grinned it off. He beckoned with his fingers. "Try again."

"Chloe, damn it!" Lysander slammed his hands against the bars. "Let me out!"

She dropped the gun and fumbled in her pocket, coming for the cage door. The keys shone on her fingers. So close. Seconds. Just seconds. She rummaged through the keys, searching for the right one.

They fell from her fingers, clattering to the floor.

Dokul's grin grew.

Chloe muttered in her own language, words he didn't understand. A prayer perhaps, to whatever god she worshipped. It had better answer.

Dokul sauntered closer.

He'd kill her. And then Lysander.

"Hurry," Lysander hissed.

She picked up the bundle of keys and searched for the right one, hands shaking. Her fingers clamped around a key he recognized. She pulled it free. Her eyes met Lysander's.

Dokul slammed into her from behind, crushing her against the bars. She screamed, eyes wild and searching. Lysander could do nothing but watch. Dokul grabbed her by the back of the neck and pinned her still beneath him. He yanked her head to the side and bit down, his teeth tearing into her neck, choking off her screaming.

Lysander backed up until he hit the rear of the cage. In moments, she was dead. If she was lucky, Dokul would make it quick.

Blood flowed freely from between Dokul's teeth and down, over Chloe's shoulder, soaking into her shirt. Dokul lifted his eyes and pinned Lysander under his gaze as Chloe's thrashing faded. The son of a breeding-bitch ground himself against her, his eyes burning into Lysander's. Only when she stopped fighting did he free his teeth from her neck and fling her aside.

The bite had been deliberate, one dragons performed as a proclamation of sexual dominance. It was meant for Lysander. He hadn't fucked her. He was saving that for Lysander too.

Chloe gasped where she'd fallen against the floor, her panting breaths came fast, but strong. That was good. If she stayed quiet she might survive.

"I tore the world apart looking for you." Dokul plunged the key into the cage lock. "And here you are." The mechanisms clunked and the door swung inward.

Lysander eyed the tiny gap to freedom, but it lasted only moments before Dokul's bulk filled it. The male took the door and slammed it shut behind him, locking himself inside. He lifted the keys, knowing Lysander's only chance was to retrieve them, and tucked them into his trouser pocket beside his obviously engorged cock.

It had been too much to ask for it to be Mirann who found him first.

"And here I was the whole time..." Lysander circled left and Dokul followed, chest heaving. Rivulets of perspiration ran down the male's chest. Lysander couldn't get away from the pungent smell of him, sweat and metal and now sex.

Lysander could have faked attraction before, could have managed his way through some rough sex, but not now, not like this. The raw, terrible need in his eyes? It was dragon. Dokul was barely thinking at all.

Lysander curled his fingers into fists. If only Chloe had believed him... And now there was no escaping what was coming next.

Dokul lowered his hand and stroked his cock, his golden pupils widening as he pleasured himself through the fabric. "You going to be easy, prince, or hard?"

In the corner of his eye, Lysander spotted Chloe slowly dragging herself away, leaving a trail of smeared blood behind her. *Yes, go, run, fucking survive.* Someone had to.

Dokul's hand worked. Maybe the male would overexcite himself and get it done without Lysander having to get involved.

They'd circled back around to the cage door. Lysander gave it a tug. It didn't budge. Not surprising, considering how his luck was going. "So, you came all this way to make me watch you jerk off?"

"I've waited a long time for this." Dokul stepped right, ending the circling, trapping Lysander in the corner. "Nowhere to go. You're all mine." The wall of muscle surged forward.

Lysander ducked and pushed off the bars, easily avoiding Dokul's lumbering attack. The male growled and rebounded, starting after him again. "The more you try to escape, the more I want you, *Lysander Bronze.*"

"About that name—"

Dokul darted right. Lysander feigned left, then bounced back, leaving Dokul off-balance and open for the fist Lysander planted across his jaw. It was well-aimed and hit hard, if the retort of pain blasting up Lysander's arm was anything to go by. The problem was, hitting Dokul was like trying to knock out a mountain, and the male swung back, slamming a fist into Lysander's middle, instantly blasting all the air out of his lungs.

Black spots swam in Lysander's vision. Dokul's steely fingers clamped around his neck and the male's free hand was at Lysander's waist, desperately pulling on his belt. Lysander's head spun, lungs burning for air. This was happening. Fuck, this was happening... after everything, after years of fighting him off.

Dokul pushed Lysander face-first into the bars and growled into Lysander's ear. The rod-hard press of Dokul's cock shoved against his ass. With too many clothes between them, Lysander had time to stop this if he could just breathe again. He focused on that, breathing in, breathing out, as Dokul's rough hands fought with his belt and trousers. Passing out wouldn't save him from Dokul's fit of lust, he'd wake again with Dokul on him, *in* him.

Blurred spots began to clear, his lungs inflating again, his body coming back to him. There was still time.

Dokul's blunt teeth sank into his neck.

He let out an involuntary cry and clutched at the bars. The teeth sank deeper. Lysander pushed back, but Dokul was too big, too heavy, and with his teeth in his neck, the rough movement forced Dokul's teeth deeper still. Blood flowed and a sick, twisting sense that he'd already lost slithered around him. Dokul's growls grew heavier and suddenly his efforts spent on Lysander's clothing paid off. Lysander's belt and trousers skimmed down, over his hips. Cold air hit the back of his thighs and with it came the shock of reality. The male's hand was gone, his body easing off. Lysander bucked, cracked his head back, striking something. Pain flashed. Dokul shoved against his shoulder. The hard thrust of the male's cock dove between Lysander's ass and thighs, the male's haste the only thing saving him from penetration.

Lysander growled through his teeth. Thoughts pulling together, he summoned the magic that would free his true form, and yanked all the power into him, releasing the shift in a sudden, furious blast that tore him open and at the same time remade him into dragon.

Dokul must have recognized the signs the second Lysander called to the magic, and the bronze chief responded in-kind. Mid-shift, Lysander registered the taste of metal and old magics. A smothering weight pushed in from behind and another crushed his chest until Lysander thought his bones might all shatter at once. Then the cage bars exploded outward, spilling him into the warehouse with Dokul—all wings and claws —behind him.

Lysander whirled, tucked his good wing in, and charged at the enormous bronze's middle, slamming into the beast's chest and driving on, through a wall, out into a world of smoke and fire and burning bodies. Bricks and dust bounced off his scales. He couldn't let up, not for a second.

Dokul's enormous dragon form scrabbled in the dirt for purchase, his claws digging up great furrows of earth. He dug in and twisted, tail lashing like a whip.

Lysander struck at his neck, teeth snapping together too late with a resounding crack. He'd missed.

Dokul's mountainous weight slammed into Lysander's broken wing. White agony snapped up Lysander's side, momentarily burying him in nowhere and nothing, wrenching a roar up his throat and out. He needed to turn this around, to fight back, to focus, but Dokul's clawed foot came down, clamping on Lysander's neck, pinning him to the ground. Air lodged in Lysander's throat. Fire churned, trapped behind Dokul's weight. He snapped and snarled, trying to bite and tear at the heavier dragon's grip.

Dokul spread his vast wings, flung his head skyward, and bellowed toward the skies.

Pain fizzled and snapped down Lysander's spine. He writhed and bucked, tried to claw at the dirt, to dig in and buck Dokul off, but the bronze was a crushing weight on his neck, choking off his consciousness.

Dokul's smothering weight shifted, settling between Lysander's wings, and the foot on his neck was replaced by rows of piercing teeth. Each of those teeth sank through scale, plunging into Lysander's flesh. An ill-timed twitch from Lysander and Dokul's bite would tear out his throat. Pinned, beaten, Lysander's panicked thoughts tumbled over, searching for a way out, for escape. This couldn't happen. He hadn't spent a lifetime fighting for Dokul to win now.

Pain and pressure pushed at Lysander's rear, beneath his tail—a hard, barbed rod spread him open, forcing inside. Lysander locked his jaw and gritted his teeth together so hard the ache in his head almost overcame the ache *below*. Unbidden growls burbled through his chest, but with his throat clamped, he couldn't roar out the hurt. His foreclaws sank into the dirt, digging deep as Dokul fell into a sickening, pounding rhythm. The beast's rapid grunting filled Lysander's head, forcing its way inside, just like the rest of him. Splintering pain broke him open until his whole world became Dokul's weight, his grunting, and the agony he dealt with every thrust.

But inside it all, a new fire made of hate burned, a fire so furious it could burn the world.

~

THE ENORMOUS BRONZE brood had abandoned their warren across the ocean channel for the fields of Northern France. They'd excavated a huge crater, forming a nest, and although exposed to the winter elements, it didn't seem to bother them. Bronze were nothing if not resilient. They huddled together, fucked and snapped at one another in close quarters, like the animals they were.

And now Lysander was among them, his scales green against their golden hues. He hated that too, that he was jeweled and they were metal. Carline had once told him his green scales were rare, a freak of dragon genetics. He'd laughed at her words, so fitting were they. Trapped in the nest, he wondered about her sometimes, the old wise one who had always been there for him. He wondered about Amalia too, the sister he'd loved. Her death had been inevitable. Like his was. He wondered about Mirann, and why she was not here. Perhaps she had stayed behind, or perhaps Dokul had killed her. He wondered about Akiem, alone on their mother's throne. Akiem wanted him dead, but he could not find it in himself to hate his brother for that—for surviving in a world where enemies were killed or fucked into submission.

Dokul padded back into the nest and all around his dragon brood rolled over, exposing their bellies, nipping and snapping, teeth exposed in strange, nervous grins. Lysander lay still and waited for the weight on his back, the teeth in his throat, the thrusting cock, and when it happened, he sent his mind far away, to another time, when he had soared above the forest canopy in a dream that felt like freedom.

roan

THE WAR COUNCIL consisted of assassins from across the lands, chosen by their village elders and sent to Ashford, and Eroan was among them. In the days that followed, they spoke of how weapons were being tested with Eroan's dragon-teeth designs. Days quickly turned to weeks.

"I'm afraid we can only do so much." Others around the table nodded their agreement with Alador, the male who had spoken. An elf as old as oak, as old as any elf Eroan had known. Older than Xena, and likely just as wise. With his wolf-gray hair pulled back into a tight horse-tail, he wore a heavy gray cloak and hood. When he walked to the tree in the central atrium to bathe in the light, others bowed their heads in respect. He kept his words to a minimum, but what he did say was always concise and usually right.

They tittered and tossed ideas around.

It's not enough, Eroan thought. The weapons, the meager successes. They weren't enough to make any real difference. Chipping away at the dragons never had been enough. And nothing they had said or done, had softened the dangerous edge of Eroan's thoughts. The one Seraph had sharpened, the one that told him his place was no longer here, among them, but somewhere else, in a land far away, beyond the ocean channel.

"Eroan... what do you suggest?" Alador asked.

He blinked at the faces looking to him for answers, considered his next words, and rose to his feet. "There is no use in attacking the tower without a substantial force alongside us. Dragonkin numbers are almost immeasurable. When we strike, we do so with everything we have. And to that end, I volunteer to return to France and rally the humans. We can't succeed without them."

To their credit, they didn't lose their composure like the villagers of Cheen would have. But stern-faced Order elves looked back at him. Elves who had trained to die for their cause, elves who lived and breathed the art of violence against the dragonkin.

The silence was so thick it was almost painful.

Alador broke it, his measured voice a throaty rumble. "The last time we trusted humans, we lost everything."

"That is true, but that was many generations ago. The humans recognize their mistake. I partnered with them at the bronze wall and the wall fell. We are stronger together."

"Their *mistake* made the dragons stronger. In case you had forgotten your lessons, Eroan, or perhaps you are too young to care about our ancestral past, but the humans unleashed their nuclear bomb on the dragons, causing this jeweled mutation we battle with today. The jeweled dragons wouldn't have existed at all if not for their haste to throw more fuel on the fire. Their inventions, their tools, their methods... it is not our way."

Alador held Eroan's gaze to the point where Eroan wondered if there was more to the elder's denial than stubbornness.

"What choice do we have?" Eroan asked.

"We could strike in smaller cells, pick the dragons off one by one," came an accented female voice.

"And lose the element of surprise?" Eroan asked her, then skimmed the grim faces around him.

"And survive." Alador's eyes were cold, flat. They reminded Eroan of his own. This elder would not be easily swayed.

"With human numbers bolstering our own, we can turn the tide of this war."

"The humans assured us of victory once before." He breathed in and slowly sighed. "They abandoned us this side of the channel. Thousands died. They are responsible for more elven deaths than any dragon since."

He had been there, Eroan realized. The steady depth of Alador's gaze, the quiet, measured way he spoke. He was holding himself in restraint because he'd witnessed the infamous battle that had torn elves from humans. Elves could live many seasons, just so long as their life strings weren't prematurely cut. For Alador the human betrayal wasn't a distant story, it was his life. Alumn, he was as old as the Ashford tree, maybe as old as Cheen's memorial tree.

Briefly, doubt nipped at Eroan's resolve. If Alador thought him wrong, then perhaps he *was* wrong. But he'd seen the humans fight. They were ingenious, and as courageous as any elf.

Agreeing murmurs grew louder. Eroan was losing them. "I have worked among them. Some are still reckless, but others are honorable and brave. We would be fools ourselves to dismiss them when our numbers are so few—"

"Your insight is appreciated." Alador interrupted. "But the decision must be a group one."

The vote failed. Eroan had known it would. The rift between elves and humans still remained and it would take more than the victory at the bronze wall to heal it.

He dismissed himself from the proceedings and returned to his room. After bundling up his traveling kit, weapons, and coat, he knocked on Nye's adjacent door.

Nye opened the door shirtless, blinking sleep-weary eyes. "What is it?" He ruffled a hand through his hair.

Eroan stalled, his mind eagerly recalling the many times he'd woken with Nye looking just as bedraggled beside him and how they'd shared those sleepy mornings together. "It's late... I didn't realize..." He'd been so caught up in the Order proceeding's he hadn't stopped to think about the practicalities of leaving at night.

Nye rubbed a hand down his face, noticing Eroan's coat and bag. "What happened?"

"Nothing. That's the problem. I'm leaving. You can sta—"

"Now?" Nye turned away from the door, threw on a shirt and gathered his bag. "Why now?"

The door on the room next to Nye's creaked opened and Seraph appeared, already in her coat and boots. Listening-in again. Eroan tossed her a thankful smile. She adjusted her bag and sword and grinned back.

"We need help," he told them both, "whether the Order will admit it or not. I have some... ideas. But first, we'll return to Cheen."

Nye tugged on his coat and flicked his hair up, out of the collar. He still looked bed-ridden and mildly dazed. "The humans?" Nye guessed.

"You're going to France?" Seraph's tone jumped, her eagerness showing.

"Yes."

"For Lysander?"

"Not for him—"

Nye's brow furrowed.

"But you'll try?" she asked.

"The prince?" Nye grimaced, tossing his bag onto his shoulder. "Seraph, your fixation with this dragon is disturbing. It's a matter I'll be discussing with Curan on our return. I've heard it's not uncommon for victims to get attached to their captors..." Nye trailed off under Eroan's glare. "... that is, if you mention him again," he back-tracked. "If not, I'll forget the matter."

Seraph stared at Eroan, waiting for his answer. When Nye pushed ahead of them, Eroan nodded, short and sharp. Hope lit up Seraph's face.

She nudged him in the arm and whispered, "You're going for Lysander?"

She knew him too well. "I'd never forgive myself if I didn't."

CHAPTER 9

roan

TEN DAYS LATER, Eroan left Nye and Seraph at Cheen, slipping out in the dead of night to avoid either of them insisting they accompany him to France. Both were still likely to try and follow him, so he made sure to muddy his tracks and traveled through the night, without rest, until he came upon the abandoned bronze wall. Exposed to the elements, and with no dragons to repair the gaping holes, the bronze warren and surrounding battlements had fallen into decline. Eroan had expected to encounter some resistance, but the skies were clear and the dragons long gone.

A discarded skiff on the shoreline provided him the means to row the thirty or so miles from shore to shore. The return journey to France had been far easier than he'd expected, but its ease set his nerves on edge. There had been no reply from the last message into human territory and no dragons at the wall. The signs were ominous, and as Eroan trekked the last few miles to Chloe's outpost, it became clear why.

The acrid smell of ash in the air was the first indication all was not well, and as he approached, the outline of crumbled buildings and piles of rubble told the rest of the story. He'd expected some human losses since the assault on the wall, but not total devastation.

Toeing through the debris uncovered scorched bones and little else. No entire bodies. The fires had been so hot the flames had devoured most of the remains. Or perhaps dragons had.

Inside the warehouse where he'd expected to find the dragon-sized cage, mangled iron bars lay strewn across the floor. Their angle suggested the cage had been blown apart from the inside.

Eroan wandered through the debris, shifting aside fallen roofing sheets. The far end of the warehouse lay open to the elements, the roof and walls collapsed. His eye snagged on patches of dark marking the floor. Old blood. Something terrible had happened here.

He turned the evidence over in his mind. The dragon they'd kept inside the cage had shifted and escaped, laying waste to the entire outpost, killing dozens, maybe more. Maybe all of them.

Had Lysander done all this?

He swallowed, tasting ash.

There had been many times in the tower when he'd have gladly killed every dragon he could have gotten his hands on. He had willingly and ruthlessly cut through many during his escape. Could he blame Lysander for doing the same to his human captors?

A part of him didn't believe it, but how well did he know Lysander? They had shared little more than fleeting moments fraught with risk. He'd deliberately used the prince to get to the queen. What was to say Lysander's motives for freeing Eroan weren't similarly self-serving? What if Lysander *was* dragon and Eroan had fallen for the act and now here he was, hundreds of miles from his own land and people because of a gut feeling?

Disturbed crows cawed outside the warehouse. Cracking open the door, he freed the dragonblade and peered through. A human woman wandered the road running between abandoned buildings. Her hair was shorter than he remembered and as she turned her head toward the fields, he spotted a bandage on the side of her neck. Chloe. Eroan scanned behind her, waiting for others of her pride to emerge. None did. She stumbled and almost fell.

Opening the door, he whistled.

She looked up. Through the soot and dust blackening her face, he couldn't make out her expression.

Eroan sheathed his blade and approached. "Chloe? What happened here?"

Her face fell, and then the rest of her fell too. He caught her and sank to his knees, clutching her close as she trembled and sobbed.

"Bronze..." she said. "It was bronze..."

"I'm sorry you came for nothing." Chloe picked at her roasted chicken bone, her face turned downward, lit only by shifting campfire light. The same light made shadows dance on the walls of the abandoned building they now sheltered in. A lazy line of campfire smoke drifted skyward through the gaping hole in the roof.

"I'm sorry I was too late," Eroan replied, wanting to say more but unable to find the words. He poked the remains of his roasted chicken around on the piece of slate he'd used as a plate, looking for his appetite.

The time he'd spent in Ashford had been necessary, but if he had left just a few weeks earlier he could have been here, could have tried to save her people. The restlessness, the need to move on: Alumn had shown him his place had been elsewhere and he'd ignored the feeling.

Chloe tossed her finished bone onto the fire and looked up. Her tears had dried, but their tracks still showed through the soot. "We can't save everyone."

"That won't stop me from trying."

She smiled at his defiance, though there seemed little to smile about. "There is nothing you could have done. The bronze chief was..." Her gaze defocused. "Everything we fired at him just..." she skimmed one hand against the other, "ricocheted off. He was... *le tempête*," she tried again to find a word he'd know, "a wild storm."

Eroan stayed quiet. Having been at the mercy of the bronze, he could readily imagine what it was like to face a beast like Dokul. The bronze were bigger than amethysts, heavier too. Slower, but more armored to compensate. Before the assault on the beach, Eroan had never killed one. The beach had only been a success because they caught the bronze brood unaware. Facing a fully-armored bronze flight? There was only ever going to be one outcome. It was a miracle Chloe had survived.

"He did this." She pulled her collar away from her neck, exposing the medical gauze. "He'd have done more if Lysander hadn't been there."

Eroan slowly swallowed a bite of chicken. It went down hard. He'd been waiting to ask about Lysander, but the right moment had eluded him. Part of him didn't want to know what had happened, fearing the worst. If he didn't know, then he still had hope. Chloe's next words might end that hope.

"What he did to Lysander was worse," she whispered.

Eroan's instincts knotted. "Why didn't you kill Lysander on the beach that day?" He wasn't sure if he'd buried the quiver in his voice.

She looked up, eyes widened in surprise. "I saw an opportunity. I didn't know he... you and he were friends."

Friends? He didn't think they were that, but he'd spent so long deliberately not thinking about Lysander that his own feelings toward the dragon were a muddle he dared not untangle.

"How could I know? You're..." she waved a hand at him. "... you're you and he's dragon. He was the only dragon in human form and my only chance to capture one." Her tone pitched high, teetering on distress. "If I'd known he wasn't like the rest, I wouldn't ha—"

"It's all right. The mistake was mine that day, not yours." *Kill him. Make him suffer.* "What happened with Dokul?"

Her gaze shifted again, glazing over. "I should have let him out. He told me... I did not believe the things he said. Dragons have always lied. They are monsters. Trusting him would have been foolish..." She paused. Eroan let her settle her thoughts. "The bronze wanted him. I just... I..." Her voice cracked.

Every pause, every hitch in her voice, drove a new guilty nail home, making Eroan wince.

"He was a bronze now, Lysander Bronze, so we assumed that meant they were family—a brood, that they cared for him, and that's why the chief was looking for him." She laughed. The short, sharp sound echoed off the walls, but there was no humor in it.

He couldn't blame her for keeping Lysander in her cage or for what had happened after. "Dragons don't care like we do," Eroan said quietly. "What did Dokul do to him?"

"H-He tried to rape him, right inside the cage. Lysander fought him but... There was no way out. *Mon dieu*, I could not reach him..." She brushed back her bangs, fingers shaking. "I've never seen anything so animal before, not even from them. They both turned dragon in the cage. Broke its bars open. *C'est horrible... vicieux.* They tore half the warehouse down and..."

Eroan closed his eyes. This would be the moment she said Lysander was dead, that Eroan had been too late. He knew—inside, he already knew...

"Dokul had him anyway, pinned him down and... He tried to get away, but the bronze is..." She shook her head. *"C'est un démon inarrêtable avec le visage de la mort.* When it was over, Dokul took him away."

Her words sank in like a barbed hook and rooted there. "Lysander's alive?"

"*Oui.*"

A silence settled over Eroan's thoughts, turning them icy. He'd known what would happen if Dokul caught Lysander. Seraph had told him as much. He'd been a victim of bronze brutality. All this time, he'd known Lysander's fate... and he'd waited, trying to convince elves to do the right thing—trying to convince himself he'd been doing the right thing.

"Where are the bronze now, do you know?" he sounded distant, as though the words belonged to someone else. Icy rage crackled and hissed inside his head. All Lysander's life, he'd been abused. Eroan had known that much from everything he'd witnessed in the tower, and now Elisandra was gone, still the abuse continued. *No one has cut my ropes.*

"I know where they are, you cannot miss them in daylight, they're a swarm of hornets from a distance. But as for where Lysander is ... he was hurt... bleeding. They eat their weak..." She swallowed hard. "I keep telling myself he's still just dragon, that what I saw was normal for them. They're all the same, aren't they?"

"No." Anger grated at the edges of the word.

Chloe sniffed and looked up, right at him. "You told me a dragon helped you once. It was him, wasn't it?"

He set the make-do plate down by his boots and reaching over his shoulder, he pulled the dragonblade free. "Lysander helped me and others in countless ways. This sword is—was his."

Tears brimmed her eyes. She muttered something in her language, words Eroan didn't understand, but when her tears fell, he didn't need to understand her words.

"He said you knew him. I called him a liar... Everything he said was true. I was so stupid. He begged me to free him. He's dragon, I kept telling myself that he's dragon, and not to trust him because of that." She flicked her tears away. "Eroan, on the beach, you said to kill him?"

"A mistake." The words tasted foul. "Don't misunderstand me. I'll kill any dragon I can, just not him." To hear it out loud... it sounded right, just like Seraph had said it would. He'd been a fool to ignore his own instincts, to deny the way he felt when he thought back on Lysander. Maybe he still wanted to believe that the feelings he had for the dragon weren't real, but at the very least, he owed Lysander more. As soon as he'd handed over the information to Ashford he should have turned on his heel and made for France, saving weeks, saving people, and maybe saving Lysander from Dokul.

But it wasn't over. He'd find the nest, find Lysander, somehow help him... He knew now, in that part of him he trusted, that saving the prince was the right thing to do.

"We found Gabe, my father, on the beach," Chloe was saying, "he survived for a little while..." She smiled fondly, her memories warming. "He spoke of you, in the end. Said you would bring change to both sides."

The memories of her father were warm ones for him too. The old human had been more open-minded than most elves. "I have tried but change is not easy..."

"I'm sorry I cannot be of more help," she said. "Everyone was killed, I only survived because Dokul got what he wanted. Now we're gone, the remaining outposts will move their operations, so they're not compromised. I'd take you to them, but I don't know how to find them."

Finding humans to fight alongside elves would be a task for another time. He had a dragon to save. "Tomorrow, at dawn, will you take me to see the bronze nest?"

"*Oui*, but you can't get close without being seen."

He'd find a way, he wasn't leaving France until it was done.

~

THE VAST ROLLING grass plains made the bronze flights easy to spot. A swift wind rippled the grass heads toward where Eroan and Chloe crouched in the dip of an old track, pushing their scents away from the horde. Birds chirped nearby, but most sounds were the barks and yips of dragoncalls.

Chloe handed Eroan her spyglass. He propped himself

onto his elbows and peered through the ingenious contraption that brought the dragons much closer.

"See them?" she asked.

He did. Dozens of bronze. Some in the sky, some fighting over the carcass of something that had died a while ago and no longer resembled whatever it had been while living. Others lay coiled in a nest, a collection of heads and tails and the occasional stretched wing. Among bits of metal debris, teeth flashed and scales shined. The entire nest seemed unruly and chaotic. There were too many to tackle head-on.

"I don't see Lysander though," Chloe added.

Eroan scanned the mass of beasts. Their colors ranged from brown to tarnished gold, and any shade between. Lysander's green scales would have been instantly recognizable.

He wasn't there. "No."

But he did see the biggest dragon he'd ever lain eyes on. At least twice the size of the lowers, the creature lifted its head from deep within the nest and yawned wide, its gaping mouth large enough to swallow one of the humans' wheeled machines. Eroan had only seen Dokul in his human form but there was no mistaking the absolute bulk of raw muscle as the bronze chief. "But I see their leader."

Chloe stilled.

He handed the spyglass back and watched the now-smaller dragons come and go, specks in the sky. "Lysander's not among them."

She raised the spyglass and observed them again. "He's not dead. We'd have seen the body."

"Do you know if they bury their dead, like some of the amethyst do?"

"They don't seem to, but we've never seen inside their

warren and I haven't observed them gather so openly like this before to know their inner workings."

"Perhaps he escaped."

Chloe lowered the glass and turned to look at Eroan. "You saw his wing?"

Eroan dropped his gaze. The chances of Lysander escaping were slim to zero. "He could have shifted and slipped away?"

"It is... possible."

But unlikely, he heard. "Go, there's no use us both being out here. I'll watch them some more."

"I'll stay." She handed the glass back. "I have nowhere else to go."

Eroan observed their comings and goings until his body ached from lying flat on the ground and the light had dropped low behind far hills. Twilight saw the big bronze climb from the nest and shake sleep off, then spread his wings and take to the skies, dwarfing all others already airborne. He headed north and only when he was out of sight did Eroan breathe again.

He nudged the dosing Chloe awake.

She jolted and rubbed at her eyes. "Anything?"

He shook his head. There had been cycles to their movements. They never left alone and preferred to fly out in flights of three or four. The smaller, lower beasts did most of the fetching and carrying of fish or roaming live-stock while the bigger bronze seemed to prefer to lay about and do little else. Nightfall might bring different behavior. But if Lysander were here, they'd have seen him.

There was no point in staying any longer. "He's not among them. We should leave."

"Wait... hand me the glass." She took the glass off him and held it up, adjusting the sights. "There... look."

He took the glass again but saw only the same heaving mass of dragons as before. "What am I looking for?"

"Wait... look deeper in the nest."

A flash of green among gold.

Eroan steadied the glass, focusing toward the back of the nest where one of the bronze appeared to be caught in a scuffle. The beast flailed, wings flapping, clearly disturbed, and there, in front of it, almost completely hidden by the commotion, was a mass of glassy-green scales. The dragon lay low in the nest, almost buried.

"*Alumn*..." Eroan breathed.

"Is it him?"

"I can't tell." The bronze was snapping and snarling, upsetting the rest of the brood, but the emerald lay still. It had its jaw open, teeth bared in a clear signal to back off. If Eroan could see its wing, he'd know.

More squabbling started until the entire nest was upset. Half of them decided to take flight, blocking Eroan's view for a few moments. Once the dragons cleared, he saw why the bronze had fled. The emerald had torn into the troublemaker and pinned it beneath his claws, either dead or dying. The emerald's snout and teeth glistened scarlet with blood. And the wing, Eroan saw, lay clamped against its side, twisted along its main branch.

"It's him." He hadn't expected the sight of a dragon to ever kick him in the chest in the same way seeing Lysander did. He watched him a while, watched him guard his kill like a trophy to ward off the others. Lowers snuffled and yipped around him but didn't venture closer. Lysander was a survivor.

"Do you have any of your mechanical vehicles left?" he asked.

"Dokul burned all the cars."

"Explosives?"

"Some, but not many, not enough to do any real damage to them. Why?"

"We need a distraction. Something to tempt them all away."

The bronze chief flew in low and alighted nearby, scattering his brood from his path. What little sunlight was left sparked off the male's scales, briefly blinding Eroan through the glass. When he looked again, Lysander had his head down, jaws open, and appeared to be guarding his kill, but the position was clearly a submissive one. Dokul's upper lip rippled, and although Eroan couldn't hear the snarl, he imagined it readily enough. The bronze drew his head back, lips pulling back, showing all his teeth, then he plunged in, tore the carcass from Lysander's grasp and tossed it outside the nest. Lysander snapped at the beast, but the attacks weren't anything more than warning shots. The bronze settled beside Lysander, blocking him completely from Eroan's view.

The exchange hadn't looked willing.

What if he wants to be there?

"You wouldn't doubt it if you'd seen the fear on his face like I did." Chloe said, clearly seeing him hesitate. "He'd rather be dead than with them."

"If we're wrong, *we're* dead."

She sucked in a deep breath. "If I had listened to him and let him out, my friends would likely still be alive. Let me help you save him."

CHAPTER 10

$\mathcal{L}$ysander

BEING FUCKED by Dokul was one thing, but when the others decided he was fair game, Lysander reminded them exactly how he dealt with dragons who forgot their place. He might have been Dokul's bitch, but he was still the amethyst prince. Of course, killing a bronze was dragon catnip to Dokul. The bronze chief got off on murder and seeing his dead kin, or any other violent and insane thing he happened to witness. If Lysander didn't act, the lowers would fuck him. When he did act, Dokul fucked him.

The blood-soaked and odious oily taste of the chief had firmly rooted in Lysander's throat. He couldn't move for feeling *him* smothered close. The bronze was everywhere, inside Lysander's head, his thoughts, his body. He'd known what awaited him was bad, but the reality of it was a fucking never-ending nightmare. When Dokul left, the others closed in, waiting for a weakness to show itself, for Lysander to drop his head and let them have him. There was no reprieve. Day and night, he endured, until it all blurred into one long, hateful dream peppered by his mother's harsh words, *"You think you know savagery. You have no idea."*

The bitch had been right.

He'd never given in, never let anything beat him. He'd survived Elisandra, survived the attempts to have him killed, survived everything amethyst could do, but even the worst of it hadn't been like this. He could not give in to Dokul now. But the fight for his body was never-ending and the one in his head? That fight he feared he was losing. He'd send his thoughts far away and lay still and unfeeling, like stone. There was nowhere else for him to go but inside himself, but he could not survive there forever.

A vicious runt of a bronze with a damaged crown approached him. Every time Dokul left, this one made a move. The runt had backed off after Lysander had killed others, but he was back now, skirting the fringes of Lysander's vision, trying to place himself behind while he believed Lysander dosed. A warning growl tried to bubble up Lysander's throat. He dampened it down and stayed quiet. Clearly it was time to remind them how he'd become amethyst's flight leader. It certainly wasn't by allowing lowers to fuck him anytime they pleased.

Broken Crown slunk outside of Lysander's field of vision, though he could still see the male's tail, pressed low, and tucked among their dozing kin for camouflage. Lysander's lip quivered, instincts pushing through his restrain.

The lower struck, a clawed foot landing between Lysander's wings, his open jaws aiming straight for

Lysander's throat. Rage built and snapped apart, driving Lysander's aching muscles into motion. He rolled, exposing his belly to Broken Crown's claws in a move no sane dragon would willingly execute, and used the lower's brief surprise to clamp his teeth around the beast's snout and bite down.

Claws raked at Lysander's belly. Lysander sank his teeth in harder, using the muscles at the back of his jaw to constrict his mouth and crush the runt's nose, one bone-snapping break at a time.

Fire leaked from between the lower's teeth, sizzling against Lysander's tongue. The lower heaved, grunted, scrabbled in his panic to get free, and all it did was give Lysander's curved teeth better purchase. Deeper and deeper, Lysander crushed, until the lower stopped fighting altogether.

It wasn't over.

The others were awake, dozens of pairs of golden eyes trained on Lysander, to fuck or to kill. They hissed and spat their displeasure at one of their own being killed by an amethyst.

Lysander twisted, dropping Broken Crown's panting body between himself and them, then planted a foot on the lower's back, clamped his jaws around a wing, and ripped it free to the sounds of wrenching flesh and popping bone.

The lower might have screamed had his mouthparts not been too ruined to vocalize the sound. The mangled noises he ended up making sent half the brood scattering.

Lysander wasn't done.

He hooked his claws into the creature's belly and sliced, spilling the beast's stinking, hot insides among them all. The remaining lowers barked and yipped, snapping back at him, fearful and angry. Lysander finally let his growl bubble free, then sank his teeth into Broken Crown's throat and tore the column of muscle and sinew free.

Dokul would approve of the bloodbath he now rolled in. That realization soured the victory and made anger fray his thoughts. Maybe he could kill them all and see how Dokul reacted then.

He lunged at the nearest one in the nest and sent it flailing into the field. Then another, when it tried to stalk around him. Most took to the air, where he couldn't reach them. He spread his one good wing anyway and snapped at them as they mobbed him from above. Their screams and calls filled his head, driving his mind to madness.

Fire churned low in his throat. Fire and hate and disgust, and with it came the furious raw power he'd felt when killing Elisandra. It lit him up inside, made him burn like he *was* fire. He freed the flame, fanning it far and wide, setting the grass ablaze and curtains of heat haze and smoke into the air.

Lysander didn't hear or scent Dokul until it was too late. He saw the flash of golden wings through the fire and turned too late to defend himself from the claws and teeth that sunk into his back, dislodging scales and pinching his spine. Then the chief was smothered everywhere, wings spread, burying Lysander beneath everything Dokul. The anger and power spluttered and fled, his fight broken.

And so the nightmare began again.

He didn't know how long it lasted this time. The hours didn't pass like they used to.

When an explosion sounded, Lysander was lost in that nowhere place where the pain couldn't touch him. He registered the ground trembling and the burst of light but ignored it until Dokul stirred beside him and barked an alarm that sent the brood skyward.

Then the chief was gone too, and for a few blissful seconds, he could breathe easier. Until the few remaining lowers began to close in.

CHAPTER 11

 roan

WHEN CHLOE'S EXPLOSIVE DETONATED, the sound thundered across the open plains, just as she'd said it would.

Eroan lay low in the tall grass, as close as he dared get to the nest, and watched with the spyglass as the dragons burst into the skies. Dokul's head appeared over the crater's edge, then his wings spread, encompassing the entire nest, and he launched himself into the skies.

Eroan shifted onto his feet and cut low through the tall grass, heart pounding. The late evening light would keep him in shadow until the scorched and smoking last hundred meters.

Dragon calls sounded above and behind him, toward Chloe's outpost. By now, she'd safely be in hiding. But he didn't have long before the brood returned.

This is madness, the voice of doubt niggled at him. *He*

was clearly insane because no elf in their right mind would do what he was about to.

The tall grass abruptly ended in singed tufts. Lysander's huge mass of green scales was now clearly visible in the nest, surrounded by four bronze brutes.

Eroan gritted his teeth and clutched the dragonblade at his side. *Madness.*

He'd come all this way. He wasn't leaving until it was done.

He bolted out of the grass and sprinted across the blackened earth. Ash and embers smoked around him. A dragon—one he hadn't seen or hadn't been there moments before—galloped closer, its golden eyes fixed on Eroan.

He ran harder, lungs ablaze, legs pumping. These were either his last moments alive or the most foolish moments of his life. Maybe both.

The ridge around the nest was a few strides ahead.

Dragon jaws snapped together inches behind him, so loud and close, a bolt of adrenaline soared through Eroan's veins. He vaulted over the nest's edge and skidded into the pit, landing crouched, pinned beneath the sudden collective gazes of four dragons. He'd hoped for less of them, but he'd killed more in the past, just not all at once. Or on his own.

Madness.

He straightened, his blood on fire, mind sharp. He lived to kill these monsters and none would escape him today.

"My name is Eroan Ilanea." He flexed his grip on the sword, swallowed the ash-coated choking knot in his throat and narrowed his eyes. "And that emerald dragon is mine."

CHAPTER 12

*L*ysander

LYSANDER HEARD WORDS. They made no sense, not least because they came from a tall, angry elf, but it didn't matter, the dragons had all turned their backs on him and that would be their last mistake.

He let loose the reins on his rage and attacked. The first went down after a swift bite to the neck severed its spine. The second was on him in a blur, all snapping jaws and tearing claws, but as it was the smaller of the brood, Lysander easily sank his teeth in and tore it free, flinging it outside the nest. The third, a female, moved fast for a bronze. Lysander snagged her wing, tearing through the membrane before yanking her into his waiting jaws. She went down twitching. The fourth seemed to be distracted by the elf. It was all the hesitation he needed to pounce on its back and sink into the soft spot behind its crown, leaving it paralyzed and on its way to death.

He didn't see the fifth until it was almost on the elf. The blond-haired sword-wielding elf flitted out of the path of a huge swipe, catching the beast in an upward slice of his blade—a blade that shook loose a memory in Lysander's mind—but there was no time to think on it. The fifth dragon reared, narrowing in on the elf for the final bite, when Lysander turned his head and plowed into the bronze, sending it skidding into the burned grass.

Clouds of dust and ash rolled skyward, obscuring the view of the returning brood.

Panting and maddened by the kills, he waited for more dragons to lunge out of the dust clouds. But none came.

The call of the nearest, still a mile out, signaled it wouldn't be back for a few minutes. He was alone for the first time in what felt like forever.

No, not alone.

He swung his head around and bared his teeth at the elf, rumbling a warning low in his throat. The little creature stared up at him, sword in hand, sky-blue eyes wide.

Prey.

roan

UP CLOSE, as dragon, Lysander was everything Eroan's life-long training demanded he kill, and when Lysander's green eyes fixed on Eroan, narrowing into slits, for a terrible, breathless moment, Eroan's heart stopped. He'd made a terrible mistake. Whatever was left of Lysander behind those dragon-eyes, he didn't recognize Eroan, or didn't care.

These would be Eroan's final moments after all.

He lowered his sword, heart sinking with it. *Alumn, I was too late.*

A growl trembled through the beast's chest and bubbled up his long neck, burling through his tight lips. A warning. A threat. Any second, he would lunge and it would be over.

Then what was the point of all of this if this was how it

ended? The people he'd lost, the battles he'd fought, surviving the dragons as a child, and grown, … for what?

"Shift," Eroan said, voice hard. This would not be how it ended.

Lysander lowered his head. His lips rippled, the growl growing deadly.

"Shift now."

Dragon calls rolled across the plains. The bronze would be on them soon and all would be lost. He had to reach Lysander now.

The beast's whiskered chin rubbed at the ground, bringing its snout within arm's length. Lysander's huge head was all he could see. The gnarled, rough skin, the long, shining teeth, and a crown of bone made for a prince. Eroan's heart beat too hard and too fast. He should run, but his whole world had become this moment, focused on green gem-like eyes. The stench of dragon-blood burned the back of his throat. A reek he knew all too well. But he would not step back, he would not give in. He had not come here to be turned away. *Until it is done.*

The snout came so close, Eroan's racing breaths would surely trigger the creature's instincts to hunt. He briefly closed his eyes. *Alumn, guide me.* Lysander's snout shoved him in the chest, knocking him back a step. Eroan opened his eyes. *Teeth.* Close racks of teeth, each one half Eroan's size and capable of slicing him in two.

Lysander huffed, blasting him with hot air, the meaning clear: Back off. But it was Lysander who eased back, stare pinned on Eroan.

Eroan bared his teeth. "You know who I am," he lifted his free hand, still clutching the sword in the other, and reached out, fingers trembling. The lattice of scale on Lysander's nose shined like it was wet and cold, but when his fingers touched those scales, they were rough, dry, and curiously warm. He spread his touch, absorbing the warmth and feel of dragon beneath his hand.

Lysander's eyes suddenly flared. With a jolt, he jerked backward, lifting his head high, as though he might flee or strike. Fire glowed behind the scales low in his throat, filling the firepit. The touch had startled him.

Eroan's heart stammered. "You know me, dragon!" he barked, using the same tone he'd take with young, unruly elflings. "You hear me. I'm cutting your ropes."

Light blasted hot and white, scorching Eroan's eyes. He staggered, and when the flare faded, Lysander was on his knees as man, head bowed, shoulders heaving with his every labored breath. He tried to stand, got a leg under him, then stumbled onto his hands. His long mane of knotted hair fell forward, his shirt gaped, clothes filthy and torn.

Dragons screeched. Coming closer.

Lysander flinched and slowly lifted his head. Pain clouded his green eyes and twisted his face. "Eroan?"

Eroan lunged in and heaved Lysander to his feet, bearing his weight. Lysander's weak fingers slid around Eroan's waist and clamped on.

"There's... no way out," he said. The broken, wrecked growl of a voice sounded nothing like Eroan remembered.

"Hold on to me. Don't look back. I have you."

Lysander's weight grew heavier, his steps messier, and it was all Eroan could do to keep him moving forward. If they were spotted now, there was nothing else he could do to save Lysander or himself.

Alumn, if there is any hope left in this world, help me save this dragon.

The calls grew louder, closing in, coming faster.

Clouds of ash thrown up from their battle began to settle.

One step. Another. Following his earlier path through the grass. They just needed some hope and a little luck. Wasn't it time Alumn favored him with a chance?

"Just a few more steps..." he whispered. He could do this. He had to do this.

Lysander growled something in reply, the words indecipherable.

In the tall grass, Eroan eased Lysander over a small ridge in the earth and pulled him down to his knees. The dragon's lashes fluttered, but his gaze was unseeing, his mind somewhere else.

"Lysander... you need to get down—"

A bronze screeched high above them. The sound triggered Lysander to jerk back, suddenly clawing and shoving at Eroan. Eroan grabbed his arm, trying to get him under control. Lysander broke free and twisted. Eroan snagged his wrist, but Lysander pulled, and suddenly he was up and running through the grass.

Eroan bolted after him, tackled him low in the back and knocked him hard to the ground. Lysander writhed beneath him, grappling Eroan's hands, trying to shove him off. Wide, panicked eyes still didn't see.

"Stop..." Eroan pinned his wrists. Lysander tore his right arm free. A sloppy punch hit Eroan square in the jaw. Eroan grabbed that flailing arm, pinned it again, and pushed in, making it so Lysander saw only his face. Nothing else. No dragons. Just him. Breathing hard, he clamped Lysander still. "I need you to stop fighting me."

Panting through his nose, chest heaving, Lysander glared back until, second by second, the madness clouding his eyes thawed. "Eroan?" he croaked.

"Are you going to run?"

Mouth open, he seemed to be trying to say something, but failed.

"Keep your head down." Eroan eased off and, grabbing Lysander's hand, pulled him into a crouch. "Follow me. Can you do that?"

Lysander followed, still breathing too hard and on the edge of panic, but he was here, in this moment, and thinking, not running.

Eroan grabbed the wooden pallet he'd used earlier to hide the hole dug into the ground and pulled it aside. "We're getting inside. We'll be safe. Do you understand?"

Lysander's gaze darted, nostrils flaring, and Eroan wondered if he might shift again, right there. He grabbed the prince's jaw in a firm hold and held him still, forcing him to see only Eroan. "Trust me. I won't let anything happen to you."

Lysander's eyes glazed over, his focus shifting, mind wandering. He was going into shock. With a curse, Eroan pulled Lysander close, maneuvered himself and Lysander deep into the hole, and pulled the pallet over them, sealing them in the dark.

Dragons cawed and barked, and among them, the bronze chief's ground-shuddering roars were the loudest, sending shivers spilling through Lysander. Eroan closed his arms around Lysander, tucking the prince beneath his chin, so close Lysander's trembling became his own. If he could have shared the burden, he would have, but now, all he could do was hold him and hope that was enough.

CHAPTER 14

$\mathcal{L}$ysander

THE MALE ELF smelled of freedom, of the forest, of good things. He did not smell of dragon.

Lysander dug his fingers in—not claws; he didn't want to hurt this one—and breathed in the smell of elf. The strong arms folded around him wouldn't let go. He trusted that. Trusted him. When the shaking started, the arms tightened and Lysander pulled him closer, wanting to hide inside this safe place and never leave.

"I have you," a voice rumbled in the closed, quiet place.

Those three small words broke him open, laying him bare. And for the first time in a long time, living no longer hurt.

CHAPTER 15

roan

IN THE EARLY HOURS, when dawn was still a hint on the horizon and the night at its coldest, Eroan moved to another hole in the ground. Their escape couldn't be rushed. Dokul would search far and wide for Lysander, forgetting to look closer to his own nesting site—or so Eroan hoped.

Another few hours, another hole on the ground, leading away from the abandoned outpost to a copse of trees, then down, deeper into the hidden valley Chloe had shown him.

They weren't safe yet, but with every passing hour, their chances increased.

Lysander hadn't spoken since the nest. He sat propped on a rock at the edge of a small, burbling stream. His filthy, torn clothes hung off him, his skin gray and his cheeks hollow. Matted knots bunched his dark hair and he clearly favored his right side. The scent of spoiled blood lingered around him, but when Eroan suggested he take a look at the wound, Lysander hadn't replied, and approaching without his permission had already triggered him to fight or flee more than once.

"We need to keep moving." Eroan took a broad laurel leaf and dipped it in the stream, cupping water inside. He handed it back to Lysander.

Lysander blinked at it.

"Drink."

And blinked again. He swallowed, wet his cracked lips, only then noticing Eroan. His expression broke for a moment, twisting in confusion.

"Drink," Eroan urged again.

Lysander took the offered leaf, sniffed at the water, his eyes watching for any trick. Eroan nodded encouragement. The way Lysander moved, his eyes darting and body cumbersome as though he didn't fit inside the flesh, Lysander's dragon-self remained close.

Finally accepting Eroan wasn't about to poison him, he lifted the leaf and swallowed, spilling some water from the corners of his mouth and down his chin. He brushed the wetness off with a sweep of his hand, smearing dirt.

"I er..." The words were a growl. Lysander coughed and cleared his throat. "I... I've been dragon so long... speaking..." His voice broke. He winced. "It's taking ... time to come back."

"You don't need to explain." Eroan refilled the leaf, handed it back, and watched Lysander readily drink. He reached out for the leaf again, but Lysander had frozen, staring back at him, his mud-smeared brow furrowing.

"We need to move again," Eroan explained. "Deeper

into the valley. There's a ruined farmhouse. Chloe will meet us there."

"Chloe?" Lysander asked, face vague.

"The human—"

He was on his feet suddenly and stumbling into the trees. He hit a tree trunk and fell, then retched up the water. His fingers, clasping the tree next to him, turned white.

Eroan waited. He'd seen elves deeply traumatized. Rushing him would do no good, but they did have to keep moving. When Lysander's heaving subsided, Eroan took a wide-arc around him, approaching from the front. Slowly, carefully, he settled a hand on Lysander's shoulder. Tremors rattled through him. He clutched at his side where damp patches of blood stained his filthy shirt.

"Let me help you."

Lysander's glare burned.

Eroan withdrew his hand, expecting him to shift at any second.

"We keep moving." Lysander dragged himself to his feet. He made it another three steps before collapsing face-down in the dirt.

ysander

THE TOUCH OF WARM, rough hands roaming over the raw, sensitive bruise on his side, and the rumble of a deep, familiar voice roused Lysander from a dark and cold place. The voice came and went like the ebb and flow of a tide. He should know the words, they were important, but he couldn't cling to them long enough to make sense of them.

When he finally did blink awake, it was inside a room he didn't recognize. Stone walls, a roof, a fireplace. Was this even real? Piece by piece he slotted his broken thoughts back together. Was this the tower? Trying to sit set the wound on his side alight again, dropping him breathless back onto the bed.

Probing with his fingers, he found a gauze and bandage stuck to his side where he'd expected to find the deep gashes one of the lowers had left him with. He couldn't even remember which one. They'd all blurred into one long string of dragons he'd killed or tried to. All but the worst one.

Thoughts of Dokul twisted his mouth. He rolled his tongue, finding it parched, and swallowed. Shit, how long had he been out? Flopping a hand over his eyes he tried to think back and reassemble the mental wreckage from the last few days. Something about being buried alive, and hearing that same voice...

"Water?"

Lysander jumped. Fucking hell, Eroan was here. The stupid, stubborn, impossible elf was really here. He hadn't dreamed him up.

The wound barked at him to quit moving. He winced and squinted up at the very elf he'd been thinking of. Eroan looked perfectly at home standing beside the bed, cup in hand, long blond hair neatly bound in a tail slung over his shoulder and wearing earthy-colored traveling clothes.

"How long have you been standing there?" he croaked out. He had to blink again to be sure Eroan wasn't about to vanish. When he didn't disappear, Lysander awkwardly propped himself on an elbow and reached for the cup.

The elf's mouth lifted at one side. "Not long."

The water went down nice and smooth, leaving a cool, clean trail all the way to his belly. He had a feeling he'd soon wish it was wine, but water would do for now, although it wasn't going to do much for the memories crowding the back of his thoughts, waiting to pounce.

Eroan pulled up a chair and made himself comfortable. He leaned forward, resting his forearms along his thighs. Now Lysander's thoughts were coming together, he could see how Eroan's clothes were scuffed and marked in places, and how similar grazes marked the elf's chin and jaw. Dust and dirt darkened his face in places. Not so immune to everything, it seemed. How was he even here?

"How long have I been out?" Lysander set the cup down and tried to twist onto his side. The wound fired up again, dropping him back. "Damn..."

"On and off, two days."

He blinked and Eroan stood over him suddenly, face lit only by flickering candle-light. Eroan leaned in and probed at the gauze. Lysander's chest tightened with something like fear as the elf's fingers lightly brushed his lower abs and plucked at the gauze's sticky corners.

Eroan's eyebrows slightly knitted, creating a tiny, imperfect crease. "I'm not going to hurt you."

"I know." He had answered too quickly. It was a lie. He *had* been afraid. It was a horrible, gut-loosening fear, one he hadn't felt before. If Eroan heard the lie, he didn't react, and Lysander resigned himself to laying back and letting him do whatever he wanted. In the state he was in, he couldn't fight anyone, even if he'd wanted to.

"The wound was infected," Eroan said. "Had you left it any longer, it would have killed you."

Lysander breathed out a heavy sigh. Typical, it'd be something so menial that would kill him, after surviving everything else.

"You're easier to nurse when unconscious," Eroan added, his tone lightening.

Was that a smile on the elf's lips? Why was he even here, in a near-derelict house hundreds of miles from his home, after he'd given the order to have Lysander killed? What was this exactly? A rescue, or something else?

A small part of his pride, whatever bits of it he had left, demanded he push the elf off and lick his wounds himself, but he found, in this quiet moment, he didn't care what Eroan's reasons were. Being here was better than anywhere he'd been in months. Here was safe, for now, and felt just fine a place to close his eyes and rest a little while, knowing he didn't have to fight for his life when he next woke.

When he next looked about the room, the light had changed and the candle burned down another inch. The chair was still at the bedside, but no Eroan. He stared at the empty seat, thoughts rolling over, then poked at his side again. This time, the wound didn't bite back. He shoved upright, using his arms to push up instead of his abs to pull and managed to prop himself into a sitting position. The room spun, vision blurring, body warring with him to lay back down and sleep, but two days' rest was long enough. Dokul would be coming and an old building like this one would eventually draw the dragon's eye.

Lysander found his boots and tugged them on without doing himself any further damage, then made a brave attempt to make it to the doorway. The neat little scene greeting him in the adjacent room beyond was one that took a few moments for him to unpack: Eroan, standing by the fire, arm resting on the mantle as he spoke low and quietly to Chloe, the human, seated in an armchair full of holes and spilling its fluffy filling all over the floor. They looked... familiar. Content, even. Friends. More?

Eroan looked up, concern widening his eyes before his expression settled somewhere around mildly irritated. "You shouldn't be up."

From his tone, he was clearly used to speaking and having others obey him.

"Yes, I am aware." Lysander propped himself against

the doorframe in the hope he didn't give away how he was about to fall over. "Thank you. Both. But you need to leave me. When Dokul finds you, he'll kill you."

Chloe chewed on her thumbnail and turned her face toward the firelight. She'd seen much of what Dokul had done to him, Lysander realized. Maybe most of it, and she'd lost everything. He'd fucking warned her.

Eroan's eyebrow lifted in question. Though Lysander had no idea what that question might be. "I didn't run into a bronze nest only to leave you behind now," the elf said, tone still lofty.

Lysander felt a smile lighten his lips. Eroan would be a bastard to argue with. "What you did was the height of stupidity. It's a fucking miracle you weren't killed."

"I told him he's insane," Chloe agreed. "But he's *Eroan Ilanea*. I don't think he knows how to listen to anyone but his own ego."

Eroan bowed his head and watched the firelight, the hollow of his cheek flickering.

"Why did you do it?" Lysander had to know. Nothing and nobody gave a damn about him, ever. He was a tool, a bargaining item, property to be traded. There was a reason Eroan had risked his life and it had nothing to do with *cutting his ropes*, it couldn't. No creature was that noble. What did Eroan want?

Chloe looked up, clearly wanting an answer too.

"You ordered me dead," Lysander pushed. "Second thoughts?"

The wince was real, pulling at Eroan's mouth, briefly revealing a flicker of those sharp little elven teeth.

"Make him suffer." The words dripped from Lysander's tongue. "I heard it all." He shoved off the doorframe and surprised himself by managing to stay upright until he bumped into a table and used that to root him to the spot. "Well? You had a change of heart? Because from where I'm standing, none of this makes sense. Elves don't save dragons."

A tiny pulse twitched over Eroan's eye, as though the words truly ate at him and it drove Lysander crazy wondering why.

"The three of us can change things," he finally said. "Human, elf, dragon. We're together, in this room, talking. This is change, right here. We have an opportunity."

Right.

That had to be it.

See, too fucking noble for anything but a righteous mission from his blessed Alumn. Of course it was something reasonable like trying to talk peace or saving the fucking world by bringing them all together.

Lysander groped for an old, rotten chair and prayed it held him up when he dropped himself into it. Dust puffed into the air. He coughed and winced. His side hurt. Everything hurt. But his stupid heart hurt the most. Sweet nights, what was he thinking? That Eroan had come here for no other reason than to *save* him because he what... liked him? He could hear his mother's laugh and pressed a cool hand to his flushed forehead. Eroan ordered his death. He needed to get over the insane fantasy that he felt anything besides hate toward Lysander.

"You can't negotiate with dragons, if that's what you're hoping. Humans tried that a long time ago. The first great metals ate all the negotiators." He looked down and filtered his fingers through his hair, snagging on too many knots. He stank too. Of dirt and blood and worse. By the Great Ones, he was a fucking mess.

"I have to agree with the dragon," Chloe said.

Lysander threw a hand in her general direction. "The human sees sense." While they were sitting here *talking*, Dokul was closing in. He could be on them at any moment. Chloe would die after narrowly escaping him the first time and Eroan... Damn Eroan for even being here. Lysander couldn't think past him. All his thoughts hustled right back around to the elf standing across the room, still so strong and proud, like death itself couldn't touch him. But it would. If Dokul found them, knowing it had been Eroan who took Lysander away... He'd ruin Eroan in the way only the bronze could, with tooth and claw and blood.

"... Lysander?"

He looked up into two faces waiting for a reply to a question he hadn't heard. Eroan should be with his people. Chloe with hers. And Lysander... He had no people, and with only one working wing, he didn't stand a chance in the wild. Akiem should have fucking killed him when they fell from the tower.

"I don't know what you want from me." He'd meant to address both of them, but his gaze found its way to Eroan as if the male held a magical pull all of his own. Even bruised with weeks' worth of travel on him, Eroan still looked like some impossible dream. The earring high in his tipped ear winked emerald green. That was a new addition since he'd last seen him. Lysander's thoughts fell to those final moments. Not the beach, that didn't count—his head had been covered, he'd only heard Eroan's cruel voice deliver his execution order. Before, when Eroan had been tied to Elisandra's bed, Lysander's mouth on the parts of him that were as hard as they were smooth. *Don't be sorry.*

It was all lies. Eroan had wanted to escape. Anything else was his own wishful thinking.

Too much time had passed and nobody had replied.

Eroan knelt to stoke the fire, his thoughts clearly elsewhere.

Maybe these two didn't know why they needed Lysander either. What good was he anyway, broken as he was?

"Are you well enough to walk?" Chloe asked.

"Maybe."

"*Bien*. We continue. There are other hidden outposts like this one with more medical supplies, some pain medication, if needed. I don't know how it'll impact a dragon but it's there, if needed." Lysander nodded his thanks and scratched at his whiskered chin. A bath was what he needed, and then a whole lot of mead and somewhere dark to curl up and lick all the hurts away.

She passed by him and out of the room. In the quiet that followed, Eroan poked the fire with a stick, dislodging the larger logs, embers sparking.

Eroan should leave now, Lysander realized. He'd come for some grand idea about uniting the three races with a warrior woman and an amethyst prince. Instead, he'd found a broken prince and a warrior woman with no warriors of her own. If he stayed with Lysander, he'd die.

"There's nothing here for you," Lysander muttered. "Go back to your people, Eroan Ilanea."

Eroan's throat bobbed as he swallowed. He tossed the stick into the fire and headed for the door, stopping beside Lysander.

Lysander stared at the flames, not wanting to see Eroan's sorry face. But he felt his closeness as a warming of the blood and with it came the memory of being held somewhere cold and dark, being buried in the ground. The smell of wildness filling his head, of cut pine and all things

Eroan, and hearing the thump of the elf's strong, steady heart. By diamonds, he wanted that place to be real.

The hand suddenly on Lysander's shoulder gave a gentle squeeze, choking him up. "Don't let them break you, prince." Then, Eroan was gone too, leaving Lysander alone, watching the fire's dying light.

CHAPTER 17

roan

THE DAYS LENGTHENED, heavy clouds thinned, and after every nightfall, Lysander was able to walk farther between rests. True to her word, Chloe's outposts offered safety, warmth, and a place to eat the rabbit and pheasant they caught during the day. Dragoncalls became few and far between until they stopped hearing them altogether.

"I've been thinking," Chloe began, picking up her jacket from the ground and flicking off grit and moss. Behind her, a shallow river burbled through the creek. Sunlight sparkled off its surface, making the water shine.

Eroan scanned their immediate surroundings from his vantage point atop a flat, rocky outcrop, soaking in the sun's rays while he could. They'd rested up here a while, collecting fresh water and eating what supplies they had left. The little creek was a good place to stop. Well hidden from above and their voices didn't carry far beyond the trickle of running water.

"Yesterday, we passed by some fresh boot tracks," Chloe continued. "My people are nearby. I want to head out and find them but..." She tugged the coat on and fumbled with the buttons.

Eroan knew what she would say. Her people would likely welcome him, with some caveats, but not a dragon.

"It's all right," Lysander's gravelly voice drew Eroan's eye. He leaned against the largest of the surrounding boulders. "I don't expect charity from humans." He'd knotted his hair in a loose bun, but long, dark strands had escaped. The warm breeze had them sweeping near his shadowed jawline. The messy appearance was a stark contrast to how Eroan remembered him in the tower, with all his fine clothing and long, carefully measured looks, giving nothing away. He wore no such looks out here and let Chloe see the solemn acceptance on his face.

Chloe's eyes said *sorry*, but Lysander looked at the trinket he turned over and over in his hands, probably a pebble picked up off the ground. He dropped whatever it was into his pocket and straightened. "You've both already done enough."

She picked up her rucksack and slung it onto her back. "But it wasn't enough, was it..."

Lysander shrugged, making light of the past between them. He gave her a guarded look; the same one he'd used on Eroan when he didn't like what he'd heard. "What do you want me to say?"

"I'll ask them if they'll take us all—"

Lysander laughed. "Given my past experience with humans, I won't hold my breath."

She swung a respectful nod up at Eroan. "Will you come with me?"

He cast his gaze far upstream.

There's nothing here for you.

Lysander didn't know how his words had cracked open Eroan's doubts and exposed them to the harsh reality. He should go with her, help rally the humans, share knowledge and tactics and bring word of it all back to the elves. They were all stronger together.

He lifted his face to the sun. Every waking moment of his life had been devoted to one thing: destroying dragons. His target had been the queen. With her gone, his purpose was still a clear one. Keep on killing until there were no dragons left to stain his blade. It was an assassin's duty. His duty. The desire sang in his blood. It was who he was. Eroan Ilanea, bane of dragons. The answer to Chloe's question was simple.

"I can approach them first, if you like," she said. "Wait here a few days and I'll return with their answer."

There's nothing here for you.

"Very well," he agreed. "I'll wait for their answer. Two days."

Chloe sighed, clearly relieved, and made her way to where Lysander stood. She offered her hand. "You did what no other dragon could have. You made me see your kind as something other than monsters."

He stilled and looked at her hand, then took it, giving it a firm squeeze, but when she tried to pull back, he held on and spoke low. "Your monsters are real and I'm one of them." His broad smile and sudden gleam in his eyes rattled her enough that she pulled her hand free and made a hasty retreat, nodding Eroan a farewell and trekking upstream until the sight of her vanished into the trees.

"Why frighten her now?" Eroan asked. They'd been on the road for two weeks and in that time, Lysander had been nothing but kind to Chloe, if wary of the human. He'd given no sign of a threat, nothing untoward. If anything, he'd been the model patient, although worryingly subdued. Until now. Eroan had his own theory but wanted to hear the truth from Lysander.

The dragon squinted into the light bouncing off the water. "It'll keep her alive."

Always protecting others. And yet nobody had protected him. Eroan studied the male in the stark daylight. Any sign of his ordeal had vanished from his exterior. His clothes, cleaned and patched up along the way, fit snugly again around broad shoulders and powerful arms. If anything about him had changed it was the hardened edge to his glances and cutting tone to his words. His smile, so readily available before, was a rare thing now. The bronze had damaged him, that much was clear, but how deep did the cracks go?

Eroan hopped down from the rock and picked up a hazel branch about five feet long, likely washed up on the riverside during the last rains. He tore off any protruding twigs and tossed the branch at Lysander without warning. The dragon snatched it out of the air and raised an eyebrow.

"How's your range of movement?" Eroan asked.

He rolled his right shoulder, stretching his wounded side. "Better."

Eroan set the dragonblade down below the outcrop, picked up a second branch, this one longer, and snapped it underfoot. He lifted the now-shorter branch in both hands, testing its weight, then gave it a flick from one hand to the other. "You think so?"

Catching on, Lysander shrugged off his jacket and tossed it aside, then refreshed his grip on the hazel, flexing his fingers around the staff. "Rules?"

"First blood."

The dragon's brow arched again. His smile slid sideways. "Are you sure you want to test me? The last time we fought, I kicked your—"

Eroan struck fast, swinging the staff low to get a wide, upward tilted arc that, had it hit, would have cracked Lysander under the jaw and likely ended the fight before it had begun. Only Lysander was fast, Eroan hadn't forgotten that, and as the dragon appeared to twist away, he thrust his own makeshift staff downward in both hands, blocking Eroan's attack with a loud *crack* and holding him there.

The dragon's eyes had darkened and fixed on Eroan's and for a few moments the only sound was that of the bubbling river and their breathing. "You stopped?"

"You winced." Eroan withdrew, backing up. "You're still in pain."

"I did not wince, elf. The sun was in my eyes."

"Another day, perhaps." Eroan turned his back, ears pricked. The dragon's clumsy footing gave him away. Eroan whirled, deflecting Lysander's staff, then used the bottom section of his own to jab at Lysander's thigh. Had he been aiming to hurt, he'd have struck at where he knew the prince was wounded, and wouldn't have missed, but the jolt in the thigh was enough to pluck a hiss from between Lysander's teeth and force him back a step.

Lysander twirled the staff and circled around, grin widening.

"Don't like to be told no, *prince*?" Eroan asked.

"Just warming up. It's been a while since I've used a stick to beat an elf."

Eroan narrowed his eyes. Like that, was it? Maybe he wouldn't go so easy on the prince. "I've been meaning to ask... How many elves have you personally killed?"

Lysander's mouth ticked. "Well, if you will keep sending them over my tower walls to play with, the numbers soon add up. How many dragons have you killed?"

Eroan kept his face blank. "I don't count. A dead dragon is a good thing."

"We have that belief in common." Lysander's dark chuckle tugged on the line of wicked lust Eroan had been denying in himself since watching the prince sleep and heal, since he'd washed the wound on Lysander's side and lightly run his fingers over the ripple of Lysander's abdominal muscles, touching the forbidden in secret. It had started as nothing, a curiosity, no more. Lysander had been out cold and feverish and Eroan had only meant to clean him up and treat the wound. But what he'd felt while examining the prone prince was more than curiosity. To touch him, it had been a visceral reaction, a deep need and a shocking attraction that had stolen his breath. And it had been wrong, he'd known it, not least because Lysander had been unaware, but it had felt too good to deny himself such wicked pleasure. That same flickering delight shortened his breaths now: the forbidden, the wrong. It had seeded in him when the queen had him tied down and Lysander's smart mouth had worked him into a creature made of panting need. That same wicked root was still knotted inside, growing, stretching, becoming more, *needing* more. Lysander was the enemy. And Eroan had never wanted to touch, taste and explore someone as much as he did him.

There's nothing here for you.

But such desires could not be made possible. He'd channel the need elsewhere, into this moment. It was as good as any, and might be their last if the humans welcomed him in.

Lysander struck, pivoting off his back foot and twisting in the air, bringing the staff down like a blade. Eroan's heart stuttered, adrenaline spiking at the last second, driving him to the side. He flicked his weapon back, blocking a second upward strike, but his balance was off and the beach rocky. He stumbled. Lysander's staff cracked down, into his shoulder, earning the hit. Eroan pulled away, forcing distance between them and room to bring his weapon in and back under control.

Lysander's open-mouthed grin was the kind seen on dragons before they went in for the kill. He barely left a moment for Eroan to catch his breath before swinging the staff overhead in an unnecessarily flashy move, one Eroan took full advantage of by jabbing the prince in the gut and kicking out, sending him staggering backward. Only Lysander wasn't the type to let a minor trip unsteady him. He turned the unbalance to his advantage, dropped low, and swung the hazel staff into Eroan's weight-bearing knee.

Eroan buckled, stabbed the staff in the beach and danced away, until finding his staff was suddenly gone— flicked out from under him. Eroan found himself on his back, staring up the length of the hazel branch pressed at his throat, into a dragon's gaze filled with cunning and delight.

"Still got it, elf."

The whole exchange had taken seconds.

But it wasn't over.

Eroan chuckled. "I went easy on you."

"That's your mistake." Lysander's gaze dropped, the

staff shifted, moving away from Eroan's throat as the prince's attention wandered down, over Eroan's heaving chest.

Eroan waited, soaking up the warm look in Lysander's eyes like he soaked up the sun. Then, when he was sure the dragon was fully distracted, he grabbed the end of Lysander's staff and thrust forward, crunching the handle into Lysander's nose. Blood bloomed. Lysander barked a curse and stumbled back, losing his staff to Eroan's grip. His hands flew to his battered nose.

"*Gate gogs, elmf!*" He threw Eroan a glare and spat blood onto the rocks.

"First blood," Eroan reminded, getting to his feet.

Lysander's narrowed-eyed glare flicked to the right, to the rock Eroan had been resting on earlier and the sword beneath.

Eroan's chest tightened. *He wouldn't...*

Lysander bolted for the blade. Eroan lunged, the stakes suddenly higher, and Lysander had the sword in his hand. He swung, cut through the staff in a blur, and pinned Eroan back against the boulder by the tip of the blade.

The prince's green eyes had lost all their jovial shine. There was nothing there now but cold, ruthless focus.

Eroan lifted his hands and plastered himself against the rock. Still, the blade pushed in. Its sharp edge gripped his neck, threatening to cut.

Lysander altered his grip, lifting his elbow, and leaned in. Blood ran from his nose, around his mouth and down his chin. Behind that scarlet wetness, white teeth flashed. "Why are you here?" Lysander asked, leaning in.

They'd been here before. Months ago. The queen's chamber. Eroan's one focus to kill the queen. Now... now he didn't know what he was fighting for or why he was here, not really. Since the bronze wall fell, he'd been lost.

"Tell me," the dragon prince growled. His thigh pressed against Eroan's, then the firmness of his hip dug in until there was nothing between them but the sword and blood. A small wet drop tickled down Eroan's neck.

"You coming here..." Lysander bowed his head, bringing his chin over the top of the blade, his face inches from Eroan's, "... makes no sense."

Eroan gritted his teeth. The answer was one he couldn't speak, one he didn't understand, but Lysander was right, it didn't make any sense.

"Why?" Lysander growled.

Eroan tasted blood in the air, pinned as he was, smothered by dragon, the parts of his mind that had buried it all began to turn over, disturbing the past, bringing the horrors of his time in the tower back to the surface. But the heated rush through his veins had nothing to do with fear or anger, and when Lysander bared his teeth in a warning snarl, Eroan parted his lips, needing more air.

When Lysander tilted his head and brushed his cheek against Eroan's, Eroan lost all his thoughts in the powerful feel of having him so close.

Lysander's bloodied mouth brushed Eroan's cheek and drifted lower, sweeping to the corner of his mouth. "What do you want from me?"

CHAPTER 18

$\mathcal{L}$ysander

Own, take, bite, fuck. Each need thumped in time with his heart. *Own, take, bite, fuck.* The dragon was too close to the surface, muddying his thoughts. And the elf was doing all the wrong things. Even now, he still fought, his fucking silence like a bolt screwing down deeper and deeper, driving Lysander toward madness. His own blood wet his tongue. The smell of it mingling with the dribble of blood running down Eroan's neck, into his mess of blond hair braided at one shoulder.

Tilting his head, he breathed him in, drawing Eroan deep into his senses where the sensation of him sizzled, driving his stirring dick fast toward painfully hard. The blade between them was the only thing stopping him from acting on the rabid needs tearing him apart. *Own. Take. Bite. Fuck.* He pushed his hips in, biting into his lip as the pressure rubbed him the right way. Without the blade between them, this wouldn't have been as civilized.

Eroan's hard, powerful body began trembling, and it was all Lysander could do not to throw the blade away and fuck him, whether he wanted it or not. It *was* a madness he realized. A dangerous one.

He wasn't Dokul.

He wasn't his mother.

He wasn't some fucked-up bronze that took whatever he wanted like a rabid animal.

Oh, but he could be.

Maybe he should be.

Hadn't all the bad happened because he'd fought his nature?

What if he gave in... just stopped fighting... and became what everyone expected of him?

His mouth was at Eroan's jaw, just below his ear. If he pulled the blade free, he could sink his teeth in and own him, do what his body so desperately wanted.

Own. Blood pumping.

Take. Need raging.

Bite. Soul aching.

Fuck. Instincts demanding.

Become what he'd never been, become dragon in every way.

But the blade was there... a blade that had once been his. One of the two he'd taken from his sister's carcass. A sister, so light, so full of hope. Amalia. Blades he'd had on him constantly, blades he'd kept to remind him of how he could be, how he should be, that no matter the weight of darkness bearing down, he could never let it smother him. For Amalia, for his own soul, if he had such a thing.

He broke through the desire-filled shackles and flung

himself away from Eroan, throwing the sword at the rock. It clattered and bounced, ringing its alarm.

He needed to move, to get away, to kill, to fuck, to do something to stop from going out of his damned mind. Before, he'd have taken to the skies, beat his wings and flown until there was nothing left of the madness to chase him.

The only escape was the forest. He left the beach, hesitating at the deliberate noise behind him. "Don't follow me, elf! I'll kill you if you do."

He didn't look to know if Eroan listened. The warning was enough, and he'd meant it. He stumbled on, into the trees, where the air was cooler and the sunlight fleeting. Falling back against a tree, he growled out the pain. Muscle and blood boiled. He wanted out of his skin, to shift and roar at the world.

What had Dokul done to him?

But it wasn't all Dokul. Before... there had been times he'd needed the release or he feared what he might have become without it. With Mirann, he'd fucked her because he'd have killed her if he hadn't. He had killed Elisandra, and in that moment he hadn't felt like himself.

He dropped his hand and cupped the unrelenting erection, gasping as desire flooded low in his groin and emptied his thoughts of all the bad shit. Eyes closed, the taste of blood on his tongue and the image of Eroan firmly lodged in his mind, he freed his wretched dick and clamped it in hand. *Fuck*. He needed the madness to break apart, to free him again so he could think. The pre-slickness came quickly, easing his efforts to ride the pleasure out. Just get it done. Own. Take. Bite. Fuck. Sweet nights, things would be so much easier if he was like the rest of his fucked-up amethyst brood. But he didn't want to be like them...

He remembered his mouth on Eroan's silken cock, imagined the elf arching beneath him, driving his cock deeper into Lysander's throat and remembered the taste of his need. Lust coiled tight to the breaking point, and Lysander imagined, back by the river, how he would have held the elf down and fucked him every way he could, made him come, screaming for more. Pleasure built in its final moments, Lysander's hand pumping harder, tighter, to the point of pain. Then it burst, free, unspooling, waves of mind-numbing ecstasy rolling up his spine, spilling bouts of hot seed onto the forest floor. Own. His cock pulsed. Take. His heart thumped. Bite. Hips jolted. Fuck. His mind cleared, dumping him in the reality of how close he'd come to destroying the only thing in this wretched world he loved. Eroan Ilanea.

CHLOE RETURNED A DAY LATER, talking beside the water with Eroan where the sound of the river muffled their voices. Lysander lay back on a sun-baked rock, resigning himself to the fact Eroan would leave with her—as he should, especially after Lysander had fucked up their not-so-friendly sparring session the day before. At least Eroan hadn't seen him jerk off in the woods like some rampant bronze.

Anxiety nibbled on his nerves, and with it, the fluttering of his heart, like panic, was setting in. He knew the signs. Fight or flight. Since Dokul, his entire body had been a treacherous wreck of sickness, doubt, weakness and a fuckload of other shit he'd once dealt with by drinking copious amount of wine, or mead, he wasn't fussy.

You think you know savagery. You have no idea.

A cloud lumbered its way in front of the sun, chilling the spring air. Lysander turned his head and watched an elf and human discuss their future.

It wasn't so bad. There were other dragons in this land. He'd occasionally caught their light scent on the breeze. They smelled different from amethyst and bronze. Nothing close enough to worry those two with it. Maybe these different dragons would be open to taking in a lost amethyst prince? Or maybe he could pretend to be a lower and hide among the working ranks. Easier said than done with scales as green as grass. Right now, he didn't have a whole lot of other options.

Chloe and Eroan embraced and Lysander's withered heart flipped over. This would be it, they'd go together, and maybe someday soon act on that look in her eyes she sometimes gave Eroan when he wasn't watching. Fuck knows Lysander probably gave Eroan the same look often enough.

He watched the human warrior woman walk away while Eroan hung back. He'd no doubt follow her later. The humans would be fools to turn him away.

Eroan turned and Lysander pretended to be engrossed in watching the skies while keeping Eroan's approach over the rocks in the corner of his eye. Lysander shamelessly admired the sight he'd probably never see again after today. The elf moved like he knew his body was a weapon, and every inch of it could kill. He'd gone easy on Lysander yesterday, before things got... complicated. That had been his mistake. You could never go easy on a dragon. It'd turn around and eat you.

As the cloud cleared and sunlight poured into the creek again, that same light brightened Eroan's near-white hair, braided in one thick tail, a few locks curling free here and there. Blue, keen eyes, glittering with intelligence. Lysander was going to miss that sight.

"When do you leave for their camp?" He propped his head and watched Eroan pick up the dragonblade, admiring the hard line of his thigh, hip, and ass beneath his snug leathers.

"I don't." Eroan kicked over the campfire, smothering the flames.

He wasn't going? It couldn't be because the humans had said no. "You should go with her."

Eroan straightened, stared into the woods, then said simply, "Yes, I should." And with that, he strode into the woods on the path they'd arrived on some days ago.

Lysander dropped off the rock and frowned at the retreating sight of the elf, the sword jostling against his back, braid swinging.

"Are you coming, prince?"

Lysander kept his pace steady. So Eroan wasn't leaving him? It didn't mean anything, just that Lysander was valuable in some way.

Eventually catching up with Eroan's long-legged lope, he kept his voice level and asked, "Where are we going? To your people?" He laughed at the insane idea.

Predictably, Eroan didn't answer, just swept on, soundlessly striding over the gnarled roots and weaving between trees.

"Where *are* we going?" Lysander asked, the silence killing him.

"You can get into the amethyst tower?" Eroan glanced

behind him, brow raised. It wasn't so much a question as a statement.

"Do you mean dead or alive, because my brother likely wouldn't care either way."

"There are tunnels, correct? The ones we found were always well-guarded. We weren't able to penetrate them." He stepped over the trunk of a fallen tree, utterly familiar with the terrain. "But you can."

Lysander clambered over the mossy trunk, trying to unpack Eroan's words. The tower was riddled with tunnels from the old times, when it had stood at the heart of a great human city. Those old foundations were still beneath the surface. Most were closed off, but some remained. He'd used them a few times while visiting the lowers for *relief*. Could he get inside now without being seen? "Perhaps."

Eroan stopped, one boot propped on a tree root, and hesitated. When he looked over, intent flickered in his eyes. "Your brother is by now amethyst king, don't you think?"

"He is," Lysander confirmed, wondering where this conversation was now headed. "At least in name." The amethyst brood would need more convincing for Akiem to stay king. There may even have been internal fights, other strong amethyst who believed they could take the rule from Akiem. Lysander knew of a few candidates from the flights he'd trained who were strong enough to tackle Akiem... but not win. Akiem was no pushover.

"How do you feel about that?" Eroan asked it like it was a simple question and required a simple answer but nothing inside the amethyst brood had been simple, and Lysander's feelings about his brother were no exception.

"Why?" he asked.

"Do you care for him?"

His own laugh surprised him and startled a roosting murder of crows that took to the air, cawing. *Care?* "Did you not see how I lived?" The dry acidity in his tone was a surprise too, though it shouldn't have been.

Eroan's expression hadn't changed. He merely waited for Lysander's emotions to settle and jerked his chin, asking, "Are you loyal to the crown?"

"Loyal to the crown?" A growl bubbled through his words. "I am prince by blood but not in heart, that is all. And do I care for my brother?" He rubbed a hand over his chin. Why ask these questions now? What did he hope to achieve here? "I had a sister. A real sister from the same clutch of eggs, not just a brood sister where we're all thrown together." He leaned a shoulder against the nearest tree and peered up through its green-tipped branches. A squirrel bounded along a branch and out of sight. "If you don't fight in amethyst to keep your head above the shit, you'll drown in it. She fought but somehow kept her spirit."

Eroan's eyes softened. He shifted the sword, rolling his shoulders so it settled back into place. Lysander's gaze fell to the curved blade—Amalia's tooth—before skipping away. Telling Eroan why those swords had meant so much to him seemed pointless now. Besides, this proud, stubborn elf wore the sword well. It seemed right that he should have it. Amalia would have approved.

"Akiem loved her, I think. At least, as much as he's capable of. They would play... He laughed more back then." Lysander waved his own sentence off. Eroan didn't want to know how Amalia and Akiem had spent the days and nights together. To him it likely seemed normal to have a sister to love. "Do you have kin, siblings, parents?"

Eroan's quiet continued long enough that it seemed he wouldn't answer. "No."

Right, Eroan had told him before how Order assassins were unencumbered by loved ones so they could willfully throw themselves into killing.

"I *had* a family," Eroan added. "I remember my mother's laugh. A younger brother she carried in her arms... but our home was destroyed. I alone survived. My village, my people, they are my family now."

The way he spoke, Lysander sensed this was information Eroan didn't readily offer. He stashed it away like a precious gem. It wasn't too much of a stretch to imagine what had destroyed a young Eroan's family. Orphaned young, Eroan had survived, thrived among his own kind. Lysander envied elves and their fierce protective instincts. What must it feel like to be surrounded by people who cared for you, loved you?

"Mother got some idea in her head that Amalia was Akiem's favorite," Lysander continued. "She planned to breed Amalia off but Amalia wouldn't submit. Elisandra crippled her—crushed her front leg—and exiled her. It was a death sentence. The same as my wing." Lysander watched for Eroan's flinch, but none came. Instead, he listened, attentive and undeterred. "I happened upon her carcass weeks later while patrolling. Her death, more than all the other shit we dealt with, broke Akiem."

Eroan processed the information, his sharp mind likely turning it over and storing it for later use. He hadn't forgotten this elf had made it his life's purpose to kill dragons. Lysander had found himself telling Eroan too much before. He hadn't cared about the consequences then and didn't now. "You asked me if I care for my brother. It's not as simple as that. Dragons don't *care*. We think in stages of *how much can I use this creature for*? I don't want to kill Akiem, but he *will* kill me. He must, if he wants the brood to respect him. It's why he left the tower and came to the bronze line."

"He searches for you," Eroan said. "He tracked Seraph and I. Demanded to know where the humans held you..."

"You didn't tell him?"

Eroan's left eyebrow twitched higher. "I believed you were dead at the time."

"Well, you did order me killed."

And there was the wince and the little flicker in his cheek. A dead giveaway the elf was hurting. Lysander smiled at the sight of it. Eroan wasn't as invincible as he made out. "Seraph is alive?" Eroan nodded and Lysander sighed his relief. "I like her. She has spirit—"

"Will you help me end this war?"

Lysander almost laughed. He coughed and clamped his teeth together. Had the elf lost his mind? "How are you going to go about that? There are a thousand dragons in that tower. Countless others in nearby territories. Immeasurable wild ones in the north. Hundreds of thousands in lands like this one."

"And I have their prince right here."

Definitely lost his mind. "Besides the little problem of Akiem, I don't have any authority over my kin. You saw what my life was like with Elisandra."

Eroan wasn't going to be so easily dissuaded. He had that same stony determination about him now that had gotten him through months of torture. "You led her flights in battle," he said. "Your reputation as their most proficient fighter still holds."

"That's different." Lysander pushed off the tree. "It was a different time. I was different..." Why wasn't Eroan listening? Didn't he remember how Elisandra had sold him off to the bronze as breeding stock. He wasn't the same amethyst prince who had fought Eroan outside Elisandra's door. Dokul had driven him into the ground like a fucking nail through a board. Whatever authority he'd had was long gone. And even to think of facing his kin now after *that*, it made him want to throw up the breakfast of berries and fish.

"It's a chance," Eroan persisted. "Which is more than we've got now. So will you help me?"

Lysander shook his head, more as a reflex than answer but Eroan wasn't done.

"The dragon Carline said you're the future. She told me to protect you. I thought she was mentally unsound, but your path continues to cross mine, again and again. Alumn has her reasons. I cannot afford to ignore the signs any longer."

"*Alumn*, huh?" Lysander wished he had such faith in someone. "Carline told you I'm the future?" The old dragon had been spouting nonsense his entire life. Mumblings about potential and destiny. Frankly, he'd thought it all horseshit and she was just screwing with him because she had nothing better to do.

"Come back with me," Eroan urged.

Lysander scratched at the niggling worry-spot in his chest. This was insanity. "Your people will kill me on sight. Your elf friend in the woods, you remember her? She would have killed me if Elisandra hadn't... you know... eaten her."

"I remember well enough, dragon." He looked away. "If my people want me back, they'll hear me out. I'm not saying it'll be easy. It won't. But they're reasonable people."

Where was this coming from suddenly? Weeks on the

trek and now suddenly they were turning around? "What did Chloe say to you?"

And there, that flash of something was back in his eyes. Frustration, anger, Lysander couldn't be sure. "The humans are scattered," Eroan said. "Any ability to mobilize a resistance force is months away. I'm done waiting for others to decide when we die and what for. I have an opportunity right here..." He fixed his sharp gaze on Lysander. "You."

Lysander held that look for as long as he dared without falling into those intense elf eyes then blinked away. "You want to use me to get your forces into the tower? That's what you're asking?"

"I'm asking for your help to stop your kin from sweeping elves and humans from this world. What you do with that is your choice."

When he said it like that, he made it sound like some kind of destined choice, like they really could change the world, just the two of them. No wonder elves followed him. He could have told Lysander to roll over and close his eyes and he'd have considered it. The elf had a way about him that inspired others to act, made them want to follow his lead. "You'll try to do this without me, won't you? If you take a pride—or whatever your flights are called—into the tower, the guards will trap and kill you all. I know. I trained them to do exactly that."

He didn't reply, but something like admittance made him look away. And now Lysander could see why Eroan might have been kicked out of the infamous Order assassins. He'd do whatever it took to win. Any sacrifice, any cost. He'd go too far when everyone else was afraid to.

He chuckled to himself, pushed on down the track

leaving Eroan behind him, and said, "Do you ever stop taunting death, Eroan Ilanea?"

"I'm an Assassin of the Order, death is my life," came his reply from close behind.

Of course it was. "Your elf ass is going to get me killed."

"Will you help?"

The thought of saying yes lifted his heavy heart. He couldn't recall the last time he'd had a clear answer in his mind, the decision so right. "You expect me to drop everything from my obviously busy schedule to help you stop the war?"

"If you have something better to do, prince, by all means, go do that," the elf's smooth, taunting voice drawled, feeding a direct line to that feral part of Lysander's brain that very much wanted to spend every hour he had left with someone who had spent their entire life honing skills to kill dragons just like him. That very same person had held him close at a time when he'd needed nothing else more.

"I'll help you." He said it and knew immediately it was right. Carline, wherever the old crone was, would be cackling hard at the amethyst prince about to follow an elf's insane plan to end a never-ending war. "I can't think of anything else I'd rather do." *Or anyone I'd rather be with.* He was fairly certain this decision would get him killed but there was nothing and no one else he'd gladly die for.

CHAPTER 19

roan

BREAKERS THUNDERED against jutting coastal rocks. Over the expanse of angry looking water, Eroan's homeland interrupted the horizon. He'd crossed the expanse of water a few times now, but by boat. There were no boats here. Some debris, perhaps enough to make a raft, but that would take too long.

"Can you fly, elf?" Lysander smirked, apparently amused by the stretch of water blocking their path.

"Can you?"

Lysander chuckled and the soft, rolling sound set off a small cascade of flutters low in Eroan's belly, the kind of fluttering that led to wandering distractions and forbidden thoughts.

A raft it was then. But not tonight. The sky bled red. There were only a few hours of daylight left and the time was better spent making a camp.

"You know..." Lysander scratched at his nose and gave Eroan the kind of wicked look that told he wouldn't appreciate the next words. "I can swim it."

And die. "It's miles," Eroan dismissed. "Swimming it nearly killed me."

Lysander rolled his eyes. "Obviously, not as man..."

Oh. Dragons were likely buoyant and given what he'd seen of Lysander's dragon-physique he had the strength. "And how am I supposed to cross it?"

"You want me to spell it out for you?" Lysander crouched and picked up a pebble. He tossed it into the churning surf. "I'm guessing it'll take a few hours under the cover of darkness. If you ride up high, behind my crown, you'll be protected from the surf. I'll try to—"

"I'll make a raft." It would be easier than... what Lysander suggested. A few boards, some unraveled fishing net. Everything he needed was right here. He began looking for debris among the rocks and ignored his pounding heart.

"Afraid to get up close and personal with a dragon without sticking your sword in it?"

The words pulled Eroan up short. He turned to find Lysander casually tossing more pebbles into the bubbling surf. "With good reason."

Lysander threw him a low-lidded glance, the kind that invited further games to be played. "I don't bite. Often." He straightened and brushed sand from his hands. "Had I wanted to eat you..." his mouth fought with a smile, "I'd have done so at the nest when I wasn't in my right mind. You did look delicious at the time."

Afraid? Eroan adjusted the sword at his back. It wasn't a fear, more a healthy desire to stay alive coupled with the curiously playful look in Lysander's eyes that had

Eroan wondering if he was about to regret agreeing to this.

"You can swim that distance?" The opposite coastline was a long way off and the water foreboding.

"Are you doubting my word?"

No, my own sanity. "And I'm supposed to just... climb on?"

"You're making this more difficult than it needs to be." Lysander's smile was the kind that teased. "We're wasting time. Say the word and I'll shift."

Lysander wasn't some small kit. Since the bronze nest, Eroan had dreamed of standing in front of Lysander as dragon, his hand spread over the dragon's nose and the shock on Lysander's dragon-face. "You're comfortable doing this?" The touch had startled Lysander out of whatever killing madness had gripped him then. What if he went wild halfway across the channel? What if he decided he no longer liked an elf clinging to the back of his head?

"Just so long as you don't take that sword and stick it in my skull, yes. If you want to trust me, you must trust all of me. I am dragon, that's never going to change. Do I have your word you won't stab me, elf?"

Behind the crown was the most vulnerable spot on the dragon. One Eroan had exploited countless times. He'd taught dozens of elves the same. And now he was about to clamber on a dragon and allow it to ferry him across a huge body of water for a few hours. In the dark. With no boat or buoyancy aid.

If Lysander did turn on him, he was in the most advantageous location to make sure he didn't turn vicious. Eroan recalled a tale, of sorts, from when he was young. A fox and a scorpion wanted to cross a river. The scorpion stings the fox halfway across and they both die. Eroan had told

Curan that the story was a terrible one. Now it made a whole lot of sense. But he wasn't sure which beast Lysander was. The scorpion, who dooms them both because it's in his nature to kill, or the fox who trusted a killer. Maybe they were both scorpions. In which case, this would not end well. It all came down to one thing: trust. If he was going to trust Lysander with helping his people, then he would have to trust all of him, not just the man, but the dragon too. This crossing was the perfect time to test that trust.

"All right. I won't stab you so long as you don't try to kill me," Eroan agreed. "Shift then, dragon, and let's get this done."

He wasn't prepared for the blast of power. No human or elf could be. The light, the sudden pressure against his ears, the crackle of energy lifting the hairs on his neck and arms, and the shiver that tracked down his spine. *Magic*, it was called, but never fully explained. It just was, like the warmth of the sun that fed Eroan's soul, or the shifting of the seasons. And then, of course, the sight of the beast towered over him. Lysander's scales looked almost black in the fading light, but his eyes took the low light and refracted it, making them glow green.

Eroan resisted the urge to grab for his sword. *Just a dragon.* He'd seen plenty of them. The queen had carried him in her clutches. He'd killed dozens. This one was Lysander, the prince who'd protected him, even if he did now look like every elf's nightmare.

Lysander slowly brought his head down, planting his whiskered chin softly on the pebbles and huffed through his nose, signaling he was ready.

Eroan had climbed hills smaller than this. The crown Eroan was supposed to cling to was a ridge of spiked bone that flared up, presenting a fearsome appearance. Lysander's was one of the most impressive he'd seen. The spot behind, as well as being the most vulnerable spot, was also the most protected, at least from the front and sides.

Lysander huffed again and shuffled his belly lower in the sand, trying to make himself smaller. Eroan appreciated the effort but the thought of climbing a dragon wasn't getting any less daunting.

He walked the length of Lysander's snout, passed the enormous shining green eye with its wide, dark pupil tracking his every move, and stopped behind the curve of his jaw. The ridge of bone followed the angle of the jaw upward, its spikes getting progressively larger the higher they climbed.

It was just a few hours. How bad could it be?

He touched a scale twice the size of his hand. Warmth soaked into his palm. He pressed his other hand in and deliberately ran his touch over the scaled surface, riding the bumps and smooth, polished sections.

A deep rumbling started up somewhere inside Lysander's bulk. Not a growl, but a softer sound. A purr? A small smile tugged on Eroan's mouth. Lysander liked to be touched and he had to admit, the lattice of scales were fascinating up close, and the *thud-thud* of a dragon's enormous heart beat like an elven drum.

Lysander grumbled a reminder to hurry.

Eroan caught the lowest spike and heaved himself— one crown-spike at a time—up the dragon's head to straddle his broad neck. When Lysander lifted, Eroan's gut sank, the swift movement and sudden height reminding him that elves were not meant to ride dragons. He clutched on, pressed himself to the smaller scales behind the crown, and listened to the crash of waves and the beast's enormous thudding heart as Lysander took to the water. Salt water spray cooled his face and hands, numbing his grip. He clutched tighter, tucking himself in behind the ridge of bone. If he survived this, Seraph would never believe him.

~

THE CHANNEL CROSSING was relatively painless besides a few rogue waves that had nearly tipped him off and Lysander's huffing and shifting to keep him balanced. Lysander had been the model of good behavior. No stabbing required. But scaling the cliffs below the abandoned bronze wall had been an entirely different challenge. Weakened from the endless traveling, scaling the cliff left Eroan's body aching and Lysander—now back as man— visibly shivering.

Dragoncalls peppered the night, keeping them moving, until the warm dawnlight filtered through green-leafed trees and the calls had thinned to just one or two distant barks. Lysander still trembled, despite the day already warming. He watched the skies through the waving leaves.

To his shame, it took Eroan too long to understand why Lysander had fallen quiet. It had nothing to do with the cold and everything to do with the dragons in the skies. This was bronze territory. Some had likely remained, or perhaps they'd returned since Eroan had taken Lysander from their nest. Either way, Lysander wasn't cold, he was terrified.

A hollow opened ahead where a huge oak had fallen, ripping up the ground. Eroan recognized it as the temporary camp he and Seraph had used before winter set in. The circle of rocks marking the campfire was still in place and right there, Eroan starkly recalled how he'd sobbed in Seraph's arms on hearing his home was gone and how he'd ordered the death of the dragon who now shivered beside him. "We rest up here."

"Why waste good daylight?" Lysander mumbled, but he didn't look up. He'd seen the cold ring of stones and looked at it as though seeing more. His hair had escaped its knot again and fallen forward. Eroan fought the urge to tuck those locks back, to tell him he was safe here, that he'd meant his vow to protect him.

"We can afford to rest a while," he said instead.

The fact Lysander didn't argue and slumped down in the divot, against the bank, validated Eroan's concerns.

Lysander stretched out a leg and dropped his head back, but kept his arms wrapped around himself. His eyes closed.

The arduous last few weeks showed on the lines around Lysander's mouth and the permanent knot in his brow, but beneath the dirt and frown, the prince was still there. Somewhere. His mouth wasn't as quick to smile as it had been, but the smiles that did shine through were real, unlike the ones he'd thrown Eroan's way in the tower. His eyes too, when open, held a brittleness to them that hadn't been there before, as though he were walking the fine edge of a blade. Eroan had seen the evidence of that when Lysander had pinned him against a rock. It would take time for him to heal, and it would not be easy. Xena's words reminded him of a time when he'd suffered. She'd seen him volatile and wracked with guilt even if Eroan hadn't seen the signs himself, but he saw them in Lysander now.

Lysander's lips parted. His breaths deepened, as though sleeping. Eroan's gaze tracked over that smart mouth, remembering again how Lysander's tongue and lips had woken Eroan's darkest desires in the worst of times.

A short, sharp dart of lust cut off those thoughts. "I'll find us some food," he said, unsure if Lysander was awake to hear.

There would be no room for lustful thoughts once he was home. Elves did not want the things Eroan wanted. They were not aroused by being held down and threatened by a dragon. As for the rest of Eroan's thoughts... Maybe it was Elisandra's doing, some power of hers leftover from his time in the tower? It had to be. There was no other explanation, other than the one he couldn't afford entertain, that he might feel more for Lysander than he had any elf.

Hunger knotted his belly. He freed the blade and went in search of prey.

CHAPTER 20

$\mathcal{L}$ysander

THE SUN WAS WARM, the forest quiet, the breeze full of springtime scents, and with no further dragoncalls, Lysander's shivers subsided. He'd waved off Eroan's concerned glances, telling him it was the strain of the crossing, but the shivering hadn't started until he'd seen the dragons in the sky.

He hadn't feared them before. Not even after the coupling or Mirann's mind-fucks. But now... Terror clutched at his heart and drenched him in cold sweat. Nobody *wanted* to be afraid, to feel their body betray them, and Lysander had always hidden it, controlled it, used it. Any sign of fear would have killed him long before now if he'd allowed it. But that was before the cage, before Dokul. He could still taste the bastard at the back of his throat, and if he let the memories claw at him, the bronze *beast* was inside him all over again.

He swallowed. His gut rolled and his mouth watered. The shivering started up again. Would it ever fucking end?

Maybe Eroan's people would be kinder? They couldn't be any worse. He was under no illusions. They weren't going to welcome him in with open arms. In fact, Eroan's optimism seemed too short-sighted. Maybe elves were inherently hopeful, but Lysander had been around long enough to have hope beaten out of him. The fact remained Lysander had killed elves. Many of them. And those he hadn't killed, he'd left for Elisandra to toy with. Killing assassins, protecting the queen, rallying the flights, those were the things he'd excelled at. Either Eroan had forgotten or he was kidding himself.

A musky scent tickled his nose. He opened his eyes and sniffed at the air, parting his lips to draw the taste across his tongue.

Wolf.

Jolting to his feet, he plunged into the brush after Eroan.

CHAPTER 21

roan

THE ROE DEER had its head down, delicately munching the soft grass and mosses between the trees. There was enough meat on it to fill both Eroan's and Lysander's belly for the long trek back to Cheen. The logistics of cooking it would be interesting, but he'd deal with that problem after he'd slain it.

Crouched low, hood up, he waited for the deer to wander closer. Its ears flicked and a dainty hoof sank in the moss, inching forward one leisurely step at a time. Occasionally it lifted its head and looked about, its poor vision skimming right over Eroan's motionless form.

He'd approached downwind, preventing his scent—a mix of elf, sea salt, sweat, and dirt—from giving him away. Janna would have caught it and butchered it by now, but then Eroan had never had the patience for a long stalk.

The deer started, jerking its head up. A distant buck

honked, and the roe bolted away through the bushes like an arrow. Eroan dropped his head. No venison for dinner.

A rumbling growl sounded a second before a huge weight slammed into his back. He hit the ground cheek first. Grit dug in, shearing off a layer of skin. He pushed up. Teeth clamped around the back of his neck. Reaching behind him, he sunk his fingers into rough fur. The wolf shook, trying to rattle the life out of him, but the coat in its jaws loosened and he twisted himself free and backward. The huge wolf mauled his coat, ripping strips from beneath its paws.

A new pair of yellow eyes loomed from the dark behind its pack-mate. This one had its head down, stalking in low. One wolf he could tackle, but not two.

His sword glinted in the dirt between him and them. The first attack had torn it free of his back. He could choose to go for the sword and fight or run for a tree and hope he made it before the wolves snapped at his heels.

The first wolf was done with its prey of coat and swung its attention back to Eroan.

A rustle of movement from behind pricked Eroan's ears. Three wolves. And now he had no choice at all. He lunged forward, grabbed at the sword, looked up to see the wolf galloping in, and thrust the blade forward, striking the beast in the belly. The animal let out a whimpering cry, curling around the sword, snapping its teeth at the blade.

He yanked the sword free and whirled away, straight into the sights of another. Then a different rumbling growl poured in, deeper than a wolf's burble and full of threat. The wolf eyeing Eroan dropped low on its haunches, plastered its ears flat against its head, the white of its eyes showing as it turned.

Eroan followed its gaze.

Lysander emerged through the undergrowth, eyes fierce. The dragon growls rumbled on, not from the man he appeared to be, but from the truth of him, far bigger than the wolves and the clearing.

The wolves whimpered away under the weight of Lysander's presence, leaving their pack-mate bleeding out.

Eroan rubbed the back of his bruised neck and stumbled to his feet. The skin wasn't broken, he'd been lucky his now-ruined coat had taken the worst of the bite. Lysander was looking at that coat now and the dead wolf beside it, hands clenched and trembling at his sides.

"Thank you."

Lysander twitched, waking from whatever thoughts had him gripped. His cold, flat look had Eroan wondering if the threat hadn't left, it had just gotten bigger. Then Lysander came closer, crossing the small clearing in a few strides, setting Eroan's heart racing. He eased back a step. Then another. A dribble of blood tickled his cheek. He swiped it away with the back of his hand.

Lysander tracked the movement, then the male's hand hooked around the back of Eroan's bruised neck and suddenly, breathlessly, Lysander's hot mouth was on Eroan's, his tongue thrusting in, taking what hadn't been given.

A fire burst alive inside his chest, one raging with lust and fear, with a sudden, terrifying need so visceral that Eroan's lifetime of training kicked in. He brought his hands up between them and shoved hard, pushing Lysander back.

Staggering, Eroan tasted dragon on his tongue, like he had before, when dragon was all he'd been able to taste and see and smell. Disgust stoked the fire inside now, but that wasn't all. His body stirred in other ways, responding to Lysander like fire licks at fuel.

Lysander's glare blazed with his own raging flames. This wasn't the weakened prince, nor was it the smart-mouthed joker who made light of his terrible life.

He lunged in again, catching Eroan by the neck and yanking him forward. Eroan's chest slammed against Lysander's, the dragon full of rough demand. Eroan growled, pulling his head away. Lysander twisted and Eroan's shove slipped off. He didn't—couldn't—want this.

Lysander's fingers squeezed at Eroan's throat. Eroan's back hit the hard, rough tree bark, stopping his retreat, and suddenly Lysander pressed in and all over, just like before, only there was no sword between them now, just Lysander's fingers clamped around Eroan's neck, his leg between Eroan's, his chest an impenetrable wall.

Lysander's rough jaw scratched Eroan's grazed cheek, his lips brushing Eroan's ear. "If you want to stop me, use the sword in your other hand." The words hissed and Eroan's mind skipped over the thought of stopping this to the dark thought of needing more. "You hate me, right? I'm a tool to you. A way to get back at everything my kin did to you. We killed your family, we tortured you. Then fucking use me, Eroan." He dropped his hand and thrust it against Eroan's groin. "*This* says you want to."

The ball of Lysander's thumb pushed in, grinding against Eroan's painfully swollen arousal. His fingers plunged lower, seating near Eroan's balls, and rabid lust surged through Eroan's entire body, funneling right to where Lysander's hands had him gripped, by the neck and cock.

Lysander's lips brushed the corner of Eroan's mouth and Eroan found himself turning toward that teasing question, needing its answer. Wherever Lysander's rage had come from, whatever had caused it, Eroan recognized the need behind it all. He'd felt the same often enough. The need to rage at the world, to fight because the alternative would be to fall in the dirt and let the world rage at you.

Lysander nipped at his lip and Eroan tried to seal the kiss, only for Lysander's to hold him back. Lysander's mouth teased. He flicked out his tongue, tasting. The soft, intimate wetness had Eroan's arousal pulsing, his denials leaving him as his hips canted, driving his erection harder against Lysander's stubbornly motionless hand.

Lysander's hot breaths warmed Eroan's neck where blood pulsed close to the surface of his skin. As wrong as this was, Eroan's entire body ached to be touched and owned by this male, like it had in the queen's tower. Never had he wanted someone to control him like this. A sudden madness had smothered him, robbed him of reasonable thought. He'd always been the one in control. Always. But here, Lysander had him trapped, turning what should have been fear into a ferocious longing. "If you're going to fuck me, dragon, do it," he snapped, flashing sharp teeth.

Lysander's grip left Eroan's neck, then his hand caught Eroan's fingers and guided them to the hard rod trapped inside Lysander's trousers. Eroan molded his fingers around the erection as much as the fabric would allow. The dragon's eyes flared, more fuel on the fire. Lysander's low, bubbling growls shivered through Eroan, igniting the lust he'd worked so hard to deny.

Eroan was falling ever faster toward the insanity. He yanked his hand free, grabbed Lysander's rough jaw and attacked his mouth with a kiss so barbed it hurt. His sharp teeth cut, and Lysander took it, giving back the same assault.

Eroan wanted to strip this male bare and taste every forbidden inch of him. He wanted it now, all of him, everything. He tore at Lysander's coat, needing to feel warm, smooth skin, when Lysander suddenly caught both his hands, lifted them over Eroan's head and pinned his wrists to the tree.

Trapped, Eroan groaned out his frustration at being denied, then Lysander's tongue swirled at his neck, making him forget how he wanted to touch and allowed him to just feel.

Lysander's free hand rubbed at Eroan's erection, but none of it was enough to quench the heat between them. "Harder," Eroan demanded, capturing the dragon's gaze with his own. "Take me. Now."

CHAPTER 22

$\mathcal{L}$ysander

RAMPANT DESIRE LED Lysander's thoughts to the edge of a precipice and when Eroan looked him in the eyes, fierce demands falling from the elf's snarling mouth, it was all he could do not to turn him around and mindlessly fuck him against the tree. The elf was a heated, writhing, vision of temptation. His mouth wicked, the fire in his eyes like some personal torment designed just for Lysander. To have Eroan would be to capture a wild force, one Lysander would do anything for. The primal part of him wanted to fill him and fuck him until the world fell away, but he was afraid of how far he'd go, afraid he'd hurt him, or worse.

"Alumn damn you, dragon!" Eroan arched, giving himself to Lysander's hand.

His words had a direct link to Lysander's cock and every damn thing he said had him twitching and leaking, needing to be sated. So much anger flared in the elf's eyes and danced along the cruel twist of his lips, Lysander wanted to lick that anger off his trembling, sculpted body.

He hadn't planned on this, but the wolves, the fear that he'd been too late, and realizing one day Eroan wouldn't survive, had clicked over that switch inside that told him to fuck the rules, the fear, the wrongs and the rights. And then Eroan had fought him, shoved and pushed, denying the truth that was alive and hungry between them, making Lysander lose his mind.

Even now, trapped beneath him, Eroan was a stubborn riddle of denials. He'd fight until his last moment, but his body didn't lie. The male's straining cock grinding against Lysander's palm didn't lie. He wanted this, to be taken, to be owned. Eroan *liked* it.

Lysander had seen that flicker of fire when Eroan had been tied to Elisandra's bed. Oh, but that fire raged now. Uncontrolled and free and oh-so-fucking-hungry.

A dragon's roar thundered above. Birds startled. And all the lust, the need, the delight, fell off Lysander, making way for a sudden, bone-chilling fear.

The shock of hearing the call and what it did to him, stunned him into numbness. He let Eroan's wrists go and stumbled back, lust replaced by sudden, sickening cold. The shift almost poured through him, right there, like some weak lower unable to control himself.

Eroan said something, but suddenly all Lysander could hear was Dokul's rumbling laughter alongside the seductive song of his mother's voice.

The dragon in the skies let loose another roar, getting closer, and Lysander dropped to his knees, needing to get low, to submit. It wasn't Dokul. He knew that. The cry was bronze but not the chief's, but the fear didn't care. It had him now.

Eroan's fingers curled around Lysander's bicep. The smell of elf soothed his rattled mind, guiding him out of the fog. He blinked up at Eroan, at the pity in his eyes, and felt shame slither beneath his skin.

"Can you move?" Eroan whispered.

The bronze was close. Wing beats thumped above. The bronze had found them, those beats said. Dokul would be close behind. Eroan would die and it would be Lysander's fault.

"Lysander..." Eroan's mouth brushed his ear, the soft way he said his name brought him back from the loud place in his head. "Come with me," Eroan whispered. The elf's warm hand brushed against Lysander's neck and his lips teased against his cheek. "I'm not leaving without you."

CHAPTER 23

roan

LYSANDER HAD WITHDRAWN after the incident with the wolves and after, when the bronze had almost found them. And as Eroan stood before the Cheen's elders, he was no longer sure this was the right thing to do. Lysander was safely tucked away far from Cheen and waiting for him to return, but bringing him here after everything he'd been through could be too much too soon.

"It is good to see you have returned, Eroan," Anye greeted. He nodded politely. The last to arrive, she took her seat at the head of the table. "What is so urgent it could not wait for you to get settled before calling this meeting?"

He'd arrived less than an hour ago and come straight to the elders, avoiding Curan's demands to be briefed first. The Order leader sat off to the right now, among dozens of his prides. No Nye or Seraph. They were likely on patrol.

187

"I bring news from the humans and an opportunity."

He quickly told them of how the bronze had devastated the human ranks, but said they would recover in time, then they waited for him to present to them the real reason for him marching in after two months away.

"I have Lysander Amethyst in my care."

Gasps sailed about the hall. They all knew the name. Lysander Amethyst had caused the death of their loved ones. The queen's younger son had a reputation. Although a warped one, twisted as it passed from elf to elf. Eroan let them chatter and grumble, reminding himself of how the first time Eroan had seen Lysander, he'd have given anything to drive a blade through his heart. He couldn't forget his people would feel the same way.

"Quiet!" Anye called, settling those in the hall before fixing her stare on Eroan. "In your care? Would you please explain, Eroan?"

"I know you will find this difficult to believe..." He told them all he dared. Some Curan knew—too much, in truth —but the Order leader stayed quiet. Eroan told them of how Lysander had helped him escape the tower and kept him alive several times before that moment.

"He's not like the others." Seraph's voice rang from the back of the room. Eroan hadn't seen her enter but found her among the rowing crowd now and nodded his thanks. She dipped her chin in return. "He kept me safe from the bronze," she added. "He's the reason I'm here today."

"It seems this dragon has a penchant for saving elves," Anye remarked, but not in humor. "As convincing as this all is, the fact remains he is an amethyst prince. His motives are likely unkind ones."

If only she had seen Lysander save Eroan from the bronzes' sexual appetites, or the countless other times he'd helped in some way. Chloe had come around but only after it was too late.

Eroan began to fear being told Lysander was good was not enough, but it was all Eroan had to give them. That, and the truth. "I did not kill the dragon queen, though I was there." The crowd was twittering again. He sighed, the truth finally free. "Lysander broke her neck."

The twitter turned into a riot of noise that took too long for the elders to control again.

"And what is it you're suggesting, Eroan?" Anye finally addressed him.

"He has no love for his own kin. He'll help us fight them." The crowd exploded, but not in joy. Fear. Eroan had brought a dragon to them, one strong enough to kill their queen. This wasn't working.

Eroan caught Curan's keen glance before leaving the elves to their riotous outburst. It wasn't often his people got swept up in fear, but a dragon challenging everything they thought they knew was enough.

Eroan loitered by a water pump, idly watching elflings splash about under the sun. When they saw him, they cowered. He'd forgotten he was caked in dust from his trek.

Their big eyes watched him approach the water pump. He crouched, pumped out some water and splashed it over his face and down his neck, then flicked the rest over them, sending the little group into fits of giggles.

"More!" they squealed. "More, more!"

He pumped out more water into both hands and tossed it over them, stamping and dancing in the mud. They were young, just a few years old. At their age, he imagined he must have been like them, believing nothing could hurt them. Until one day everything had changed.

He hoped these little ones never had to suffer like he had.

"When I heard there was a riot in the hall," Janna said, startling him from the game. "I should have known you'd be in the middle of it."

He stood. "Janna, you look... well."

Her green-tinted hair had darkened, and her belly rounded, leaving no doubt she was in the family way. She still wore the bow slung over her shoulder. Being with-child wouldn't stop her hunting.

"I'd hug you, but you stink and this," she fondly patted her belly, "gets in the way."

He cupped her face and lightly kissed her forehead before quickly withdrawing. "Congratulations." Color touched her cheeks. He should have said it months ago, should have said a lot of things. "A summer babe?"

"She will be." She blinked up at him and the same fondness warmed him at the sight of seeing her safe. Brushing her hair back, he took the opportunity to gently flick her ear. She swatted him away with a laugh, one that brought a smile to his lips, until he spotted Ross casually pretending not to watch them from his sentinel position by the gate. The look on the male's face was more assassin-worthy than fisher-folk.

"She kicks," Janna said. "She's strong. Definitely female."

"I'm happy for you." Eroan gave Janna a few feet of space, lest Ross decide to put some weight behind his glare.

"So, what trouble have you gotten into now?"

"The usual..." he hedged, but as her smile faded, he guessed she'd already heard all she needed to.

"Is the dragon nearby?" she asked.

He didn't answer. Janna wasn't an assassin, but she could have been. And although he'd told her about the prince who had helped him, she didn't know it all. Every elf here would want Lysander dead. Worry niggled at him again. He'd been thinking of the future when he'd asked Lysander to help, but in doing so, he'd forgotten to consider Lysander's part in all of this. The risk to him was great, maybe too great.

"He's not bad, Janna. He saved Seraph for no other reason than because it was the right thing to do."

She searched his face and nodded. "I believe you but there are others who... They worry you've been alone too long..."

"I wouldn't bring him here if I didn't believe he would protect us."

"I know." She dropped her gaze and worried her lip between her teeth.

Eroan spotted Ross making his way over. "How I left things between us," he said hastily. "It was wrong of me." In truth, he hadn't intended on returning from France at all, and their time together that night before his leaving, it had been more of a parting gift to her.

She looked up, her soft smile genuine. "I've always known who you are, Eroan Ilanea, and would never dream of changing you. Now stop worrying over me and go upset the elders some more. They haven't had this much excitement in years."

When he was summoned back to the hall, only Anye and Curan remained.

Eroan told them of his plan to use Lysander's knowledge to get deeper than ever inside the tower and strike from within, ideally hitting at its heart: Akiem. When done, Anye's face had grown severe and a vein pulsed in Curan's neck.

"He is not like the others," Eroan added softly, hoping to give them the nudge they needed.

"You want us to risk our entire prides on the word of a dragon?" Curan asked, worryingly calm.

"Yes."

"You go too far, Eroan." His voice trembled. Color flushed around the scar on his cheek.

"That may be so, but if we can bring down the tower, and continue to employ the ballista, these southern lands will belong to elves once more. Isn't that worth the risk?"

Anye placed her hands together on the tabletop and glanced at her Order leader. Curan gave his head a firm shake. She sighed. "Eroan, please excuse us. We'll let you know the decision shortly."

"Know that if you do not admit him, under my care, then I'll not be returning to the Order."

Anye failed at hiding her shock, but it was Curan who spoke, "Perhaps *that* is for the best."

CHAPTER 24

*L*ysander

EROAN RETURNED in darkness with a length of rope and a hessian bag. The last time he'd had a bag over his head he'd almost been executed. "Really?"

"It's not my choice." At least Eroan looked apologetic.

Lysander offered his wrists. "You know I can break that rope in a blink." He could think of a far better use for the rope and imagined looping it around Eroan's wrists while he lay beneath him, all stretched out, naked and wanting. Only along with that thought came the memory of pinning Eroan to a tree, and how he'd spectacularly lost his mental-shit right after.

Eroan looped the rope ends around his wrists. Lysander took the time to study Eroan's face. The pinched eyebrows and distant gaze weren't inspiring. Lysander's gut clenched. "On a scale of one to ten, how much do your people want to kill me? Ten being they'd like to gut me and hang my carcass from their biggest tree and one being we'll all sit around the campfire drinking hot milk."

Eroan took too long to think about it. He cinched the ropes tight. His light eyelashes flicked up, framing blue eyes. "Eight."

"Oh, eight. Lovely. And I suppose those who don't want me dead are you and Seraph?"

"Something like that."

Eroan parted the bag and lifted it onto Lysander's head, drawing him in close.

"Wait..." Lysander's heart skipped. Eroan hesitated, the bag still raised. Lysander worried his lower lip in between his teeth. Eroan's eyes, speckled with silver in the low light, tracked the movement. "The last time I had a bag over my head you said—"

Eroan's mouth was on his suddenly, the kiss slow and leisurely, like a long, lazy summer day and Lysander immediately forgot the question, forgot it all, and reveled in the sweetness of elf and the tease of the male's tongue. His hands were tied, else he'd have them exploring by now. Since the *incident* a few days ago, where Eroan had clearly wanted Lysander, he'd kept his distance. But now, this teasing little kiss reignited Lysander's galloping feelings all over again, and the relief that Eroan *did* want him. Then the bag came down with a rapid shunt and all he could see was filtered darkness. "By the Great Ones, elf, you are a vicious tease."

"Shut up and walk, dragon." Humor lifted his order.

Lysander's battered heart swelled.

roan

EROAN LED Lysander by his roped wrists through the lines of gathered elves. They parted ahead of him and closed in behind, too afraid to get close, but too curious not to see the dragon prince. A few whispers hissed between them, but their words were lost against the sound of flickering torches. Most were silent, which felt worse.

Eroan was to take Lysander to the food-store and tie him up inside, as agreed with the elders. With every step, he prayed to Alumn that his people would be understanding, that they would not judge this lost prince for his name alone but by his selfless deeds. But so many he passed had vengeance in their eyes. And his assassin brothers and sisters, watching on from the shadows, would be the hardest of all to convince.

Once inside the store, Eroan tied just one of Lysander's

wrists to a structural floor-to-ceiling beam and pulled off the bag.

Lysander wet his lips and ran his glassy gaze over Eroan, darting it to the assassins behind him. The prince's jaw hardened and Eroan imagined what he saw on the elves' faces was the same lust for vengeance Eroan had recognized on the walk in.

Lysander pulled on the rope and looked questioningly back at Eroan. "I trust you."

Eroan swallowed. He had made costly mistakes before and prayed this would not be another. "This is temporary."

Lysander's attention wandered to the neat pile of fresh clothes, bucket of clean water and another bucket for Lysander to relieve himself in. The food-store wasn't a windowless tower dungeon and the single rope wasn't a pair of wrist shackles, and yet the sickening wrongness Eroan had felt on the walk in came down hard on him now. *Just temporary*.

Turning, he caught the eye of the two guards and nodded. He knew them well, as he knew most of Cheen's Order. They were more than capable of dispatching one restrained dragon before he could shift. A flung dagger to the throat would do it. "He is a guest and should be treated well. This is a formality."

They nodded, eyes forward, faces blank.

Eroan had to convince his people of Lysander's loyalty, and fast. Lysander's life depended on it.

CHAPTER 26

$\mathcal{L}$ ysander

EROAN LEFT the food-store without looking back. He did trust Eroan... to be exactly who he was: an Order assassin who needed him to strike at the dragonkin.

Lysander took up the washcloth and water and cleaned the dirt from his face and neck, as much as he could without stripping naked. The two silent elves watched on. One female, one male. Like stone statues against the far wall, dragon-teeth daggers at their hips and ankles. Their reception was decidedly icy, though he supposed he couldn't blame them.

They were the ones taking the risk here. He could shift and destroy half their village before they got a lucky strike in with one of their shiny new dragon-teeth swords. The bag over his head had been a waste of time too. He could smell the ocean, the forest too. It wouldn't take him long to orientate himself if he could get his head above the trees. Besides all that, he couldn't stay awake night and day and he would be vulnerable at times. Eroan might not want him dead, but from the looks of these two guards, the rest of the elves certainly did.

Different guards switched in through the night. Lysander dozed, his back against the beam, half-alert to the two new dragon-killers watching over him. Sometime near dawn, the door rattled and a familiar elf strode in, a wide grin on her perky face.

He blinked away the weariness and got to his feet, working the restraining rope up the beam.

Seraph shifted from foot-to-foot, glancing between Lysander and the guards.

"Hey," he croaked, letting a warm smile slip through. She looked decidedly better since he'd carried her unconscious body away from Dokul.

She sprang, and Lysander readied for a dagger in the gut or across his throat. She crashed into him, flung her arms around his neck and dragged him down, into a full-body hug.

"Huh, we're hugging...? All right." His muscles unlocked and carefully he looped his free arm around her back, pulling her close. Gods, she was a little thing.

The guards' collective gazes burned. Lysander displayed a middle-finger and the male to the right silently bared his teeth.

Seraph hugged him closer. "You're alive..."

So little, but full of fire. She smelled like the forest, like Eroan, and for a few moments he allowed himself the warmth of just being held by another with no ulterior motive, just kindness. "No biting this time?" he grumbled with a chuckle.

She plucked herself free, realigning her clothes to settle her composure. Her eyes were like Eroan's, pupils full, her lashes dark and sweeping. Her face still had a little roundness to it that she'd soon grow into. "I thought... I thought you were dead." She sniffed and blinked at the ceiling, chasing off unshed tears.

"That seems to be an ongoing theme with elves. They either think I'm dead or want me dead."

She glanced behind her at the stoic guards.

"They don't say much," he added.

Awkwardly smiling, some of her elven hardness returned, the guards having reminded her of her position and responsibilities. "Your hair got longer."

"So did yours." He backed against the pole, easing the pull of the rope on his wrists.

"I'm growing it out to annoy Curan." She combed her fingers through her mass of dark locks. "Our Order leader... he says I'm too much like Eroan."

Lysander could see that. "Maybe if more elves were like Eroan the war would have ended before it began." His casual words landed hard and her smile fell away.

"I'm sorry... about all this." She gestured at the bucket and clothes. "They're afraid. I told them they didn't need to be."

"It's all right. It's warm, it's dry. This is luxury compared to my last lodgings."

She stepped closer, clearly wanting to move in again. "If I'd known you were taken sooner, I would have found you myself. Eroan stopped me..." Tugging at her sleeve, she frowned down at her feet.

"He did, huh." He tried not to read too much into that. Eroan had likely been trying to protect Seraph. And what could she have done? The bronze would have killed her on sight, or worse. Eroan had been right to stop her. But Eroan could have come sooner? Could have but hadn't. His place was with his people. It was a miracle he'd come at all.

"He says you can help us. Will you?"

Lysander dropped his head back against the beam and sighed, suddenly so tired with it all. More cages. More questions. He was here by choice. It felt like that should be enough, but he understood why it wasn't. "If you'll let me."

"I've heard him in the hall, speaking with the elders." She lowered her voice. "He's trying to make it so you don't have to be tied up but Curan is... He... er..." She glanced behind her again. "Eroan told him some things from before and he thinks you're... you know..." She made some interesting clasping motions with her hands. "... *involved*."

By her odd tone, he assumed *some things from before* were probably bad things from Eroan's time at the tower. This *Curan* would be the one to convince if Lysander had any hope of staying alive here.

"He'll talk them around. Anye likes him, like Xena used to. He'll make it so you don't have to be tied up much longer."

She sounded confident, but she also clearly worshipped the ground Eroan walked. It was all on her face, every bit of admiration, every fearful piece of concern. Her honesty was a refreshing change to the lies and deceit he'd matured among. Her being here made all the difference in the world. "It's good to see you again, Seraph."

"You too, dragon. And thank you... for everything you did."

Funny how a simple heartfelt thanks could chew him up inside. She'd survived. He'd done something good with his life. It almost made all the pain and hurt worth it.

The door opened and an elf dressed head to toe in black marched in, his demeanor rod-straight and unforgiving. Seraph's back instantly straightened, her chin up.

"You should not be here," the dark elf told her.

"Nye, I was just—"

"You have patrols."

She nodded quickly and headed out.

"Seraph." His tone yanked her to a stop. "If I find you here again I'll inform Curan and you'll be struck from the Order."

"Yes, sassa." She ducked out the door, gently closing it behind her.

The two guards acknowledged Nye with short, sharp dips of their chins. This elf had authority. He was respected and his words held weight.

He was well built for his role as assassin, dark hair, dark clothes, dark eyes, even his skin was a shade darker than most elves he'd seen. A little shorter and slimmer than the others, but what he lacked in height he clearly made up for in attitude.

Nye studied him with a cool, calculated appraisal. Whatever the outcome, he kept it from his face and addressed the guards with a single glance. "You may leave."

"There are to be two of us here at all times. Curan's orders," the right-most guard replied.

Nye didn't argue, so he was no higher in rank than the infamous Curan, it seemed. He took a few moments then stepped closer, careful to keep outside lunging distance. "Amethyst?"

Disgust rode his tone, but more than that, a quiet thread of anger ran through it too, just beneath the surface. Lysander's being here seemed more personal to this one.

"Your queen, your mother, fixed a collar on Eroan."

Lysander shuffled through all the possible replies and denials and settled on silence. He wasn't yet sure who this elf was or what he wanted.

Nye came closer, deliberately stepping within range. Eroan had that same look about him when Lysander had first seen him, chained to a dungeon wall: defiance, strength, and a hate so pure it ran like blood through his veins. Eroan could have happily killed him back then. The array of weapons strapped to this elf's shins and thighs might swiftly find their way to a dragon's heart.

"The scars on his back... Whip scars." The elf's top lip quivered. "The things you did to him." His eyes narrowed. "You're an animal."

A right hook swung in, quick and fast. Pain smashed into Lysander's jaw, but it was the surprise that had him hesitating. Nye hadn't broadcasted his intent to attack. A skilled fighter, this one.

Lysander reeled, tasting blood. Nye's fist locked in his shirt and shoved, forcing him back against the beam. The cool kiss of a blade touched Lysander's throat, freezing him still.

"I could cut you open and let you bleed out. Nobody will save you and by the time Eroan knows, you'll be dead."

The elves behind him watched on, faces blank. If Lysander died here, they'd likely tell their elders how he had lashed out, how Nye was defending himself. He could shift but that would ruin everything Eroan was fighting for.

He stayed quiet, careful to measure each breath. Nothing he said would stop this elf if he truly wanted him dead.

Blood pooled in his mouth. He swallowed. Another

time, another place, this would have been over already, but that time was not here or now. Eroan's gamble, his dream, was worth too much to throw away.

Nye leaned so close the colors in his dark eyes sparkled. "You're not worth it." He spat, and the warm wetness landed on Lysander's mouth and chin.

Still Lysander stayed still, stayed calm. Perhaps he should feel something, anything, maybe even be afraid?

Nye finally pushed off and strode out the door, slamming it closed behind him.

Lysander wiped a hand across his face, sweeping off the spittle. The two remaining elven guards wore new smiles.

roan

"THE DRAGONS ARE COORDINATING their attacks like nothing we've seen from them before." The Ashford messenger had arrived moments ago, prompting a summons to the Order hall. Breathless and filthy, she looked as though she hadn't stopped for a single night during the trek. "They're systematically scouring the forests and laying waste to all settlements they find. The Ashford Higher Order has dispatched elves to the remaining villages, bolstering their defenses. They're warning all other settlements to prepare."

Eroan listened, seated beside Curan. The attacks were unusually organized for amethyst but not surprising. They had a new king, one eager to prove himself.

The messenger went on to reveal the number of dead. Too many.

Elisandra had never bothered to attack so methodically. She'd seemed content to ignore elves, for the most part. But Akiem was clearly not his mother.

The messenger left and Eroan listened to the elders' concerned murmurs. They'd respond by limiting the hunts. Food would be rationed. They'd be prisoners in their own village and hope Akiem overlooked them. It was the same behavior that had gotten so many killed in the past. Frightened rabbits going to ground. "We should prepare for an assault on the tower," he interrupted, "as I've suggested."

"Preparations for an assault will take too long," Curan said. He leaned forward, resting an arm on the table and waited for all eyes to turn to him. "The new dragon king is looking for Lysander."

Fear skittered down Eroan's spine. Curan wanted Lysander gone. "We don't know that for certain. He's just as likely to be hunting us as a sign he's in control of this region."

Curan's frown shadowed his face. He rolled his lips together and finally looked at Eroan. "Akiem appeared to you on the way to Ashford. You neglected to mention this when I asked for the details of your excursion. Why was that?"

Eroan held Curan's glare as panic fluttered inside. If he hadn't kept Akiem's appearance on the trek to Ashford a secret, Curan would have assumed he wanted to return to France to find Lysander. "I didn't think it important."

"You didn't? And now we're another fifty elves dead as he searches for the prince you've brought into the heart of our village."

The collective weight of a dozen angry elves drilled into him. "I brought Lysander here for a reason." Those watching this exchange likely knew most of Eroan's past by now, of the things that had transpired in the tower, and with that knowledge came a tightening in his chest. The gazes judged him, thinking him compromised. "He has knowledge of the amethyst tower that we'd never have obtained without him."

"Where is this knowledge? It's been a day. What do you have from him?"

Eroan licked his lips and looked to Anye. "I can't ask him to help us tied up like he is."

"Why are you asking him at all?" This came from Nye, seated at the far end of the table. "They tortured you, we should do the same to him. Get all the answers we need that way."

Agreeable mutterings joined in, rising in volume. Nausea wet his tongue. Were elves animals now? Where was their honor? Where was their compassion? These were not the elves he'd trained his whole life to protect.

"No!" He thumped a fist against the table, silencing their useless twitterings. "No," he said again, softer. "We are not like them. Torture is not our way."

"The fact remains," Curan interceded, "we do not have enough time to build a force and assault the tower before more villages burn."

Eroan rolled his tongue over his teeth and swallowed. They would have had enough time had Curan listened to him in the beginning.

"We have what the king wants," Curan continued. "We don't need to assault the tower, risking hundreds of lives. We need simply use his brother as bait, drawing Akiem into a waiting ambush."

Eroan closed his eyes and fell back into the chair as the others argued and discussed the fate of the dragon tied in the food-store. His heart thudded, his gut telling him this was wrong. He hadn't brought Lysander here to use him as a tool like he'd been used his entire life. He'd brought him here as an equal, as someone who could help them, protect them all. They were supposed to work together.

He looked around the table at the faces of his kin as they discussed handing the dragon over or torturing him, and Eroan's heart sank. He had hoped it would be different, that they would see the sense in having Lysander as an ally, but all they saw was dragon.

He pushed from the table and left, ignoring calls to return. He couldn't do this, couldn't use Lysander in this way. His feet carried him to the store, but he lingered outside, trapped between his duty and what his heart told him he must do. An Assassin of the Order stood for more than killing. This wasn't about sacrificing one dragon to save elven lives, they just wanted him gone and were grasping at anything that would see it happen. Lysander would die for their ignorance.

He pushed inside the store and barked at the guards to leave.

"Two guards at all times," one snapped back.

Eroan narrowed his eyes at them both. "Who was it who gave you those blades at your hips? Who taught you how to build and unleash the ballista?" They wavered, glancing between themselves. "Leave," Eroan dismissed. "I can handle one dragon."

They finally left, closing the door firmly behind them.

Lysander stood by the beam, his brow pinched. A new bruise blackened his cheek. Someone had struck him.

The fear, the rage, the injustice—it snapped inside Eroan. He crossed the floor, ignored the prince's widening eyes, and took him in a kiss that stole the worry away. Lysander moved with him, capturing his mouth and working it, responding like flame to kindling, and Eroan knew in that moment he could never use Lysander like his people wanted. He deserved more from them. He deserved to be heard, to be seen for who he was, not what he was. And he knew bringing him here had been a mistake.

CHAPTER 28

$\mathcal{L}$ ysander

THE ROPES at his wrist strained, pulling taut as Eroan withdrew and Lysander tried to move with him. His lips tingled, the kiss still there, lingering like an unfulfilled promise.

Eroan brushed a thumb across his mouth, his gaze tilted downward, lashes soft and low, and Lysander silently wished him to look up, to see, so he could read the truth in Eroan's eyes.

A dangerous hopeful spark stuttered his heart.

He wet his lips, tasting Eroan's sweetness. "What is this thing between us?"

Eroan looked up, but the sorrow in his eyes made Lysander wish he hadn't asked. Something had happened. Something bad to drive him here, like this. He didn't want to know it, couldn't bear the next terrible thing, whatever it might be.

"Kiss me again."

And Eroan did, moving in like the assassin he was, attacking Lysander's mouth with his. Eroan was everywhere, pushing against him, warm and strong and so very much alive. He pressed in, chest to chest, hip to hip, and rocked, grinding the hard length of him in a way that had Lysander breaking away and gasping. The elf's tongue flicked at his jaw, then his mouth sealed the kiss and roamed down the sensitive column of his neck, and all the while he rocked against Lysander, driving him to the point of mindless desire. Lysander's cock ached to be touched, and as Eroan's hip rubbed, pleasure sparked. He hissed in through his teeth. He wanted to hold him, bite him, taste him, until all he knew was Eroan. "You drive me wild," he breathed. Then Eroan's mouth was on his again, kissing him like he couldn't get enough.

But all too soon he slowed and doubt cooled Lysander's desire. He couldn't bear it, to have this male and then let him go. It would break him like nothing else had.

He touched Eroan's face, hating the fraught look, as though Eroan had failed or been defeated. The world would try to take Eroan from him. Lysander knew it, he'd known it all along. Eroan was too good for him, too much the dream he could never hold. But sweet nights, he wanted him here and now. Fuck the world. Just this once, he wanted to feel something that was real, because what he saw reflected in Eroan, the heat, the want, the need, it was everything, and he could not let that go.

"Could you ever love a broken thing like me?"

Eroan's rough hands suddenly clutched at Lysander's face, his eyes flared and lips pulled back. "You are a light in the darkness, a diamond in the rough. After everything you've been through, surviving your kin, you still smile. You're kind, and brave, and compassionate. I do not think I would be the same had I suffered as you have. I admire you. For that, and for many things, prince. You are not broken. You are the strongest of us all."

"Eroan, what..."

Eroan froze and it took a moment for Lysander to realize someone else had spoken, someone who had seen them like this, maybe even heard Eroan's words. Precious words Lysander clutched at and hoarded against his heart lest they be stolen from him.

Slowly, Eroan's hands dropped and he turned to reveal an unfamiliar elf inside the doorway, flanked by the two guards Eroan had earlier dismissed. A scar ran the length of this new elf's cheek.

"Curan—" Eroan began, his tone already begging.

The older elf freed two blades from his thigh sheaths. The guards behind did the same. "You would choose the life of this dragon over those of your own people?"

Lysander's protective instincts simmered awake. He would not allow them to hurt Eroan.

Eroan lifted his hands and side-stepped, drawing the three killers away from Lysander. "We don't need to do this."

"The Eroan I knew, the elfling I raised, he never left the queen's tower."

Eroan's face fell and Lysander felt that blow as though it were his own. Curan meant more to Eroan than the others. "Curan, if you'd listen—"

"You liked what they did to you... That's what you told me. And now this?" He flicked a dagger tip toward Lysander. "Did the dragons let you go so you might infiltrate us, so you could bring him here and free him among us?!"

The words struck Eroan, every one making him wince. Lysander's instincts to protect pushed through his thoughts. He clenched his fist and pulled the rope tight, making it groan. But the noise drew Eroan's eye. He shook his head, warning him not to act. How could he not? Eroan might not see it, but Lysander did. They'd turned on him. On them both. Elves were not so different from dragons.

"You're one of them, not one of us." Curan signaled the guards. "Deal with the dragon."

"Wait! What are you going to do with him?" Eroan demanded.

"A trade for peace. No more elves have to die."

"No... Curan, don't... you can't hand him back—"

Curan attacked, but all Lysander saw was Eroan avoid the first slash of daggers before the two guards blocked his view. One jabbed the handle of his blade into Lysander's forehead. His ears rang. A hard fist landed in his gut. Both strikes hit hard and true. Lysander fell into the blows, letting it happen, fighting the urge to shift and tear them all apart, because Eroan was here... and if he turned dragon now, he'd kill them all.

roan

CURAN CAME at him with all of the ruthless efficiency of an assassin who had lived too long. Eroan dodged the blades on the first lunge, but without his sword—left in his hut—his only weapon was the single dagger, plucked from its thigh sheath.

"Curan, wai—"

Curan slashed again. Single-minded focus burning in his eyes.

Eroan shied backward, out of Curan's reach. His back hit a wall.

To Eroan's right, the guards lay into Lysander. A fist in the face and another low. He doubled over, the hits landing again and again. He spat blood. He'd shift. Any moment now there'd be a whole lot of dragon in the food-store.

Pain zipped up Eroan's arm. He jolted his dagger up, clashing with one of Curan's blades, leaving his middle open for the killing blow. Curan hesitated, making the choice between life and death, and cracked his fist into Eroan's jaw. Blood burst across Eroan's tongue. His skull rattled. And Curan was on him, his blade pressed to Eroan's throat, freezing him still.

"You were a son to me." Curan grabbed at Eroan's shirt, yanking him close. "You had everything, and you threw it away for a dragon." His words trembled. Moisture shone in his eyes. "He's using you to get to us. How can you not see that?"

Eroan heard the words, but Curan was wrong. The guards had Lysander on his knees but he hadn't broken free. He could kill everyone here, could lay waste to the entire village, but he wouldn't because he was better than all of them.

One of the assassins punched his blade into Lysander's thigh. Lysander grunted, and Eroan's heart splintered. This was wrong. He strained against Curan's hold but the old leader had him pinned. "You do not want to make an enemy of me, Curan. Let Lysander go before it's too late."

The older elf's expression slowly crumpled. "Eroan Ilanea is dead. I don't know who you are anymore."

Curan's palm hit Eroan's forehead, jerking his head back. A flash of pain blinded him and then he was falling, the world suddenly dark and cold.

SICKNESS ROILED in Eroan's gut. His head throbbed, hot and heavy. He dabbed at the back of his skull, feeling the tender bruise, then gently poked at his sore jaw. Curan hit like a hammer. Clearly, he'd kept up his training.

Lysander's length of rope was now knotted around

Eroan's wrist and tied to the same beam, but Lysander wasn't here now.

He worked his tongue around the sour taste in his mouth. Curan could have killed him. Had Eroan been in his position, protecting the village, he would have killed the threat.

Eroan got to his feet and pulled the rope up the beam, trying a few different angles in the hope he could force his wrists free. When that didn't work, he tried brute force, and leaned away, putting enough strain on the rope for any frayed pieces to unravel. One or two sprung free, but no more.

"Hey!" he called, then listened for a reply outside the food-store. Either there wasn't anyone out there or they had instructions to ignore him.

Anger burned through his veins, boiling away the chilling reminders of the last time he'd been restrained. He would have never believed Curan would tie him up.

He pulled again at the ropes, yanked and snapped at them, tried to unpick the loops with his teeth. More unraveled, and he might manage to escape that way.... in a week.

Lysander didn't have a week.

Eroan trusted these people, he loved them as his own, and they had let him down, proving they were no better than the amethyst dragons they fought against.

Cowards. All of them.

He twisted the rope around his elbow, propped a boot on the beam, and heaved. Pressure tore at his wrist, zipping open grazes in his skin. Blood streamed. The beam didn't move, and with a frustrated shout, he dropped the rope and fell against the beam. He couldn't stay tied up like this, like before, but that time he'd had shackles around his wrists. This was different. This wouldn't last.

The door latch rattled.

Eroan spun, shading his eyes against the sunlit dust clouds. If it was Curan, he'd lay into him, demand to be released. Eroan was an Assassin of the Order, he couldn't be kept like this. This was not the elven way.

But it wasn't Curan. Janna left the door open and walked a few strides into the room before meeting his gaze. Her eyes glistened, edges red. On seeing him now, her lips twisted and twitched, as though she fought to hold back all the things she wanted to say.

He hadn't meant to hurt her. Or anyone. Everything he'd done, he'd done to protect them.

"Janna, please... you have to convince Curan to let me go. He's lost his mind. I haven't done anything wrong. I can't... I can't stay like this." He showed her the rope around his bloody wrist. "He can't do this to me. Tell him to come, to listen."

She bit into her lip and rested her hand on her belly. "You're here by the unanimous agreement of all elders."

Eroan straightened. That couldn't be right. They'd all agreed to keep him here, locked up like some animal? "Who told you this?"

"I was there, Eroan. There was a vote."

"A vote? On what?"

"You're to stay here until the dragon is gone and then you'll be... exiled."

He recoiled, the word as harsh as a slap across the face. "No..." *Exiled?* After everything he'd done for them? "Why... I don't... I don't understand. What did I do that was so wrong?"

A single tear fell. "Curan saw you with the dragon."

Her lip wobbled, as though the words alone disgusted her. "All of it."

Eroan closed his eyes. *All of it.* The words of hope he'd shared with Lysander. Bright words, honest words. What was so wrong in that? His whole world had just fallen apart. "It isn't what he thinks." But it was. When he'd left the hall, he'd planned on setting Lysander free, but he'd wanted just a moment between them, something to cling on to and the kiss... the kiss had been everything.

He covered his closed eyes with a hand and tried to steady his breathing, but the ropes, the darkness, and everything he'd ever fought for had turned its back on him. He was falling again, breaking inside like before. "Janna... You know me. Whatever Curan said, he's wrong—"

"He says the dragon has bespelled you with his magic, like they used to do with humans, made you... love him. Is that true?"

He laughed. He couldn't help it. Then the laughter turned cold and he saw his friend's face fall and didn't care. "Lysander has done nothing but good." His voice broke.

"He's killed dozens of us," she said quietly.

But he was different now. Why could they not see that? "He's the only one who dares fight for what's right and he's constantly punished for it. I brought him here thinking I could show you how he's different, and none of you listened. You think he's a monster."

"He is a monster!"

"No," he sobbed, thick emotion choking him, and didn't care. "He's no more a monster than I am."

"It's true," she whispered. "He has some kind of hold over you."

Eroan snarled. "It's not fucking true! His mother... she

had some power, but Lysander doesn't. How many times do I have to tell you? Why won't you listen to me? We've been friends all our lives and suddenly you don't trust my word? What did I do to make you hate me so?"

Her hand touched her belly and her tears fell freely now. "I came to say goodbye." She turned for the door.

"No, wait—wait! Janna... just..." He watched her standing there, staring out of the door, wanting to be anywhere else but with him. "Just tell me, please... Where is Lysander? Where did they take him? Is he alive?"

She closed her eyes. "They're taking him to the estuary. He'll be left there for his kind, then the dragons will leave us alone."

His heart jumped. "That won't work."

"It's happening." She slammed the door behind her.

"Janna! Wait!" He tugged at the rope, hissing as raw sores reopened. "Janna, get Curan! I need to see Curan!" Akiem wasn't just going to leave with Lysander and call it finished. If Curan believed that, he was a fool. And even if Curan was setting up an ambush—as Eroan assumed—without vast elven numbers, it wouldn't work. All they were doing was exposing themselves and Cheen. Akiem was too clever for a trade. Cheen would suffer. All elves would suffer.

And all because they didn't trust a dragon who could save them all.

He yelled until his throat was hoarse and pulled on the rope until its strings were thick with blood, and still nobody came.

CHAPTER 30

*L*ysander

THEY'D BOUND his hands behind his back and loosely tied his ankles, apparently believing a few ropes could stop him. It was clearly wishful thinking, but Lysander went along with it. The bag was back on his head too as they shuffled him along an uneven path. The briny smell of exposed, wet mud grew stronger. Distant seabird calls reminded him of the times he'd flown along the coast, riding the thermals spiraling up from warm coastal waters.

That old familiar ache returned, the heartfelt loss of no longer being able to fly. To stop the despair from sinking through his bones, he recalled Eroan's kiss back in the storage hut. A real kiss. Not forced, not taken, but freely given. He wallowed in the memory of Eroan's lips on his, his mouth opening, coming together and how every damn trial they'd been through had suddenly seemed worth it. That kiss had sparked alive a different madness, a good one, if anything, it had slipped right beneath all of Lysander's defenses and struck at the part of him he kept so well hidden, he'd wondered if it was still there: his heart.

"Keep moving, dragon..."

Something blunt and cold jabbed him in the back, shoving him out of the memory. He swallowed a growl. They were taking him somewhere close to the sea. *A trade for peace.* Maybe that would work with elves, but not with dragons. They were likely walking into a trap. He'd tried to tell the leader, Curan, as much, and received a swift kick in the ribs, then had a rag stuffed in his mouth and the bag dumped over his head. All of this was starting to feel eerily familiar.

He heard no dragon calls now, so perhaps this was some other part of the plan.

Hands tugged and pulled him down a slope. He slipped and hit soft, wet mud. One of the elves cursed.

"This would be easier if I could see," Lysander grumbled through the rag.

Nobody listened. He was pulled onto hard, wooden boards and marched along the uneven surface.

"Take him to the end," Curan said. "Watch the skies. If any arrive that aren't black, immediately retreat."

Hands pulled him along. He had a dozen questions on his lips. Some remarks too, ones that would probably get him another punch in the gut. He was beginning to wonder if, like him, Eroan wasn't like his people either.

The bag pulled up and off his head, and the rag was yanked from his mouth, leaving fluff and threads behind.

He spat and peered into the sunlight. Seabirds swirled above, but no dragons.

The dark-haired elf who had gotten the first punch in glared right at Lysander. "I hear dragons don't suffer weakness in their own broods. Maybe we'll get lucky and they'll kill you right here."

"You're a piece of work, elf," he grunted. The only other elf here was the old, grizzled one with the scar. Curan.

They stood at the end of a wooden boardwalk designed to float when the tide washed in. As the estuary river was out, the boards sat on the mud and led a path back to the estuary bank where the forest provided plenty of cover. He couldn't see them, but there would be elves back there, camouflaged out of sight.

"If you hope to meet my brother—"

Curan nodded and Nye's fist found a new home in Lysander's gut, doubling him up, then his hand gripped him by the hair and pulled. "You don't get a say in any of this."

Lysander's nerves frayed. This was a mistake. Akiem didn't negotiate. "He'll. Kill. You."

Another punch, and his breath left him, dropping him to a knee. He tasted blood again, likely from the cuts on the inside of his cheeks from the earlier beating they'd dealt him. He spat in the mud. "You have no idea who you're dealing with. This deal reeks of desperation. He'll draw you all out—"

Nye pulled on his hair, arching Lysander back. "I've been killing dragons my entire life. I know the monster we face."

A black cloud sailed across the sun, blotting out the

warm light and sweeping in a sudden chill. Lysander saw it over Nye's shoulder and realized with a start that it was no cloud. Akiem swept in, upriver, almost near-silent and filled the sky above them, his long reaching wings beating at the air, whipping up salty water.

He dwarfed them all, made them look like pitiful ants standing before a god. In the light of day, Akiem's obsidian scales absorbed the light. He didn't shine. No light could touch him.

Akiem's golden eyes scanned the tree line, looking for the trap. Of course, there would be one. Nye's words had implied enough. But Akiem hadn't lived as long as he had by trusting elves. Or anyone, for that matter.

His penetrating gaze fell to Lysander and the angle of his wing beats shifted, whipping the air into a swirling frenzy as he came in low to land in the mud. The second he set down, the shift rolled through him, black smoke knotting and lashing, until the man strode from the magical storm, sparks shivering off his form. Long, smooth black hair flowed over his shoulders, not a single strand out of place. His face angular and pale, eyes dark. A thin, jewel-encrusted band sat low on his forehead—a subtle crown and a reminder of who these foolish elves had summoned.

Lysander, still on his knees, hands and ankles tied, breathed heavily through his nose and tried to steady his racing heart. In their time apart, Akiem had changed in subtle ways. A few more lines had collected between his brows, making his face seem sharper. There was much of their mother in him, so much in fact, Lysander could almost feel her here with them, her glare shaving off layers of his armor.

"Brother," Akiem acknowledged, standing ankle deep in mud and not caring.

Lysander became very aware of his trussed state and peppering of bruises. Being beaten by elves was a new low, even for him.

Nye caught his arm and yanked him to his feet, and that too reminded Lysander of his apparent weakness. He wondered if Akiem could smell Dokul on him. He'd wanted to stand proud when he next saw his brother, like he had in the bronze warren, but now the time had come and his instincts just wanted him to drop and roll, exposing his belly and neck to the king. That too was Dokul's doing. The son of a breeding-bitch had ruined him.

"Take him and let us be," Curan said, tone typically lofty.

Akiem slowly slid his glare to the elf, then to Nye, "Did you beat him, elf?" he asked, sensing animosity.

"He resisted," Nye replied.

Akiem's dark eyebrow shot up. The lie was obvious. Had Lysander resisted they wouldn't have been here making a trade. To prove the point, Lysander tugged on the rope binding his wrists. It groaned, snapped, and fell to the boardwalk. He snapped the rope around his ankles next. Both elves valiantly attempted not to let their surprise show and failed. Lysander watched the older elf in the corner of his eye, hoping he realized he'd *allowed* them to beat him and what that meant.

"Why did you not fight them?" Akiem asked Lysander. "You could easily have broken those ropes much sooner than this."

Akiem wouldn't understand. He never had. "I'm tired of fighting."

The elves either side of him shifted nervously, sensing they'd been played. Lysander wanted to tell them to believe him, like he'd tried with Chloe. She'd realized too late to save her people, but these elves still had a chance. "Let them go, Akiem."

His brother puffed a gentle laugh through his nose and spread his hands. "Do you see any shackles? They are free to do as they please."

Unease crawled down his spine. There was more to this. Akiem would never arrive alone. He knew the elves were armed and he'd come prepared to fight. If the dragons weren't in the skies, then they had to be in the forest, closing in from behind.

"Do you *see* any dragons?" His brother smiled a cold reptilian smile and Lysander's heart constricted. They'd all die, and nothing would change. He had to stop this before it began.

Stepping forward to the edge of the boardwalk brought him almost eye to eye with Akiem. They'd had their differences, but that was the way of dragons. Fight or die. Akiem was just another survivor. "Don't harm them and I'll submit in every way." Akiem's top lip twitched. "Leave them all alive today and I'll follow your every word, brother. You will have my support in everything that you do, as king." A fractional narrowing of Akiem's eyes told Lysander he was getting through his brother's armor. But it wasn't enough. The sickness was back, coating Lysander's throat. He knelt and bowed his head. "You will be my king. Just let them walk away." He hoped the Order leader Curan heard every word and heard the sacrifice behind it. He likely wouldn't understand what Lysander was doing, not for a while, but someday soon he'd remember and perhaps it would be enough.

Akiem placed a gentle hand on Lysander's head. Relief lifted his heart. The elves would live to fight another day. But then his brother leaned down and whispered, "But I am already your king, and they are already dead."

roan

SERAPH'S ARGUING tones from outside the door dragged him from a heavy malaise. He couldn't make out the full sentences, but she seemed to be urging the guards away. Dragging himself to his feet, he watched the door and waited. Curan would never allow her to be here. She was taking a huge risk. He'd tell her to leave. She could still have a promising future in the Order but not if she associated with him... a *betrayer*.

The door flung open and Seraph strode in, sword at her back, it's twin in her hand. "You have to get to the estuary." She wasted no time in bringing the sword down on the rope, cutting him free from the beam. Then she took the bindings at his wrists and gently used the sharpened tip of his blade to pick them apart, finally freeing his bloodied and sore wrists. "They've taken Lysander to

Akiem. They're all there right now, ballista trained on the sky. As soon as Akiem takes Lysander, they'll fire on both."

Eroan rubbed at his raw wrists and took his sword from her, grateful for its comforting weight. "Thank you... I won't forget this."

She nodded, eyes narrowing. "Go save him, Eroan. Like he saved us."

He ran from the food-store, veered into the forest, and plunged deeper into the brush.

Save him. Like he saved us.

The seconds raced along with him and he feared, with every beat of his heart, that he was already too late.

CHAPTER 32

*L*ysander

THEY'RE ALREADY DEAD...

Whatever agreement Akiem had made with the elves, it was a lie. His brother was a predator. Words meant nothing. Bargains with elves meant nothing because elves were nothing.

Lysander lifted his face and Akiem trailed warm, rough fingers down Lysander's cheek, the touch curiously light. The look in his eyes easily mistaken for brotherly compassion, but Lysander knew it for what it truly was: pity.

"Run," Lysander said.

Akiem blinked. The words weren't meant for him.

Lysander whirled to Curan, *"Run now!"*

The elves backed away, but they weren't moving fast enough. Why weren't they running? Stupid, stubborn elves. "Run, damn you! He has you where he wants you. Run now or die!"

They mutely scanned the skies and all around, but with no sign of any dragons, why would they run? Lysander felt the same sinking realization he had with Chloe. Akiem was right. They were all dead. Lysander didn't know how his brother was planning to kill them, but Akiem rarely failed.

Akiem's laugh was a rich, dark seduction, growing deeper and more luscious as he stepped backward through the mud. "You always did spoil my games, *brother*." Akiem's teeth snapped together.

The mud at either side of the boardwalk bubbled and heaved, and fear plummeted through Lysander as he suddenly understood his brother's game. Mountains of mud lifted out of the estuary beds. Wings tore free, enormous heads lifted, crowns poking through, eyes blinking out from beneath their camouflage. The amethyst flights had been here all along, buried in the estuary mud.

"Run!" Lysander yelled.

Nye and Curan bolted back along the boardwalk, but while his flight had pulled themselves from the mud, Akiem had shifted. His suddenly enormous dragon form slammed a foot down between the elves and the shore, smashing the boardwalk and cutting off their retreat. He lowered his head, golden eyes narrowing in on his prey, and roared a skull-splitting roar loud enough to shake the world to its knees. Curan and Nye skidded to a stop, baring their tiny knives like they believed they truly had a chance.

Lysander started after them. If he got between them, Akiem might hesitate.

Akiem's tail swept in from the side, slamming into both elves, throwing them off the boardwalk and into the mud, straight into the boiling, heaving mass of emerging dragons.

roan

THE FOREST TREMBLED beneath the weight of a powerful roar. Eroan heard his kin shouting commands. He was too late. The dragons were here. Through the trees ahead, mud-caked mounds appeared to heave out of the estuary, coming alive before his eyes. And among the flapping mud-coated wings, Akiem's matte black scales gleamed.

"Lower the ballistae!" the elves yelled.

"Aim them down now! Down! Not at the skies!"

Eroan halted, breathless, and took in the chaotic scene. The ballistae weren't aligned. He scanned the line for Curan or any sign of leadership, but nobody seemed to be directing the assault.

"Where's Curan?" he asked the nearest ballista operator. The male ignored him, consumed with the effort of trying to wind down the angle of the enormous weapon.

"Fire! Fire!" The shouts bounced around the line.

Some freed their huge arrows, but their aim was off and ill-organized. The arrows flew, missing their targets. And now they were exposed.

Dragons turned toward the tree line—toward the hidden elves.

"Assassins!" Eroan yelled. *"Aim at the king, at the black beast! No other!"* Striking Akiem was the only chance they had. If they could bring him down, the others would scatter. *"Those not on a ballista, form up!"* He pushed forward, ahead of the ballistae, elves falling in-line behind him. *"Protect the ballista lines!"*

Dragons slammed into the tree line, waves of teeth and claws charging closer, and Eroan's assassins roared toward their end.

CHAPTER 34

ysander

ENORMOUS ARROWS ARCHED through the skies and punched into the mud. Some found their dragonscale targets, but not many, and now the dragons were turning toward the elves, intent on digging them out of the trees. The screaming started. More arrows flew in. Dragon-fire would soon strafe those trees. Elves would die.

Why did nobody listen to him?

Lysander turned his attention to Akiem. Stopping him would stop the assault. Akiem had no interest in those on the shore. He'd found one of the fallen elves in the mud and was plodding toward it, dragon-eyes fixated on the stumbling male clutching at his side.

Wading through the mud, Lysander lumbered closer. Arrows smacked the mud beside him. Cold globules splattered his face, blurring his vision. Screams confirmed what he knew to be inevitable now. They were all dead, they just didn't know it yet. But if he could stop Akiem, there was a chance he could pull the flight back.

Akiem circled the mud-coated elf, hunched low, watching his tiny prey try and struggle. The elf stumbled, falling forward. On turning his face, his white scar confirmed him as Curan. It was no mistake Akiem had singled out the elven leader to torture.

The dark elf—Nye—thrust a dagger at Lysander, but with the mud sucking at his legs, the elf's attack came up short. A growl bubbled inside. Lysander let it lose, warning the elf off. "Get in my way and your Curan dies." He pointed at the cat and mouse game. "Go back to your elves in the trees, help them survive. You cannot do any more here."

"I can kill you," the vicious elf panted, eyes burning through the mud mask.

"Not today. Now leave!" Lysander pulled himself forward, listening for Nye's attempt to stab him in the back, but when it didn't come, he plunged on, clawing at the mud, dragging himself closer.

Akiem's growls drowned out the sound of dying elves. He reared up, firepit bubbling, then brought a foot down on the elf, crushing him under the mud. The Order leader's hand flailed, desperately seeking something to cling onto.

"Akiem, stop!" He had to get Akiem's attention. "Stop! Stop and I will ensure there's no dissent in your flights. Kill him though, and I will turn the amethyst flights against you. Your rule will forever be a fragile one. Is that what you want?"

The dragon huffed and lifted his foot, but not from

submission. He had Lysander in his sights now. *Better yet*, those golden eyes said, *I kill you here.*

Lysander looked for signs that the elf was alive, saw his fingers twitch, and feared the worst. Whatever happened now, he'd done all he could do to save Curan. Now he had to save himself.

The shift rolled through him, stretching him open, filling him out, until he was a mass of super-heated rage and ancient instinct. He planted his four-legged stance over the fallen elf and fed all of the fury into the firepit low in his gullet, feeding the flames until the heat beat like an enormous second heart, too hot and too powerful to hold on to. Akiem lunged and Lysander unleashed the fire.

roan

AN ORANGE HUE poured over fallen trees and broken bodies. The dragons had ripped great holes in the forest, through the elven line, and now dragon-fire boiled the air, igniting remaining trees.

Eroan hunkered down, shielding himself from the heat, and turned toward the source of the flame.

Lysander. He fought Akiem. The dragon king was distracted, turned away, exposing his back and crown to the elven line.

"FIRE!" Eroan yelled. "Fire at the king now!"

The ballistae let loose their dragon-teeth tipped arrows. They soared, arching higher, then converged on the black beast's head.

Die, you scourge.

Arrows plunged into his neck, and the beast wailed, but none had hit below the crown.

"RELOAD!"

A wall of scale and claws slammed into the line from above. From one moment to the next, Eroan was face-down in the dirt, ears ringing, his body a beating mass of pain. He fumbled through the grass, crawling forward, and rolled onto his back.

An amethyst loomed over him, eyes narrowed to slits and pinned on Eroan. It pulled its head back and filled its firepit so the scales low on its throat glowed hotter and brighter.

Eroan scrambled toward the beast, ducked beneath its chest and thrust the blade up, through the beast's scales, into ribs, to the hilt, then heaved every ounce of strength into tearing the blade free. A clawed foot swung in. Eroan rolled, narrowly escaping. Then Nye was here, high up on the creature's neck, blades flashing as he plunged both down behind the dragon's crown. The dragon twitched, its eyes rolled, and it fell with a ground-shuddering thump, throwing up clouds of dirt and debris.

Nye emerged from the raining dirt and clasped Eroan's reaching hand, pulling him to his feet. "They have Curan."

Eroan heard him, but the devastation sprawled in all directions briefly tripped his thoughts. The ballistae were shattered. Dead elves lay among huge, fallen dragons. By Alumn, this should never have happened. So many dead... "It's over."

Nye blocked his view of the devastation. Mud and blood smeared across his face and his eyes held a haunted sheen. "It's not over. We have to save Curan."

"Go to ground!" Eroan bellowed for anyone left standing, his voice fracturing mid-way through the order. Those still alive echoed the retreat order through the elven ranks. They would not yet return to Cheen. It was too dangerous.

Instead, they'd scatter, losing any dragons on their scent and only return home once it was safe. Cheen *would* be safe. But the losses were devastating.

The dragons, perhaps sensing their victory, had withdrawn and now seemed to be gathering in the mud, converging around Lysander and Akiem.

"He's out there, Eroan." Nye gestured through the burning trees. "We have to help him."

Eroan sheathed his sword. "We wait."

"No, we have to help him now!"

At least twelve dragons filled the estuary. There was no way to get through them. In all likelihood, Curan was already dead. "It's suicide."

Nye's mouth quivered in a snarl. "That's never stopped you before. It's Curan, Eroan. We can't leave him."

Curan's last words echoed in Eroan's mind. *Eroan Ilanea is dead to me.* "His fate is in Alumn's hands."

CHAPTER 36

$\mathcal{L}$ysander

AMETHYST DRAGONS CLOSED in from all sides. Less than Akiem had arrived with, but enough to do him some serious damage.

Akiem hadn't escaped unscathed. A gash on his rear leg oozed dark blood. It wouldn't be enough to stop him, just piss him off.

Lysander padded in a circle, keeping the fallen elf beneath him. Alive or dead, it didn't matter, he had to keep this one elf—their leader—safe. He snapped his teeth at any amethyst who dared come too close, like he had the bronze. But his own brood moved differently. More lithe and slippery, they arched their long necks, lashed long, sharp, barbed tails, and teased with the promise of purple dragon-fire burning in their firepits. Then, Akiem was in front of them all, staring Lysander down.

He remembered Eroan's words about getting inside amethyst, and the hard look in his eyes when he'd spoken of Akiem. Eroan wanted more than the amethyst threat gone, he wanted Akiem dead. Wasn't Lysander better able to help the elves from inside the tower? Better that than his life ending here, dead in the mud.

Reluctantly, with the fire still churning low on his throat, he dropped his head, exposing the vulnerable spot behind his crown. Submitting. It shouldn't have felt so wrong. After Dokul, this was just dragon-play, but it still tore him up. But submitting now would save him. Akiem needed complete authority. He needed Lysander to bow.

Akiem struck. Hard, long teeth sank into Lysander's neck an inch below the soft spot behind his crown but close enough that Lysander couldn't help the fearful yelp. Akiem's powerful jaws twisted, forcing Lysander onto his side, crushing his bad wing beneath him and exposing his belly. Akiem spread his broad black wings, Lysander still in his jaws, and heaved them both into the air. The amethyst flights followed, filling the sky with wings, shaking off their mud camouflage, leaving behind a scarred landscape littered with the dead.

roan

SOUP-LIKE TIDAL WATERS had swept in and covered much of the mud, leaving just a few banks exposed. Eroan's fingers ached, numbed and cold from digging out the dead. Wordlessly, he and Nye dragged elven bodies out of the water, to the relative safety of the dry bank so at least the river didn't take their remains. Their families would come for them, once it was safe.

Wet, cold clothes clung to him, heavy with mud, but the seething rage warmed him through. He'd spent too many hours of his life collecting the dead and broken dire news to too many loved ones.

This slaughter could have been avoided.

Wading through thigh-deep water, mud sucked him down, urging him to stop. His bones ached. So did his soul.

Nye gasped and staggered forward, toward a lump of

driftwood stuck in a raised mudbank. The gnarled bit of wood moved, twitching. Eroan surged forward.

Curan was half-buried, but enough of him lay exposed for Nye to desperately try to stem the blood-pumping wound in his gut. Thick, almost black blood mingled with dirty water and oozed between Nye's fingers. Most of Curan's middle was a shredded mass of flesh and bone. He would not survive.

Curan lifted a trembling, pale hand. Eroan automatically took it, kneeling beside him. The male's grip was ice.

"Eroan...?" Blood dribbled from the corner of Curan's mouth, its color so bright against the male's milky skin.

"Don't speak." Eroan tried to smile, to offer some kind of reassurance, and failed. Curan's old eyes leaked. He knew he was dying. "You're not alone, sassa."

His face contorted in pain. His hand tightened on Eroan's but his lashes lowered, focus drifting. "...So... sorry."

"Don't speak."

"So sorry... *son*."

Eroan's vision blurred. Grief tugged at his chest, trying to rip out his heart. He cushioned Curan's head in his free hand and gently lowered his forehead to the male's, so close he could almost fall into his soul through his wide, pained eyes. "Be at peace, Curan. There is nothing to forgive."

"I was... wrong," Curan whispered. "... about your dragon."

Eroan squeezed his eyes closed. Cool, quiet tears fell.

"You must lead them." Curan switched his grip from Eroan's hand to his arm, and pulled, suddenly fierce in his conviction. "Lead them to victory. They will follow you, Eroan. It was always going to be you." Curan's trembling, mud-covered fingers cupped Eroan's face, smearing his tears. The old assassin smiled. His trembling slowed. "Xena told me once... how you will save us all."

"Yes..." He wanted to say more, but the words lodged in his throat.

Curan's eyes defocused. His grip slipped and fell away.

"No," Nye whispered.

The world shifted around him, despair spiraling in. *Son.* Running a hand down Curan's face he closed his eyes and lay the only family he'd ever really known to rest. He pressed his forehead to Curan's. "May Alumn's light embrace you..."

CHAPTER 38

*L*ysander

NOTHING HAD CHANGED in the tower. He hadn't really expected it to but had foolishly hoped Akiem's rule would be different to Elisandra's. Lysander's chamber was cold, dust-filled and strewn with cobwebs. He stood staring at the emptiness, wondering where the Lysander who had once lived here had gone because he didn't feel like him anymore. That creature had stumbled half-drunk through life, under his mother's thumb, raging at a world, expecting it to change for him. Elisandra had been right, he hadn't known savagery, hadn't known anything.

He was alive, so there was that.

But at what point did just surviving become too much of a torture?

A knock rapped on the door behind him. "Akiem will see you in the throne room," a stranger said.

Lysander nodded, sending the lower on his way, and followed moments later to find the throne room packed wall-to-wall with Akiem's amethyst subjects. A sprawl of amethyst females lounged around the queen's old throne, Akiem the center of their attention. The harem wasn't servicing him, like they would have been Elisandra, but the sight of Akiem in their mother's place, wearing the same slanted smile, startled Lysander's thoughts. Apparently, it was good to be king.

As he walked up the center aisle, idle chatter dwindled. He stopped in front of Akiem, the silence suddenly suffocating.

Akiem leaned forward. He flicked a hand toward the floor. "Kneel, brother."

The nape of his neck prickled, unease still there. Unless he wanted to challenge Akiem's rule, he had no choice but to do as ordered. This was no different to how he'd submitted at the estuary. Slowly, he knelt. Moments passed. Lysander looked up to find his brother smiling down just like Elisandra used to. Nerves roiled in his gut.

"You smell like bronze filth."

Lysander worked his jaw around the things he couldn't say. "Is there a point to having me on my knees?" When Akiem didn't answer, Lysander's nerves twitched. "Or maybe you'd like me to suck you off, brother? For old times' sake."

A dangerous tick pulled at Akiem's hard mouth.

Now it was Lysander's turn to smile. They had never talked of the time Akiem had invited Lysander's affections in a way their mother-dearest wouldn't have approved of—it had been a shared rebellion, a way to slip around Elisandra's hold, or maybe Akiem had gotten curious about males. He'd liked it too. Akiem had always been better than Lysander at hiding his desires.

"Bind him," Akiem ordered.

Guards rushed in, grabbing at Lysander's arms. He growled at them, males he knew, males he'd *taught* and fought alongside. He couldn't fight a whole tower full of dragons. Predictably, chains rattled across the stone floors. They clamped shackles in place, weighing his wrists down behind his back.

"You had better lock them tight," Lysander warned. "I escaped some just like these during the bronze coupling."

"Oh, I know..." Mirann's smooth voice sailed through the grumbling crowd.

A guard jerked Lysander's head back so he had no choice but to see the golden-painted bitch saunter toward him, sliding a cat-o-nine-tails whip through her hand. It had been so long and her presence here so shocking, he briefly forgot the shackles, the amethyst watching, and forgot about Akiem until his brother moved from the throne and landed a punch to Lysander's ribs.

The breath tore from his lungs and a cool numbness spread outward. "For abandoning amethyst," Akiem snarled.

Not a punch... He looked down to see a dagger hilt protruding from his chest. That couldn't be right. Why would Akiem stab him... What had he meant, *abandoning* amethyst? Gods, it hurt.

"That should make it a little harder to shift..." Mirann crouched in front of him and used the whip-handle to turn his head, settling her whisper in his ear, "Shift, and that blade might migrate to your heart, my pet, and we can't have that."

His head numbed, as though he'd downed too many

bottles of wine. No, this wasn't right, this wasn't fair. Akiem was harsh, but not like this... This was Mirann's idea. Her doing. Revenge, perhaps, for the fall of the bronze warren. He didn't know, and now his thoughts were softening, melting away through his fingers. Unconsciousness was coming, and then he'd be at Mirann's mercy. This hadn't been the plan. Akiem wasn't supposed to do this.

Power writhed beneath his skin, trying to roll over and spill free. "There is nothing you can do to me, Mirann, your wretched father hasn't already done," he slurred, losing his grip on reality.

Mirann's golden eyes sparkled, like pools of molten ore trying to pull him in. "Challenge accepted, Lysander Bronze."

"Take him deep beneath the tower," Akiem ordered. "Do with him what you will but let it be known throughout my kingdoms, I have no brother."

Bitter betrayal lanced adrenaline through Lysander's veins. "You son of a bitch!" He bucked against the hands holding him. Pain lanced through his chest, sparking into some vital part of his body and drenching him in weakness. "I will serve you! You don't need to do this!"

Akiem's growl rumbled through the room. "You are an elf sympathizer. You are a weak and broken creature." He settled back onto this throne and allowed the members of his harem to slither closer. "But worse than all of that, you killed Queen Elisandra. Be grateful Mirann argued for your life. You are hereby disowned by amethyst. I intend to let you rot in the bowels of this tower for the rest of your miserable existence."

The guards manhandled Lysander back down the aisle, dragging him when he kicked out, and Mirann led the way like a golden snake winding her way through amethyst brood. Lysander struggled for as long as his body held out, even managed to slip their grip once only to get as far as a sudden wall of snarling amethyst lowers. He bared his teeth and growled back at them, but then the guards had a hold of him again, dragging him down into the cool, dark confines of the lower tower foundations. They threw him into a cell eerily similar to the one Eroan had been kept in. Panic clutched at his heart and the dagger in his ribs ground against bone, snatching his breaths away. Chains rattled, but he was on his knees again, staring at the floor, trying not to let the thumping ache in his head and chest take him under.

"Hold him still."

Her voice drew his attention back into the room. That voice, as smooth as honey.

Hands gripped his shoulders, holding him down. Warnings growled up his throat. "Touch me and I'll fucking kill you all."

"There, there... darling, pet." Mirann held up something clear and cylindrical about the width of her thumb with a needle on the end and a plunger on the other. Filthy brown liquid sloshed inside. "This will make everything better."

He'd never seen a device like that before. She pointed the needle toward the ceiling and pushed the plunger. A dribble of liquid spilled from the sharp end. The hands on his shoulders pushed and Lysander hissed through his teeth at the lowers. "You think you have me? You've no fucking idea who I am now. Do this, and I'll hunt you all down and kill your broods, making you watch."

A fist struck his right eye, reopening the elves' scabbed wounds.

"Hold him, I said!" Mirann screeched.

A hand clamped around his jaw, holding his head rigid, and fingers squeezed into his upper arms.

Mirann moved in, her needle device poised. "You're all mine now, Lysander Bronze." She pressed the tip of the needled against his neck. It pierced his skin and a cool, alien sensation spilled into his veins, shivering through his chest, down his arms, sinking into his gut. "And with you..." she whispered, stroking her cool finger down his cheek. "All amethyst will soon be under me."

The cold feeling shocked his heart, spasming through muscle, then he was falling without ever hitting the ground.

HE DREAMED of silver and bronze, of blood in his mouth and cold hands scorching his skin. Waking was worse. The tremors wouldn't stop. Whatever she'd dumped into his veins was trying to eat him from the inside. He shivered, hot in the dark, hearing his mother's laugh and Akiem's words over and over. *... a weak and broken creature.*

It wasn't true. It wasn't. But the words hammered in, over and over, chipping off his armor. Then more of that poisonous shit was forced into his veins, leaving him breathless and lost, curling into himself to keep out the cold.

"Oh my kit... what have they done to you?"

He recognized the voice as someone he should know, someone important who had always been with him, but he searched the dark only to find he was alone.

"Don't let them break you." He heard Eroan and sobbed, clawing at the dirt-encrusted stone floor.

There were others here, some faces he knew, some he

didn't. They seemed like phantoms, and he couldn't fix them in his mind to know if they were real or dreams. Amalia was here, her laugh like the light he chased. Then Mirann was there, her hands forced between his thighs, around his throat. She whispered things, things he couldn't wrap his mind around, about his being emerald, about power and control and things he didn't understand.

He didn't want to be here. He wanted to be on the wing, soaring far and free from the darkness and pain. He wanted to feel the warmth of an elusive elf beneath his hands and see his soft smile again. The dream of Eroan was replaced by Mirann, her body a weight on his hips, her hands on his chest. He rolled his eyes, reality dragging his heavy body up from beneath the surface. Cold stone bruised his shoulders and hips, Mirann's every movement driving him deeper. She slammed her mouth over his, shocking him awake, and suddenly he felt it all. Her cunt riding him, his body a tool beneath hers.

With his hands still tied, all he could do was buck and twist, but the strain left him weak, his head spinning. She was all over him again, and this time her hand locked around his throat. *Just like her fucking father...* Ice coated his skin and chilled him deeply, taking him to the faraway place. Let the bitch have him now, he'd make her pay for it all... just as soon as... he could find himself again and stop the horrible hollow ache in his heart.

"You'll bow to me. You'll submit in every way to me and so will your pathetic jeweled brother." She showed him the needle and waggled it. "Tell me you're mine."

He bared his teeth. "Take out... the dagger." It still protruded from his chest, beating hot and hard like a second heart, killing him with every hour that passed. Or maybe that was her poison carving out his death.

"Oh, no no no…" She straightened, looming over him in her tarnished bronze lamé gown, all of her nakedness exposed beneath. She'd touched him all over, inside too. "Tell me you're mine."

"I'm not anyone's."

"The coupling… do you remember that? You're my emerald now, to do with as I please. Dokul shouldn't have hunted you, but it doesn't matter. I have you now."

His head was a jumble of broken things. Everything smelled of metal and blood. His gut heaved, his body a wrecked weak thing.

"Maybe just a little more of this to help you surrender —" Her weight straddled his legs, leaning in close to deliver the poison again. Lysander swallowed, breathing her blood-like scent in through his nose, letting it fuel his rage, and then, when the needle pricked his skin, he thrust his head forward, crunching against some part of her face, both hard and soft.

She screeched, but instead of backing off, her teeth sank into his neck, piercing deep. Lysander jolted still, the dragon in him suddenly and utterly subdued.

Then the needle went into his thigh and the cycle began all over again.

~

"Fix him."

Someone new had arrived. She smelled like woodsmoke and mead and reminded him of when he was a kit, his body sore and cut up from another fight. Lysander rocked. No more… he couldn't take any more of the poison in his veins and her hands all over him.

"He's useless like this." Mirann's boots clipped the stone floor until the sound faded.

The chamber door slammed.

No more...

Make it stop.

A hand touched his tingling shoulder. With his arms still bound behind him, the small touch burned. He turned away, tucking himself tighter into the corner.

"Listen to me... listen... You're a survivor."

He blinked, wondering if she was real, this new female with a bundle of gray hair and kitchen robes. Of course he knew her. She'd always been there after he and Akiem had fought, always been ready to heal his and his brother's wounds. "Carline?" he croaked.

"Yes, my dear kit..." Her hand settled on his shoulder again and this time he let her turn him toward her, let her pull him close and wrap her arms around him. "It's all right. It's almost over."

"... hurts."

"I know. You must be strong. You can survive this too."

He wanted to crawl into her lap and hide there, wanting to shift and bury himself under his wings, but shifting would be worse. The knife was too close to his heart. "She's in my head, her and... Mother. Make it stop, Carline. Take the knife out or push it in. Don't care. Just make it stop."

"Listen to me, and listen hard, Lysander." Carline's warm, healing hands touched his face and that warmth poured through him, filling out his bones, chasing away the pain. "You are not like them. You never were. But you weren't a mistake. You are the answer to everything." He squeezed his eyes closed. Her hand stroked his head, over his hair.

"... weak." *Broken.*

"No..." she crooned. "No. You are the strongest of them all."

Tremors clutched his body again, leaving him breathless. "I c-can't."

The door swung open. "Enough!" Mirann snapped. "Get out!" She pulled Carline away from him and shoved the old dragon toward the open doorway.

"It was never meant to be this way," Carline growled. "He'll be your end. The end of all of us."

Mirann laughed. "*That* will be the end of us." She pointed at him and the shivering started up again. "His mind is mine. The rest of him will follow."

"You play a dangerous game, bronze. Does your father know what you're doing to him? He is of the old ways. He will not allow—"

"Get out, old hag."

Carline cast him one long, steady look, probably trying to convey something, but Lysander failed to grasp it. After she'd left, he stared through the open door. Freedom had never felt so far away.

Mirann's outline grew until she was his whole world. She straddled his legs and crouched to look him in the eyes. "Feeling better, pet?"

He wet his cracked lips. "Take out... the dagger."

"Hmm..." She cupped his face. Her hand warm against his feverish skin. "Ready to stop fighting me?"

Thinking felt like rummaging through broken glass. "Stop the drug... Let me think."

Rocking onto her knees, she leaned in and nipped at his lip. "Or maybe it's time for a change of tact." She moved so fast it made his vision blur. But he saw the whip, saw her smile, and turned away too late to avoid the worst the nine-tails could deliver. Agony tore down his face and neck. He gasped, the pain too bright and too fast to think around.

"You." Again. His body screamed. "Are." Again. Rage and power tore through him, burning out the poison. "Mine." Again. The urge to shift loomed. Death would be a release from this. The dragon in him stirred, revitalized by Carline's healing touch. He took the raw power, shaped its weight, used it and funneled it, pouring that vicious intent into his arms, straining against the shackles around his wrists.

A link snapped, his wrists separated.

Lysander shot out a hand, catching the whip's tails before she could land them again.

Mirann screamed her rage.

With his free hand, he pulled at the dagger handle. It slipped free with a wet, sucking sound.

Freedom.

Mirann was on him, smothering and heavy. Her needle device flashed. He caught her face in his hand. The needle slammed into his shoulder, poison sinking in, but it was too late. Thoughts icy calm, he smashed her skull against the wall. Once. Twice. Bone cracked. A thrill raced through him.

Her sickening poison tried to get its claws in and send him reeling, but he was on his feet now, the shift reined in, but lending him the strength to fight. He staggered, the room tilting, and dropped Mirann in a heap.

She panted. Her fingers twitched. Her eyes rolled.

She wasn't dead.

He needed her to be dead.

Picking up her whip, he circled around her, watched her writhe and twitch. She rolled her golden eyes up, seeing him. Icy calm wrapped him in nothingness. He brought the whip's tails down with a vicious crack. She bucked, still alive, mumbling and reaching. Begging. Good.

He swung the whip again, again, needing to grind her existence into the stone floor. She grunted. Again. The whip bit, tearing, spilling blood through the links in her metal dress. Again, the tails cracked, breaking bits of Lysander's own armor off with every strike. Blood rained and pooled, and it wasn't enough. It would never be enough. Again, he beat her, roaring out all the hurt, until nothing about the noises he made was human.

He came back to himself oddly calm, sitting across from the mangled wreckage of Mirann. The air reeked of blood and shit and he probably should have cared that he was coated in all of those things, but his head was quieter now than it had been in forever. She wasn't dead. Death was a release, and she hadn't earned hers. She would suffer, like he had. But first, he had a message to send.

He hauled himself to his feet, tucked the dripping whip into his belt, fingers slick with blood, then scooped Mirann's motionless body off the floor, over his shoulder, and walked from the chamber.

NOISES RUMBLED from the feasting hall. His feet carried him up through the bowels of the tower, toward the sounds of a gathering. Lowers scattered from his path or cowered, hoping to be unseen. But he saw them. Saw every single one and marked them in his mind. He would not forget their betrayal.

Either none had dared run ahead and tell Akiem or his brother hadn't cared, because when Lysander entered the hall and carried Mirann's body among them, it took a few minutes for the shock waves to ripple through their number.

Akiem was sitting where their mother used to sit behind the long feasting table, goblet in hand, leaning casually to the side, an ample feast spread before him. When he caught sight of Lysander, his smooth, seductive smile cracked.

Nobody dared block Lysander's path. He wasn't sure what he'd have done to them if they had. He stopped beside the table, reeking and blood-soaked, breathing hard through his nose. *Get a good look, brother.* And his brother did, guarding any reaction from his face, but his stillness was enough. Akiem saw him. The real him: the beast years of mental torture had made.

Lysander gripped Mirann's deadweight and dumped her body on the table, sending plates of food toppling. Her arms flopped out, broken fingers falling open near Akiem's lap.

"You think you can get rid of me that easily, *brother?*" He peeled his lips back from his teeth and stoked the growl to life. Mirann's poison still burned through his veins, but so did the imminent shift, mixing into a white-hot, all-consuming power. He was more than this human camouflage, more than the dragon contained within. In that moment, he could almost reach out, capture the sun in his hands, and swallow it. For the first time in his life, he was the one in control.

Satisfied Akiem wasn't going to do a damn thing, Lysander turned to regard the room. Hundreds of his kin stared back. Their collective fear tingled on his tongue. Spreading his arms, he let them get a good look at their blood-and shit-covered prince. They'd always reveled in his failures before, so why not his victory too?

"If any of you fuckers so much as thinks of challenging me, I'll do to you what I did to this bronze bitch." His voice echoed through the hall, filling the gaping quiet. "Look at me wrong, and I'll rip your gods-be-damned wings off and eat them."

"Is she dead?" Akiem finally spoke, drawing Lysander's heavy gaze back to him.

Lysander's muscles twitched, the dragon within stretching its claws. "Afraid of the bronze response?"

His brother's cheek fluttered. Still leaning to the side, he rubbed his thumb and forefinger together, thinking.

Oh, he was afraid all right. Lysander had just started the war Akiem and their mother before him had tried to avoid. *War*. Lysander fucking wanted it. He wouldn't rest until every last bronze was ripped from the earth. And then he'd start on the amethyst, and every other dragon who dared stand in his way.

Grabbing Mirann's smooth, hairless head, he leaned in, held his brother's glare, and licked up the bitch's neck, tasting coppery blood. It dribbled from his tongue. He wiped her blood across his chin. The heat of Akiem's gaze didn't wane. Lysander's message was clear. *Don't underestimate me, brother*.

Lysander planted a boot on the bench and climbed onto the table. The eyes of the amethyst elite were all on him. Leaders of the flights he'd trained and led in battle against the dragons of the north, dragons he'd once called friend. They'd quickly abandoned him once Elisandra made her intentions clear, but she was gone and Lysander was not. He grinned and threw his arms up. "The bronze bitch suffers for crossing amethyst!"

Thunderous cheers erupted, bloodlust alive in his kins'
eyes.

Hopping down, he threw a smile at Akiem's guarded
face. "Our flights were always mine."

His brother lunged across the table and snatched
Lysander's wrist. "*Kneel to me now.*"

Right, because they needed to see Lysander follow
Akiem like a good little kit. Lysander plucked his brother's
grip free, leaving smears of blood on Akiem's smooth
fingers. "Help me kill every fucking bronze alive and I'll
kneel. For now," he replied.

Akiem glanced at those around him, their loyalty only
as strong as the strongest dragon in the room. He could
shift and throw down here, but to do so would be a sign of
weakness. Akiem had his pride. He nodded tightly, enough
for only Lysander to see.

Lysander lifted Akiem's hand, addressing the frenzy of
dragons. "Your king!" Kneeling on the bench, he bowed his
head, listening as the cheers rolled on and on.

A shudder tracked through him. Mirann's body blurred
in his vision. Fighting off the waves of weakness, he caught
Mirann's wrists and tugged, sliding her cooling carcass off
the table and onto the floor. "Lowers, she's yours."

He abandoned the body as the lowers rushed in like a
pack of starved wolves and shoved through the crowd,
letting their grasping hands slide over his arms, smearing
Mirann's blood. "You..." he barked at a stunned lower
about to leave the hall. "A bath, my chamber. Now." The
server hurried off.

Lysander made it a few more steps before stumbling
against a wall outside the hall. His vision tipped, doubling.
The power, the drug, the abuse, all of it conspired to drop
him to his knees. He shoved forward, forcing his feet to

move. Just another step and another. He could do this. He just had to hold himself together until he reached his chamber. The shudders were back, shaking his hands, then the sickness flushed waves of hot and cold across his skin.

For once he was grateful for his chamber's cold darkness.

At the window, he fumbled with the latch and threw it open, freezing in the blast of cold, fresh air washing in and over him.

Don't let them break you.

He bowed his head and closed his eyes, trying to keep his guts from heaving and his mind from splintering apart. He was afraid, he realized. Not of them, not of Mirann or the drug or his brother and maybe not even afraid of Dokul, not anymore. Nothing back there could hurt him.

He was afraid of himself and what he was becoming— what he needed to become to survive the war to come.

CHAPTER 39

 roan

"THE AMETHYST ARE MORE active now than we've ever seen them," Eroan said, addressing the forty assassins gathered around Cheen's meeting table. After sending messengers to nearby settlements with a call to arms, more assassins were arriving daily. The Order ranks had swollen to the point where they'd outgrown the Order hall and had adopted the main village hall. Although many of the faces here were young, they were each capable dragon-killers, many with double-digit kills to their names. "While they seem to be focusing on patrols, I'm not convinced they've forgotten us or what happened at the estuary a month ago. We must ready our forces. We cannot afford to wait. Waiting costs lives. It's time to act."

Cheen's messenger entered the hall, fresh from the journey by the ragged look about him. He strode straight to Eroan at the table's head and dug out a note from inside his coat.

"Trey," Eroan greeted, taking the note. The male's fingers brushed his and Eroan caught the long look in his eyes. "Will you see me after this meeting?" Eroan asked, breaking the wax seal on the note.

"Of course."

"Rest first..." Eroan's order trailed off as he read the scrawled words.

Fifty

2 days

Chloe

The humans had answered his call. Eroan's heart stuttered. He closed the note and regarded the assassins watching him, waiting for his word. Seraph was here, waiting as patiently as the others, and Nye at the far end of the table.

With his dying breaths, Curan had told him to lead them, and that was exactly what he was going to do. "Trey, how are you with dragonblades?"

"I... er..." He cleared his throat and skipped his gaze over the gathered assassins. "I get by."

"Speak with Nye. I need you in the Order. Events are moving fast and we need more numbers."

Trey blinked and cleared his throat. "I'm a better messenger than I am an assassin."

A smile tried to pull on his lips. "Let's see if Nye can change that."

Trey was a good messenger, but for Trey to survive the long treks from village to village alone, he did more than just get by with a blade.

Nye would see what the messenger was made of.

"Appoint your successor and tell them to come find me. I need to get a message to Ashford. The rest of you..." He eyed the assassins in turn, pride swelling his heart. "When you're not patrolling, you're training. More blades are being shaped and Janna is working on teeth-tipped arrows and quivers for all of you."

"Do you have a plan for assaulting the tower?" Nye asked.

"I'm working on it."

He dismissed the group and pulled Trey to one side outside the hall. Village life bustled around them, startling normalcy in the spring sunshine. "I know you don't want this, but I need strong, capable individuals in the Order."

"Is that the only place you need me?" the messenger drawled. Oh, Eroan hadn't forgotten anything about Trey's *other* talents and could happily lose himself in the promises Trey's sultry eyes suggested. Given the half-lidded look on Trey's face, he wouldn't object if they decided to make some more memories just like the ones from a few years ago. Before Lysander, Eroan would have been tempted.

"This isn't personal," Eroan said, nipping his own wandering thoughts in the bud. "I need people like you for the assault on the tower."

Trey's lazy smile faded. "I know. I have nothing but respect for you and everything you've done for Cheen. I'd be honored to pick up a blade and fight alongside you."

"Thank you." He squeezed the male's shoulder. "Go see Nye when you're ready, but be warned, he won't go easy on you."

Trey chuckled. "I'd expect nothing less from the Order."

Events were in motion, but a small seed of doubt had

Eroan wondering if things were moving too quickly. Humans working with elves? It hadn't happened in generations, and with good reason. But the past was dead. They had to look to the future. Curan wanted Eroan to lead, and this was how it would be done.

At his hut, he changed into darker camouflaged leathers, snatched up his blade and spyglass, and headed out while the sun was still high in the sky. The path he took was one he could walk with his eyes closed. He'd trekked it so many times during the past few weeks that he'd trampled the brush underfoot.

The land climbed and the trees thinned until he emerged at the very edge of the forest where fallen trees marked the boundary with the barrenlands. Tucking himself into his usual nook between two fallen trees, he lifted the spyglass and watched the tower far in the distance. It was still too far away for him to pick up any detail, but he'd seen enough to recognize various patterns in the flights coming and going from the tower grounds.

Setting the spyglass down, he picked up the little shaped piece of wood and whittling knife from where he stashed them daily, and began to carve, occasionally looking up when any dragon calls sailed across the land to see them spiraling higher and higher above their land.

The sun was getting low when he heard the soft press of weight against earth from the tree line behind him. "Seraph..." he said.

"Every time," she grumbled then crouched on the other side of the trunk to his right. "How do you hear me?"

"I don't have half an ear missing."

Scowling, she playfully flicked his ear, the one holding her stud earring. "Be nice."

He chuckled and handed her the spyglass.

"Any change in them?" She took a look through the glass, as she did every time since the first day she'd followed him out there.

"No." He chipped away at the wood. "I don't like it."

"I got that from the meeting."

He huffed through his nose and took some small chips off the head of the creature he carved. Its wings still needed work, they didn't sit quite right, and the crown needed detailing, but he'd do that last. The little dragon carving sat neatly in his palm. Tiny, really. He'd started carving it to give his hand and mind something else to focus on while watching the dragons.

"What did the note say?" Seraph asked.

"Human reinforcements are close."

She lowered the glass. "That's good."

He nodded.

"Isn't it?"

"Yes."

She glared, trying to uproot the truth. "But something is bothering you."

"A great many things bother me." He set the dragon carving down and took the glass from her hands to focus again on the tower. "I need to get in there."

"Elves that go in there don't come out... apart from you, I guess."

Something was terribly wrong behind those tower walls. The dragons had always flown far and wide, but lately, they'd stuck close, and more and more were taking to the skies, like they were restless. Were they building toward something? Akiem had stopped rooting out the elven villages. Why? What was he planning now? The king hadn't forgotten the estuary.

Seraph picked moss from the rotting log. "The others think you're coming out here to watch for any changes."

"I am."

She arched her eyebrow. "Horse. Shit. You're watching for..." she lowered her voice and whispered, "Lysander." Like the name was a dirty word. Among elves, it was. It didn't matter how many times Eroan had argued that Lysander had nothing to do with the massacre at the estuary, only that he was caught in the middle of it, they still blamed the prince. Eroan had stopped arguing his innocence, aware of his fragile new-standing among his own kind. They would never come around to thinking a dragon was anything other than an elf-killer, but perhaps he didn't need them to. He needed his people united, not worrying if their leader was embroiled with the enemy.

Seraph was different, though. She knew Lysander, she understood. "There's nothing you can do," she said.

Eroan lowered the glass and let his head drop. If he hadn't convinced Lysander to walk into his camp, bound by the wrists, none of that disaster at the estuary would have happened. But worse than that, the memory of the hope on Lysander's face, like perhaps together they really could make a difference. And all Eroan had managed to do was hand him back to his brother. And he was in that tower now, right back where he started.

"I'm afraid for him, Seraph," he admitted. "How can anyone survive what he has and not have it break them?"

She folded her arms on the ground and propped her chin on them. "If anyone can, it's him."

But for how long? "There must be a way to get a message inside... something. I need to know if he's... I just need to know." He heard the pain in his voice and didn't care. If she didn't know his feelings went beyond some need to do the right thing, then she hadn't been paying attention, and Seraph had always been the most attentive in lessons.

She puffed a sigh, stirring her bangs. "You can't let the others know how you feel."

Curan had discovered enough to see him exiled. He'd only escaped that fate because Nye witnessed Curan's last words. "I don't know how I feel about him."

"You don't?" She snorted. "Typical. *Eroan Ilanea. Can't see what's right in front of him.*"

"Remind me again why I like you."

"Because I'm the second most bad-ass elf in Cheen." She preened.

"Nye might disagree."

She laughed and went back to thinking. In truth, he was terrified of the insatiable need to be near Lysander. He wasn't even sure when it had gotten its claws into him or if it was even real. It felt real. It felt right, this strange, primal desire to protect the prince. After he'd saved him from the bronze and felt the male's trembling, locked in his arms, that's when he'd known for certain—that he'd do anything to keep Lysander safe. Alumn would be ashamed of him. What kind of elf sacrificed everything for a dragon? These strange feelings for Lysander made no sense, they broke all the rules, and still Eroan couldn't stop the swell of his heart when he recalled their last kiss in the food-store. Lysander so willing and open, so completely vulnerable.

"No elf can get in that tower and live," Seraph was saying. "Anything bigger than a bird they eat, especially elves."

Eroan looked up at the birds sailing through pale-blue skies, unmolested by dragons. "You told me once, Janna's mate, Rowan... Ray?"

She chuckled. "Like you don't know his name! *Ross*."

"He has hawks?" he asked, thinking aloud.

Seraph arched an eyebrow. "Yeah, he does, for fishing."

"They're well trained?"

"I guess..." She followed Eroan's gaze toward the tower.

CHAPTER 40

$\mathcal{L}$ysander

HE WENT THROUGH THE MOTIONS, doubling-down on the brutality to make up for being half-dragon. Elisandra would have despised him, no matter what he became, and the hate in Akiem's eyes had solidified, becoming a visceral thing between them. Akiem was king, but Lysander had a hold of his flights, just so long as he could terrify them into submission, but with every passing night, as Akiem took to the skies, Lysander could only watch on, destined never to be among them, or among anyone. Loneliness clawed at him. And in that loneliness his mind began to tear itself apart.

As the tower shook with dragon roars, Lysander descended to the kitchens, discovering Carline seated at the window, gazing through filthy glass.

"I wondered when you might come to me, kit." She

brushed away the creases in her apron. "I hear you dealt with the bronze."

Her warm tone belied the edge of ice beneath. She had never approved of Elisandra's methods, and now those methods were Lysander's. Her disappointment was so thick, he could almost taste it.

"Mirann lives," he said. "They have her in the lower nest, likely doing to her what the bronze chief did to me." He wandered about the room, not really seeing much of anything, his mind a black and hungry place. "I used to wonder sometimes if Elisandra was once good like Amalia was good. Now I know Mother always had the darkness in her, rotting her from the inside out. When the humans fired their monstrous weapon on our ancestors and the killing dust rained from the skies, that poison twisted the great metals into us... Made us all... *wrong*." *I have that broken root in me too, a thing all twisted and foul, that is not meant to exist.* "I fought so long to keep it at bay... I'm not fighting anymore."

The old dragon sighed. "This wasn't how it was supposed to be."

She'd said that before. Many times. The same nonsense she'd been spouting for years. "How are things supposed to be exactly?"

He knew she wouldn't answer. She never had.

He approached, seeing her thick eyebrows draw together, her eyes revealing a new fear. Of him. "What's done is done." He sounded cruel, like his mother, and couldn't find it in him to care. "Carline." She dragged her gaze up to Lysander's face. "I need to fly again."

She shook her head. "Lysander—"

"Don't tell me it can't happen."

"I tried—"

"You didn't try hard enough!" He had a hand around her neck in the next second, squeezing her throat closed. She gaped, her fear so thick now he could roll in it. "It's killing me inside. You don't know what it's like."

Her eyes misted. *"I suppose.... I don't."*

Something inside his mind jolted lose and Lysander saw the image of himself prepared to choke an old dragon, a healer, one of the few people in his life who had helped him. The shock of his own actions shoved him free. He looked at his hands, killer's hands. He'd beaten Mirann into a bloody mess. He'd have done worse if he hadn't handed her over to the lowers. He'd punished lowers, made them beg. *Own, take, bite, fuck.* Who was he? He stumbled backward against a kitchen countertop. "I'm losing my fucking mind." There were two parts to him. The old Lysander and the new. The drunken prince was gone now. This new side to him ruled with iron teeth and claws.

Carline rubbed at her neck and rose from her chair. "Losing it?" she groused. "No. You're allowing others to take it from you."

"Allowing?" He should never have come here. "I've fought them all. I'm sick of it. Sick of fighting something I can't win. So I am them now. And because I can't fly I have to be worse than them. I took..." he swallowed around the crack in his voice, "I took a whip to a lower yesterday. I don't remember when he died, exactly, just that when it was done, I felt nothing..." He still felt nothing and that seemed wrong. Amalia would have been disgusted by him. "I need to fly again. I can't be this thing and not fly, it's turning me into Mother."

"Being able to fly again won't change your nature. Only you can do that."

But he couldn't. Not anymore. With a snarl, he headed for the door. "Nothing can change my nature, old woman. It was a mistake to come to you."

"What if there were a way for you to fly again, prince?"

He stopped in the doorway, hard fingers gripping the frame. "Suddenly you recall one?" When she didn't immediately answer, he turned. She merely blinked back at him, the picture of patience. "What way?"

"The price is high. Perhaps too high. It may cost you the one thing in this world you love."

His heart thudded harder. He'd pay it. He'd pay anything to soar again, to lead the flights, to watch the world scroll beneath his wings before he burned it all. Besides, he didn't love anything, so the price was nothing.

"Tell me."

Old knowledge flashed in Carline's eyes. "Your mother's amethyst eye."

$\sim$

BLINDING Elisandra in one eye had been one of his better memories. She'd punished him for weeks after, but it had been worth it. When he'd recovered, she had worn an amethyst stone in place of her flesh and blood eye. Too wrapped up in his own hurt, he hadn't thought much about it.

According to Carline, that amethyst wasn't just a pretty jewel, but it held the key to fixing his wing. And she knew where it was. Far beyond her reach, beyond the reach of anyone in the tower. But Lysander knew how to get it. And she'd been right, the price was high.

Dawn flooded light into the tower through the open window as he returned, thoughts a muddle of possibilities.

A hawk screeched at him from the foot of the bed. He hadn't seen it, so deep were his thoughts, but he could hardly miss the thing now, all red feathers and puffed out chest. It flapped a little as he stared back at it, taunting him with its wingspan. He stepped closer and the bird shifted, turning its head to eye him with one yellow-ringed eye.

"Easy there..."

Closer, and the hawk spread its wings, making itself bigger, and there, strapped to its leg, was a tiny roll of paper. A note.

Lysander slowly eased off his jacket, held it out and inched forward. Before the bird could take flight, he threw the jacket over it. The creature turned into a squawking, flapping ball of feathers. Lysander grabbed at its taloned foot and plucked the note free, then let it up. The hawk flapped about the room before taking up residence on the back of a chair, glaring at Lysander as though trying to figure out the best way to eat him.

"You've got balls coming here, bird." He broke the seal on the note. Elegant, flowing handwriting led his eye across the paper.

> *Meet me?*
> *Dusk at the fallen oak.*
> *- Eroan*

He read it again, to be sure, then flipped the paper over, looking for the trick, the lie. The sweet smell of cut wood and pine needles drifting from the paper, soothing his thoughts, reminding him of the days he'd trekked through the woods, behind or beside Eroan, watching him carve through the undergrowth, perfectly at ease in the wilds. He knew the oak Eroan referred to, the same one they'd stopped at on the way back from the coast. The one where the wolves had ambushed Eroan.

He slid down the edge of the bed and slumped to the floor. The trek to Eroan's village felt like so long ago. The last time he'd seen Eroan, Curan had knocked him out, and the estuary had happened.

Eroan was alive.

He was all right.

He lifted the paper to his nose and breathed in.

What if it was a trap? The thought dampened his mood. The elves would likely want to lure Lysander out. They may even have heard of his more recent reputation as Akiem's vicious flight commander.

"Is this a trap, bird?" He, or she—he had no idea how to tell male or female hawks apart—ruffled her feathers, apparently comfortable where she was.

The paper had Eroan's scent all over it. If it were a trap, then he was explicit in it, willingly or unwillingly. There was only one way to know.

He shoved to his feet and stopped at the window. Clouds had rolled in, but he could just make out the tree line far beyond the barrenlands. Eroan was out there, somewhere.

On horseback, he could make it to the fallen oak before nightfall.

A knock at the door announced a lower's arrival. "The dawn patrol has returned. A flight of bronze are making their way up the coast. They'll be here by sundown."

Dusk at the fallen oak. Right when the bronze would arrive. Dokul would be among them. Acid coated his tongue, chasing away the taste of bronze. He cursed. Could nothing go his way? He couldn't leave. He had to be in the tower with his flights on a long leash, had to be standing alongside amethyst when Dokul arrived, or all of this was for nothing. Revenge was in his grasp.

He screwed the note up in a trembling fist, held it over the window ledge, and let it fall.

"Sire, there's a hawk... right there."

"I'd noticed." Lysander flashed the lower a forced smile. "Breakfast."

CHAPTER 41

roan

DUSK FELL EARLIER in the forest where shadows were thick and long. A few early stars began their twinkling above swaying branches and rippling leaves. Eroan lowered his gaze to the small campfire, feeling like a fool. There was a chance the hawk had been killed, or intercepted, in which case, the fallen oak note would mean nothing to anyone else. Or Lysander may not even still be in the tower, or he'd received the note and chosen not to come. There could be a thousand reasons for why Eroan found himself alone, but that last one cut the most.

And after his people had turned on them both the smart thing for Lysander to do would be *not* to come to this meeting.

It was for the best. An elf and a dragon was an impossible thing.

He stood and kicked the fire over, stamping out the

remains to keep the wood from reigniting. The humans would be at Cheen soon. If he hurried now—

"Now how will we keep warm?"

Eroan had the sword out and his glare trained on the cloaked figure before recognizing the deep, gravelly voice as Lysander's. "You're late," he chided.

Lysander skidded down the furrow, into the depression beneath the oak's upturned roots, and lowered his hood. "It's a long ride."

Then he must have left his horse outside the camp somewhere. Eroan wondered about wolves until he saw Lysander crouch, take the firestarter from his pocket and begin to rebuild the fire. A few sparks from the firestarter and the hot wood was burning again.

Lysander looked up, seeing the query in Eroan's eyes. "I'm not shifting just to relight your puny fire, elf."

"You kept it?" Eroan asked, replacing the sword in its backsheath and shrugging it off to set it down beside the fallen oak's reaching roots. He'd recalled Lysander holding something in his hand at the creek in France, turning it over and over. He'd assumed it was a pebble. Lysander had kept the firestarter this whole time.

"It's not always convenient to turn into a thirty-thousand-pound dragon to roast some rabbit." Dry humor still underlined Lysander's voice in a tone he used to cover all the hurt.

The firestarter was more than convenience. The tool had been with them since Eroan had stolen it from the bronze. For Lysander, a dragon apt at fire, to keep it all this time... it meant something to him.

Eroan circled around the campfire, rolling up his sleeves to absorb the warmth and light. He kept Lysander in the corner of his vision. There was something different about him, a difference that had Eroan's instincts on edge. The dragon carried a new stillness, some other hardness that had stolen the light from his eyes. Eroan's heart raced. He had vowed to protect him and failed.

"If you keep looking at me like that, elf, I may act on the promise in your eyes."

Eroan's chest briefly constricted at the predatory drawl to Lysander's words. He'd been about to sit across the fire from him but now reconsidered that thought. Staying on his feet provided a quicker chance to react, if he should need to.

"The elf at the estuary... did he make it?" Lysander used a stick to poke at the fire.

"No." Eroan fought off the memory of Curan bleeding in the mud. Many elves had died that day. Many dragons too, but not enough. And not this dragon, thankfully.

"I'm sorry... I tried to stop him..." Lysander pinched the bridge of his nose, wincing at some unseen pain. "I tried to warn him. Elves are too stubborn for their own good."

"He lived long enough to speak of how wrong he was... about you."

"He did, huh?" He continued to nurse the fire, lost in thought. "That lesson always seems to be learned too late."

In firelight, Lysander's face took on a new menace. Eroan searched for the glitter of humor he'd found so fascinating, or the teasing lift of his mouth, but there was none. He wanted to go to him, sit with him, listen to whatever he wanted to say and anything he didn't, but the gnawing doubt held him standing firm on the opposite side of the fire. Even when Eroan had been in chains, there hadn't been this gulf between them.

"Why did you ask me here?" Lysander asked.

Why had he? He had a dozen reasons he could use; for information, for a way into the tower, to know if Lysander would still help him. But more than all of those, he'd needed to know Lysander was alive and well. Lysander was alive, but clearly all was not well.

"I asked you once and I'm asking again..." he said, when Eroan had waited too long, "what is this thing between us?"

The hardness with which he asked exposed Eroan's own fears. He brushed Lysander's question away with one of his own. "Do you know of any disused or unguarded tunnels?"

Lysander's mouth tilted sideways. He tossed the stick onto the fire and watched the flames twist it until it snapped. Then those dark, flame-licked eyes lifted to Eroan. "Is that all you want from me?"

No, it wasn't all. It wasn't even the real reason Eroan was here. "Lysander, this... us," he sucked in a breath, "there is no place for what I want. There can't be."

"And what do you want?" He unclasped his cloak, shrugged it off his shoulders, dropped it to the ground and stood, stepping around the fire, bringing his shroud of darkness with him, like he was a hunter and Eroan his prey. Only Eroan had never been prey and had no intention of starting now.

Eroan stepped in, jolting Lysander to a stop, and in that moment of confusion, Eroan sank his fingers into Lysander's hair, cupped his head and pulled him into a kiss that said everything words alone could not.

CHAPTER 42

$\mathscr{L}$ysander

INSTINCTS DEMANDED HE PUSH AWAY, but then Eroan pulled, and the elf's mouth was on his, and all Lysander could think was how warm and soft those lips were. He wanted more. So much more. His surprise, his confusion, turned into a heated need to take and own. He speared both hands into Eroan's hair, captured him completely and plundered Eroan's mouth, driving his tongue in, taking all he wanted. Lust lit him up. When Eroan arched into him, giving just as much as he received, Lysander sank his free hand down the elf's solid back and clutched him close. He was made of hard, smooth muscle, of masculine strength in a way that demanded to be stroked and kneaded and *tasted*. Lysander's fingers curled in, owning.

Eroan's warm, light hands touched the nape of Lysander's neck, holding him firmly cradled, while tangling the fingers of his other hand in his locks, tickling his face and neck.

It was everything Lysander had ached for since Elisandra had first denied him the chance to love, and this time, Eroan gave it freely.

Eroan broke away, making a deep, guttural sound low in his throat as he tilted his head back, inviting Lysander to mouth his neck. Lysander tasted Eroan's hard jawline and trailed his tongue lower to a spot that strummed Eroan, sending a jolt through him. Eroan tilted his hips, grinding his hardness against Lysander's hip. Fuck, Eroan was undoing him from the inside out.

Lysander dropped both hands and captured the elf's hips, feeling him twitch and shift, his body a song of demands and needs that Lysander would gladly answer.

"You come alive in my hands..." Lysander breathed, setting free the words he'd so long wanted to speak. Lysander wanted nothing more than to maneuver his hand to where he knew Eroan would groan for him, but not yet. He'd been a creature who takes, and he'd hated every second of it. He wanted to give, he wanted this moment to last forever knowing it never could. "It's never been like this before..." He kissed his neck, tasting the salt and sweetness of elf. "You slay me."

Eroan pulled Lysander's head back and gently nipped at Lysander's neck. Sharp, tiny teeth pinched, sending a painful rush of heated lust right to where his cock ached. To make it worse, or better, Eroan shoved, driving him back against the fallen oak's towering roots. Something sharp and awkward nudged him in the lower back. "Ah, fuck..."

Eroan laughed that wickedly seductive chuckle of his.

Lysander hooked his leg around Eroan's, and pulled, dropping the elf—still laughing—in the dirt. "You think this is amusing?" He straddled his thighs, planted his hand right over Eroan's bulging crotch, and watched lust flash a warning in the elf's eyes. Eroan's breath shortened. His smile turned serious and it was all Lysander could do not to act on the rabid desires to *take* this impossible creature. He brushed his rough cheek against Eroan's smooth jaw, filling his head with the smell of elf, prompting an automatic rumble low in his throat.

Eroan jerked beneath him. The laughter was back in his beautiful eyes. "This really isn't funny."

"Dragons *purr*."

Lysander brushed his forehead against Eroan's, losing himself in the fine lines and long lashes of Eroan's eyes. "Only with you." Eroan's brow pinched and Lysander feared he'd said too much, but then the elf hooked his arms around his neck and pulled him down, arching beneath him, to rise and meet Lysander's chest with his own. Eroan's hand dropped down Lysander's back, seeking his ass, and squeezed, pulling down at the same time so Lysander's cock crushed against Eroan's hip.

A gasp betrayed Lysander's fraying control and Eroan's warm, rough hands found their way beneath his jacket. Skin on skin, on his lower back, set off an array of delicious tingling that made him wish they could go somewhere safe, somewhere warm, and lose himself in the naked feel of Eroan moving beneath his hands, stretch out beneath his body. "Do elves purr?"

"Want to find out?"

He wanted too many things and all of them now. He tore at Eroan's jacket, flicking open the fasteners, and Eroan's wet mouth was on his neck again, at the point that rattled his nerves, sending them into freefall in a way that felt so fucking right.

"You like that?" Eroan whispered, meeting Lysander's gaze. With low lashes and bright eyes, Lysander forgot the question as he admired the marvel of Eroan, the line of his nose and sumptuous, take-me mouth. His mass of near-white hair pillowed behind his head, strewn with twigs and leaves. How had he resisted him this long? The truth was, he hadn't. He'd wanted him since he'd first lain eyes on the dragon-killer who'd come to kill the queen.

"You free me, Eroan Ilanea." He bit at Eroan's lower lip, teasing the softness between his teeth as he broke open the jacket and eased his hand up beneath Eroan's shirt, dancing his fingers over the hard, lean ridges of muscle, feeling smooth scar tissue beneath his fingertips. Eroan sucked in, and Lysander dropped his hand to the plane of Eroan's stomach until he brushed that light trail of silken hair farther down, to the heat below Eroan's belt.

He flicked his eyes up and eased himself lower, brushing the bunched shirt at Eroan's chest, feeling and hearing Eroan's panting beneath him.

A little voice at the back of his mind told him he had somewhere else to be, a war to fight, questions to ask, that he had to be *someone* else, but he cared more for the male spread beneath him than any war or mission.

Unlacing Eroan's fly, he worked the male's cock from the undergarments and closed his fingers around the impressive swollen shaft, his own restrained arousal throbbing with want, and shifted down enough to hold Eroan's cock firmly at the base and flick his tongue over the flushed head. Eroan's sharp little teeth came down on his own lower lip, and his eyes fell closed, surrendering to Lysander's mouth. Obliging, Lysander took him in deep, rubbing the smooth head against the roof of his mouth, and this time there was no Mother leaning over him, no ropes holding Eroan down, and no audience to watch. Eroan's sweetness laced his throat. He took more, before withdrawing and sliding his fingers in a building rhythm.

"You taste so fucking good, elf."

Eroan's abs stuttered, pulling in, and Lysander imagined his pleasure tightening low in his back, through the base of his balls and shaft. He felt his own tight pressure riding higher. By diamonds, he'd dreamed this so often he could hardly believe it was happening.

Eroan's hips twitched and a small groan rumbled through him. "Alumn," he groaned, eyes fluttering open. That gaze fixed on Lysander with unwavering intent. Lysander's withered and broken heart swelled. He could allow himself this one blissful moment knowing it would likely be his last.

CHAPTER 43

 roan

EROAN FELL into the feel and taste of dragon. The male's hand on the most personal part of him, his mouth on his exposed hip, roaming and teasing as he pulled Eroan's trousers lower. He was falling and losing his mind at the same time, giving himself up to the beast. He'd never surrendered, not to anyone. Until now. Falling had never felt so good.

When his gaze locked with Lysander's, the raw, heated look in the male's eyes ignited his own savage desires and when Lysander next went down on him, Eroan threw his legs up, locking Lysander's shoulders between his thighs and rolled, flipping the dragon onto his back with Eroan above him, pinned at the chest. Eroan attacked, throwing himself into a kiss that distracted Lysander enough for Eroan to pull open his shirt where he'd wanted to with his hands since admiring Lysander's unconscious body all those weeks ago. The dragon purred again, and something told Eroan his sound of contentment was a rare one.

Eroan planted both hands on Lysander's bare chest and pushed up. The racing *thud-thud* of Lysander's heart warmed his palm. Lysander's sultry look promised all the wicked desires Eroan's mind could think of. He leaned over him, pinning him beneath him. Eroan's hair, now free of its band, fell over one shoulder and trailed finger-like over Lysander's pectoral muscle, making it twitch. Eroan kept his eyes up and ran the wet tip of his tongue along the hard ridge of that muscle, then roamed it lower to flick the nipple. Lysander's hand shot into his hair. His hips jerked and Eroan gripped the offered cock, capturing Lysander's gasp in his mouth.

He was everything an elf was not. Pure, restrained strength. Power, dammed behind a wall of muscle and control. Eroan strummed the hot, writhing body, plucking apart all Lysander's restraints, revealing the truth behind.

For a moment, Eroan simply stared at the terrible, wonderful male. A creature so foreign and dangerous that Eroan could not hope to fully capture all of him. But he could try. "Will you come for me, dragon?"

The purr became a growl, fraught with want. Eroan nipped at Lysander's ear, freeing a cascade of shivers through Lysander, pinned and writhing beneath him. To have this devastating creature at his mercy teased all the dark thoughts and wants from the corners of his mind. Eroan ached to mindlessly taste and explore this compli-cated treasure, to whittle away the hours beneath the stars until there was no inch of him left unexplored. If it was a madness, then let him be insane, because nothing had ever felt so right as this.

Eroan listened to Lysander's shortening breaths, caressed Lysander's hard arousal until the breaths became ragged, and switched to a faster pace, bringing Lysander to the very edge, where his entire body trembled with need. Moonlight spilled through the trees, glistening on Lysander's shuddering chest and catching in his dark eyes. Eroan drank in the sinful sight and brought the dragon to the final moment. His back arched, mouth opening. Eroan dropped his head and tongued a line down Lysander's cock.

Lysander bucked. "Fuck." He growled out a wrangled cry, his seed spurting into the hollow of his stomach in three shuddering spasms. Eroan swept his tongue through the thick, salty wetness, and gently milked the last few sensitive strokes from Lysander's cock, making the dragon jerk and hiss.

"Fucking diamonds, elf." Voice gruff and breathless, Lysander roughly grabbed at Eroan's shoulder and pulled. Eroan met the fiery kiss with an insatiable one of his own, tasting Lysander's seed on his tongue. Lysander's warm, tingling fingers found Eroan's neglected erection. Eroan jerked into Lysander's hand, clasping the dragon against him, leaving only enough room for Lysander's hand to caress and stroke as the kiss turned hard and demanding.

Somewhere in all the mindless lust, he lost all sense of where he ended and Lysander began, and became a thing of raw need, hips thrusting, fucking Lysander's tight grip until he lost himself to the racing pleasure and came so hard, he sank his teeth into the male's shoulder to keep from crying out.

Blissful shudders spilled through him.

Lysander mouthed at his neck and jaw. "I am nowhere near done with you," the dragon growled.

Eroan smiled into Lysander's shoulder. He had a hundred places his people needed him to be, a thousand responsibilities on his back, but none called to him like this precious moment and the moments to come.

THE RATTLE of a woodpecker deep in the forest brought Eroan around from the warm, contented sleep he'd been cradled in. A heavy leg lay hooked over his, the thigh warm but hard and positioned as though to claim Eroan from behind. A smile eased onto Eroan's lips. Lysander had thrown his cloak over them both sometime in the night, keeping out the morning chill, and the mossy earth beneath them made a fine bed. Eroan's trousers hung around an ankle, trapped by one remaining boot, and his shirt had bunched low down his arms and back. He was a mess of twisted fabric, leaves, twigs, and the rich smell of sex and dragon, and he couldn't think of anywhere else he'd rather be. Despite there being many places he *should* be. With no word from him, the Order would start looking. If he left now and traveled fast he'd be back by nightfall. It would be the sensible and responsible thing to do.

He didn't move.

The raw way Lysander had looked at him last night? He couldn't leave him while he slept, not even for the Order or the barrage of questions he'd get on his return. Lysander had probably seen the same desperation in Eroan. He must have certainly felt it in their touches.

What is this thing between us?

It was a dangerous question, one Lysander kept asking and one Eroan was too afraid to answer.

The woodpecker rattled again. Lysander stirred against

Eroan's back. With his shirt wrenched down, Lysander's rough chin grazed Eroan's shoulder, making him shiver. Old scars tingled. Lysander's fingers touched the raised welts and Eroan hissed in a shuddering breath. "*Alumn...*" It hadn't hurt, his skin had been too damaged to feel much of anything, but he wasn't used to having anyone linger on those marks.

"I didn't want to do this," Lysander whispered. "Had it been any other, they'd have killed you."

Eroan pulled his mind from the dark memories. "I know."

A soft kiss settled on Eroan's shoulder. Lysander trailed his fingers lower, over Eroan's hip, sparking off tight little flutters low in Eroan's belly. "Tell me of your goddess, Alumn," Lysander whispered.

"Alumn?" Eroan sighed and let his attention pool exactly where Lysander's curiously gentle fingers roamed inward. But, instead of venturing around his hip, to where Eroan's arousal was hardening, he stroked his fingertips back up, along Eroan's waist. "She is the light that feeds us, the hand that guides us. She is in the hearts of us all."

"Even dragons?" he asked.

Before Lysander, he would have said no. "Perhaps."

Lysander's touch danced over Eroan's shoulder and down his arm again, reigniting delightful sparks of lust. Eroan shivered, his skin suddenly sensitive. Lysander's dry chuckle rumbled. Those wandering fingertips roamed back up again to the nape of his neck, where they gathered Eroan's hair back, making room for the soft warmth of Lysander's mouth. His wet tongue probed just below Eroan's ear, at his jaw.

Eroan leaned back and fluttered his eyes closed. The

open kiss became hungry and the firm press of Lysander's arousal nudged at Eroan's hip.

Eroan had learned how Lysander knew exactly how to disarm with his mouth and tongue, and how he used the rest of his shockingly seductive body to empty Eroan of every thought, leaving just the feel of a dragon worshipping every inch of him.

"I'll never forget how you saved me from the bronze nest..." Lysander whispered, breaths hot on Eroan's neck. "And the hours after. In the dark. In the ground."

Neither would Eroan. He'd been afraid Lysander would shift and crush him, afraid a bronze would find them, afraid of so much, and the only thing he could do to stop it all was hold Lysander and pray Alumn would spare them.

Had Lysander ever been loved? He couldn't imagine such a thing as love existed among dragons. Would the prince recognize love should he be given it?

"You never gave up on me," Lysander whispered, clutching Eroan's hip and pulling, giving him an anchor to grind his erection against Eroan's back.

"I never will." Nothing had felt truer.

Lysander stilled. His stroking touches vanished. The cloak shifted and Lysander's warmth disappeared.

Eroan looked behind him at the sight of the dragon in dawnlight. His skin was much darker than most elves, and where the light lapped at his abdominal muscles, Eroan readily remembered mouthing those molded ripples, making Lysander's breath hitch.

His shirt hung loose as he hitched up his trousers, over his hips. Then he went hunting the camp for his belt. Eroan figured he could watch him all day. Dappled sunlight touched small elf-bites on his toned arms and firm shoulders. Lysander noticed one of those bites on his forearm, his mouth teasing into a smile. "Dragon bites never felt as good as yours."

He considered pulling Lysander back down and deliberately losing himself in him again, just for a few more hours. The world and its war could wait. But he'd already been gone too long and the last thing they needed was a pride of elves stumbling upon them together.

Eroan tossed the cloak off and shrugged his shirt back over his shoulders, leaving the laces hanging lose. Where Lysander's mouth had scorched him, the remaining tingling sensations made his skin fizzle. Lysander had a true healer's touch. Eroan had known it, but after last night, he'd felt its evidence. Magic moved beneath the male's hands. There was magic in him now, even as human. That lemony twang, the one that added a kick whenever he'd nipped at Lysander's back and shoulders. *Alumn*, Lysander was like a drug, like something forbidden. Eroan's body tingled, coming alive just thinking about tasting him again. He needed that dragon with him for longer, much longer. A night was not enough. But such things were impossible.

He dressed, distracting himself with raking his fingers through his hair, freeing leaves and twigs, then rummaged through the pockets of his coat for the wooden carving. They would part ways soon. This might be his only chance to give it to him. Eroan clutched the small wooden dragon in his hand, lingering in uncertainty, until Lysander approached, throwing his dark cloak around his shoulders, readying to leave.

There wouldn't be better time.

He pulled a leather lace from his shirt, tied it around the dragon carving, making a necklace, and offered it to Lysander.

"What is it?" Lysander asked.

"A gift."

"Gift?" His face darkened, which hadn't been the reaction Eroan had expected. "What for?"

He took Lysander's hand and dropped the necklace into it, then folded his rough fingers around the carving.

"I have this," he touched Seraph's earring in his ear, "from a friend, to remind me I'm not alone. Now you have that." Eroan released his hand and concentrated on fastening his coat with Lysander beside him, looking down at the necklace in his hand like it might come alive and bite him. "It's an elven custom to give parting gifts—"

An odd look of horror came over the dragon's face.

"It's freely given," Eroan explained. Had this been a mistake? He hadn't meant to distress him. Had nobody given him a gift before? It hadn't even crossed his mind that something so small would cause Lysander pain.

He swallowed and bundled his hair back in a band, giving his hands something to do.

"You carved this?" Lysander asked, face pained.

Eroan nodded. His chest tightened. He regretted giving it. "If you don't want it—"

"I can't take this." Lysander held it out at arm's length, mouth twisted as though disgusted.

"Keep it," Eroan said. "It's no good for anyone else."

"You don't understand..." Lysander backed off, stumbling in his haste. "Why are *you* like this?"

Like what? Where was this coming from? Why was a gift so wrong a thing to give? Something had triggered Lysander. The gift, or something else? "I... didn't mean for it to hurt you. A gift is a good thing."

Lysander dropped the necklace into a pocket, whirled on his heel, snatched Eroan's sword from its place by the oak's roots, and pulled it free of its scabbard, all in one, swift moment. A panicked, wild look crossed his face.

"Wait..." Eroan lifted his hands. What was happening here? "What is this?" Lysander bore down on him and Eroan backed up, boots snagging in tree root.

"This..." Lysander hissed. "This is necessary."

Eroan planted his boots. This could only be a misunderstanding, something that could be remedied. "I meant no offense. It's just a small gift. It means nothing—"

"Good, because all of this..." Lysander gestured wildly at the camp. "All of this means nothing." His teeth flashed as he spoke, the words bubbling with fury.

The concern Eroan had felt the previous evening returned. The same darkness he'd sensed then lurked behind Lysander's eyes now.

"Where's the amethyst stone, Eroan?" he snarled.

Eroan's thoughts stuttered, tripping over his heart. This male bearing down on him now was not the same male he had spent the entire night with. The sudden switch in behavior scattered Eroan's instincts, numbing him inside. "I don't understand."

"You don't? Let me spell it out for you, *elf*. The night I killed the queen, you took something from her chamber, something that belongs to amethyst—belongs to me. I need it back." Lysander pushed forward, driving Eroan against a tree.

The dragonblade tip dug in, just above the pulse point in his neck. He could taste the beat of his own heart. "I took the swords." The sword tip pricked, burning.

"My brother doesn't have it. He searched that tower high and low. The only other soul who could have taken it is you."

Then Lysander coming here, and last night, it was lies?

Eroan lowered his hands, narrowing his eyes. A cool, sharp chill filtered through his veins, encasing his heart in ice. "That's why you came?"

Lysander laughed. "What, did you think I came to kindle some doomed romance with a fucking elf?" The cruelty in Lysander's laugh almost matched that in his eyes. "You trust too easily, Eroan Ilanea. Tell me where you have the stone and I won't return to your village and burn it down to its foundations. I spent long enough there to find it again... All I have to do is follow the stench of elf."

That same elven tale of the scorpion and fox crossed Eroan's mind. One having trusted the other, and both dying because of it. Lysander was the scorpion, after all. "Don't threaten my people." Eroan's lips quivered around a snarl. "Whatever this is, I know you. *This* is not you."

Lysander was on him suddenly, the blade crushed between them, Lysander's weight a solid wall of muscle. Only this time the look in his eyes was one of cold-blooded murder. He grabbed Eroan's jacket in a fist. "You have no fucking idea what I've done or what I'll do. You took the amethyst eye. I need it back."

They'd broken him, Eroan realized. The worst had happened and now he was the monster Lysander had tried so hard to fight. He'd been so strong, but that was before Eroan's people had handed him back to his brother, before Eroan had failed him. Something terrible had happened after the estuary, something he could not fight. "Lysander, what did they do to you?"

He pulled and slammed Eroan back. Pain cracked up Eroan's skull. He cried out and hissed through his teeth. "I lost the amethyst when Akiem burned my village. It's gone."

The backhanded blow burst a flash of stinging heat

across Eroan's face. Shock more than pain momentarily stunned him. Then Lysander's grip closed around his throat. "Don't lie to me, bitch."

He pulled his lips back, baring his teeth while slamming internal barriers down to guard his heart. "You let them win after everything you've fought for?"

"I didn't *let* them do anything." Fire spilled into Lysander's eyes. "Tell me where it is or your precious new home burns."

There was nothing of the Lysander he knew in him now, and maybe there hadn't been since last night. Bitter failure burned Eroan's throat. Lysander's failure to hold back the dark, and his own for promising to keep him safe and failing. He swallowed. "I'll bring it to you."

Between one blink and the next, between assuming Eroan had taken the stone and knowing it for certain, the hurt showed in Lysander's eyes.

Eroan had betrayed him.

"I found it," Eroan admitted. "When she fell, it fell too." He recalled the glint of purple stone under the queen's bed, remembered the wrong feel of it in his hand and how it had chilled the blood in his veins. "I took it, and after your brother burned my home, I went back and retrieved it from the ashes." Lysander's grip loosened. He let go and backed away. Eroan dabbed at the sword's bite on his neck. "I'll bring it to you."

"No," Lysander said. "We go now and you take me right to it. No tricks."

"If you walk into Cheen, the Order will kill you."

"And I'm supposed to believe an elf like you doesn't have his secret ways in and out?"

Eroan watched Lysander become cold, become something else—someone else. Someone with no choice but to become what he despised. But Lysander was in there. Last night had been proof of that. "It doesn't have to be this way."

"In your world, perhaps not. But it my world, there is no other way."

CHAPTER 44

$\mathcal{L}$ysander

HATE. Disgust. Betrayal. These things knotted in Lysander's gut, twisting and tightening, trying to choke him. He didn't deserve Eroan's gift, not before, and definitely not now. He needed that gem. It would change everything. He needed it so he could stop the bronze, stop all of them, and what he felt for Eroan... That all-consuming need to be with him, to taste him, feel him, to have his arms around him... When Carline had warned him that he'd need to find Eroan again, he hadn't expected this to feel so wrong. Hadn't expected to feel at all. He'd stopped feeling much of anything. But now none of his physical wounds had hurt this bad—the loss of Eroan was the terrible price to fly again, to be free, to destroy the bronze, but it was a price he had to pay. With both wings, and with a new reputation, he'd finally do more than just survive. He'd thrive.

"Keep walking, elf." He jabbed Eroan in the back, pushing him onward.

The march through the trees went on and on. He hadn't wanted this, but it was the only way. This thing between them, this push and pull, it would get Eroan killed, either by dragons or by Eroan's own people. He was too bright a thing to die for Lysander. This way, Eroan survived. He'd hate him, but he'd live, and go on with his life, destined to be the infamous dragon-killer. The hurt Lysander saw in Eroan's eyes when he'd turned on him, that hurt was a gift too, it would fuel Eroan. Make him a better killer, a better leader.

By now the bronze would be at the tower. War may have already begun. Lysander's absence would be noted. He needed his mother's gem. That was the only thing that mattered now.

"Hurry." Another jab in the back.

"I should kill you for this," Eroan snarled.

Lysander laughed to cover the hollow feeling those words opened. "You already tried once." The words tasted like ash. Everything tasted like ash on his tongue. The memories of last night had burned up in the self-hate now fueling every step. He was dragon. This was what was expected of him, and if he played it to the end, he'd make it count and bring the entire dragonlands down around him. And all it cost him was the only person who ever understood him. *The price is high.*

They trekked along the same path Lysander had willingly taken with Eroan back to his village before. He watched the elf's back, watched his steady gait through the brush. Lysander was under no illusion, he'd made a powerful enemy in Eroan. But if that was his legacy, so be it. Eroan had been right, this thing between them could not happen.

"You don't need to do this," Eroan said.

"You have no idea what I need."

"I know what you're doing, pushing me away. You believe you're not worthy. I'll not play your game."

"My life is no game."

"Had you just asked—"

"You'd have handed the gem over?" Not a chance, Eroan was too wily for that. "The eye belongs to amethysts. You stole it. I told you before, we do not suffer thieves."

The elf's ears ticked at the familiar words. He stopped on the path and turned his head a little just enough to catch Lysander with a scathing look, then he crouched low, waving Lysander down to a crouch and out of sight. "Patrol."

Lysander knelt and listened, hearing nothing but the breeze. Eroan knew the gem was worth more than it appeared, else he wouldn't have bothered with it. He'd seen the queen wearing it, maybe even wondered how she was able to rule and if the gem had anything to do with the strength of her reign. The elf was too sharp to let something of power slip through his fingers. He'd figured it out before Lysander had.

Lysander admired that sharp mind of his. Admired more than that, like the way he was poised now, on the cusp of fighting back, about to pick his moment to strike.

Lysander slid the sword's edge up the back of Eroan's coat, denting the leather. "Easy now, and everyone gets to live."

"Was any of last night real?" Eroan whispered, keeping his face turned toward the trees.

All of it. Every touch, every kiss, every delicious taste. Even now, Lysander's body sang with all the ways he wanted Eroan. The dozens of tiny elven bites hummed, each one a reminder of where Eroan's mouth had marked him, *owned* him. His cock semi-hardened from the memory. But last night had been about more than sex. In Eroan's arms, he truly felt safe. Eroan alone had the power to chase the wrongs and the hurts away. And Lysander had ruined it all. But he'd save the elf again. One last time. Save him from Lysander.

He leaned in, his mouth close to Eroan's neck, like it had been last night, when he'd kissed him there, made him groan Lysander's name. "You were the sweetest one-night fuck I've ever had." Eroan's cheek fluttered. Lysander's heart cracked. "We're keeping elves alive today, remember. Get in, get me the gem, and none of your kin gets hurt."

Eroan led him around the outskirts of the village, staying far away from the palisades to avoid the eagle-eyed elves watching the walls, and in through a dense line of undergrowth to a hut that had that same cut pine smell Lysander associated with Eroan.

Lysander kept Eroan in sight and kicked the hut door closed behind him. The place was small, a chair, fireplace, table, a bed at the back, an out-of-place trail of metal pipes running across the ceiling beams.

A flicker in his vision. He lunged to the side to the sound of a dagger thrumming in wood and then Eroan slammed against him, plowing him into the wall. *"I never miss!"* The right hook split the inside of Lysander's cheek, spilling blood onto his tongue. He backed up, hit a wall, threw his arm up to block another vicious-looking dagger from slashing across his throat and retaliated with a low left punch, striking Eroan in his gut. The elf grunted, slashed. Lysander caught his wrist and twisted his arm around, almost popping it from the shoulder socket. Eroan barked a cry. Lysander kicked him forward, against the table, still clutching the dragonblade sword in his right hand—deliberately unused, he did not want to hurt him.

He pinned a hand between Eroan's shoulders, shoving him down onto the tabletop, Eroan's ass angled against his groin. "Don't piss me off." Eroan bucked. Lysander dropped the sword with a clatter and caught Eroan's other failing arm at the wrist, trapping both at the wrists at Eroan's lower back.

He had the elf pinned and still he fought. Wild darts of lust plucked on Lysander's beastly instincts, pooling molten heat through his cock. Eroan's struggles only served to wind him tighter.

"I need you to stop fighting me," he hissed, words from a part of his past, a part that tried to dig in and demand he stop this now. "Or you won't like where this goes." But if this did happen, there would be no going back. *Save him from me and my world.*

Eroan calmed, face turned to one side so he could pin those hate-filled eyes on Lysander. Only, the glare wasn't as vicious as Lysander expected. Despite Eroan showing his teeth, his muscles straining against Lysander's hold, the sharp challenge in his eyes steered Lysander's thoughts far off course. Eroan liked to fight, in life, and in love. And now Lysander had him trapped beneath him, the rules of the game had changed.

He tightened his fingers around Eroan's wrists, warm skin against warm skin, and purred, "Or maybe you will like where this goes?"

roan

THE KILLING RUSH sped through his veins, setting his blood alight. The things Lysander had said cut him to the bone, but even now, the feel of Lysander's weight against the backs of his thighs re-stitched the part of his brain that told him this was wrong and made it feel right. Teeth gritted, hands wrenched behind him, shame tried to dampen the lust. Then Lysander deliberately canted his hips, shifting just enough that Lysander's hardened length shoved against his ass.

"You had your chance to fuck me," Eroan snapped. "You'll not get another."

Lysander pulled Eroan's hip closer and thrust a hand around Eroan's waist and downward, searching. His fingers found the evidence he needed and cupped Eroan's firm arousal hard enough to steal Eroan's breath. There was no hiding his desires now. *Wrong*, his mind tried to tell him, but his body had already betrayed him. Lysander's eyes were cold. Last night... it hadn't been anything like this. Last night, Lysander had been loving. That wasn't man, this was dragon.

Lysander's fingers tugged at his fly, unlacing it. Eroan made a small effort to pull his arms free. Lysander's grip on his wrists tightened and so did the hand on Eroan's cock, pleasure cresting. Anticipation spun through him, lighting him up.

Then Lysander's hand was gone. Eroan's trousers jerked down, exposing his ass and Lysander's spreading hand, the male's tingling touch a temptation all of its own. Eroan had never taken another male in. He'd always been the one in control, always the leader, never led.

Pressure pushed at his hole. Lysander eased a wet finger in. Eroan shifted, wincing as an uncomfortable pain opened him up. Doubt stoked a little fear alive but then Lysander's hot mouth fell to Eroan's neck, his hand once again back on Eroan's cock, working him into a mind-numbing frenzy, emptying out those fears. Then Lysander's moistened hand vanished from his cock, leaving Eroan panting and writhing and aching, his mind and body a wreck of warring needs. He barely felt Lysander's arousal nudge his opening until Lysander pushed, and a new, luscious pressure sparked off an intense pleasure, one that took all the fear and sense of wrongness and made it so very right.

"Damn you for feeling so good." Lysander's raw voice touched the back of Eroan's neck and Lysander pushed himself in deep, filling Eroan, igniting a new kind of heat. When he eased out, Eroan groaned at the loss and chased that sensation, needing to be filled again.

"Tell me you want this..." Lysander's weight smothered

his back, crushing his trapped hands between them. "Tell me," Lysander growled.

By Alumn, he wanted it, he wanted Lysander so deep that he'd forget who he was and what he was supposed to be and not be. He wanted that feeling of being filled, being taken and owned, the feeling of freefall and the pulsing, building ecstasy. "*Yes.*"

Lysander thrust in. Pleasure and pain crackled low in Eroan's back, jolting a sharp dart of pure pleasure through him. More. He wanted—needed—more. Lysander's thrusting pace grew urgent, his grunts coming rough and hard and that too rode Eroan's desires higher. A new, sensual pleasure arched up his back, the pressure and closeness making him feel connected to another like never before. The delicious feel of having a male inside of him touched places he hadn't known could feel so good.

He squeezed muscle around Lysander's cock, heard the dragon's rolling groan and clamped again. Lysander's thighs relentlessly slapped his ass. Then Lysander fell forward again and matched his frantic beat to that of his hand gripping Eroan's erection. The gem, the war, the hate, his people, the risk, the hurt, it all fell away, buried beneath the rawness of having Lysander fuck him into the table. Alumn, this was a madness, one he willingly took and made his own.

Lysander's breaths shuddered, rhythm stuttering, the hand at Eroan's cock suddenly jerking. Lysander's grip on Eroan's wrists tightened toward pain, but only for a few moments, then Lysander's final thrusts spilled his seed.

Eroan shoved back, ripping a gasp from Lysander. The dragon's grip hardened around Eroan's needing erection, worked him harder, his expert hand suddenly directly linked to the animal part of Eroan's mind. Ecstasy built, higher and higher. The release crested over him, sparking up his back, coming harder with Lysander's fullness still inside. He thrust into Lysander's grip until he was spent, breathless, wrecked and trembling.

Lysander pulled free too soon, wet seed spilling from Eroan's hole, and for a few long, sensual moments, Lysander teased the slickness between Eroan's thighs and up, pushing a finger in, touching him intimately, before inching out. "Still want me dead, Eroan Ilanea?" the dragon purred.

Eroan yanked his wrists free and kicked back, turning to show Lysander the truth on his face. He pulled the table drawer open, plucked out the gem and threw it at him.

Lysander fumbled the gem as it bounced against his chest, but managed to catch the lump of shining, purple crystals. Whatever that rock was, Lysander looked at it like it held all the answers. Eroan knew how it throbbed with darkness. It was not a tool for good.

"I hope it's worth it." Eroan sneered, tucking himself away. "Get out."

Lysander tidied himself and retied his trousers, his face back to its hard, impenetrable mask. He backed toward the door, shadowed gaze lingering on Eroan like he wanted to say more, but it was too late for words.

The dragon's touch still scorched his thighs and wrists and now it was done, he wondered if this thing between them was now broken for good. "If you ever hurt my people, I'll put a blade through your dragon-heart and your head on a stake."

"I'd expect nothing less from Eroan Ilanea," Lysander grumbled. He tossed the gem in the air, caught it, and turned toward the door, but before leaving, some indecision held him back. "There's a disused tunnel running beneath the tower to the northwest. A collapse years ago made it almost impassable. It's unguarded." Then he was out the door and gone.

Eroan waited for the barks of alarm to sound from outside, for the Order shouts, but when the alarm didn't come, he slumped against the table.

Dampness gathered between his legs. He reeked of dragon. Roughly tugging off his clothes, he dove into the shower.

Water hissed into his hair and pounded against his shoulders. Leaves and grit swirled around the drain. Eroan watched the dirt vanish, his head spinning so much, he reached out and braced an arm against the wall, letting cool water rush down his back and legs. His wrists burned, the ghost of Lysander's grip still there. *Tell me you want this...*

He had a way into the tower. If Lysander was to be believed...

Damn Lysander... Damn him to Ifreann and back. Eroan had given himself completely, even crafted that dragon token like a lovestruck fool. Had it always been a game to him? Had he ever needed saving or had his life been exactly the way he wanted it? He recalled the drunken prince from the tower and the cry for help in his eyes. That plea wasn't there now.

What was it the old female dragon at the tower had said to him... that Lysander wouldn't ask for help, and he'd fight Eroan? Was this that challenge, or had she been messing with his head too?

The mocking things Lysander had said, Eroan could hear them again now and still his wretched heart clung onto the threads of hope thinking... thinking what? That Lysander was still good?

If he wasn't good, what did that make Eroan? He'd just allowed Lysander to fuck him and *liked* it. He'd more than liked it. What if Curan had been right? Was Eroan broken somewhere inside and it had started with the queen, with the prison and the chains? Started and never stopped. He would know if he was compromised, wouldn't he?

Was any of last night real?

You were the sweetest one-night fuck I've ever had.

He hissed in through his teeth, and let the cold water numb him through. It didn't matter. He couldn't let it matter. The humans would soon be here. More from the Order were arriving, and they were all looking to him for the future. Lysander was gone. Eroan had to let it end there.

You never gave up on me.

I never will.

He gently thumped a fist against the wall and rested his forehead against the wood. Lysander needed him more now than ever but Eroan had no idea how to save him this time, or even if he could.

"Eroan?" Seraph's voice penetrated the hiss of the water. "You there?"

"I'll be right out." He sounded normal, didn't he? A bit gruff, perhaps.

"Are you all right?"

He cleared the hitch in his throat, switched off the water, and poked a hand out the door. "Hand me a towel?" Soft fabric landed in his grip.

"When you didn't return, Nye sent three prides out looking for you."

"I had an encounter." He ruffled the towel over his hair and down his face, hoping the muffle hid any other tremors. "I dealt with it."

"I thought I smelled dragon..." Closer to the door, she whispered, "Did he show?"

He knotted the towel around his waist and stilled, hardening his heart. Seraph liked Lysander. If she knew how he'd changed... "No."

He pushed all thoughts and feeling about Lysander far away where they couldn't undermine what had to be done going forward. The humans would be here soon with their ingenious weapons and now he had a way to get inside the tower—a parting gift from Lysander. It was time to strike at the dragons' heart.

CHAPTER 46

$\mathcal{L}$ ysander

LYSANDER SLOWED when the forest cover thinned and the risk of a keen-sighted elf seeing him had passed. Echoing dragoncalls broke the quiet and the taste of ash landed on his tongue. He stumbled against a tree, charred bark coming away beneath his hands, and closed his eyes, trying to steady his breathing. But behind closed eyes, he saw Eroan's furious face, heard Eroan's scathing words, felt him warm and hard and tasting of freedom. Pushing him away had been the right thing to do. Lysander had to believe that because there was no getting him back.

He sank to a crouch and thumped his head back against the tree. Once. Twice. A bite of pain chased the guilt away and a knot clogged his throat, bottling rising emotion behind it. If forsaking Eroan had been so right a thing, why did it hurt so bad? After Mirann, after Dokul, the dungeons, after every-fucking-thing, there was no room in his world for stupid, stubborn, honorable elves who didn't know when to quit. After last night, he'd known Eroan would follow him into death, because the damn elf knew no other way. Eroan would get himself killed for him. And Lysander wasn't worth that sacrifice.

He shoved a hand into his pocket and scooped up the amethyst. The gem throbbed warm and strong, like a living, pumping organ. It didn't have the same feel to it as his shifting magic, but it had power. How else could a rock feel alive? Only this mattered now, and getting his wings back. The fantasy of last night was over. He had to return to a reality, survive it, and somehow thrive inside its dark heart. This gem was the key to that. The gem... and forgetting Eroan existed.

He left the tree cover and headed across the open barrenlands toward the tower jutting out of the horizon. Bronze wings caught the blood-red sunset, making the usurpers look as though they were ablaze. He'd considered sneaking in after dark, but stealth wouldn't solve whatever he found inside. Clearly, the bronze had arrived in huge numbers and showed no signs of leaving. As he drew closer to the tower grounds, the lookouts barked their warnings, but none flew down to stop him.

Inside the tower's many corridors, the smell of wet metal assaulted his nose. Faces he didn't recognize watched him pass, expressions blank. He made sure to match their indifference with his own.

The fire in Carline's kitchen grate had burned down to ash and the dragon's chambers were empty. He'd never known her to be anywhere else. In fact, he'd never seen her outside the tower.

Standing in the chamber doorway, he felt the gem

throb in his coat pocket. Without Carline, he didn't know enough about it to utilize whatever power it held. He had to find her, and fast.

"Lysander Bronze, you're required in the feasting hall."

Anger fizzled at the end of his nerves. He turned his head and fixed the lower in his sights. Just another metal-stinking male. Itching restlessness had him wanting to throw the fool against the wall. Their presence here was an insult, a disrespect. It was an act of aggression, of war and while Lysander felt no more part of amethyst than he did bronze, these walls *had* been his home.

"Did you hear me?" the lower asked, brow rising.

"I heard you, bitch," he snarled, rounding on the lower. The stranger wore a large hoop earring and metal bands across his biceps. When he spoke, a piercing bobbed in his tongue. Just the scent of him made Lysander's gut churn, a scent he'd been buried in for weeks. A creeping thread of fear began to work its way through his anger. He stamped it down, burying it under the hate for the bronze. "Where's my brother, *the king*?"

"Waiting in the hall..." Malice lit up the bronze's eyes.

What else was waiting in the hall for him?

A moment passed between them. The bronze was twice his weight. He might even get a few pendulum swings in. Lysander was faster and better trained. Lysander could take him but fighting a lower would only delay the inevitable meeting with Dokul. He dropped a hand into his pocket to find the beat of the gem. His fingers brushed the wooden dragon carving and regret stabbed him in the chest. The past was done. He had vengeance to sate. "Take me to the hall."

When the lower turned his back, Lysander followed, lifting the necklace free and fixing it around his neck. He tucked the token out of sight, inside his shirt, and breathed in the teasing scent of fresh wood and pine needles, absorbing the familiar scent before it could escape. He'd use the memories of being wrapped in Eroan's arms to keep the dark at bay. A dark he willingly walked toward now. There was no room in this world for the dragon he had been before, the dragon who had watched the stars drift across the sky while a proud elf slept tucked against him. He knew that now, and with every step toward the feasting hall, he cast off that vulnerable outer shell, building himself a new layer of invisible iron.

HE COULDN'T DECIDE if it was blood he tasted in the feasting hall air or just the stench of metal. His boots clunked through trails of sticky, shining black ooze: arterial blood. Snaking trails of it led to the dead. From the large number of bodies, bronze had hit hard and fast, killing many amethyst before they'd had a chance to draw their weapons or shift. The rest of amethysts' more powerful flights were in chains, heads down and lined up as though facing their execution. The sight of those chains, the smell of the massacre roused the primal part of him, stretching power into his veins. He was going to need it. At the back of the hall, perched on the edge of a table, sat Dokul.

The formidable male—all shimmering smooth skin and tarnished metal—wore a broad smirk and leaned on one drawn-up knee, rubbing his thumb against the fingers of his right hand, probably remembering what it had felt like to have Lysander in his claws.

Fear tried to sink its talons into Lysander but that too

he blocked off, welcoming a shallow numbness. He could master fear now. Dokul was just another monster he'd already survived once.

A female dressed in a simple lowers' gown sat at the bench beside the bronze chief, her smooth head tilted downward, hands cradled in her lap. It took a few moments for Lysander to recognize her. Mirann. She'd healed some, at least on the outside, but her shoulders and arms were riddled with the scars Lysander had inflicted.

The fear inside Lysander tried to twitch free of its bindings. He held firm, stopped his approach in front of Dokul, and wore the same mask he'd always used when his mother went searching for a reaction.

"The prince returns." Dokul's deep voice rumbled about the vast hall. "We did wonder if you'd fled? You can't fly..." He chuckled. "So perhaps you ran like humans would?"

A few of the gathered bronze snickered. Lysander cast a glance over the hundreds here. All bronze. Any surviving amethyst lower would likely be deeper inside the tower, the bronze bastards having their fun with them. The amethyst flights on their knees could still shift and rip free of the chains, but to do so would be seen as a weakness and none had yet given into that temptation. Whatever he thought of amethyst, they had pride.

"In your absence, the tower was left to this one..." Dokul swept a hand to his right and the crowd parted, revealing Akiem in royal robes, on his knees, chains bound around bloody and raw wrists. Blood dripped from his dark hair. Smeared, bloody fingerprints had dried across his cheek and jaw. He'd been cut and beaten, and fuck knew what else. Akiem didn't look over. He only had eyes for Dokul. Lysander wasn't even sure if his brother knew he'd arrived, or maybe he just didn't care enough to acknowledge him.

Dokul heaved his bulk out of the throne and stood, slowly approaching Lysander. "Akiem never had enough authority over Elisandra's flights—that was always *you*." He pointed a thick finger. "Didn't have the balls to back up his short-lived reign either." Dokul shrugged his broad, pauldron-capped shoulder. "Balls that now belong to me." The male grinned and his eyes sparkled with slippery glee. "Yet I doubt he'll be as much fun as you."

So he hadn't fucked Akiem. Yet.

Lysander's mouth twitched. He should have been here last night. The bronze might not have broken through the amethyst flights had he organized their defense. Akiem was likely thinking the same, if he was thinking at all. Lysander had abandoned them at precisely the right time for the bronze to attack. Lysander *Bronze*. Akiem probably thought he was complicit in all of this.

"I intend to ruin this whelp who calls himself king," Dokul explained. "An eye for an eye, for what you did to my daughter." Dokul tilted his head, eyeing Lysander side-on. "I might make a bronze of you yet." Holding out a hand, he added, "Daughter, stand."

Mirann rose like a ghost. Dressed in a tight-fitting slip of a gown, she looked small, vulnerable. Lysander took more of his regret and shame and used it to reinforce the wall around him.

Dokul offered his hand and his daughter stepped forward, her hand on her swollen belly, red-eyes glassy and pupils wide. The tracks on her inner arms suggested she'd been given the same poison she'd inflicted on Lysander. Or perhaps she chose to take it as an escape to whatever the amethyst lowers had done to her.

Dokul watched closely for a reaction. Lysander gave none, although a fluttering panic at the sight of her belly tried to break his armor down. Given her size, the clutch she was growing inside had to be a few months on, the timing right for having been impregnated at the coupling. He hadn't cared enough to notice her change before, and once she had him drugged, he had been incapable of seeing much of anything, but now there was no mistaking her distended belly, ripe with eggs.

"Half of amethyst fucked her," he dismissed.

A muscle twitched above Dokul's right eye. "She's too far along for the clutch to be any but yours."

By the great gods, the last thing he'd wanted was more dragons—stronger dragons. Bronze and amethyst hybrids. The spawn would be monstrous. In all of this he'd hoped, after the coupling, that his seed was as broken as the rest of him. It made sense for it to be that way. Clearly, that wasn't the case. "Should I care?"

"Care? No." Dokul laughed along. "When they're hatched, you'll understand." He left Mirann's side and approached Lysander. "Why do you think she so badly had to fuck you, prince?" He reached out a hand, thick fingers wavering close.

Lysander lifted his chin. In his pocket, he closed his hand around the gem. "Touch me—I'll break your fingers and worse."

Desire lit up the brute's eyes. "Tempting threats. I hear you've gained a reputation since returning from my care. Fond of a whip, the lowers told me. Now there's a kink I didn't expect, and one I'd be delighted to explore..."

Lysander swallowed a bubbling rage before it could blind him.

"Do you not wonder why your mother kept you dumb?

Why she so badly wanted your coupling with a bronze? Or why my Mirann was so focused on having you? You're pretty to look at, but you're hardly a fierce specimen. But as dragon... As dragon you are..." He paused, searching for the right words. "Something else. You are *emerald*, and that, Prince, is priceless."

He was done with hearing Dokul's bullshit. "You need to leave this tower. Take your bitch of a daughter and your fucked-up metal brood with you."

"And who is going to make me? You?" Dokul leaned closer. His metal-capped teeth shining. "Your flights are scattered, in chains, or dead." He raked his gaze down Lysander, mouth parted, eyes full. "All those years when she could have trained you... Such a waste... She was afraid. Did you know?"

His teasing taunts weren't going to work. "What do you want, Dokul?" The growl came unbidden, rumbling up from Lysander's chest.

Dokul's smile flashed. "You. Beneath me. Your hybrid brood raised as my own. All of amethyst below me, where they belong. There is a whole world to rule. Not just these lands, but lands beyond, where people still fight and human cities clutch at life. Diamond, onyx, ruby, sapphire. With you, the last emerald at my side and your brood as my weapons, they will *all* be under me. I alone will be king."

He was mad. Lysander had known it, but now he saw that madness as clear as day, glittering on Dokul's tarnished golden eyes. Dokul couldn't rule them all, and what sense did it make to even try? Because the bronze had an insatiable need to take, to own, a need Lysander recognized in himself. All dragons had it, but some allowed it purchase in their minds, allowed that need to control them. Dokul was a creature of singular purpose. There would be no reasoning with him, Lysander realized. Only his death would end this nightmare, and after him, the death of all the bronze. But to do that, Lysander needed both wings working. He needed more time.

"And if I refuse?"

Dokul lifted a hand and one of the bronze dragged a captured amethyst forward. The male struggled against the chain, his eyes flicking hopefully to Lysander. He missed the bronze free a knife from behind his back. The blade slashed fast and true, opening a bloody smile in the amethyst's throat before he could invite the shift. Blood spurted, splashing the stone floor. The bronze dropped his prey and landed a kick in the male's side. He likely didn't feel it, the light in his eyes faded as quickly as the blood left his veins.

A deep, trembling growl bubbled to Lysander's left. "Kill another and I'll shift right here," Akiem warned.

Dokul's smile twitched. "And destroy your own seat of power in the resulting fight? You fought me once and limped off with your tail between your legs. This tower has stood longer than amethyst have existed. Your mother ruled it, the grand matriarch before her, and before her... The great metals did not need towers to rule from. You can't fight me, Akiem. Vicious you might be, but you're no match for my bite. You'll not risk it, *prince*."

Dokul's heavy hand landed on Lysander's shoulder. "Submit to me and this slaughter ends."

His golden eyes pulled Lysander deeper. The ancient creature stirred behind that glare. A creature so old it was a wonder it could reason at all.

Lysander dropped his gaze to Dokul's thick hand, remembering how the chief's calluses had grazed his hips in the human-made cage, how he'd tried to fuck him and failed then, but not later. Dokul didn't care who Lysander was, he realized. It was nothing to do with the crown at all. He wanted *what* Lysander was: Emerald. "Why me, Dokul?"

"Why you... that's the question, isn't it?" The big male's voice boomed about the chamber. "We learned to kill all emeralds the moment they broke from the egg. Better that than allow them to grow to maturity. When you hatched, your mother believed she was cursed. She should have killed you herself. Too afraid, she encouraged your whelp of a brother to finish you."

Akiem didn't hear or didn't care. He continued to glare at Dokul, his cheek fluttering.

"When he tried and failed, she instead thought to use you, as she used many things in her life, but she could never control you, not fully."

Lysander's attention lingered on Akiem. One of his brother's dark brows flickered. Whatever Dokul spoke of, Akiem knew it too. Mirann's distant gaze was too far away to read, but it was true that she'd have done anything to ensure the coupling went ahead. Everyone wanted a piece of him. A piece of emerald. The only difference between him and the rest was his healing ability, but even that was weak, and dragons had never cared for such skills. "Why?" he asked Dokul again.

"Kneel to me, submit to me as mine, and I'll tell you everything." Dokul's thick, slick fingers brushed Lysander's cheek.

Bile burned the back of his throat. He met the male's penetrative glare with his own, offering a challenge. The bronze's grip twisted, clutching the left side of Lysander's face.

Instincts tried to pull Lysander from the male's grotesque touch and spill dragon into his veins, but that too, he pushed down, building more and more layers of armor around it all, until all that was left inside was cold iron and the throbbing, roiling fire of vengeance.

Lysander grabbed the amethyst gem in his fist, holding it so tightly its jagged edges cut into his palm. Leaning closer, he clamped a hand around the back of Dokul's warm, gritty neck and yanked the male close enough to kiss. "You come into my territory and take my flights as your own, you kill amethyst like they are nothing, and you chain up my brother, the king. You are a thief, Dokul Bronze, and I do not suffer thieves." Dokul's mouth twisted. Lysander continued, "I will never kneel to you. I'll fight you and your bronze with every breath I have left. Do you hear me through all that madness? You will never reign over amethyst and you will never reign over *me*."

Dokul roared himself free. "I *have* taken it, whelp!" he announced. "Like I took you, my teeth at your throat and my cock in your ass." He grabbed his crotch and snarled. "You will all kneel to me as it should have been in the beginning before you wretched jeweled were spawned from chaos. You are all mistakes!" Spittle flew. The male's face flushed red, veins bulging. "You were not meant to be! I was a first. I OWN YOU ALL."

He plunged into the line of restrained amethyst and grabbed one, dragging her twisting and scrabbling on her hands and knees to the front.

Carline.

A dangerous edge plucked on Lysander's armor, threatening to break it open and spill power, tooth and claw into this hall, into him.

"Don't!" Akiem tried to stand. His bronze guard struck him across his cheek, knocking him back.

"I've finally found someone you both care about... Interesting." Dokul flung Carline to the floor and stalked around her. "Some lower hag? Or something else?" Around and around he walked while Carline kept her head bowed, her silvery hair sprung from its bands and fallen about her face, hiding her expression. "There's something familiar about you... The mother figure the princes never had?" Dokul grinned, reading his answers on Akiem's face. "Maybe I'll fuck her right here, in front of you all, rip her open so you can see what it is to deny my claim."

"Let her go," Lysander warned, mental restraints straining to hold the shift within.

Dokul grabbed a fist of Carline's hair and yanked her to her feet, against his chest. She didn't cry out, didn't protest. "Kneel, whelp," he ordered Lysander and switched his glare to Akiem. "Both of you submit to me, *now*."

Carline's compassionate eyes widened. In them was a plea not to let Dokul beat him. She threw the same look toward Akiem and Lysander heard his brother's growl simmering again.

The gem in his pocket, clutched tightly in his hand, throbbed in time with Lysander's heart, pumping power and blood and lust and rage through his body. He couldn't hold it back for long, but perhaps just long enough to get close enough.

Lysander stepped forward.

Carline's gaze turned fearful. She thought he was going to kneel. The entire gathering of amethyst likely feared the same. He was bronze anyway, but not by choice. Never by choice.

He pulled the gem from his pocket and threw it to

Carline. She reached up a hand, neatly catching it. Her soft, aging face instantly hardened, then before Lysander's eyes, she dropped the gem. It *tinked* against the stone, drawing the gaze of everyone in the hall.

The old dragon brought the heel of her boot down with a ringing slam, smashing it into countless glittering shards, tinkling across the floor.

Lysander's heart stuttered. But... his wing?! She'd told him he needed it to fix his wing... She'd said it would change everything. He'd betrayed Eroan's trust for that gem.

"No!" Akiem lunged, not toward Carline, but for the glittering remains of the gem. The bronze holding him struggled to keep him, and Akiem tore free, then fell to his knees, wrist shackles rattling, and scooped up the broken pieces as though he could somehow miraculously slot them all back together.

He swung his glare to Lysander. *"What have you done?!"*

The worst of it was, he didn't know, but it felt like something terrible and the cruel, twisted smile on Carline's face confirmed it. A smile that warped and twitched as magic poured into the space Carline occupied. That magic tasted like death, like wet rust and doused flames.

Dread sank in his gut.

Mirann's laugh clawed at Lysander's mind, but he couldn't look away from Carline's transformation as threads of power unwrapped her human form and filled the air with golden scale. Some part of his brain told him to leave, to run and not look back because the creature emerging before him *was* death and decay and the end of all things.

Akiem slammed into Lysander. His hands snagged on

Lysander's wrist and pulled, but still he couldn't look away, as though this emerging creature demanded to be admired. Scale built on scale, crafting ladders over enormous muscles and then it was there, too big, too surreal, too much a legend for Lysander to wrap his thoughts around. *Gold*, was all his mind supplied. *She is gold.*

"Run!" Akiem pulled, tugging Lysander back from beneath the golden beast's shadow.

He looked up and up to a monstrous head gnarled and jagged with scales, and to the crown: its spears thrust back, shining golden, the greatest of metals. The first terrible queen to claw through the thawing ice and breach the human world.

When she opened her enormous mouth and roared, the noise barreled through him, jolting his body into action, but skewering his power deep inside. Rock rained from the ceiling, the floor cracked and the walls shifted, dust exploding into the air. More dragons shifted around them, claws and wings suddenly thrust into the air. He ran hard and fast, dashing through gaps and out into narrow corridors behind Akiem.

Carline was—is—Gold.

I freed the Gold.

It didn't make any sense. Why hadn't she revealed herself before? Why was she here?

The gem.

Elisandra's gem.

Carline hadn't wanted it to fix his wing, she'd wanted it to free herself from a prison nobody had seen.

Akiem threw back a wall tapestry, revealing a hidden door behind, and pulled Lysander into the dark. A spiral staircase twisted downward. The sound of their boots thundering on steps accompanied the frantic beat of Lysander's racing heart.

"Where does this lead?" he asked, startled to hear his voice carry far into the dark ahead.

"Out."

A roar shook the stairwell, raining dust from above.

"Wait..." Lysander slowed. "Akiem, wait..."

His brother pulled up short and glared up at him. "What?!" He strained against the wrist shackles, tried to yank them apart and swore when they held.

"Back there... I... I didn't know."

"Didn't know what exactly? That Dokul was coming for me or that Carline was Gold?"

"Both, neither. I knew the bronze were coming—"

"And you left." Akiem fell back against the damp stonewall. "I could not fight them all. Too many amethyst would have died..."

"I had planned to return before he—"

"You're my brother. Where were you?!"

With Eroan. "I'm your brother now?! Kin means shit to you. You threw me in that fucking dungeon!"

"Because you're bronze!" Akiem snarled back. "You son of a breeding-bitch. This is all your fault." He stepped forward, fists clenched. "Everything is your fault. Amalia... this. All of it." The fight faded out of him. He stepped back and fell against the wall. "Why couldn't you have just died when we were hatched?!"

Amalia? What? "No. I didn't do this. The gem, I thought... I didn't know its power held hers."

"Of course you didn't," he sneered. "We need to keep moving. Dokul and Carline together..." He stared down the steps, into the dark. "Two Great Gods. We must get as far away as we can."

Lysander descended a few more steps, stopping on Akiem's level. His eyes flared a warning for Lysander to back off. "You knew about Carline?"

"I guessed," Akiem admitted. "A long time ago. The matriarch, our grandmother, had her trapped... the gem was hers, then Elisandra's. I only know because I found it and Elisandra... She did not react well." Akiem rubbed at his forehead. "We must leave. It's not over. Together they are stronger than us."

Akiem's eyes seemed brighter in the dark, but from fear. The only time Lysander had seen fear on Akiem's face was the night Amalia was exiled. "Why is Amalia my fault?"

"It doesn't matter..."

Lysander grabbed Akiem's chains and pulled, snapping the links. Akiem didn't linger to thank him and continued the descent. "The jeweled stole our reign from the metals. They will destroy this tower, destroy all of us, it's all they know."

"Why was I not told about any of this?!"

"Because you're a fucking *emerald.*"

He kept hearing this accusation, like it was a crime. "What difference does the color of my scales make?"

Akiem stopped and sighed, shoulders heaving. "I only know that what Dokul said was true, Elisandra feared you." When he glanced back, his gaze skimmed. "Come."

He followed Akiem into the dark, knowing his brother had just lied.

roan

THE BAND of humans traipsed through Cheen's open gates, their clothes bedraggled and faces grim. An Order pride instructed to escort them the last mile flanked the column, the obvious racial differences suddenly stark. Humans stomped, bodies stockier, heavier, with a physical strength echoed in the dragons. Whereas elves seemed both harsher in appearance and yet more fluid, the difference between maces swung in battle and well-balanced swords. All around, elves watched the humans arrive, studying their visitors as those visitors studied the elves. Hundreds of years and generations had passed since humans and elves had fought side-by-side, hundreds of years since humans had abandoned elves mid-battle, since their devastating weapon dropped, changing things forever. Eroan hoped to change things forever again, but for the better. It couldn't get much worse.

Chloe led the column, her face lifting the moment she spotted Eroan.

Anye, in her white robes, approached first. "You'll find my people friendly and welcoming," the elder greeted, her smile warm but not without its own thin edge, "just so long as you return the courtesy."

Eroan half-listened to the pair exchange polite greetings but kept his gaze on the assassins still flanking the humans, each one a formidable presence. The humans were armed with what appeared to be pistols, their hands resting close by to those weapons. Eroan smelled dragon on them, which likely accounted for the skittish look in his pride's eyes. Dragons had once routinely infiltrated humans, another reason for elves to distrust these outsiders. The scent likely came from various scuffles along their journey.

Change had to begin with trust.

Catching Nye's eye, Eroan nodded him over. "Tell the Order to withdraw. These people are no threat to us. But stay observant."

Anye arranged a meeting in the hall once the band was settled and allocated a number of elves to help them find lodgings. He watched the group separate and nervous smiles bloom. The anxiety would pass, given time, but time was in short supply.

A short while later, Eroan met with Anye, Chloe, and a tall, slim man with skin the color of charred wood who constantly shifted on his feet. Not from anxiety though, more from excitement.

"Eroan, *mon dieu*," Chloe's arms briefly settled around him. "It is good to see you again." He embraced her, breathing in the smell of the sea and human. "This is Ben." She withdrew and gestured at the man beside her.

Ben's grin lit up his friendly face. He extended his hand. "I've heard a lot about you."

Eroan took the hand, giving it a firm shake. His accent was easier on Eroan's ears than Chloe's. Familiar, but different.

"American," Chloe explained.

Eroan had no idea what that word meant, but he recalled Chloe's father mentioning the land across the great ocean called something like *American*. If Chloe trusted him, then Eroan was sure the male was worthy, although his constant gestures and fidgeting made Eroan want to sit him down and order him to stay put.

"We have much to discuss." Chloe added, "Details I could not put into letters. Ben is a scientist, of sorts. He's here to exchange knowledge, after we're settled, if that's acceptable with you?"

Ben took that as his cue to explain, "More of a dracologist, I guess. I've made it my life's work to study all races of dragon." He spoke quickly, as though desperate to impart that knowledge to all.

"Have you found any weaknesses?" Eroan asked.

"Some. There are various quirks to their physiology." He laughed, short and sharp, although Eroan had no idea what was so amusing. "I could spend days explaining. For instance, different dragons produce their own unique type of fire. Some, like diamond, don't produce fire at all, but a plasma-based semi-liquid substance. It burns through surfaces like fire."

"But we understand we don't have much time?" Chloe interrupted, addressing Eroan and Anye.

"The number of dragons at the tower is increasing daily. We're concerned they're preparing for an attack," Anye began, then nodded to Eroan to continue.

"We've recently discovered a disused tunnel. We have scouts observing it now. If it proves to be accessible, it could be the way in we've been looking for. And with your numbers now joining our ranks, we could very likely deal a devastating blow to the amethysts, but we must act quickly."

He'd told Anye how he'd discovered the tunnel by accident after observing the tower with the spyglass from a distance. It was a good lie, one that sat easily with Eroan. Better a lie than the truth, that the amethyst prince had told him as a goodbye token, right after fucking him against a table.

Chloe removed a fist-sized cylinder from inside her coat and set it on the table. "I was hoping you'd found a way inside by the time we'd arrived. This is something Ben's team has been working on. The aerosol inside, when released in a confined place, brings a dragon down inside of fifteen seconds."

The can didn't look at all deadly. He'd seen similar containers buried in the earth and overlooked them as metal from the human age. Eyeing the can in disbelief, Eroan frowned. It didn't seem possible something so small could bring down a dragon. "Kills it?"

"No, unfortunately," Chloe replied. "That is where you come in. The gas inside will render dragons unconscious for up to ten minutes. At least, it does with the dragons we've been able to test it on."

He reached out for the cylinder. "May I?"

"Go ahead," Ben agreed. "Just don't pull the tag. It doesn't do much to humans but make them drowsy. I'm not sure of the effect on elves. I've... er... I've not met one of you before to... you know, test it."

The cylinder was heavier than it looked. Eroan

weighed it in his hand. Carrying more than three would slow an elf down. "What dragon-types have you exposed to it?"

"Diamond, mostly. They're the predominant race in Spain and northern Africa, where I was stationed before traveling north to France."

"No bronze? Amethyst?"

"One amethyst, but it was young and already disorientated. The gas worked in an enclosed space. We haven't tested it on any metals. You have bronze here?"

"Yes, many," Anye said. "There's increasing bronze activity at the tower."

Ben nodded, thinking it over. "I haven't personally encountered a metal before, but as long as their physiology isn't too different to the jeweled, the signs are good that the gas will work on them. It's the best shot we have right now."

They discussed the risks while Eroan considered what he'd seen of the tower layout. In a confined place, a deployable gas could sweep through the corridors almost undetected, and even if it was discovered, fifteen seconds wasn't enough time for the alarm to be raised. Once the dragons were down, killing them was a matter of thrusting a blade into the skull behind the crown. Ten minutes was more than enough time. "This could be the perfect solution." To Anye, he said, "Have our outfitters make us some masks. Use charcoal to filter the gas."

Chloe's eager expression mirrored Eroan's racing heart. "How soon can you be ready?" he asked her.

"A few hours of rest and we'll be ready."

Eroan handed the canister back to Ben. "How many of those do you have?"

"Over a hundred. We found a stash a few years ago in

an abandoned military base in Gibraltar," Ben replied. "Enough to flush that tower if we can get deep enough inside before the radiation dose gets too high."

"Radiation?" Eroan had never heard that word before.

Ben glanced at Anye and found another equally baffled expression. "Your entire south coast is radioactive, we assume from the nuclear fallout—the danger-zone is to the west." He said it as though surprised Eroan wasn't aware. "You've likely evolved a resistance to it, or it could be elves are naturally immune." He scratched at his nose and smiled nervously again. "I'd like... I mean, I'd love to, you know... get a closer look at you." Anye blinked back at him. "At elf physiology, I mean. Strictly for ... science."

Nuclear? Radiation? These words and their meanings were alien to him. "The human weapon fell generations ago." Chloe's father had shown him huge maps with a great spread of darkness from the Whitelands out at sea. "The blast was to the west, in a land out at sea, far from here."

"The fallout has dissipated some," Ben went on, "which is why life thrives here. But the entire landscape will remain radioactive many more thousands of years. The jeweled dragons have abilities not recorded in metals. Their mutation came from the use of nuclear weapons, producing all sorts of quirks... The radiation is what made the jeweled, not the blast itself. I wonder if it altered elves?"

"Altered us?" Anye asked. "In what way?"

He chuckled again, and glanced at Chloe, looking for help. "Without studying your history, it's difficult to know."

"Oh..." Anye blinked and looked to Eroan, although he

couldn't imagine why, before darting back to Ben. "Do you mean we may have changed after the blast?"

"Yes, it's possible. You get your energy from the sun, right? You need light to live. Were you always that way?"

"Yes, but... there was a time it was said elves once had magic. Nothing like the dragons, more... a natural touch. A way to enhance naturally occurring things. Old stories... Much of it is thought to be myth, but now I wonder if those tales aren't rooted in more?"

That was news to Eroan, although he'd heard fantasy tales of the like as an elfling.

"Do you think it could be possible the human weapon took magic from us?" Anye asked.

"It's possible, sure," Ben grinned. "Do you think you might be able to answer some questions and maybe I can find out more? We could learn a great deal from each other."

Chloe cleared her throat. "Later, Ben. We must prepare."

"Oh, yeah, right, sure. When you can."

Both females smiled at Ben's shy charm. "I'd like that," Anye agreed.

Eroan frowned at Anye's obvious flustering. "After the attack," he said, not wanting their focus wandering. Eroan guarded his expression and tempered the rush of hope at having these people here and the possibilities they brought with them. He'd always believed humans and elves together would be a force strong enough to bring down the dragons. This could be the beginning. All eyes had turned to him. He nodded. "Rest up from your journey. Provided the latest reports from the tunnel lookouts are clear, we attack at first light."

~

EROAN SPENT the night making sure every member of the Order had been briefed. The last time he'd had a pride rally around him, he'd been the sole survivor. But assassins were trained to fight and to die for the cause. And they'd do the same at the tower at dawn. He trusted every single individual would give it their all.

Stealing a quiet moment a few hours before dawn, he wandered the meandering path leading to the old, gnarled oak found deep within Cheen. One flame torch lit the clearing on approach to the oak, making the countless ribbons tied among the tree's branches dance with light. The leaves were full now and vibrant in daylight, but shadows crowded the enormous tree in the dark.

Eroan pressed a hand to the rough bark and looked up. Ribbons flittered, one for every branch, it seemed. One for every severed life-string. He'd tied many ribbons to Cheen's tree in his time. Too many. Curan's was there, as were all those belonging to the elves he'd dug out of the mud.

Had anyone thought to remove his when he returned, or did it still flutter in the breeze as a sign of things to come?

He knelt among the roots and bowed his head. Alumn's tree hummed with life. It had sprouted from an acorn long before the dragons, when human monuments reached into the skies. Its roots traveled deep into the ground, where humans had once boarded great snake-like machines to travel through tunnels on vast distances. If this tree had survived for so long, then so could his people.

Alumn, please let this be right.

The soft noises from the village drifted to him on the breeze, a gentle reminder of what he fought for.

He'd already lost a home. He couldn't lose another.

And it all rested on Lysander's word.

The word of someone he believed he knew. The word of his enemy.

What if it was a lie, a trap? What if he was taking hundreds of elves and humans to their deaths tomorrow because Lysander had been truly broken?

If you want to trust me, you must trust all of me. I am dragon.

Eroan had trusted him. He did still. Didn't he?

The last moments they'd shared in his hut, that hadn't been Lysander. A part of him, yes. The necessary part, the part he built to survive behind. But not all of him. Lysander, the prince with a heart, was still inside the male he'd become. Eroan had to believe that. He would not give up on him.

Gentle footfalls alerted him to Nye's stealthy approach. Eroan kept a hand pressed against the tree, head bowed, praying to Alumn that he would not be adding more ribbons.

"Seraph wants to come tomorrow." Nye's voice was soft, like the times they'd lain together and Nye had talked about his life, his dreams, his nomadic family he'd left behind to pursue life as an Assassin of the Order.

"Why wouldn't she come with us?"

"I'm concerned about her attachment to the prince. It clouds her judgment."

Concerned about her attachment or Eroan's? "She is as worthy as any other. I'll not have her left behind." Eroan sat back on his legs, bringing Nye's standing figure into the corner of his right eye. He stared up into the tree canopy, probably thinking of the dead. "The tunnel?" Eroan asked.

"Clear. I took a pride inside a little ways. There's no sign of dragon activity and hasn't been for a long time, but it has good airflow. There's a way out." Nye stepped forward, pressed his hand to the trunk, muttered a few words to Alumn and crouched beside Eroan. "It's overgrown and a long way from the base of the tower. The mouth collapsed a long time ago. It's invisible unless you know to look for it."

Good. Exactly as Lysander had said.

"And you stumbled across it by chance..." Nye added.

The unspoken hung loud between them.

Eroan held Nye's gaze, waiting for him to finish the accusation.

He sighed and raked a hand through his hair. "I'd follow you into Alumn's light, Eroan, but this is reckless and foolish. It's not like you."

"What *this* is, is our last chance."

"Tell me the truth." Nye's gaze searched Eroan's, looking for the cracks. "How did you come to know about this tunnel?"

"Last night, after the encounter, I—"

He shook his head, looking down, cheek fluttering, clearly seeing through Eroan's lie. "I can't let you do this."

Eroan tightened his fingers on his thighs.

Nye lifted his head to the tree for guidance. "I can't let you walk them all inside that tunnel without knowing the source of the information."

Nye would never let it rest. He was too observant for excuses and vague answers. "What does it matter how I came by the information?" Eroan asked. "The tunnel exists. We must do this."

Nye's mouth tilted into a flat smile. He even laughed a little before looking Eroan in the eyes. "Do you think they'd follow you if you told them the dragon was the one who revealed the tunnel?"

His heart thudded too fast and too heavy. Nye was going to ruin everything. Eroan loosened his grip on his thighs, stretching his fingers. "No, which is why I can't tell them. This has to happen."

"I can tell them. And I will."

Nye thought he was doing the right thing. The righteous pride in his eyes was Eroan's too. It belonged to all elves. Made them stubborn, made them strong. But Nye could not win this. "Nye, see this as the opportunity it is. We have everything in place. In a few hours, we'll strike a devastating blow to the amethyst forces. With Ben's gas canisters, maybe even kill them all. These lands will be ours again, our homes safe for generations. The risk is great but the rewards are worth it."

Nye swallowed, reached out, and gripped Eroan's shoulder. "A dragon told you how to get inside the tower. Not just any dragon, the amethyst prince. Why would he do that?"

"You don't know him—"

"And you do?" He shuffled closer and eased his grip down Eroan's arm. "You think you know him?"

"I..." The right words failed Eroan. "Better than most, yes."

"You told me once that dragons are not like us. They don't think like us, they don't care like we do." He shook his head and raked his hair back from his eyes. "Is that where you were last night? Were you with him? And while you were together, he told you about this tunnel?"

Eroan winced. This conversation was one he'd planned never to have with Nye or anyone. As welcoming as elves were, the estuary had taught him his people's compassion didn't extend to dragons. No elf shall aid a dragon. None of his people could know he'd seen Lysander again. It would ruin everything. He'd be cast out, an exile, and elves would continue to die. More ribbons would be added to the tree—he looked up through the long, reaching branches—and all because they thought him tainted by Elisandra. Her threat lingered long after her death.

"Nye, please trust me."

"That's exactly what happened, isn't it? You met with the dragon." Nye's mouth twisted. "Tomorrow is a trap." He scrambled to his feet. "Anye must know." He was leaving and in moments, the whole village would think Eroan was compromised. The humans would leave. An alliance wouldn't happen. Everything he had worked for would be over.

"Nye..." Eroan got to his feet. In a few strides, he grabbed for Nye's arm, catching his sleeve to turn him around. "Curan saw what Lysander was like."

Nye yanked his arm free. "Curan died because of *that* dragon. Lysander is dragon, Eroan! They've killed thousands of us. He's likely killed dozens of your own prides. Tortured friends, people we loved. Dragons left you an orphan! You trained your entire life to kill them. How can you... *be* with one?"

Bitter anger burned his throat. "He's not like that."

Nye's gaze desperately searched Eroan's until his eyes suddenly widened. "Oh, Eroan... You think you love him, don't you? You do..." His face crumpled. He thrust his hands into his hair and staggered back. "Alumn... I couldn't understand before, but there it is..." He laughed, but the sound was ugly and dry. "You love him and he's using that. It's not love, Eroan. Love is... Love is being there for someone even when it hurts. Love is understanding them, all of them, even their mistakes, in a way no one else can. It's bone deep, not some twisted infatuation leftover from what they did to you. That's not love. It's abuse." Nye waited for denials that weren't coming. "Tomorrow will be a massacre—" He cut off, turning away.

Eroan's patience shattered.

Looping an arm around Nye's neck, he pulled, clamping the male's throat against his bicep and squeezing. Nye tried to twist, kick, and buck free. One well-aimed elbow dug into Eroan's side, landing a dull thud. Eroan tightened his grip, feet planted, and waited, his own breath ragged.

Nye's struggles slowed and in the quiet, the male's heaving softened, until the fingers gripping Eroan's arm fell away.

It had to be done. There was no other way. Nye would have ruined his plans, plans that would save them all.

He leaned in, slung Nye's weight over his shoulders, and carried him to the dark side of Alumn's tree. Setting him down among the roots, Eroan quickly listened for breathing. Nye's soft fluttering breaths touched Eroan's ear. Not dead.

"I'm sorry." He cupped Nye's face. "Your hatred is a price I'm willing to pay to stop amethyst." Backing up, he lifted his gaze to the tree. Thousands of ribbons gently fluttered. Mothers, fathers, children. Entire generations lost. It ended tomorrow. "Forgive me, Alumn."

THE TUNNEL'S concrete walls had held up well considering water seepage had eroded the floor into a slippery gulley.

Cave-ins hindered the silent line of elves and humans, but only for minutes until the rubble was cleared.

Seraph moved alongside Eroan, her glances occasionally reflecting the light from the humans' ingenious electric torches. *"They are blessed. They carry Alumn's light with them,"* she had said on the approach to the tunnel entrance. Her awe echoed in the eyes of the others. Now inside, no one spoke, as were his orders. Each elf carried a mask, ready to be deployed as soon as the gas was released. All they had to do now was get as deep as possible into the bowels of the tower.

Eroan's mind reached back to when the bronze had taken him from Elisandra's clutches, and the similar sounds of dripping water coupled with the bite of cold air. He'd been here before, or in a tunnel just like it, and took that as a sign they were on the correct path. The tunnel wasn't huge, too small for an adult dragon to squeeze through unless in human form but wide enough for his prides. And any dragons they encountered in human form could quickly be dispatched before the alarm was raised.

This would work. It had to work. It had cost too much to fail.

Nye would never forgive him.

Neither would the elders, once they learned the truth, but by then it would be too late.

Seraph had asked after Nye, as had Trey, currently at the back of the line. They'd swallowed the lie about him staying behind to guard what would otherwise be a virtually unprotected village. *Necessary*, he told himself.

A roar shook the tunnel, bouncing tiny rocks into crevices. The line hunkered down. The sound was a long way above, but formidable enough for Seraph to check

Eroan. Once it was quiet, he nodded and waved the line on. There was no turning back.

He wondered if Lysander was inside and prayed to Alumn that he wasn't—if Alumn would even listen for a dragon. There hadn't been time to get a message to him and even if he had been able to, the contents would have been too much of a risk should it fall into the wrong hands.

The tunnel opened ahead in a structure similar to Ashford's buried architecture, but smaller, with three tunnels branching off. He'd expected as much and directed each pride into the new tunnel mouths. Chloe went with Trey. The male acknowledged Eroan with a small dip of his chin. First day in the Order and he was about to be part of something larger than them all.

Eroan led Seraph, two more Order assassins—Jex and Cannel—both highly capable of slaughtering dragons, and three humans deeper armed with gas canisters into the tunnels. More rumbling shook the walls, closer this time. Whatever had stirred them up would hopefully keep them distracted long enough for the gas to circulate.

Eventually, the humans' torch beams skimmed over a small side-tunnel leading off to the right.

By Eroan's estimate, they had to be beneath the tower. He nodded at the group to take the branch, and donned his mask, checking Seraph did the same. White muslin covered her mouth and nose, making her dark eyes bright. She tucked both straps behind her ears to keep the mask secure and stuck her thumbs in the air in a sign he'd seen the humans perform. He rolled his eyes. Hers crinkled with silent laughter.

The tunnel narrowed, only wide enough for two to pass, and led up a steep incline, around a sharp corner, climbing ever higher. Eroan paused, halting those behind him, and listened. A constant rumbling had grown behind the walls. It reminded him of waves on the beach or the rumble of a waterfall, but there was nothing like that this far inland. Which left the rumble of fire and dragons.

The sound of boots scraping against dirt ahead of them.

Eroan clicked his fingers and the order elves formed up. The humans took their canisters in hand. Eroan shook his head. *Not yet.* There was no point in freeing the gas too soon and losing their advantage.

The sound of boots hammered closer. Then a male appeared, running right toward them. Seraph flung her dagger. The blade struck the beast mid-chest, right over the heart. His footing stumbled. He collapsed on the blade. Dead before he'd realized he wasn't alone.

Pride swelled in Eroan's chest. He couldn't have dispatched him any quicker.

Seraph kicked the body over, retrieved her knife as easily as pulling a stem from an apple, and continued without missing a beat.

They came across another, almost colliding with her as she bolted around another sharp corner. Jex was on her, dagger across her throat, taking her down in a blur.

"Maybe we don't need the gas..." one of the humans mumbled. Eroan ignored him. Killing one or two as they happened upon them wasn't enough. They needed the gas. He just wanted to get a little deeper.

"They're all running toward us," Seraph whispered behind her mask.

The dragons were distracted. He hushed her. "Makes them easier to kill."

CHAPTER 48

ysander

AKIEM GRABBED one of the remaining swords from the
weapons rack. The armory had been stripped, probably as
soon as the bronze had arrived. Lysander eyed the
remaining blades and picked up a rusted short sword. If
they were going down into the tunnels, a smaller weapon
would be easier to swing than Akiem's choice.

He tested the blade in his hand. Too heavy for its size
and the balance was off. Still, it was better than nothing. "I
don't believe Carline will hurt us."

Akiem straightened and winced, clutching at his side.
The smell of blood tainted the air, wounds Dokul had
inflicted upon him had reopened. "Why?" he asked.
"Because she was always kind to us? What choice do you
think she had in that? She's metal. All they know is
destruction."

Lysander wasn't buying it. Carline had always helped him, sometimes in ways she tried to hide, or believed he didn't notice. Sometimes when he didn't want help. But in the turbulence of his life, she'd been a steadying hand. "But she's Carline... she's spent more time healing both of us than hurting us."

Akiem set the sword against a table and opened his jacket, bloody fingers slipping on the fastenings. "Elisandra had her controlled with that gem. We were her ticket to getting free. Stop looking for the good among us, brother, it'll get you killed."

Like it did Amalia. Akiem lifted his shirt, revealing a latticework of cuts and deep, oozing gashes. Dokul had sliced him over and over.

Akiem peered through his lashes at Lysander, conveying a query and disgust in one glance, as only amethyst could.

Lysander sighed, tucked his blade hilt first against his lower back, and pressed both hands to Akiem's lower waist and over his ribs where the worst of the wounds pulsed blood. He didn't speak. There was little to say. Akiem had tossed him in the dungeon knowing what Mirann would do to him and Lysander hated him for that. Hated him for a lot more than that. But in all the times Elisandra had unleashed her wrath, Akiem had been there afterward, not to comfort, his brother wasn't capable of such things, but as company.

Lysander breathed out and awoke the strange, warming sensation near the middle of his chest, the area he tapped into when he'd helped heal Eroan alongside Carline. As a kit, he'd learned early on not to mention his healing skills. To do so only invited the whip and his talents weren't anything as strong as Carline's. "She said she'd fix my wing," he said softly, letting the tingling warmth soak through his shoulders and down his arms, through both palms and into Akiem.

Akiem's eyes fluttered closed. "She lied," he hissed through his teeth.

"I don't believe that." Lysander focused on the cuts and moved his fingers through the blood, stimulating the skin to repair itself.

"Nothing can fix your wing." Akiem growled, riding out the pain. "We must leave the tower and regroup with amethyst. We'll fly north..." Realizing his mistake, he opened his eyes and trailed off.

"The dragons to the north are rabid," Lysander said, ignoring the slip. There would be no flying anywhere for him and to be carried would be shameful. Dokul had carried him and he preferred never to experience that again. "And ferocious." He'd spent much of his life dealing with those wild dragons—creatures that had spent so long as dragon they had forgotten how to reason.

Wiping the blood aside, Lysander skimmed his fingers along pink and raw freshly healed wounds. "You'll have scars."

"We'll take the tunnels," Akiem said, yanking his shirt down. "It's a maze but we won't be stopped. There's no other way out."

... for me. There was for Akiem. All he had to do was shift and fly.

Wiping his bloody hands on his trousers, Lysander stepped back, and waited for Akiem to fasten his jacket. "Why don't you just leave me here?"

Akiem's dark-eyed glance stubbornly revealed nothing. He scooped up his sword. "We leave together now, or not at all."

He wasn't by Lysander's side out of some newfound brotherly love. Such things didn't exist.

"Why did Mother fear emeralds?" Lysander asked, following Akiem down another spiral staircase.

"She never told me," he replied, gaze shifting. Another lie.

Akiem wanted whatever Lysander was, so did Dokul and Mirann. All Lysander had to do was figure out what he was before that happened.

Rumbling sounds of distant roars trembled through the walls. Akiem left the armory and Lysander followed, silently vowing to get the answers he needed from him before his own ignorance got him killed.

CHAPTER 49

roan

WHEN THE GROWLS grew vocal and the number of fleeing dragons increased, Eroan gave the order to deploy the first canister. Rolling clouds of gas filled the narrow tunnels, funneling upward, driven by the drafting air. After checking their masks filtered efficiently, he waved his pride on. Moments later, the gloom revealed its first trail of unconscious bodies. The pride went to work on the sleeping dragons, killing with cold efficiency. A slash to the throat, a blade in the heart.

Eroan led from the front, checking the faces of the fallen weren't any he recognized, and praying each time a body loomed out of the haze it wouldn't be Lysander's.

If the other prides were having the same level of success, they'd kill hundreds. The gas worked. The dragons were dying. This was the affirmation he'd needed.

Body after body after body they left bleeding in their

wake, and with each new kill, the taste of vengeance sweetened Eroan's tongue.

When the tunnel widened and split, Eroan took a canister and split the pride in two, sending the other team off, leaving Seraph with him. If she was at all fazed by their actions, her face behind the mask showed no signs of it. When the gas thinned, Eroan grasped the remaining canister in one hand, thumb poised on the release, and his sword in the other, and pushed deeper into the tower.

Splatters of cooling dragon-blood plastered his clothes against his skin. Seraph's clothes were dark with it too, evidence that this was right. The thirst for vengeance fueled him. For the hours spent chained by the wrists, for every cut he'd suffered, every lash of the whip, every indignity. His only regret was that Nye wouldn't be a part of this.

"Eroan?" Seraph whispered, gaze dropping to the canister.

"Soon," he replied, voice muffled by the mask.

The tunnels turned to stone, lit only by flame torches. Dragon roars came few and far between now. Eroan had been dragged through corridors just like this one, barely conscious, his back turned to shreds beneath Lysander's whiplashes. The memories tried to dig in and distract him from his purpose. Those memories had controlled him once, but not anymore.

"Eroan, now?"

"Soon, Seraph."

Deeper. He needed to get deeper inside, to find their beating bloody heart, to strike a blow they'd never recover from.

Rapid footfalls sounded from the staircase ahead. Eroan crouched. Seraph followed. The sight of the male with one red eye struck at Eroan's mind and lodged there. The male's snarl—the same one that had been pressed against Eroan's cheek—the dagger in his hand—the same that had left its permanent marks on Eroan's chest and thighs.

"Now!" Seraph yelled.

No. He would not kill this one as he lay sleeping.

Eroan dropped the canister, unopened, and lunged, startling the dragon back against the wall. Their blades locked. The beast of a male rolled his eyes upward, hissing behind his teeth until his gaze landed on Eroan's face.

Eroan tore his mask off. *"Remember me?"*

Red-Eye laughed his thick, liquid laughter. Madness clutched at Eroan's mind. Seraph was screaming at him to put the mask back on. He didn't listen. Didn't care. Couldn't think of anything outside of butchering this beast.

Pouring all of his trembling rage into his arms, he used his sword to force the male's little dagger back against his own throat. And Red-Eye still laughed.

Eroan pulled his sword away and clamped his fingers around Red-Eye's throat, needing to feel the dragon's life pass beneath his grip. Red-Eye tried to twist his blade around and slash at Eroan's neck. Eroan brought the dragon-teeth blade back up, slicing into the dragon's wrist, driving his arm back against the wall until the blade was so far embedded in the male's flesh it butted against bone.

Still the bastard laughed.

"Hello, pretty elf." His thick, wet tongue darted across his lower lip, a tongue Eroan could feel now, its cool trail branding him.

He stole the dragon's little blade from his twitching partly severed hand, keeping him pinned with the sword, and thrust that tiny blade into the male's gut. Red-Eye gurgled and spat, his smile slowly fading. *Die.* Eroan wasn't done. He jerked the little knife up, opening a line in the male's belly, exposing his blood-soaked insides to the air.

"Feels good, doesn't it..." Red-Eye wheezed, blood seeping from the corner of his mouth.

Eroan pulled the knife free and stabbed it once between the male's ribs, punching it as deep as the hilt allowed. Red-Eye jerked. Blood bubbled. Eroan stabbed again. And again. And again, until long after the bloody mass had stopped moving. But he still heard the laughter, still recalled the feel of his fat, wet tongue on his body. It wasn't enough. Red-Eye was dead but he needed *more*. He needed them all dead.

"Eroan...?" Seraph's voice found him through the madness. "He's dead... Eroan? Please... stop."

The sound of his own ragged breaths seemed like the only noise in the world. He tasted blood and licked it from his lips. Dragon-blood. And now Red-Eye was inside him. He recoiled, dropping the body, stumbling as he tried to extract himself from the male's slumped carcass, falling against the opposite wall. But it wasn't far enough away. Red-Eye's body still sneered at him, even in death. And now he couldn't escape the taste of him, the smell of him.

Blood.

So much blood. But not his. Not this time. He wasn't hurt, not on the outside.

Seraph was in front of him suddenly, blocking the view of the mess he'd made of Red-Eye. Dark blood crept around her boots toward Eroan. If it touched him, he'd drown in it.

"Eroan, look at me..."

He lifted Red-Eye's knife and felt old wounds sting, as

though the sight of the blade reopened them all. The cool drag of its edge had roamed his body, finding muscle to carve and skin to slice. He wanted to drop the knife but couldn't let go. His breaths came too fast, his body riddled with fear.

Seraph snatched the dagger from his hand and tossed it down the corridor. "Hey! Don't you disappear on me!" Her little hands bracketed his face. "We have a job to do. We're Assassins of the Order. We're here until it is done."

Born in Alumn's maelstrom, forged in the fires of Ifreann. Yes. He knew who he was. He spat out the taste of blood, and panting, reorganized his thoughts around Seraph's fierce orders. The mission was all. He could fall apart afterward. Not now. *Until it is done.* "I'm here..."

"Good." She handed him the blood-soaked mask. "I don't think it's any good."

He dropped it in the blood and pushed on, heading up the stairs.

"Eroan... stop... wait. The mask... Wait, let me get the gas canister..."

Her voice trailed off behind him. He didn't need the gas. He didn't need a damned mask hiding his face. The dragons needed to see who it was delivering them the deaths they deserved. He had his sword and enough vengeance burning through his veins to kill every last one in this wretched tower.

Up and up the stairs spiraled until they spat him out in a corridor, divided by more corridors leading off, and there, at the junction, stood the dragon king, his face startled, and his princely brother: Lysander.

CHAPTER 50

*L*ysander

THE ELF that appeared from the stairs ahead like a fucking omen was painted in dragon-blood. So much of it, in fact, Lysander didn't recognize him until he got to the eyes. Those vengeance filled eyes could only be Eroan's. The elation at seeing him quickly collapsed as Akiem lifted his sword and freed a warning growl. "You!" Akiem snarled.

Eroan started forward. "There is a trail of dead dragons behind me." He brought his sword up. "And I'll not rest until you're among them."

"Akiem, no..." Lysander grabbed his brother's arm. "There's no time!"

Eroan was still coming. Lysander shoved Akiem toward the nearest corridor branching off and blocked his brother's view of Eroan. "Go before the metals find us. This is not the time to settle scores..."

Eroan would try to kill Akiem, might even succeed. But Lysander needed answers from his brother. Akiem could not die here.

Akiem searched Lysander's face then threw the elf a parting growl before ducking out of sight into the corridor.

A blur of movement dashed after him. Lysander thrust out an arm and blocked Eroan, narrowly missed getting a sword in his gut when Eroan turned on him, eyes blazing with the killing lust.

Lysander grappled with Eroan's sword hand, angling the blade away. The grip was messy and when Eroan's first swung in, it caught Lysander across the jaw. He stumbled, losing his grip on Eroan's arm. "Damn it, elf, stop."

"Stop?" Eroan shoved, forcing distance between them. "He ordered my torture!" Eroan loomed, his face twisted by rage. "He burned my home, killing my people! Because of him, Xena died. I'll not *stop*, not even for you."

Lysander offered a placating hand, trying to tame the wildness. "Just... not yet. I need him."

A second elf emerged from the stairs, drawing Lysander's eye, and in that moment divided between two killers, Eroan bolted after Akiem.

Seraph pulled her face mask down. "You won't stop him."

"I have to try." He eyed the canister in her hand, the blood splatters on her face. They had not come to save him, he realized. Not this time. They'd come to kill. "Are you going to kill me, elf?"

Her brow pinched, and with that infamous elven confidence she swaggered up to him, chin up, but still a foot shorter than him. "Are you going to make me?"

He huffed a soft laugh. "It's good to see you too."

The hard line of her mouth softened. "If you need your brother alive, we'd better try to stop Eroan."

CHAPTER 51

roan

EROAN TRACKED the dragon by scent, following the trail back down, where the walls turned to thick rock and the torches became few and far between. As a chill tried to seep into his bones, he stopped and listened. A few pebbles skittered somewhere up ahead. Water dripped. Flame torches fought against the gloom, creating pockets of light in the widening tunnel. It felt like a trap.

He tightened his grip on the sword. Dried blood flaked off his hand. Some of it had itched his face, tightening his cheek and forehead. He planned to be the last thing Akiem saw in life and then perhaps he'd earn the title of dragon-killer for his skills as an assassin instead of just for surviving. *Kill the king.*

Eroan pushed on, easing around the torchlight, keeping to the shadows, his footfalls silent. Akiem was here. Lying in wait. Akiem wasn't the type to flee. The only reason he'd left that corridor was to lure Eroan into the dark.

Something rumbled behind the walls, the sound so deep it sounded like it came from the earth itself. Eroan pushed on. The tunnel was still too small for Akiem to shift into.

The king lunged from the shadows to Eroan's left. Eroan thrust his dragonblade upward, blocking Akiem's swing, swords ringing. The force of the dragon's attack drove Eroan back, almost knocking him off his feet. He countered, planting his feet to steady his stance, and ducked to the side as Akiem swung again. His left fist crunched against Akiem's already bruised jaw, staggering the king back and opening an opportunity to drive the blade through his chest.

Eroan brought the sword in. Akiem's hand flashed. Dust burst in Eroan's face, eyes suddenly blurred and hot. Blinded, he brought his sword up as a barrier. Akiem's blade clashed against his, the force too much to bear. Eroan lost his footing, stumbled back, and went down hard.

"The infamous Eroan Ilanea." Akiem's voice rattled around the tunnel, echoing far into the darkness. "It all started the moment you showed up, planting ideas in my brother's head. Had I ordered your death instead of your torture, we would not be here now."

Eroan twisted, desperately blinking grit from his eyes. The tunnel was a blur of dancing torchlight and shadows. He got to his knees, aware Akiem's blade could sink into his back or be drawn across his throat at any time. If he could just see... the dragon was wounded or weakened, there would not be another chance to kill him. It had to be now.

Eroan swallowed, tasting blood and dirt. A dark figure filled his vision. His focus cleared. Akiem's details sharpened. Blood stained his gaping shirt and smeared his cold face. And he waited, holding back instead of finishing Eroan.

Eroan pushed himself back onto unsteady feet and tried to slow is panting.

"How did you do it?" Akiem asked, his sneer turning sharp. "How did you get inside my brother's head?"

Eroan wiped at his eyes. "I had nothing to do with—"

Akiem struck, as fast as a snake-bite.. Eroan ducked, shoved Akiem behind him and shoved the blunt end of the sword handle deep into the male's lower back. The king's pained grunt told him he'd landed somewhere wounded or vital.

Akiem turned, teeth bared, but now he bent a little, leaning into his pain. "I looked for the amethyst stone for weeks. You stole it, didn't you?"

"What happened up there?" Eroan nodded toward a ceiling he couldn't see in the dark. "Did Dokul finally claim your throne?" Anger burned in Akiem's brightening eyes, just as Eroan knew it would. "Without Elisandra's gem, you were too weak to stay king. Is that what you're all running from?"

The growl rising from Akiem's human form rumbled so deeply Eroan felt the air tremble.

"I knew it had power enough to shore up Elisandra's reign. There had to be a reason you all followed her, a reason Dokul knelt to her."

Akiem's mouth twitched around a shallow, predatory smile. "It wasn't power. It was what the gem contained. And now it's free... you helped do that, Eroan Ilanea. How does it feel to know you freed the great gold?"

Eroan narrowed his eyes, the words too impossible to be true. "Lies."

Akiem charged, bringing his sword up to clash with Eroan's, driving Eroan back. The force of the dragon's attacks shuddered through Eroan's bones, swords chiming over and over. Metal sang. Akiem fought differently than Lysander. Lighter, faster, he moved and slashed as fast and as ruthless as any assassin.

Only one of them would walk away from this. Eroan's mind focused, thoughts thinning to a single point. The dragon king would die here. That was his fate.

Akiem's swing went wide, skipping off the tip of Eroan's blade. He tried to dart away but wasn't fast enough. Eroan's blade sliced across Akiem's back, ripping a cry from Akiem's lips, dropping him to his knees.

"Eroan!" Lysander's shout tugged at Eroan's focus but he would not be stopped.

Eroan pressed the dragonblade's tip to the nape of Akiem's neck. One swing, and the sword would sever his spine. No dragon could shift out of that. This was right. He was *made* for this. *Alumn, lend me the strength to see this through.* "You were dead the moment you ordered me tortured." He lifted the blade, ready for the final downward swing.

"Don't." Lysander ordered. The word spoken so close beside Eroan's ear it was almost intimate. A cool, metal hardness dug into Eroan's lower back. Lysander wouldn't...?

Eroan held his sword aloft. If Lysander did push his blade home, it wouldn't be enough to save his brother. Akiem would still die here.

"Don't make me hurt you." Lysander whispered this time. The words fluttered against Eroan's neck, stirring desire among his thirst for vengeance. "You've killed enough dragons today." The words stroked over Eroan's jaw like Lysander's fingers had when they'd spent the night beneath the stars.

"It'll never be enough." Eroan brought the sword down.

CHAPTER 52

*L*ysander

THE SWORD SWUNG DOWNWARD. Lysander had a single moment in which to decide who to save. He needed Akiem's answers, but he needed Eroan more, like he needed to breathe. The blade sailed downward, and Lysander let it happen.

But Akiem moved too, faster than seemed possible. He dodged at the last second, throwing Eroan off-balance and in that second between letting one live and the other die, Akiem twisted, fell back, thrust his sword up...

He saw it happen, saw it play out in his head and knew Akiem's strike would be fatal. The blade would plunge into Eroan and that couldn't happen.

He shoved Eroan aside. An easy thing to do with the elf off-balanced. But in doing so, Akiem's blade found another target.

The hard tip punched in below Lysander's last right rib, and thrust upward, through something vital that stole the breath right out of his body. The cold blade went on and snicked that warm spot beside his heart—the guarded, fragile part of him he tapped into to heal.

It didn't hurt.

Looking down to see a sword sticking from his chest, he figured it *should* hurt. The fact it didn't was probably bad.

He dropped his rusted blade and wrapped a shaking hand around Akiem's sword handle. Maybe if he could just pull it out...that would make everything better? The sword blurred and so did Akiem's pale, shock-ridden face. Lysander should have been breathing somewhere in all of this, but his body didn't seem to know how. He wobbled backward, thoughts suddenly hard to hold on to.

"Take it out!" Seraph screeched.

He didn't like the fear in her voice.

"He'll bleed to death in minutes..." Eroan, always the voice of reason.

The sword moved, slipping free easier than it went in, with a messy wet gasp of its own. Akiem was all Lysander could see suddenly. His dark eyes shone too brightly, but those couldn't be tears. Not for Lysander.

"Shift, brother," Akiem urged, or was he pleading? It was difficult to know with the ringing in Lysander's ears.

Shift. Right. That might help. The magic would put the wound somewhere else. But Lysander knew wounds. He'd carried enough of them. This one was different. The upward thrust had struck a part of him that couldn't be changed and shifted, the constant at his center, where the magic lived, where his power was rooted, the part that made him dragon.

A roar shattered the air, sounding close by. One Lysander knew well. Dokul. More stone and rocks fell from the ceiling, the weight of the noise upsetting the tower foundations. The whole place was fracturing, coming undone around him. Maybe he could just rest his eyes a moment while that happened.

Akiem's steely fingers dug into Lysander's shoulder. But when he opened his eyes, it wasn't Akiem looking back at him, but Eroan, face bloody, eyes cold and mouth grim. Lysander had an urge to wipe the blood off Eroan's cheek, to see the male beneath all of the mistakes between them. "I'm sorry...." He tasted blood in his mouth, felt it, warm and metallic on his tongue.

Eroan's sculpted face began to break. "Don't be sorry. Shift."

Shift... like it was so easy a thing. Sleep first. Shift later.

"I didn't save your dragon ass a world away so you can die in this hole now."

Fingers dug in both his shoulders and shook, rattling the broken thoughts around his head.

"Shift and fight, you need to fight."

"...tired... of fighting..." He could die here, he realized. But here smelled like freedom and he couldn't think of anywhere else he'd prefer to enter the forever sleep. Only now it was cold and it hadn't been moments before. Some distant voice told him the cold was a very bad thing.

Eroan's cheek on his felt warm and soft. "Don't let them beat you. Live, Lysander. Live, for me. Shift now... Alumn, please let him *live*."

The stars were nice tonight, the forest quiet. He could lay in this elf's arms forever. He didn't have to fight anymore. He closed his eyes.

CHAPTER 53

roan

HE WASN'T DYING. Eroan wouldn't allow it. There had to be a way to force him to shift before it was too late.

More dragon roars shook the tower. Chunks of ceiling thumped to the ground. They didn't have long before the entire place came down. Eroan pulled Lysander's limp body close, only to see Seraph's stricken face and behind her, the beast who had done this. "Make him shift," he demanded.

Akiem's wracked face gave his answer.

Seraph was on the king suddenly, her small dragon-teeth blade at his throat. "You make him shift or you're dying alongside him!"

"Shifting takes energy," Akiem said. "It's not something easily done when conscious. Unconscious, it's impossible. He's..."

"Dying? Say it, because that's what's happening to your

brother, you sack of horse shit." Seraph's blade nicked the king's neck. "I should kill you now."

"I didn't want this! If he hadn't saved *you*—" He glared at Eroan. "It's your fault! Why does he keep saving you? Why won't you die like elves should?!"

A huge section of ceiling collapsed, thundering to the ground to Eroan's right, tossing up grit and dust. Behind it he heard the rumbling of a dragon's throaty growl. Too late, they had to move now.

Eroan heaved Lysander over his shoulders, bearing his limp, unwieldy weight, and followed Seraph's retreat over fallen stone, through narrow gulleys, and deeper into the tunnel network.

Akiem darted ahead. "This way..."

"Why should we trust you?" Seraph demanded.

"You shouldn't. But I no more want to be here than you do."

He led them out of the maze into too-bright daylight and a blue sky dotted with warring dragons. Globules of flame simmered on the ash-strewn ground. Eroan followed Akiem until he caught sight of his own people fleeing toward the tree line. "Go with them," he told Seraph.

She didn't answer and he didn't bother telling her again. Akiem led them into the tree cover just as two world-shattering roars filled the air and ground, sinking into Eroan's bones. He set Lysander down, cradled by tree roots, and tried not to linger on how white Lysander's skin was and how blue his lips were in daylight. *He's dying.*

Two dragons tore from within the tower walls, taking flight as rock and stone collapsed around them. Gold and Bronze. They beat enormous shimmering wings, rising higher, dwarfing every other dragon in the sky.

"Alumn save us..." Eroan breathed. Akiem had been right. The gold lived.

The metals fixed their sights on the string of elves and humans making their way back into the trees and dove toward them.

"They've seen them," Eroan whispered. The Order elves would know to go to ground to protect Cheen, but would the humans remember?

"Your village is close," Akiem said, tone unreadable. He stood safely within tree cover but off to the side, as still and unreadable as rock.

"What of it?" Seraph snapped.

Akiem's expression shadowed. He glanced at Lysander and those shadows deepened. He breathed in, something decided, then left the tree cover, walking out onto the exposed barrenlands. The shift took away the man, tearing the body apart and remaking him into the unmistakable black-winged monster. In crisp daylight, his black scales rippled with a deep purple. He spread his wings and beat into the air, heading straight for the two metals. Akiem was no small dragon, but the two metals made him seem no larger than a kit, and when he reared up in front of their path, unleashing a wall of flame on them, they knocked him aside as though he were no more to them than a fly.

"It's not enough." Eroan closed his eyes, unable to watch the bronze tear into Akiem, but that didn't stop the screeches from piercing his ears. "I have to stop the prides returning to Cheen ..." He looked at Lysander. "I have to leave him."

Seraph bit into her lip and nodded. "I'll stay. He won't go alone into Alumn's garden."

Eroan knelt at Lysander's side. He still breathed, his

chest above the terrible wound still rose and fell, but it wouldn't be long now. All the things he'd wanted to say and all the moments he'd hoped they'd one day get together... All of that was gone now.

Eroan clasped Lysander's face in both hands and pressed his forehead to his. "Rest now, brave prince. The battle is over for you. May Alumn's light guide you home."

CHAPTER 54

$\mathscr{L}$ysander

LIGHT. No, not light. Silver. He wasn't sure how he knew the difference, both shone so brightly it hurt his eyes, but the light was definitely silvery, like sun on water or snow. He smelled dragon and metal, and blood, and his own spilled insides. *Not good.* The light pulsed a warm and forgiving embrace, but it wasn't meant for him. Not yet, anyway. Two solid black eyes pierced the light, like tunnels leading into the dark. Then the beast spread its wings and the light became too much, it burned and boiled his skin from his bones, made him want to tear himself apart to stop the pain. It scorched his very soul, to the heart of him where Akiem's sword had found its mark. Until he realized this wasn't pain, not like physical pain. It was the same raw power he used to shift, the same power he'd sometimes molded to do his bidding. And gods he needed it. Grabbing a hold of that power, he let it in, let it roll through him and take him over until he filled his lungs with air and freed a roar.

Blinking dragon-eyes open, into daylight, he searched for the silver dragon, but she was gone, if she'd even been real to begin with. The barrenlands smoked. Where the tower should be, a smoking pile of rubble and clouds of dust remained. And above, countless dark wings stroked blue skies.

This wasn't death, it was real. And it was now.

Akiem was in the skies, he realized. Shredded wings rapidly beating to keep himself aloft. Dokul slashed and bit. One well-aimed strike would snap Akiem's neck. Lysander stretched one wing, his good wing, then tried the other, only to wince and clamp it closed again as twisted bones ground together. He could do nothing for Akiem, and given how his brother had almost killed him, he didn't linger on caring.

The gold—Carline—had broken off and headed straight for the trees, single-minded focus in her eyes. Dokul swept Akiem aside and dove in too.

Lysander glanced at the little elf standing by his fore-leg, gawking up at him, her eyes wide with awe. Seraph. She was safe here. He snorted, blasting her back, and tore from the tree cover, galloping over rough ground toward the fleeing line of humans and elves. There were few amethyst left and too many bronze. This battle was over, but not before he stopped Dokul.

He spread his one good wing between the fleeing people and the dragons diving for him, making himself bigger, shielding their retreat. Hunkered low, hiding how he churned fire low in his throat, he watched the enormous world-ending beasts soar ever-closer. The wound in his chest throbbed and beat out its protest. By rights he shouldn't even be alive, but as dragon, he'd dealt with far worse pains. And likely would again soon.

The humans and elves squawked their warnings behind him. Some distant part of him registered how they could attack him from behind. His crown was exposed. But if they killed him, they'd all die. Hopefully they saw that.

He swung toward Carline's arrow-like descent, reared up on his hind legs, stretched his wing, and freed the savage, thirsty fire, blasting a boiling wave of flame skyward.

Carline pulled up, her golden wings beating the air, whipping up storms of fire, ash, and dust. Old, shrewd eyes assessed him. The same eyes had always appraised him through the years. Watching, teaching, guarding. She knew him, even now, and Akiem was wrong, that look in her eyes didn't mean him harm.

Lysander bared his teeth and bubbled a warning growl, flaring his crown. *These people are mine.*

He was counting on the fact he knew her, and knew she wouldn't fight him, despite being twice his size and more than capable of knocking him aside to devastate the fleeing elves.

Carline hovered, considering, then Dokul flew in like a damned landslide, slamming into Lysander's chest, plowing him back through a hundred feet of snapping trees and digging him into the ground.

Dirt and branches rained over them.

Dokul's teeth clamped around Lysander's foreleg and shook, yanking the limb from side to side. Searing pain tried to force Lysander to his belly, but he knew pain, knew how to manage it, use it. Pain was not his master. He snapped at Dokul, clapping his teeth together inches from the male's flared snout. Then Akiem's wall of black scales towered behind Dokul, his massive jaws clamped around the back of Dokul's neck, below the crown. Dokul threw his head back, trying to protect that vulnerable spot, exposing his throat. Lysander lunged and sank his teeth into sinew and scale. Dokul's hot blood flowed over his tongue. He bit harder. Bone and muscle crunched. *Die.* He pulled, trying to rip out the beast's throat. But whatever grace Lysander had with Carline, he'd reached its limit.

Claws raked at Lysander's back, snagging on his broken wing, pouring a flash of mind-numbing agony through his thoughts. Lysander roared his hurt, releasing Dokul.

The bronze chief rolled back, crushing Akiem beneath his bulk, but he did not retreat. Lysander stared at the two ancient metals. An impossible fight. He would not win. But that had never stopped him before.

roan

HE HAD NEVER EXPECTED to see green scales again, and never expected to see Lysander as dragon throw himself in front of the incoming wave of metal monsters.

"Go, go, go!" Eroan ordered, running with his pride through the trees. A sudden blast behind him uprooted his feet and threw him to the ground, partially burying him in snapped branches and dirt. He hauled himself out of the debris to the sight and sounds of Dokul and Lysander locked in battle on the ground.

He scanned the flattened impact site. By Alumn's luck, none of his pride had been caught in the collision. Most had already fled into the trees and vanished, but several of the Order hung back, including Trey, waiting for Eroan's order.

Eroan's place was among his people. He should turn

and flee into the trees. But Lysander continued fighting, even now, outnumbered and outmatched.

Eroan palmed the sword. "I'm not leaving him!" he shouted over the thunderous roars. "Go!" he told the elves. "This is not your fight."

The assassins, each clasping their own blades, glanced among themselves. Eroan knew them like he knew all of the Order. They were each as fierce and driven as the blades in their hands. Their place was with the Order, with their people. Not with him.

"I said go!" he snapped. There was no use in all of them getting banished for his loyalty to a dragon.

They melted into the shadows.

As soon as he was sure they were gone, Eroan stared at the scene unfolding before him. Akiem had joined the brawl, tearing into Dokul from behind while Lysander attacked from the front, still partially pinned on his back in the dirt. The sight of the gold towered over all three, its shimmering wings spread as it observed the chaos. Its golden scales glowed like the sun.

Eroan snuck closer, keeping to the tree line to stay hidden. The chances of him helping were slim but at least if he was here, he'd do what he was able to. He'd told Lysander he'd never give up on him. He had no intention of breaking that vow.

Movement from across the crater in the earth caught Eroan's eye. Seraph waved, lifted the last gas canister, grinned, and pointed at the savage battle.

She never ceased to surprise him.

They had one last shot.

He nodded and held up five fingers.

The dragons battled on. The gold lunged in to take a

bite out of Lysander's back, then it clawed at Dokul, locked in battle with both. There seemed to be no reason behind who attacked who. The ground shook with their battle. The air trembled.

Eroan dropped a finger. Four.

Seraph had to throw it right.

Three.

She couldn't miss.

Two.

Dokul looked up. Bronze eyes narrowed on Eroan, their black snake-like slits thinning like two swords encased in amber.

One.

Seraph flicked open the canister, threw back her arm, and sent it in a huge arc, spewing gas among the dragons. The big metals breathed in clouds of the noxious air and hacked lungfulls of gas back up.

Eroan cupped his hands around his mouth and yelled, "Lysander, shift!"

The emerald dragon whipped his head around, startled eyes fixing on Eroan, then Seraph. The gas-cloud threatened to engulf him, and those dragon-eyes widened farther, knowing the gas would render him unconscious. He'd need to trust Eroan to save him...

Lysander's outline blurred and collapsed, rolling into itself, packing the enormous beast away—appearing to vanish beneath the gold and bronze. A lazy breeze wafted the gas over those metals, clouding Eroan's view. But he heard their angered snorting, saw glimpses of scale, then the breeze whisked the gas away, leaving the gold and bronze dumbly staggered over their own feet. Not unconscious, but enough for Eroan to venture closer.

Eroan waved Seraph into the crater Lysander's earlier impact had caused. Akiem's black-scaled body lay motionless farther into the barrenlands. Not dead, Eroan saw how the beast's eyes rolled. Good. Akiem would die one day, beneath Eroan's blade, but not today, it seemed.

Lysander lay in the dirt, out cold. Eroan first searched for the terrible chest wound he'd been sure would kill him, finding it stuck closed and on its way to healing. "Help me with him." Seraph gripped Lysander and helped prop him between them. Stumbling over rock and upturned earth, they made it into the trees. Dragoncalls and snarls faded behind them.

They'd done it.

They'd gotten him out. Eroan had no idea what would happen from here, but he knew he'd keep Lysander safe.

An assassin blocked the path ahead.

Eroan lifted his gaze to Trey's stoic face. *No...* He'd almost made it.

Then the others were there, stepping out of the shadows, blades gleaming in the dappled light.

Eroan couldn't fight them all, and he couldn't ask Seraph to put her life on the line for him or Lysander. But he'd give his own life, he realized. Even if his chances of surviving his Order assassins were slim.

"I..." he began, but no words could make this right. Assassins of the Order did not save dragons.

He flicked his gaze over each of them, seeing so much of himself in their formidable line. They were not wrong to stop him. But that didn't make them right either.

Seraph looked to Eroan for a way out, but there was none.

Then, wordlessly, Trey stepped aside, opening the path ahead. The elven pride circled around, flanking Eroan and

Seraph in a protective circle. A knot formed in Eroan's throat, stealing words of gratitude.

He adjusted Lysander's weight between him and Seraph and continued on. Together with the Order assassins, they carried Lysander to safety.

roan

EROAN STOOD at the end of the elders' long table. Half the village had packed into the hall. Those who couldn't fit inside crowded around the doors outside. The humans were here, too. Chloe, Ben, and others.

The weight of the elven gazes landed on him like lead. He had devoted his entire life to keeping them safe. Every breath, he'd used to fight for them. But did any of that matter now he'd brought the dragon prince home?

Anye was seated at the center of the elders. She had mastered her emotions, but he knew what was coming.

Nye was here too.

The only person who wasn't, was Seraph, and only because he'd ordered her to stay with Lysander and stop anyone who tried to take him.

He lifted his chin. They'd given him time to wash off the blood and change his clothes. The killing lust stilled raced through him, the leather and lemon smell of Lysander still lingered about him. His body buzzed, his thoughts churned. This would not go well.

"Eroan Ilanea, what do you have to say in your defense?"

He wet his lips. "That dragon has done more for the people of this village than any of you." And there were the gasps. He welcomed them. What did he have to lose? "Exile me, if you want, but you'll have to remove me yourselves. I will not go quietly. I've done nothing wrong and neither has Lysander."

"He's dragon," Anye said, like that accounted for all the sins of dragons everywhere.

"Yes, he is. The tower assault was a success. We didn't lose a single life. Had Lysander not delayed the gold and bronze, we'd be adding more ribbons to Alumn's tree. He wasn't going to win that fight, but he protected our prides from the dragons anyway. Every single one of us owes him their thanks, not prejudice and hatred." He made sure they all heard. If they were going to turf him out, then he'd leave them with the hard truth.

Shocked gasps and mutterings grated on Eroan's thoughts. He'd heard enough. This council was a farce. His people were hypocrites. "I told the humans of how elves are an honorable people, we are good people. Our ancestors may have lost us our compassion in the wars, but we kept our souls. I am proud to protect every life deserving of that protection, not just elven lives, but humans too, and any who deserve it. It is my duty as an Assassin of the Order to protect those who cannot protect themselves, including Lysander. Don't make me a liar."

"You are a liar." Nye's voice cut through the chitter. "You lied about how you found that tunnel. You lied about where you were the night before. The dragon prince is more to you than just another soul who needs saving. He's your lover."

Someone shouted a filthy insult. Someone else barked in Eroan's defense. The noise became too much to separate any one voice. Eroan stilled, listened to his heart thumping and let the collective crackle of anger wash over him.

Nye was right. "I lied," he raised his voice, "because at every turn, elves have refused to believe a dragon can do good. I lied because you wouldn't have allowed the mission had you known where the information came from. The fact remains, Lysander told me how to get inside the tower, and together, we won."

"You deceived the council," Anye replied, her quiet calm as sharp as Nye's accusations.

He was done holding his words back. Eroan slammed both hands against the table. "We killed fifteen hundred dragons inside that tower! With its collapse, the number is likely much higher. We struck a blow to the dragons like nothing they've seen since this war began! The amethyst have scattered. As of today, the skies are empty of dragons. We won! All because of Lysander."

Anye glared. "And now the gold has returned."

He couldn't argue that either. Alumn knew he had made mistakes, but Lysander wasn't one of them. "I'm a long way from innocent, I understand that and I'm not denying it, but I'm also not asking for forgiveness. Lysander is not your enemy. If we are as honorable as we proclaim to be, we owe him a place among us."

"You speak of the impossible," The elder to Anye's left said. "Eroan Ilanea, you will gather your belongings and leave Cheen at sunset."

"No." He straightened and eyed each of the elders in turn. "I will not."

Anye's brows pinched. "You'll leave or I'll order the assassins remove you."

"I'm not leaving. I secured us the greatest victory in living memory. You need me to win this war."

"Assassins of the Order," Anye rose to her feet, "remove Eroan from this hall."

Eroan waited for the scrape of chairs, for the hands to grip his arms and drag him away, but a new quiet had settled. Nobody moved.

"Assassins, you will follow my orders until a new sassa is chosen!"

Silence.

Eroan's heart swelled, hope was a fragile, fluttering thing in his chest. His Order, his blade brothers and sisters, had not abandoned him.

A chair scraped. "I was there yesterday," Trey said. "I saw the dragon block the metals. He stood alone, the chances of his survival slim. He was prepared to die there, for us, *for elves*." Trey paused and let that reality soak into them all. "There is no other explanation for what he did. He gained nothing from that fight. But we did. We survived. If Eroan is to be exiled, then I'm leaving with him."

Eroan opened his mouth to tell Trey to sit and not risk his future, when another voice spoke up. "If Eroan goes, so do I." Eroan knew the speaker, an older female, quiet but reliable. The elf who had killed the dragon Nye and him had sheltered inside. Another Order assassin he respected. She nodded at his glance.

Another, "We owe the dragon a safe place to heal, at least. This could be an opportunity—"

Pride and relief constricted Eroan's throat.

"Assassins of the Order have earned the right to speak for one of our own," came another voice. "Eroan does not deserve to be exiled. The tower raid was a success." Another, "I trust Eroan..." Another, "Eroan wouldn't allow anything bad to stay among us." More, "Curan said Eroan should lead..."

Anye's face fell with every protest. She could not banish her entire Order. More and more voices joined the others. Eroan bit into his bottom lip and fought to keep a knot climbing his throat.

She lifted her hands and silenced the hall. "Very well," Anye sighed. "I have always respected the way of the Order. You are our guardians. We owe you our lives and I have no wish to deny your voices. Eroan..."

He straightened.

"Your exile is withdrawn."

Honor and pride warmed him through. *This* was change. This was progress. "And Lysander?"

Her wise eyes sharpened with threat. "The dragon is your responsibility. His life is in your hands, and yours in his. If he harms us, in any way, there will be worse consequences than exile."

CHAPTER 57

*L*ysander

THERE WAS an elf in a chair in a room made of wood. Lysander remembered being in this room before, remembered Eroan throwing a knife at his head, and remembered a whole lot more right after that. Eroan had been angry then, furious even. Now he looked smug, sprawled in that chair with a tempting smile pulling his mouth sideways.

Lysander shifted beneath the covers. Someone had tucked him in so tightly, he'd woken wondering if he was once again in chains. Plucking an arm free, he loosened the sheets and realized he'd been stripped to his undergarments. Had that been Eroan's doing? He couldn't imagine any other elf would want to get so close. Which meant Eroan had undressed him and he'd slept through it. What a crime that was. "There are easier ways to get me in your bed."

Eroan's smile ticked sideways.

Breathing in, Lysander shamelessly let the smell of pine and cut wood smooth out the creases in his thoughts. Was this what being safe felt like? He rubbed at his itchy eyes. "What was in that gas?"

"Human invention. It knocks out jeweled. Didn't work as well on the great metals though."

He tried to remember but all it brought back was a sensation of fury and pain. He winced and twisted onto his side, looking back at Eroan's curious expression. "You saved me again, huh?"

One of Eroan's eyebrows jumped. "How did you come back from certain death?"

He tried to think on that moment, but a jagged, silvery stab threatened to slice his skull open. Those memories weren't ready to be examined. "Ask me again when I can think right. I save you, you save me... We must be even now?"

Eroan stood, and Lysander absorbed the seductive sight of him approaching. The sway of his narrow hips, the strength in those bare forearms—honed to swing blades— sleeves rolled up to just below his biceps. His typical leathers were gone, replaced with simple cotton trousers and a V-neck loose shirt. The plain clothes did nothing to soften his lethality. He still looked like he was either about to stab Lysander or kiss him. In Lysander's weary state, he'd take either.

"I've lost count." Eroan stopped by the bed, forcing Lysander to look up the tall length of him. A long blond braid hung over one shoulder, all neatly controlled. Lysander wanted to pull the band free and plunge his hands into that hair, and then maybe fall into a kiss that would likely get them both thrown out of this village.

Eroan's gaze flicked down to where the little dragon token rested on its string in the hollow of Lysander's throat. Lysander circled a hand around the gift. By diamonds, the things he'd said and done to Eroan.

Eroan's eyebrow flicked higher. He folded his arms across his chest and waited.

"About... before," Lysander began. "I... My behavior... the gem... I'm dragon—"

Eroan lunged, caught Lysander's wrists, pinning them loosely to the pillow either side of Lysander's head, and leaned in so close Lysander could see how Eroan's blue eyes sparkled, reminding him of the endless ocean surface. "Did you know the stone was linked to the gold?" Eroan demanded in his hard, cold, assassin voice.

And just like that, Lysander was at the mercy of a dragon-killer. Maybe he *was* about to be stabbed? "No. I was told it could heal my wing. Apparently, being emerald means my own kin keep me in the dark. You probably know as much about that amethyst stone as I do." He swallowed hard and studied Eroan's quirked mouth. Its gentle, bow-like curve, so quick to harden or soften. He wanted to reach out and trace its line with a fingertip and then, done with that, he'd replace his fingertip with the tip of his tongue and knew Eroan would open for him. Sparks of lust hardened his cock, and now that *that* part of him was awake, he couldn't ignore those thoughts and where they led him. Making his lashes heavy, he swept his tongue over his top lip, deliberately reminding Eroan exactly what he could do, and had done, with his tongue.

Eroan's sensual eyes grew sly. He switched his grip to hold Lysander's wrists with just one hand, then reached into a pocket and plucked out the firestarter, dangling it between them.

He must have left it at the fallen oak. "Keep it," Lysander said. "Call it a gift."

"You have much to make up for, *dragon*." Eroan tucked the firestarter away again. Both having a part of each other to carry with them seemed right.

"I have some ideas on how to make you pay..." The sly purr behind Eroan's words had Lysander's heart jumping. He lost control of his breathing and tried to lift his head to nip at Eroan's mouth. Eroan pulled back, narrowing his eyes as though he'd focused on his next kill.

Lysander swallowed, powerfully aroused. "Are your assassins going to burst in here and try to kill me?"

Eroan bowed his head. "Door's locked." He ran his tongue over Lysander's bottom lip. The soft wetness demanded to be answered, but Lysander held still. Eroan sucked. Drawing Lysander's lip between his teeth, and looking up, he peered through his lashes. "Anyone who wants to hurt you," he whispered, "has to go through me."

Lysander's breath caught, not from lust, but from the sudden, desperate feeling of holding on and never wanting to let go. This wild, impossible elf was looking at him as though he were his whole world. He'd never had that before, never felt *this* overwhelming sense of belonging. With anyone.

"I'm a bastard."

"Yes, you are."

And still Eroan looked at him like he was his whole world. After everything he'd done, after everything he *was*, this elf wouldn't quit on him. Ever.

All the iron armor he'd built around him cracked and fell away, freeing too much hurt for Lysander to do anything but pull his arms free of Eroan's grip and throw them around

Eroan, clutching him close, holding him tight, so damn afraid of how he'd almost lost the one good thing in his entire world. Eroan softened in his arms, accepting him like none other ever had. *"Why do you keep saving me?"* he whispered. Through all of this, Eroan hadn't answered that one simple question. Why save his enemy, why save a creature he was created to kill and keep on saving him, time and time again?

Eroan's hand tightened against his back, the touch spreading, like a warm claiming. "Because..." he said, "in the one place I expected to die, you gave me a reason to live."

"What reason?"

"You."

Eroan... cared? Not for getting ahead, not for some way of using him against the rest of the dragonkin, he just cared because he *liked* Lysander? Just a simple thing, and yet it broke Lysander's heart wide open. He pulled tighter, wracked with tremors. He hadn't felt this before and was afraid to let it go. Nobody had cared for him. From his first breath, he'd been alone. He'd fought for every second, tried to climb out of the dark, and he hadn't always won. He was dragon and he did not deserve someone like Eroan.

He should let Eroan go but couldn't. Not yet, maybe never. Besides, Eroan was too stubborn to leave. "You're the light in my dark." In the frantic need to be loved, he wasn't sure if he'd spoken aloud and found he didn't care if he had.

"You're safe..." Eroan whispered, holding him like he had when they'd both hidden in the ground.

Safe.

"What is this thing between us?"

Eroan had never answered. He didn't expect him to now.

Eroan shifted on the bed, still trapped in Lysander's arms but maneuvering so he could comfortably hold Lysander against his chest. Eroan's embrace felt more like home than any place he'd ever known. But he needed the answer from him. If this thing between them was nothing, he had to know now, before he fell too far.

Eroan's chin rubbed his head and when he spoke, his voice rumbled through Lysander. "It is everything."

He crushed Eroan's shirt in his fists, afraid to let go. He wanted so badly to believe him, wanted to be free to feel safe but this world would not tolerate what they shared.

He wasn't safe, not while Dokul was alive and hunting him, while Carline was restored as gold. And he doubted Eroan's people had suddenly warmed to the idea of having an amethyst among them. But he could pretend while wrapped in Eroan's arms, pretend this was how things would be from now on. It would never last, but he could dream, couldn't he? Dream of Eroan's light... light like the kind that had come to him in the darkest place, in a world of ice at the edge of death, when he'd fallen and finally hit the ground. That light harbored deep, black eyes, full of cold, and sharp, silver wings. And its name. He had heard its name moments before the silver dragon had sent him back to the living to change the world.

She was called Alumn.

ye

A PAIR of yellow eyes glowed among the trees. Nye freed his daggers from his thigh sheaths and waited for the creature to slink closer. Her satin-like, hairless skin shimmered from head to toe. Dark lines accentuated dark eyes. Tarnished metal rings hung from her ears and wrists, and when she licked her lips, the campfire light caught the metal stud through her tongue. As she drew closer, the same firelight licked through her semi-transparent chainmail garments, stroking over her lean limbs and warming her swollen belly.

"Hello again, little elf." She stroked her pregnant bump. "I had wondered if you'd make good on our deal or if I'd need to root you out among your little wooden huts. A mother has many mouths to feed and a village of elves will fill many bellies."

The beasts in *her* belly would hatch to be elf killers. He

should kill her and her developing eggs now before they had a chance to end any more elven lives but her cold, sly eyes watched him too closely. She'd see any attack coming before he could land it.

He hated this, that it had come to this, but clearly Eroan needed to be dealt with, cut out of the Order like a tumor before the cancer spread. Eroan *and* the dragon prince. He'd have preferred to dispatch the dragon prince himself, but this bronze—Mirann, she'd told him her name —had taken that choice as soon as she'd toyed with him during the retreat from the tower.

"There has been a change," he said. Her eyes flared and a sharp dart of panic tried to weaken him. "They're not being exiled."

She stalked closer, seeming to grow taller in the fire-light, her golden-metal dress alight with a fiery glow. "You promised me—"

He held out a hand, making her slow. "But... I can still get them to you. I just need..." He wet his lips. "A little more time, that's all... just a little more time. Nobody needs to die. This can still happen."

Mirann hesitated, and instead of closing the last few strides between him, she circled around the campfire, facing the flames. Embers drifted high. She extended her hand, disturbing the upward flowing embers. "You elves do realize the kind of dragon you harbor among you? He appears harmless, but his smiles are masks and his bite sharp. Lysander is as vicious as any in his hideous amethyst brood and just as cunning. Emerald dragons are feared among the dragonkin for a reason. He *will* turn on you. It is in his nature."

He believed every word. "I'll see to it he's cast out." Someone had to protect Cheen from Lysander, and from this bronze monster who clearly had the village in her sights. "Just... a little more time?" he asked again. It would be simple enough to turn the elves against Lysander. Eroan would be more difficult—he was still on the war council, still the Order leader—even after he'd attacked Nye—but not for much longer.

She looked down at her belly. "Time? I have a little time, elf. And I have Akiem to keep my father occupied, at least until he grows bored of him. Unfortunately for the amethyst prince, he is not Lysander." Her gaze soured. She captured an ember, turned toward Nye and set the glowing bit of dust free. It drifted between them, luring Nye into the spell of her beautiful glowing eyes. "But do not push your luck. If you fail, I'll come get my broodmate myself." Her teeth flashed behind a reptilian smile. "And you do not want that, little elf. Unless you want your precious ribbon-tree to burn?"

She knew of Alumn's sacred tree? Then she truly did know where Cheen was. He failed to hide his alarm, and with a wicked laugh she turned on her heel and strode back into the shadows.

Nye stared into the darkness long after she'd gone. Perhaps he shouldn't have tried to go after Eroan during the assault on the tower. If he hadn't, she wouldn't have seen him, but she would have trapped another elf, someone she could terrify into doing her bidding. At least, like this, he would keep Cheen safe. This *Mirann* desperately wanted Lysander and he would give him to her.

All he had to do was hand over the dragon. And where the dragon went, so did Eroan.

Nye loved Eroan. Always had. Always would. Loved him enough to end his torment under Lysander's control.

The future was all on Nye, and by Alumn, he would not fail like Eroan had.

He lifted his gaze to the sky beyond the tree canopy, said a silent prayer to Alumn, kicked the fire over, and plunged back into the undergrowth, toward home.

THE SILK & Steel series continues in Blood & Ice, due for release in late summer. To be sure you don't miss the release, please sign up to Ariana Nash's newsletter here (and get the short story, *Sealed with a Kiss*, free.)

DISCOVER EXCLUSIVE ART, snippets, and chat with Ariana at her Facebook group here.

ABOUT THE AUTHOR

Born to wolves, Ariana Nash only ventures from the Cornish moors when the moon is fat and the night alive with myths and legends. She captures those myths in glass jars and returning home, weaves them into stories filled with forbidden desires, fantasy realms, and wicked delights.

Sign up to her newsletter here: https://www.subscribepage. com/silk-steel